Die Again Once More

Mark Nesbitt

Copyright 2019 Mark Nesbitt
Published by Second Chance Publications
P.O. Box 3126
Gettysburg, PA. 17325

WARNING! The content herein is fully protected by U. S. Federal copyright laws. Unauthorized copying, reproduction, recording, broadcasting, derivative works and public performance, by any individual or company without written consent of the publisher and author are strictly prohibited. Federal copyright laws will be vigorously enforced and infringements will be prosecuted to the fullest extent of the law, which can include damages and lawyers' fees to be paid by the infringer of copyright.

ISBN: 0-9995795-4-1
ISBN-13: 978-0-9995795-4-1

This is a work of fiction. Characters, places, names, organizations, incidents and events herein are either products of the author's imagination or are fictitious. Any resemblance to actual persons, living or dead, is purely coincidental.

So as through a glass and darkly
The age long strife I see
Where I fought in many guises,
Many names—but always me.

So forever in the future
Shall I battle as of yore,
Dying to be born a fighter
But to die again once more.

—George S. Patton, Jr.

TABLE OF CONTENTS

CHAPTER 1 1
CHAPTER 2 3
CHAPTER 3 4
CHAPTER 4 6
CHAPTER 5 8
CHAPTER 6 11
CHAPTER 7 12
CHAPTER 8 15
CHAPTER 9 17
CHAPTER 10 20
CHAPTER 11 24
CHAPTER 12 26
CHAPTER 13 28
CHAPTER 14 30
CHAPTER 15 33
CHAPTER 16 35
CHAPTER 17 39
CHAPTER 18 43
CHAPTER 19 46
CHAPTER 20 50
CHAPTER 21 53
CHAPTER 22 55

CHAPTER 23	61
CHAPTER 24	63
CHAPTER 25	68
CHAPTER 26	70
CHAPTER 27	73
CHAPTER 28	75
CHAPTER 29	78
CHAPTER 30	79
CHAPTER 31	86
CHAPTER 32	89
CHAPTER 33	94
CHAPTER 34	100
CHAPTER 35	106
CHAPTER 36	110
CHAPTER 37	112
CHAPTER 38	116
CHAPTER 39	120
CHAPTER 40	123
CHAPTER 41	129
CHAPTER 42	131
CHAPTER 43	137
CHAPTER 44	147
CHAPTER 45	152
CHAPTER 46	157

CHAPTER 47	160
CHAPTER 48	169
CHAPTER 49	172
CHAPTER 50	176
CHAPTER 51	182
CHAPTER 52	186
CHAPTER 53	188
CHAPTER 54	190
CHAPTER 55	193
CHAPTER 56	195
CHAPTER 57	200
CHAPTER 58	207
CHAPTER 59	212
CHAPTER 60	214
CHAPTER 61	221
CHAPTER 62	224
CHAPTER 63	229
CHAPTER 64	232
CHAPTER 65	235
CHAPTER 66	236
CHAPTER 67	237
CHAPTER 68	244
CHAPTER 69	248
CHAPTER 70	252

CHAPTER 71	254
CHAPTER 72	256
CHAPTER 73	262
CHAPTER 74	264
CHAPTER 75	267
CHAPTER 76	268
CHAPTER 77	272
CHAPTER 78	274
CHAPTER 79	280
CHAPTER 80	281
CHAPTER 81	283
CHAPTER 82	285
CHAPTER 83	287
CHAPTER 84	289
CHAPTER 85	293
CHAPTER 86	295
CHAPTER 87	298
CHAPTER 88	300
CHAPTER 89	301
CHAPTER 90	303
CHAPTER 91	304
CHAPTER 92	306
ABOUT THE AUTHOR	308

CHAPTER 1

Sitting in this stinking bar like a steam engine with the safety valve tied down waiting to blow.
Thinking about the spring day the neighbor lady brought me into her bedroom when her husband was away at work. The hot rush, like gushing liquid pounding through my head, and Mrs. McGillis's soft puffy mounds, warm lips and tight back. How the cool breeze made her curtains fly. Head spun for a week afterward every time I passed her house and smelled cheap rosewater perfume blowing out the windows. Spun twice as fast when I saw her. She never invited me back, treated me like trash after that making me pick things up and kissing her husband in front of me, eyes wide open, looking right at me over his shoulder.
But it made me feel...alive.
Grown up since then. Couple of brandies then I don't mind having to force myself on the girls who say they don't want it. Irish girls are the best. A little sweet talk, little taste from my flask, and they giggle and tumble. Poor and smelly they change my name. "Oh, Seamus," they call me. James from the old world they say. It's easy to get away with, in a back alley, or sneaking in their bedroom windows at night. They deserve it. All just like that whore Mrs. McGillis under their skins.
This newest one, ah, she is real special. Hair the shade of the night, wheat-colored eyes, large breasts. Also married, but it matters not. Had me plenty of married women.
But she's been making excuses for not seeing me.
Older husband brought her to town six months ago. Blacksmith. Plenty of work too, with the army readying to march on the rebels in Virginia. Moving to Washington must be good for the big dirty blacksmith with the young plump wife.

Good for me, too.

Brandy number four. Going to visit my little tart just down the street. I can practically see her flat from here. Husband would be working, hammering horseshoes or whatever he did, she's bouncing about the place with nothing to do. Seventy-five cents tossed on the bar.

Well, I'll give her something to do.

CHAPTER 2

Mara McKay sat down on the floor of her rented house's living room to rest. She cracked a beer from the six-pack sitting next to her and kicked back, leaning against the one uncluttered wall. Most of the boxes were in from her car. Now all she needed to do was unpack them.

She had worked up a sweat in the mid-80 degree, mid-Virginia, mid-October afternoon. Three long pulls on the icy beer and she got a little buzz going. Whether it was the frosty chill down her throat or the familiar hoppy after-taste that brought back the memory, she couldn't tell, but there he was in her head again: "Sexy Rexy" to her girlfriends. *Rex the Ex to me.*

That's it. Bury it, girl. Jam him and his perfect body and her and her friendship and your feelings about them both into a hole deep inside and keep pushing them down. You've got too much to do, too much to write. This is your big chance to get away from it. A godsend in the form of your first book contract and it can take you away, just like it already has.

She thought: it may not be perfect, this little Virginia town, but it's away.

And it's where I need to be.

CHAPTER 3

Look around the fenced-in yard. No one saw me come up the stairs. With the brandies under my belt, I'm bold as a trooper.

Back door is wide open. I'm inside. Ginny bending over the hearth sweeping into a dustpan.

I sneak up behind. One motion and her long daydress is over her back.

She cries out, tries to stand up but I push her down across the table near the fireplace. I'm in her pantaloons and find the split in the crotch.

Unbutton my pants and try to ram it home but she's not ready and moving and that last brandy is beginning to take effect. A bit unsteady on my pins. Give it one more hard push. I enter her, she screams.

Back of my neck cracks. I hear it inside. Dirty foul-smelling hand clamping down and squeezing my neck, fingers trying to touch through my throat. I'm pulled out of the woman, fly across the room. I stumble face-first. Head hits the plaster wall, bits of dust and horsehair falling on me.

An ungodly roar in my ears. I look up. There's the blacksmith above, reaching for me. "You dog!" he growls, a huge fist comes down. Hear my cheekbone pop before I feel pain. Boot comes down on my belly pushes the breath clear out of me. Boot comes down again, misses my crotch by an inch. I have to do something before he gets his stinking hands on me or I will die.

The smith turns to his wife, screams, "Him! That is the little puke you've brought into our bed?"

Ginny bawling, trying to adjust her skirts, fumbling with the bottom I pulled loose. "Henry. Don't. Please. I tried to...but he just kept coming. I didn't..."

A roar through the pain in my head I hear him. "I knew there was someone…but him? He isn't worth the effort to kill. But I will, by God. I will kill him."

An iron poker already in my hand above my head comes down at the same time he hits me across my face. There's the old anger again—little puke, huh?—I swing much harder than I need. The thin, solid iron cleaves his skull down to his chin. Explosion of blood and brains from the huge crack. One of the smith's eyes pops from its socket lands on his cheek. Other has a funny look of wonder why his big arms won't obey his commands anymore.

Off in the distance. Ginny screams. His body drops into a pile of bloody work clothes, shaking.

She looks up at me. Breast comes loose, simple face twisted with fear, confusion. Thinking of Mrs. McGillis and the smelly Irish work-girls. Swing the poker hard and hit her above her ear. She drops a rumpled heap across the body of her husband, convulsing and gurgling. Hit her again, and again. The movement stops, her head is a bowl of black hair and bloody gray pudding. He has stopped breathing. Time for me to go.

CHAPTER 4

It was still dark. Mara couldn't tell if her eyes were open or closed, but she could smell the damp, earthy smell of freshly dug dirt. Like earthworms or mushrooms, she thought. She lay still, with her arms at her sides.

Suddenly something fell on her face and crumbled, a clod of loose dirt, some tumbling close to her nostrils. She went to brush it away. Her hand hit a ceiling of dirt just three inches above her waist. She tried to sit up. Her forehead hit the same dirt ceiling and she dropped back down. More moist earth fell on her face.

She reached to the side. Her arm was stopped by a wall of dirt. She tried to slide her arm up her body, but it got stuck at her chest against the damp earth ceiling.

I'm buried, still alive!

She tried to roll over but her shoulders would not rotate in the confined space, which seemed to be only a foot high and as wide as her shoulders. Her knees were also stopped by packed dirt. She pushed up again, trying to sit up but the crumbly ceiling wouldn't move.

Panic twisted her stomach. She vomited, and there was barely enough room for her to turn her head to clear her throat and she began to choke on the liquid. Some ran into the back of her nose. She snorted against the vile burning.

She started to scream, but the sound was absorbed by the dirt. More fell on her face and into her eyes, and still she couldn't bring her arm up to brush it away. "Help me!" she screamed. "Help! I'm still alive! Help!"

She bolted awake, sat up in her bed holding her throat, frantically brushing non-existent nightmare dirt off her face. A streetlight provided enough of a beam of light for her to see she was in her bedroom in the old house she had rented. Her dog was whining a pathetic whine, as if he wanted to help but couldn't.

She looked at her alarm clock. It was 4:10 A.M. Mara McKay would not sleep the rest of the morning.

CHAPTER 5

"Name?"

"Huh?"

The soldier whose face looks like a rusted bucket looks up from his paper at me over silver, wire-rimmed glasses.

"That was one of the more difficult questions you'll get today, sonny. Ya know, to go out and git killed for Mr. Lincoln, you got to own at least half a brain."

Arms stiffen and I want to punch the fat red face in front of me. But I need to get in the army to run away, to disappear. I put a lid on my boiling anger.

"Ja...uh, Will, that's the name." No idea where the name "Will" came from, just pops into my head.

"Yer absolutely sure? About yer own name?" The sergeant looks over his shoulder, pulls a bottle from next to the table-leg, takes a hard swig.

"Yeah, I am. Will...McGillis." Last name is easy.

"How old are ya?"

"Twenty...uh..."

"Twenty, huh? Too bad yer mother dropped you on yer head and stopped yer brain development when you were five. Where ya from?"

Arms tighten again. Stupid bastard. I'll get him, if I can. If I'm in his outfit, I'll get him.

"Maryland."

The sergeant looks up at him again. "I know that, you mule. Yer in Mary-land now. What town?"

"Uh...Rockville."

The sergeant blinks with whiskey-swollen eyelids, stares at me for a long time, shakes his head and scribbles on his paper.

"How tall?"

"Huh?"

"Now look, sonny. By the way, that's short for 'son-of-a-bitch.' I got a long line of fellers behind you there with more brains in the back of their underdrawers than you have in yer whole head. Ya pay attention or I'll throw ya out of line. How tall are ya?"

"Five foot eight." I hate the man right then and there. He'll be sorry, when I get a gun and he turns his back on me.

"Weight?"

"'Bout a hundred thirty-five."

"Eyes? That's the color, sonny, so don't answer 'two'."

"Blue."

"Hair? No, I can see fer myself. Brown. Just like a pile a shit. Now, isn't this goin' much better? You're doin' all right now...fer bein' dumber than a box of horse-turds. Now here's the toughest question of all. Course, most normal boys can answer it right away."

He winks at the line of men behind me and they all begin to chuckle. So mad I'm shaking.

"Which branch of the service you want to be in: Infantry, Cav'ry, Artillery?"

For this question, I really don't have an answer. I know nothing about the army. Care even less. To me it's just a way to disappear. Since the sergeant already thinks I'm an idiot, what difference does it make? Play the shithead's game.

"What's the difference?"

The line behind roars with laughter and the sergeant just shakes his head in disgust. "Shut up!" he yells at the rest of the men in the tent. "Half you horse's asses don't know either. So listen." He takes another long swig from his bottle, places it on the ground again. "The Artillery are the men who fire the big cannons. They'll probably put you on some easy duty, like guarding the politicians who got us into this war in the first place. Nice soft duty in Washington. The Cav'ry are the boys who ride around on their horsies all day in the prettiest uniforms in the army. They wave their sabers at straw heads and run errands for the generals. Nobody's ever seen a dead cav'ryman."

He stops to take another swig and puts the bottle back below the table.

"Now, the infantry. They do all the fightin' and dyin' in this man's army. They walk everywhere, the food is full of maggots, the water always tastes like some horse pissed in it upstream, yer officers are all cowardly idiots who don't give a damn about yer safety, and the first time in battle you will shit your pants. The enemy cav'ry, which is a hunnert times better than ours, will ram his saber right through yer eye sockets, and their artillery will rip yer guts out and spray them all over yer pretty blue uniform."

The sergeant leans back in his chair and throws the stump of his leg up on the writing desk, bouncing the inkbottle.

"Here's what work artillery does on the infantry. Gone at Manassas. Watched the ball bouncing toward me, just as nice as you please. Couldn't get out of the way though. Watched my leg tore off. You shoulda seen the blood spout. Like a fountain. Never thought I had that much in me. But I was lucky. The ball bounced after it hit me. The feller just behind me had his head ripped off. That's what it sounded like: the thump of a melon and the rip of cloth. He stood there fer a second, without no head, like he was trying to figure out what happened, with the blood pumpin' like a geyser and sprayin' everywhere, his head rollin' along the ground like a baseball, thumpin' along till it hit the legs of a line of infantry behind us. One soldier didn't see it, stepped on it. It rolled under his foot and he fell on it. Weirdest damn thing I'd ever seen, him on the ground with the head in his arms like he was some sort of two-headed monster."

He glances at us boys in line. Some of them look like they are about to puke.

"So. What branch of the service would you like?"

"Artillery."

The sergeant's eyes turn into slits. I see an evil smile grow. He picks up a rubber stamp from his desk and stamps my paper.

"*Yer* in the infantry, sonny. Move on."

I stand there for a second. "Didn't you hear me? I said I wanted artillery."

"I heard ya...Will. But anybody as dumb as you couldn't do all the things they need in the artillery. Lots to learn, ya know. You'll be lucky to learn enough in the infantry to keep alive. Next."

I stand in the hot tent, boiling for a second, thinking what would happen if I punch him right then and there. I have to get out. I pass the sergeant's desk, I reach with my foot and kick over his bottle and I can hear the contents gurgling quickly into the dirt. The sergeant yells, stumbles and hollers for his crutches, but by the time he gets outside the tent, I duck around a shed.

CHAPTER 6

Dr. Ricard Fisher's intense, out-of-body, mental reverie exploded in the high-pitched buzzing of his alarm watch.

Oh yes, he thought. That reporter is coming to interview me. That's right. That's today. I have five minutes before she's here. I need to wrap this up.

He slid some hand-written papers across his large desk. Some others caught underneath and they fanned out like a deck of cards. There, he thought. There's the one I've been looking for.

There were some calculations along the edges. Some weights in fractional grams of superconductors; some measurements of electromagnetic fields in mega-gauss; notes on human electromagnetic frequencies; "The Casimir Effect" underlined several times; a sketched whirling spiral leading from the center of the page to the bottom. Outside the spiral he had drawn some boxes indicating indeterminate power sources.

He smiled at the simplicity of it; and the complexity of the concept it represented.

He printed across the bottom of the page, "See you later." Why? Why not?

He shuffled the papers together and slid them into a manila file folder. It went into his briefcase. I'll work out the precise calculations at home, he thought.

There was a knock at the door.

CHAPTER 7

"Hello Ms. McKay. Please. Step into my office. And please forgive the clutter."

Mara was a little surprised when Ricard Fisher, Ph.D., opened the door himself and not a secretary. His face was thinner than she remembered it, but easily recognizable from what she had seen of him on television. The office was indeed a cluttered mess, but if you're the smartest person in the world, you deserve a little latitude when it comes to disorganization.

"Here. Have a seat." He grabbed an armful of folders from a wooden chair and placed them on another wooden chair, on top of more folders and some books.

"So," Mara began, "Is this the secret to your creativity?" She fumbled for her digital recorder in her backpack and flipped it on. "Do you mind?"

"Not at all. And yes, I suppose this mess does help a little. It is kind of the way my mind works: Toss a hand grenade in my brain and watch as the ideas float down. Keep reading them as they settle and maybe a few will make sense."

Okay, thought Mara. He is kind of geeky. But he is a manly geek. Kind of like Indiana Jones, wearing his glasses teaching in the classroom.

"I can empathize. That's sort of how it is when I write. But your floating ideas win Nobel Prizes. I've yet to have mine published. As I think I mentioned, yours is the first major biography I've sold to a publisher. So I really appreciate your time for this interview."

"Not a problem. Did you have any specific questions?"

Whew, Mara thought. He really gets down to business.

"Yes. Can I have a re-interview? That's if I have any more questions after this one, which I'm sure I will."

"I suppose so. That is, if you can stand me after this one."

Mara thought: For being the man many consider the brightest star in the current intellectual universe, he seems pretty down-to-earth. But there's something else about him....

"I've read a little about your background, Dr. Fisher..."

"Ricard, please."

"Okay. Ricard. Wikipedia, Internet sources and so forth, but I need it from you. Where would you say your genius comes from?"

"Well, that is an interesting question. Nature or nurture? I suppose I'm like a racehorse. Breed the best to the best, hire the best trainers and rider, and hope for the best. My parents, my environment growing up, my education and teachers, and sheer luck all had a hand in my development." He glanced around the office. "In this cluttered mess."

How unassuming, Mara thought. But there was also something behind his eyes. He reminded her of a beautiful predator—a wolf or puma—not physically, but intellectually, crouched to pounce on a false premise or bad idea. And he's rather handsome, too. No wonder he is considered charming and at the top of the list of most eligible bachelors in, of all places, Hollywood.

Mara began to feel the questions she worked on half the day yesterday were woefully inadequate. Although she had been interested in the weirdness of quantum physics as an undergrad, the math stopped her dead in her tracks. So her questions about string theory, dark matter, black holes and cosmology seemed sort of lame. Fisher's answers seemed pat. After forty minutes of interviewing she was thinking, I need something more.

She felt like the intellectual jaguar was about to pounce on her thoughts and rip them to shreds. Instead, like all successful combatants, animal or human, he gave her an out.

"I think you might get a better idea of what I'm interested in and why I think theoretical physics is so important, if I just explain my one guiding principle."

Mara was thankful for the bailout. "Please do, Ricard. I think I'm flunking my 'Interviews 101' class before your very eyes."

"Theoretical physics falls short because physicists rarely make any of it matter to people. A black hole ten thousand light years away doesn't mean much to a person engaged in everyday life, who, say, is in mourning over a recently deceased child. But if there were a connection between energy on earth and something the religions call a 'miracle'—what scientists have blown-off as something supernatural—then we have made our science relevant.

"It's like the story of the apple falling on Newton's head. It is no doubt fictional. But it *is* a good story. And so non-scientific laymen remember it and explain it to their children and create interest in the most important and least understood force we know. We scientists almost always fail to make the science-to-human connection, and yet are still self-satisfied in what we do."

Mara sat silent for a second. Yes. That's exactly what scientists need to do. She was about to say something when Fisher spoke again.

"Physics is the most important of all the sciences. It is the basis for all the other sciences, for life, for being, for the existence of matter and energy. Yet, we physicists make our calculations, write our grant proposals, publish our results in obscure journals, get our tenure and are pleased within our own little world. It all needs to come out, this connection between the great miracle that holds together the vast cosmos, as well as binds our individual cells and the atoms that make up the cells. It is a symphony that sweeps through the largest concert hall, yet is made up of individual notes orchestrated from the soul of each performer."

"Ricard. That's wonderful. That will probably go on the cover jacket." Mara looked at her watch. "And I will take you up on that re-interview, maybe in a week or two, after I've done a little more research."

"Yes. That will work. I have this feeling that I can trust you, that you can help to get my work out into the world, more than those insipid television shows I keep getting invited to appear on. I have to go now myself. I have an appointment to keep. It was nice meeting you, Mara."

Firm handshake, she thought as she walked out the door. Ricard Fisher, Ph. D., is definitely not your typical science nerd.

CHAPTER 8

This is what hell must be like. Smell alone is enough to qualify the place. Just what I get for back talking the new sergeant. Burial duty after the battle. Should be happy. Least I didn't have to go into the fighting. Wherever the hell this place is.

I know we're somewhere in Virginia. A small ramshackle town just up the hill from here. If anyone is still in the town, they must be crazy. I see some of the ghouls wandering around the fields, some soldiers, some civilians, picking at the dead for money or something else valuable. Having to bury the stinking dead, figure I deserve some of the booty, too.

They've been lying around so long that it's getting more difficult. First the rain soaked the bodies, then the hot sun turning them brown and black. Can't reach into the pockets anymore without having some of their stinking skin slide off. Now that they have started to bloat with the heat, they're likely to explode when you touch them. I saw that. Crew just down the hill dropped one of the bodies on the way to the grave hole and it burst, spitting rotten guts, gas, and bowel shit all over the men and some others just watching. Half of them puking as they wiped the swill from their faces and lips.

"Get over here. Let's go over to where they already gathered the meat."

Lucky this pard is a dolt who doesn't even know how to write his name. Look at him and I'm reminded of the time at the state fair. Went into the fun house and saw the mirrors. Looking into his eyes was like looking into that fun house mirror. Kid will do anything I tell him and not know the difference.

The men who are cleaning the rotten guts off themselves wave as they walk off. Can still hear some dry heaving. Ah. Just got a whiff of the dozen bodies dumped on the little flat space of ground. Where's my handkerchief? Where's that vial of mint oil? Makes it smell a little better, but the rag around my face makes it hard to breathe.

"Here. We'll dig right next to this one, roll him in, and cover him with the dirt from the next one's hole."

I dig, but make sure that the dolt does most of the work. Hole is only a foot-and-a-half deep. "That's enough."

"That gonna cover him, boss? He's pretty fat."

"Sure. He'll flatten out when all the gas gets out of him."

"What happens when it rains again?"

Shake my head. "We'll be long gone, Bunky. Just do what I tell you."

Look around and find a long heavy tree branch brought down by artillery fire from the battle. "Come here."

We push the body toward the small trench. Have to move to the other side because other bodies are in the way. Hook the body with an offshoot branch and it rolls into the trench, but the head falls off and starts to roll away down the hill.

"Christ! Go get it!" Stifle a laugh as the dummy runs and grabs the rolling head with its bloated lips and swollen tongue sticking out. He picks it up with both hands grabbing the ears. The dullard begins to smile when he saw me grinning.

"Okay, Boss?"

"Toss 'er in."

The head lands on the stomach of its own corpse, which immediately collapses with a loud sigh of smelly gas.

"Start digging the next hole."

We go at it for the next several hours, until all the bodies are covered. Bits and pieces fall off and get tossed into the graves.

Mounds are considerably higher toward the end of the job than at the beginning. Dullard hasn't been digging as deep. Must be getting tired since I made him do most of the work.

"Now look, Rube. That'll never do. What are you going to do about it?"

Dimwit tries to pat them down with his shovel then begins to hit them harder and harder. Finally he jumps up and down upon one until it collapses in a muffled explosion of gas. Dullard loses a shoe in the ribcage of the dead man and has to fish it out with a muck-covered hand. Just shake my head.

So much for our sainted dead.

CHAPTER 9

It was nearly closing time in the university library by the time she finally packed up her laptop, recorder and small notebook and headed for the elevator. It was a long dreary walk through a dimly-lit musty-smelling corridor. Mara's head felt over-stuffed with information. It represented a long-day's work at something she adored. It was the feeling of total mental exhaustion, a feeling most people worked overtime to avoid. Today was particularly hard.

After her bizarre nightmare, she spent most of the morning moving the rest of her belongings around her rented house, interviewed Ricard Fisher, then spent the remainder of the late autumn afternoon and most of the evening at the library researching what they had in their archives about their most illustrious professor, whom she had first seen on *Oprah*.

As she walked through the upper lobby, the old building that served as the university library was now all but empty, except for the skeleton staff who would keep the place open another hour to clean up, filling rolling carts with books left on the tables by students and returning them to their shelves according to the Dewey Decimal System. As she walked the large echoing room, she tried to humanize all that she had read about her subject and synch it to the additional upcoming interview she had scheduled. After the initial interview she began to think of more questions. Another more in-depth grilling would help now.

Her head ached dully as she entered the elevator, but she had to smile at the handsome undergrad she caught staring at her butt as she passed the returns desk. Guess I'm not too old for the college crowd, she thought. She pushed the button to take her from the fourth floor research area to the first floor exit. She leaned against the cold, metal back wall and rubbed her eyes. She wanted to plan what to do tomorrow, but she just couldn't force her mind to work anymore. When she glanced at the lighted numbers above the door, she realized that the elevator had passed the first floor and was descending into the cellar of the antiquated building.

Great. What now? she thought as she pushed away from the back wall toward the door and punched the button for the first floor again.

The elevator bounced to a stop at the cellar level and the doors began to open.

Before they had opened half-a-foot, Mara was hit by the smell: the sour stench of body odor and wet wool, fecal matter, vomit and—most frightening—the metallic smell of blood. *Grandpa's garage and dead rats.* She looked with growing panic at the scene slowly being revealed to her, inch by inch, as the doors opened.

It was a glimpse into Hell: men's crimson bodies tangled in a weltering, moist mass. Blood smeared floor to ceiling and all over men who seemed to be swimming in it. Some half naked, slimy with coagulated, purple blood and vomit. Dozens of arms weakly gestured for help in flickering candlelight, looking like a crawling, single-bodied, centipede-like creature. Some actually turned, looked up in confusion at her, their faces blood-caked masks, white eyes rolling in aimless directions. An ochre-aproned surgeon, sleeves rolled up, stood at an operating table—no more than a door placed upon two wooden barrels—rust-stained saw poised over a writhing patient whose thigh skin was pulled back with the white, bulbous fat and exposed red muscle retracted so that the surgeon could see the bright bone. Several men struggled hard to hold him down. The saw rasped against bone and his shriek stabbed her eardrums.

Her shaking hand found the buttons, frantic to push them. She paused. My God, she thought, peering into the horror. *Where am I? What is this?* A sudden wave of fear tore at her guts. She hit the button to take her to the first floor.

Nothing happened.

The doors remained open. The elevator didn't move.

From around the corner outside the elevator, not two feet from her, was the gore-smeared face and pleading eyes of a young orderly. Mara recoiled, slammed hard into the back wall of the elevator. Now she couldn't even reach the buttons. *There's no place to go.*

In his arms, like a bundle of bloody logs, he held dripping, amputated limbs of patients. Blood ran from between his fingers to the floor; his leather-soled shoe scraped across the dirt floor as he took another step, toward the open elevator, toward her. For a moment she thought he was about to dump his hideous bundle at her feet. With his eyes, he begged her: *Take me out of this place; I've worked so long already; let me go with you; or, at least, come in and help me with this never-ending work. Yes. Come in. Help!*

She launched herself toward the open door, breathed in the stench once more. She slammed her palm against the buttons. Her small notebook flew from her pack and landed with a slap outside the elevator at the young orderly's feet. She looked at it, then back into the bloodshot eyes of the young man; he took one more lurching step toward her.

Almost reluctantly, the doors began to close. She felt the jolt of the elevator as it began to rise.

Rushing into the cool night air was like someone throwing a bucket of cold water into her face. *What had just happened?* Her hands were trembling. She took several deep breaths, and realized that she must report this to the authorities.

CHAPTER 10

She found herself in a jog toward a building with a blue security light. She tried to replay the scene in her head. One thing stood out: somewhere, in the back of the filthy, blood-stained room, she saw what looked like a bright, white, pristine coat—a lab coat. There was a head and a hazy face atop it. The face looked like someone she should know, but she could not place it.

A sleepy-eyed security officer answered the door.

She stumbled over what she tried to say, half not believing herself what she had just seen.

"I'd like to report something. A group of men in the basement of the library. They are covered in what must be fake blood and they're acting like…soldiers in a hospital."

The security officer's eyes lit up. He grabbed his black ball cap.

"Great!" he said with an enthusiasm that surprised Mara. He locked the door behind him and began to walk toward the library. "A large group of men, you say? How long ago was this?"

"Thirty seconds ago," she said, trying to keep up with him. "A minute, max."

"How bad did they trash the place? Would they have had time to clean it up between the time you caught them and now?"

"Hell, no. It was a real mess."

"Good!"

They reached the library. The security officer politely opened the door. "And who are you?" he asked.

"Mara McKay. I'm a writer doing some research."

"Nice to meet you, especially under these circumstances. You'll make a great witness at their trial. I've been waiting to catch one of these rich-boy fraternities in one of their pranks. You say you don't think they'll have time to clean it up and get out?"

"Not the bloody mess I saw."

"Great!"

They got to the elevator. She tried to step in, but she couldn't. A sudden, incredible dread came over her

"What's the matter?"

"I can't go. You go."

"Ms. McKay. I need you as a witness. If you don't come with me and actually identify the perpetrators, I may not be able to make my case."

She took a deep breath. "All right," she said and reluctantly stepped onto the elevator. She shivered as the floor dropped out from under her. She was calmed somewhat by the fact that the security officer had given her an explanation for what she saw: those pesky fraternities, scaring the living daylights out of the students and faculty again. The doors began to crack. The room before her was pitch dark. She could hear her heart as the security officer reached outside the elevator to flick on the lights.

As they flared, she drew in a breath. The blood-covered surgeon, the men who were lying like butchered meat, the exhausted orderly, all were gone. In their place stood pristine, brightly painted walls and solid concrete floors. Cutting halfway into the room was a concrete-block wall covered with electrical panels.

The security officer strolled casually off the elevator. Mara cautiously followed. Hands on his hips, he turned with a sour look on his face.

"Ms. McKay, is this where you saw the frat boys playing their prank?"

"Yes. Right here." She looked around, astounded. "This is the only elevator in the building, isn't it?"

"Yes, ma'am."

"But right here was an operating table…and the surgeon stood here. And here…in this corner, was a pile of arms and feet and hands and legs."

The security officer walked over, squatted, and pointed his flashlight into the corner. "Well, there's absolutely nothing here now. How long ago did you say you saw this?"

"Two, three minutes ago. However long it takes for me to walk from here to your office and back. I swear there was a horrible, bloody scene, right here. I mean, this wall wasn't here, but…."

"You mean, a bunch of college students broke down a scene out of *Gone with the Wind*, moved it all out of here without us seeing them leave, rebuilt the concrete-block wall, repainted, all in three minutes? What was it you were researching upstairs, Ms. McKay?"

"Dr. Ricard Fisher, the professor who works here."

The security officer said nothing for an uncomfortably long time.

"And how long had you been working?"

"Oh, I don't know. Since mid-afternoon."

"I think I know what happened."

"You think I dreamed this?"

"Well, you *had* worked a long time and it's late, and the mind can play tricks...."

Mara's mind whirled. She was absolutely certain she hadn't fallen asleep in the elevator. She knew what she had seen.

The officer had already stepped back on the elevator.

She hurriedly followed him, not wanting to get left behind in that space.

"Don't you believe me?"

"Ms. McKay. You certainly had a convincing look when you came into my office. I believe that you think you saw something. Maybe in a half-sleep, and with the shadows down in the basement...well, enough said. I'm more disappointed that I didn't catch any pranksters."

He was kind enough to walk her to her car. She apologized for the trouble. By now she was doubting herself, her own senses. Maybe he was right, she thought. Maybe I did fall asleep momentarily and had a flash dream. The security officer had taken a half-dozen steps when he turned around and walked back to her.

"I just need to tell you one more thing, Ms. McKay. It may or may not help to explain what you saw."

He paused an uncomfortably long time. "Yes," she prompted.

"Well, I'm no historian, but just from living here, well, everyone knows a little history."

"Yes?"

"You knew there was a battle in and around the town?"

"Yes."

"Well, during and after the battle, all the structures in town became hospitals, with wounded and dying men lying around waiting to be operated on, surgeons hacking away at them with primitive tools, and so on. Had you ever read anything about that before?"

"No," she said, growing more interested. "I've never really studied war. I certainly didn't know that the library had been used as a hospital."

"Oh. I thought that maybe because you had read something about the hospitals and because you were so tired when you entered the elevator, I thought that maybe you, well, you know, maybe just dozed off for a second or two there and could have dreamed it."

Yeah, she thought. Maybe I did dream it. *But it was so vivid....*

"Thank you for your help and insight. I'm sorry for disturbing you."

"You know—and once again I'm no historian—but some people around here say that a place could be—for lack of a better word—inhabited by the spirits of those who died there and were not afforded a proper burial. Apparently happened all the time around here after the battle." He smiled. "But that's just a superstition, no doubt."

Mara smiled back. "Well, everybody likes a good ghost story. Again, sorry for bothering you."

"No problem. I was bored anyways. Thanks for the diversion."

CHAPTER 11

Only one man here scares me. Malachai is his name. Not certain of his last name, but from the way he acts, it should be Beelzebub.

He's bigger than most of the men in our outfit, broader and taller and heavier, and has a temper I've seen snap in an instant. Dark skinned, almost Negro. Comes from Baltimore, I think. Saw him beat a colored muleskinner half to death with the limb of a tree for giving him a funny look. Kept a twisted smile on his face the whole time he swung the arm-sized branch. When the officers became aware of the commotion, he stopped and walked away. No one would say who it was, including me. Not even the colored boy, who feigned being senseless after the attack, so as to not draw another beating.

Malachai steals things from right under other soldiers' noses, defying them to do anything about it. Bullies the smaller men in the unit, making them do the camp labor he's assigned. I'm willing to bet that even some of the officers are afraid of him. I ponder it and think it's better to stay close to a man like this than turn my back on him.

Then I make a discovery that evens us up.

It was a skirmish, but still confusing like all battles, big or small. We were moving forward, spread out along a hundred yard front with several yards between each man. Just entered some woods and began taking fire from the damned rebels standing behind a stone fence. Pasty-faced Lieutenant Randall was leading. Malachai had a run-in with Randall over a petty theft and spent a day in the hot sun without food or water straddling a fence rail, legs dangling a foot off the ground. As much as everyone hated or feared him, it made us all goosy to see him sweating buckets, squirming around on the rail trying not to end up sitting on one of his own balls. Never uttered a word, but the looks he gave the young Lieutenant whenever he passed were as evil as any I'd ever seen.

Skirmisher next to Malachai went down with a wound to his foot. I saw Malachai move over, closer to the Lieutenant. Here comes a volley from the rebs, and I quick-step toward a large rock where I could fake sickness. Got to the lee side of the rock. There, in head-high thickets, in a cloud of powder smoke, was the Lieutenant looking scared, shouting over the rattling of musketry some orders. Malachai swung the barrel of his musket level with the Lieutenant's heart and fired. When the smoke blew off, the Lieutenant was on his stomach with a hole the size of a fist in the back of his blue coat. I stand and Malachai saw me. The muzzle of Malachai's musket turned toward me, but I knew I was safe with his single-shot Springfield. Malachai scowled, I read his mind: "Say anything, and I'll kill you too." I swung my own musket around, fired at Malachai's head. Pull the trigger just as I move my aiming point an inch to the side of the big man's face, sending my bullet toward the rebel lines. The smoke clears, Malachai is shaking. I stare at him. Give him my weird, madman smile, just to confuse him, and crouch back behind my rock.

From then on I know I'm safe from him, at least until the next battle. Then I'll be behind him in the second rank when we go in. As long as Malachai knows I won't report him, my fate is in my own hands.

CHAPTER 12

"Okay," Mara said out loud on the drive home from the library. "That was a once-in-a-lifetime experience."

She tapped the touchpad on her car's radio and pulled up a mellow station, a notch above classic rock. "Ah, that's better. You've got to think about something positive. Oh, and quit talking to yourself!"

The first positive thing that popped into her mind was the contract. After years at newspapers chasing cop cars to get stories, she had finally landed her first book contract. It was a matter of the right proposal at the right time. Although the advance was not all that great, it would pay for food and rent while she researched and wrote the biography on Dr. Ricard Fisher, the brilliant, esoteric, sexy geek who was burning up the tabloids. It was, as they say, her breakout book, the first time she would have a hardcover, mass-marketed, long work by a major publisher. The proverbial foot-in-the-door.

But not if you keep using stupid clichés, she thought.

Having to move here was more than a necessity for the book. It would also help get her mind off Rex.

"Sexy Rexy" her girlfriends had called him. Yeah, he *was* that, she thought as she remembered his slim, taut, professional soccer-player's body and seemingly endless cash flow. For a while she believed that he might be the one. Eventually she had to admit that she had fallen hard for him, even ignoring the rumors. It all came crashing in, like a concrete building in an earthquake, rubble crushing her heart, when she caught him with Ramona, her *ex*-girlfriend, from the moment she walked into his living room and saw her naked, reverse cowgirl, on top of him. She left feeling like she wanted to kill them both. But by the time she got into her car, dissolving into tears, she just wanted him back.

It never happened. She was too afraid of how vulnerable she felt after that. She vowed to be careful and never let it happen again. After almost two years, she may have taken that vow a little too far....

She had to slam on her brakes, nearly passing the old house she had rented. She had trouble with the ancient skeleton key in the archaic lock, and was greeted by her always over-enthusiastic dog, Reynolds. She tossed her pack on the kitchen table.

Her pack.

She ripped open the nylon zippers and spilled the entire contents onto the table: Laptop, electrical cords, pens, pencil, recorder, note cards...where was her little notebook? It was not in her pack. She checked her jacket: not in her pockets either.

And it was not on the floor in front of the elevator once she reached the basement with the security officer. Crap, she thought. *What the hell?* Either her notebook had been picked up by a fraternity that had set the land speed record for cleaning up a totally destroyed room and re-building a block wall, or it was...somewhere that could not exist.

CHAPTER 13

 Regiment's finally through that underbrush, but our alignment is all busted by the barrel-size rocks in this field. Now the rebels are shelling us.
 The shelling stops. Orders calling down the line to halt. There's a low stone wall about ten yards ahead of us, then an open field. Other side of the field, a line of enemy infantry, muskets flashing in the sun. Looks like some infernal centipede turned upside down.
 "Damn them. And damn our officers too. Why in hell did we do all that drilling in an open parade ground when they knew we'd never fight on one. How can we keep a straight line over that busted-up ground?"
 Man next to me is just a boy really. Has the most frightened, pitiful look on his face. "What, boy? You scared? You want your mama?" He throws up on my trousers, then pees himself.
 "Jesus God."
 Here comes an officer on his horse to the front of the line. I think it's our brigade commander. Not real sure because he only came around a couple of times before to inspect us. Has his sword drawn and looks scared himself. Can only make out a few words since his stupid horse keeps dancing and twirling and turning him around, so his speech is shouted at the stone wall half the time. "Soldiers!" he yells. Then some garble, then something about God and the Country and home and wives and sweethearts. Then he turns and shouts the order to advance, echoed down the line by the officers on foot. We no sooner start to move and the enemy artillery begins again.
 Boy next to me is shaking so hard his bayonet is rattling.
 Shell explodes in the tree above us and a leg-sized limb drops. Hits the boy square on the head. His skull cracks and it sounds like

a ripe watermelon being split over my knee. He drops just as we reach the stone wall. Now's a good a time as any, I'm thinking.

I throw up my arms, drop my musket and fall behind the stone wall, snuggling my head next to the boy's. I smear some of his blood on my face. He's still alive, but most of his brains are oozing through the crack. I see his neck is broke, too.

Scoop a little more blood and run it around my face and start moaning. Rear line steps over us and then over the wall. The file closer, bayonet fixed to persuade any malingerers, gives a quick glance down at me then moves on following the line. Blood always works.

"Idiot." I hear myself say. Looking at the boy dying next to me, struggling to move and get a breath. "You, too."

CHAPTER 14

Tossing on a bulky old sweatshirt, her blue running shorts and jogging shoes, Mara managed to hook a leash to a spinning Reynolds. She had to muscle him out of the way with her knee so she could open the door to let them both out for their first morning walk. It was something she hoped to do each day to get the blood flowing for good writing.

The rays of the early morning sun cut horizontally, straight down the one main street of the town, setting the October foliage on fire. No building was higher than two stories, and the street, originally laid out for horses and wagons, barely managed to accommodate two-way traffic with parking along one side.

She turned to look at her own rented house. It was an antiquated, two-story, cottage-style, complete with an over-heated attic and musty, creepy basement. And a stubborn lock so worn the skeleton key had to be jiggled around each time before it would catch.

Some of the trees along her street had grown to mammoth proportions, lifting and buckling the brick sidewalks, and in places the macadam on the road had worn through and you could actually see red brick—and below that, some of the original smooth cobblestone that once covered the street. Modern big city planners would be aghast, but Mara thought the casual disrepair lent a certain charm to the town.

What *didn't* lend charm to the town, Mara thought as Reynolds paused to water a downspout, was the fact that there had been some battle fought nearby. She had never been that much into military history, but she was impressed—horrified, even—by the realization that along the street she and Reynolds casually strolled at one time men were slain, perhaps on the very spot where she stepped. Just outside of town, monuments to the armies and regiments and generals dotted the rolling countryside and a park had been established to commemorate and preserve the "hallowed ground."

But even without the monuments, Mara would have known something was a little weird about the place. It was something she had tried to describe as a writer, in her head, but couldn't come up with it yet. It was a different feeling, an intangible, like the sensation you get when you walk into a church. It's just a building, *but there's a feeling*....

Reynolds went berserk at a cat in a yard, jerking Mara from her reverie. She flashed back about her experience the night before and the frightening scene she apparently had imagined—or dreamed—in the elevator. She was so tired after moving into the old house, then researching the rest of the afternoon, she was willing to concede that perhaps she had dozed briefly in the elevator and dreamed the awful, realistic nightmare in just the few seconds of unconsciousness between the fourth and first floors.

And yet, the smells, the stares of the wounded men, the orderly.... If it was a dream, it was the most realistic one she'd ever had.

Other than the one she had the first morning. She shivered involuntarily at the recollection of being buried alive.

Her notebook must have fallen out of her pack somewhere in the library, or maybe on the way to her car; she would go back later and try to find it. The dream about being entombed...chalk that up to being overly tired from the drive, the move and a late meal. For now, however, she could consider herself lucky to have taken her notes on Ricard Fisher on her laptop and recorder rather than the small, lost notebook, and relegate whatever it was she saw from the elevator to overwork.

They turned left down a small side street and it was like they had slipped into a different century: ancient oaks arched across the street lined with picket fences; most of the sidewalks were brick, and the street was so narrow that cars could not park on it; the houses were all wooden clapboard; the morning mists rose from the ground and danced slowly like glowing specters.

There was a government plaque in front of one of the buildings identifying it as the site of a church where revivals were held during the war; thousands of men, for weeks before the battle, converted in the hopes of life everlasting should they be killed in battle.

"Fat chance," Mara said to Reynolds who seemed to be in his own little focused world. "Poor guys. Once you're dead, you're dead." She knew it for a fact. Her experience during the murders she'd covered working for the newspaper proved that to her. Those people, shot, mutilated, stinking, with grotesquely bloated twisted faces, were not going anywhere. But the finality of death was shown to her in an even more intimate way—by her own beloved grandfather.

Mara had to pull Reynolds, who seemed unusually reluctant to walk down that street. She noticed he stopped to lift his leg more often than usual. All she wanted to do was explore, and she figured there must be a cross street or alley at the end of this one where she could circle around the block.

But after a block the street emptied into a dirt farmer's lane that slowly began to descend into a dark sunken road. Before long she and Reynolds had plunged below ground level. The temperature dove. The mists were so thick the sun was blotted out.

Reynolds froze.

CHAPTER 15

Get back to camp with a crusty bandage soaked with the boy's blood still wrapped around my head. The blood hardened, made scratches on my head, staining the rag with my own fresh blood.

I shun the stewards who come near, acting like the wound makes me insane. I come around, get food, not talk to anyone. I'd make the Booth family proud with my performance.

Seemed an easy thing to shirk. If I'm going to keep this up, I probably don't always have to act like I was wounded. I see men straggling into camp days after the battle, with their muskets and cartridge boxes and packs. All they said was they got lost during the fighting, lost their unit in the smoke and maneuver, but fought real hard with some other boys, and that seemed good enough for the lame-brained officers. Fine. Next time....

There's a gathering at the rear of the camp. Someone's talking. I wander like I'm crazy toward the meeting.

"...and the Lord will cover you with his sword and buckler and yea, though you walk through the valley of the shadow of death, you will fear nothing...."

The company preacher. The last time I saw him before the battle, he was hiding behind the biggest rock I'd ever seen.

"...and the noble dead who have so unselfishly yielded up their lives for their Country shall rise up on the great day of resurrection, and shall be greeted by our Lord and savior...."

Noble dead? That poor stupid kid was killed by a falling tree limb. He unselfishly yielded nothing. He was unlucky, wrong place at the wrong time. Same with all the others. Forced into the battle by the goddamned file closers who would have bayoneted them in the kidneys if they stopped.

"...blessed are the meek. For they...."

Turn away and walk quickly down the company street out of earshot of the preacher. Suddenly I smell a strange smell, like rosewater, and feel heat rush in my head. Follow my nose toward the stream's edge. There she is.

One of the black contrabands that followed the army after running away from their masters. To keep them busy, the army has them wash clothes. Duck down behind a bush.

She's the daughter of one of the mammies who'd escaped hoping to end up somewhere in the north. Look around for Mammy, she's nowhere to be seen.

She's chubby. As she scrubbed the drawers, I see her young breasts flutter beneath her loose top. I begin to harden. It has been so long. Start to feel bold and alive again, ready to explode.

Move toward her on the lookout for Mammy. Behind a bush within ten feet and throw a rock into the water to distract her. In a moment I'm behind her with my knife at her throat.

"One sound, I cut you." She stops struggling begins to whimper softly. Drag her behind a huckleberry thicket. Down on the river stones she goes and I land on top of her, my knifepoint making a dent in her mahogany-colored throat. It's over in less than thirty seconds.

"Say anything to anyone," I'm panting, "I'll kill you. Understand?"

She nods her head. Push myself to my feet, button my trousers, start back up the stream bank. Turn to see her standing, looking at me. I make a quick gesture with the knife across my throat. She turns, begins to wash clothes again.

I smile and breathe deep, alive and satisfied.

CHAPTER 16

No matter how much cajoling she did, the dog would not move, but kept his eyes darting from her to something she couldn't see through the fog down the road. He whined and pulled and made such a fuss that Mara finally gave in.

"All right," she said to him as they turned back. "You win. It's okay. I don't know where this lane goes anyway." He pulled hard on the leash as they headed back. Twice coming out of that depressed lane, she turned her head, convinced she heard footsteps following.

Back at the house she again had her usual problem with the old skeleton key in the lock, but it finally opened.

She stripped off the sweatshirt inside out to let it dry and began to feed the dog. She started some coffee, pulled some milk from the refrigerator and grabbed a bowl and some cereal from the cupboard.

She had just put Reynolds's food down and was turning to set her own breakfast on the table. "What the hell…?" she heard herself say out loud.

Reynolds gave her a quick glance from crunching his breakfast, too busy eating to care.

On the kitchen table was a newspaper, folded open to the obituaries. "How did this get…"

Mara suddenly thought: *I might not be alone in the house.* She grabbed a baseball bat from a closet below the stairs. It was the only thing she had seen exploring the house on moving day that could serve as a weapon. She quickly decided to work her way from the upstairs down. She checked behind the bedroom door and the one closet built into the corner, finally appreciating the lack of closets in 19th century houses. *Nothing under the bed.*

Passing the bathroom, out of the corner of her eye she caught the movement of a body. Cold zipped up her spine. She swung into the bathroom, bat-first, and almost swatted her own image in the mirror.

Two more small rooms and the second floor was secured to her satisfaction.

As she moved through the first floor she realized that the world's best security system—the dog—hadn't made a peep at an intruder. She began to relax, checking each closet, then peered warily into the musty half-basement—a place that gave her the creeps with its inexplicable, partly-sealed indentations in the walls—then the doors, which remained locked and bolted, and finally all the windows: shut and locked. She let Reynolds out into the fenced-in back yard, listening for him to bark at an exiting intruder. Not a sound.

Sitting down at the kitchen table, she took a deep breath and stared at the paper. It was this morning's *Exponent-Sun*. It was icy-cold, as if it had come out of a deep-freeze.

There, beginning three inches above the fold was the headlined announcement of the death of 37-year-old Dr. Ricard Fisher, the pre-eminent theoretical physicist in the world.

"Oh, shit."

Even harder to believe was that Fisher apparently died by his own hand. Mara thought back to the interview. There was absolutely nothing in his demeanor that would even suggest suicidal thoughts. The body was discovered in his apartment yesterday evening. He had left a note, but its contents were being withheld. Details of the manner of death were being withheld as well. Must have been particularly gory, Mara thought.

His obituary told how Fisher had set the scientific world on its ear as the author of *Einstein, Schmeinstein*, his bizarrely-titled, iconoclastic book that mathematically, categorically disproved several of Albert Einstein's trademark theories.

The obit listed the numerous prizes he'd garnered, and said that, had he lived, it was likely there would be a Nobel Prize sometime in his life.

It said that Fisher's work was making modern physics understandable to the common man.

Still, the obit explained, even with his fame, few had known anything about the boyish genius who had been restructuring the methodology of modern human thought.

That's where I was supposed to come in, Mara thought.

She opened the folded paper and sharply drew in a breath. There, in the photo of the dead scientist, she recognized the image she had seen staring at her in her dream...or vision...or whatever it was in the elevator last night.

It was the very form in the white coat that had been standing at the back of the room observing the bloody gore with her.

She showered quickly, uncomfortably vulnerable behind the opaque shower curtain, feeling as if someone were watching her. She toweled off, fluffed her short dark hair with her hands, and pulled on blue jeans and a baggy cotton sweater.

A brief panic flashed through her head as she wondered if her publisher was still interested in Fisher now that he was no longer alive. This bio was to be her first major book. She would be devastated if it got pulled out from under her.

She picked up the phone and called her editor.

"Ackerman." Her voice was unmistakable. The years of smoking made it sound like she gargled hydraulic fluid every morning.

Yes, she was still interested in doing the bio.

"The guy offed himself at the pinnacle of his career, hopefully in some hideous way. He just made himself even more interesting. Keep at it, Kiddo."

Mara didn't even get a goodbye out before Ackerman hung up, coughing. But she did manage a deep sigh of relief that she still had the contract.

Her second call was to Mitch Landry, a long time friend living just out of town, who had set her up with the house she had rented.

She made a date for lunch in the park at noon just to catch up.

First there was some research to be done on Fisher's self-imposed death.

She jammed her laptop, digital recorder, and a replacement pocket-sized notebook into her backpack. She pulled a bottle of water out of the refrigerator—a machine that she was convinced had been there when the house was built in the early 1840s—zipped it in one of the outer pockets, and unlocked the massive oak door.

She gave the dog's head a rub and told him to be good while she was gone. She closed the door with a solid wooden and brass "kerchunk." The key worked fine this time.

Suddenly, after hearing her editor's enthusiasm, Mara wanted more than ever to finish her biography on the brilliant, ephemeral—and now tragic—genius, Ricard Fisher.

CHAPTER 17

Mara wanted to scan the newspaper archives for anything else she might be able to find on Ricard Fisher. Newspapers are notorious name-droppers. Early in her writing career she found she could pick up names of potential interviewees by perusing local archives.

She stopped in at the offices of the *Exponent-Sun*, made her introductions to the archival staff, and went to the jammed researchers' room. Amazingly there actually was a computer free and she began a search of the name Dr. Ricard Fisher.

The most recent article was written just three weeks ago. It covered an awards ceremony honoring him and his achievements in the field of theoretical physics as visiting professor at the university. His acceptance speech was a simple "Thank you," for the $250,000 award presented by BBG Software Corporation.

So, Mara thought, Dr. Fisher didn't commit suicide because he was a starving frustrated college professor.

The next oldest article covered a paper he had published the previous year revealing his newest theory on the connection between dimensions. The newspaper handled it all rather sketchily, but from what she could gather, the bottom line was that while all energy in the macrocosmic universe follows one event upon the other, in the microcosm of particle physics, the way things move, either forward or backward, is meaningless. If this works on energy, it must work on matter as well, since they are interchangeable. This tosses Einstein's theories, based upon the speed of light as a constant function of distance and time, into a cocked hat.

Whoa, she thought. What is he saying here? *Time doesn't always run from the past to the future?*

She read a little more and yes, he claimed that particles can move in one direction or the other—electrons can go either way around the nucleus—and it didn't matter. From the article she read a quote from Fisher: "Since this takes 'time' out of the speed/distance/time equation, we cannot use the speed of light with any certainty: it is not the absolute constant we—or Einstein—thought it was."

From her high school algebra class she *did* remember that every equation needed *one* constant and Einstein's equation $E=mc^2$ needs one constant or a known quantity to be solved. Einstein's constant was the speed of light. Without the "time" factor, the equation cannot be solved.

"Nor, then," he was quoted as saying, "is Matter the constant we thought. And Matter existing over the span of time, of course, is what we perceive as reality."

"This guy is good," Mara muttered, and got a look from the researcher next to her.

The next article was written about a year previous to that. It was a glowing review on his recently published book, *Einstein Schmeinstein*. It reported that while some traditionalist theoretical physicists were outraged by the work, all of them, with a couple of exceptions, had to agree that Fisher's mathematics were impeccable, that his theories were sound, and that, indeed, there must be certain forces that did travel faster than the speed of light.

Again, she thought. *That time thing.*

He had taken up the cause of a young university professor who theorized that the force of gravity was faster than light, since, if two masses were instantly created, their gravitational pull towards one another—and everything else—would be instantaneous at their moment of creation, whereas, because of the speed of light, they might not be seen at a great distance, for a number of minutes, or years. "In other words," she read, "we will *feel* the sun go out, when we spin off into space and icy oblivion, losing the gravitational pull of the sun before we see it vanish, with about eight minutes left until the world begins to darken and freeze. Conversely, we can be influenced by the gravity of things we still are not able to perceive."

The other force he proposed as instantaneous was the energy from ESP—Extra Sensory Perception.

Hold everything, she thought. The smartest guy in the world brings parapsychology mumbo-jumbo into his discussion? She jotted down in her notebook, *check goofy parapsych lead.*

The only other articles the *Exponent-Sun* had on Fisher were ones concerning his arrival at the university, and his instant acceptance as visiting scholar so that he could continue his groundbreaking research.

She began a web search of some of the papers he had written and presented at various conferences around the country. She found a few of the over-one hundred papers that he had published. They were fascinating, but once again, too technical for her. She noted them as sources, perhaps for an appendix.

Her natural writer's instinct told her that what she really needed was intrigue, some hook that showed he was a *sexy* brainiac. The story had now turned from a triumph into a tragedy, and she needed her readers to care even more about the rare bird himself, Ricard Fisher.

She had found another photo of him besides the one in his obituary. Again, a boyish grin gave his angular features an impishness she had begun to see in her interview with him. But it still wasn't the one she could use for a jacket cover. As she stared at the photo, the memory of the white-coated image she had seen—or dreamed—in the cellar of the library returned.

She needed to get deeper than the newspapers or his publications. She needed some personal stuff. *That second interview.*

Damn! she thought. Why did he have to kill himself?

She pulled out her cell phone and recalled a number from its memory. A few rings and a voice answered gruffly.

"Fosster. Yeah?"

"Oscar," Mara said in her sweetest voice. "Hi, baby. How are things?"

"Mac? That you? You on that dumb smart phone again? Speak up."

She stood and walked towards a window. "How are things going, handsome?"

"Stop right now. What do you want?"

"Why do you always think I want something, babycakes?"

"Now I know you want something 'cause you're buttering me up. The last time you did that I had internal affairs lookin' up my butt for a month and a half."

"But I did hard time for you, sweetheart."

"Hard time? You spent an hour in the holding tank because you wouldn't reveal me as a source after you practically gave up my badge number during depositions."

"But I never said your name. And you're still on the force."

She could all but hear him covering his eyes and shaking his head over the phone.

"And dinner afterwards was certainly worth it," she said.

She heard a hearty laugh on the other end of the line.

"Yeah. You stuck me with the check. And I didn't even get laid."

"But you knew you weren't going to get laid, honey bunch."

"Yeah. No shit. At least you're honest about that."

"I'm honest about everything, Oscar. You know that."

She could picture him smiling in the brief silence on the other end of the line. "Mara, it's a good thing I love you so much."

"And I love you too, Oscar. Can I come down and look at the files on Dr. Fisher?"

"What? The computer nerd that killed himself the other day? Hey, where are you?"

"I'm here, baby!"

"Oh, no! Not again. I thought I got rid of you after the trial when I almost lost my badge, my career, and my pension."

"Honey, you'll never be rid of me. I moved here to work on his bio, and now the guy just made himself totally interesting by killing himself."

"Oh, you are cold, girl. You got a publisher for this one?"

"You bet, O."

"That's my girl. Finally, huh? Congratulations. You're going to be a published author. I'm damn proud of you, Mac."

Mara could feel the sincerity over the phone. Oscar had witnessed the ups and downs from all the rejection slips over the years. "Thanks, O. You're a sweetie. Now, how about those files?"

"This is a simple one. How can I get in trouble for this, as long as I know you're willing to spend some hard time in the can to protect my good name."

"I'll be down right after lunch. See you soon, sweetness."

CHAPTER 18

"Here, son. Here's the door you want to walk into. Walk in this door and walk out a man."

Roscoe has his arm around the shoulder of a tow-headed boy who lied to his recruiter about his age. I think he's probably fourteen. Eyes are as wide as open barn doors and his face looks like his momma just scrubbed it. Through the open door I see three women. One has a red corset with bows, long stockings, high-button shoes, a red ribbon tied around her neck. Another in a full hoop skirt, like she's going to meet Mrs. Lincoln, except that most of her bosom is puffing out over the top nearly rubbing her thick chin. The last one walks through an inner door, and I see most of her rump and all of her back below and above a tiny dancer's green dress.

"Hey, Roscoe." a ruddy-faced corporal crows from the crowd. "Leave the babe alone. Can't you see he's gettin' ready to bawl."

Young man leans back against Roscoe's hand on his shoulders. Roscoe has some greenbacks waving them at the door.

"Come on, ladies. Come on and get yerself some fresh fish. Bet it's been years since you had anything that ain't been had before."

Woman in the corset smiles like she's hungry, walks to the door and reaches for the money. Roscoe grabs her wrist, pulls her into the crowd of drunken soldiers. A flurry of hands squeeze her breasts. One pops out of the corset. Other hands feel her backside, up her legs, around her crotch. Whole time she's giggling and shouting to the other girls to "get Madam."

A few seconds a huge black mammy comes from the doorway, pulls a hickory bat from behind the door, smashes Roscoe over the head, dropping him gushing blood to the brick road. As he falls, she snatches the money from his hand, waves the bat to drive away the rest of us.

She grabs the youngster by the scruff, pulls him and the whore back through the door. It slams and we all hoot.

I wish it was me.

"C'mon, boys." says Shadrack, a grizzled sergeant. "He may not live through the night. I need whiskey."

They hoist Roscoe by the arms, carry him down the street laughing at him.

I stay behind. For a few minutes I watch the door. During the scuffle I felt that old rush, my head spinning. Grew hard as I watched the girl being pinched and grabbed. Would have been in on it if I could have gotten closer. I watch the door, trying to think of a way to get in, do my business without paying any money, since I lost it earlier gambling. There's a sound like wooden boxes tumbling around in the alley next to the whorehouse.

I look around the corner. In the garbage in the shadows is Malachai. I see his hips thrusting at a dark form bent over a barrel. Once the form lifted its head. Malachai brought a fist down on it. The form slumped. Then it was over.

Malachai is out of breath, buttoning up his trousers. He begins to grin like Satan, motions for me to come over.

"Go to 'er, Laddie. My gift to you fer keepin' yer damned mouth shut."

Before I even know what I'm doing, I'm hunched over the soft, buttocks, slimy with Malachai's residue. Hear a soft grunt from the form as I enter. Know I'm not in the right hole, but it don't matter. Eight or ten strokes and it's over. I back out. Now I don't even want to touch the creature in front of me. Button my fly, wipe my hands on my trousers. Walk kind of lightheaded out of the alley into the gaslight of Pennsylvania Avenue.

As I turn the corner I'm startled by Malachai's face not a foot from mine.

"Well, Laddie, that didn't take long," he growls. His breath stinks of whiskey, cigars, garlic and fish. "Now you 'n' me, we got somethin' in common." He nods back toward the alley. "Young Private MacGillicuddy."

I turn to see a child-soldier, looking sixteen but probably no more than twelve, staggering out of the other side of the alley, trousers torn down the back. He holds them together with one hand and feels his way along the wall with the other.

"You mean…?"

"Stick with me, Laddie, and you'll taste all the forbidden treasures this war has to offer."

CHAPTER 19

A stop at a local deli, a quick hello hug and she was enjoying the glorious October day sitting on a park bench sharing a sandwich with Mitch Landry.

"So Mitch, how's things at the 'Think Tank'?"

"You mean with 'The Skulls'?"

"I can't believe you call them that. They're all geniuses."

"And still come up with sow slop for ideas." In spite of having lived in the north for a number of years, Mitch still kept his Georgia accent and his colloquialisms.

"You keep them in hand?"

"Lucky for me, for every nine ideas they come up with that are sow slop, there's that one that makes the company thirty million dollars. As long as I don't discard the wrong idea, I think I'll have a job. Speaking of which, how's the work on the bio going? Everything fall through since your subject died?"

"Actually, my editor said he'd just made himself more interesting by dying." Mara took another bite of sandwich and couldn't help but grin at the weird look she got from Mitch. "I know, the cut-throat business of publishing. But who am I to complain?"

"Your first book," Mitch said through a smile and held up his half-sandwich to clink hers in a toast. "I gotta tell you Mara, I'm proud of you. Only took nine years for you to become an overnight success."

"Well, it's not published just yet." Her mind suddenly flashed back to the horrible scene she saw—or thought she saw—from the elevator. The more she thought about it, the easier it was getting to relegate it to a flash-dream. *But here's the perfect guy to tell about it. Maybe Mitch can shed some light on what I thought I saw.*

Mara got through her account of the experience in the elevator, but made the mistake of inserting the word "ghost" in her narrative. It was fresh chum-slick strewn in the water to Mitch's shark-like thought processes.

"A ghost?" Mitch scooped spilled chicken salad from the deli paper on his lap with his finger. "You trying to tell me you saw a ghost?" He popped the morsel into his mouth, turned and grinned at Mara, a dab of mayo just under his lower lip.

"Come here, knucklehead." She wiped the mayo with a paper napkin. "Look, honestly I'm not sure what I saw. All I know is that I think I saw it." She paused at an uncomfortable thought: "Them," she corrected herself. "And I think they saw me."

"*They?* Now you're seeing more than one ghost? Look, Mara. Let me just repeat one small thing that seems to be eluding you right now: There are no such things as ghosts. Or 'haints,' as we used to call them in Georgia. Get it?" Mitch popped a chip into his mouth and grinned again.

Mara bristled at Landry's lack of sympathy, but then realized that this is exactly why she brought it up in the first place. Mara knew she would be in for a down-to-earth explanation on the impossibility of the event she had experienced being supernatural. Mitch was the perfect foil to make sense of the non-sensical.

"Well, then, what did I see outside the elevator?"

"I don't know. How about something in your eye? Blurred contacts? Sleep deprivation is always a good explanation. Maybe you had a quick bout of indigestion. Were you eating pepperoni pizza for supper again? Honestly, I don't know what you saw. No doubt it was a hallucination of some kind. There's really no other scientific or logical explanation."

"So you're saying that it really wasn't there? That what I know I saw wasn't there right in front of me?"

"Yeah. To be brutally honest." Landry sipped his soda and tossed a chip crumb to the nodding pigeons strolling around their legs, who rushed the morsel, *en masse.*

"Okay Landry. I'll give you that one. I may possibly—okay, probably—have been dreaming when I thought I saw Fisher and a couple dozen dying, bloody soldiers in a cellar, but I wasn't dreaming when I found the newspaper opened to his obit on my kitchen table."

"Maybe you were just thinking too much about doing his biography and inadvertently picked up the paper from your doorstep and tossed it inside when you left."

"It was *that* morning's paper, I never subscribed to it, and unless I was sleep-driving between 5:00 and 6:30 A.M., someone else had to have brought it to my house and laid it on the table. Without me seeing it when I took the dog out." She looked down at one of the blood-eyed pigeons. It tilted its head and looked back with one eye. "It's almost as if he is encouraging me to continue his bio," she said nearly under her breath, more to herself than to Mitch.

Landry stopped chewing, stared at her and shook his head. It took him thirty seconds to finish chewing, swallow and start talking again.

"What? Did you hear what you just said? Some guy purposely comes to you in a dream the night he commits suicide then delivers his obit to your kitchen table to consciously encourage you to do his biography. Huh?"

"I know, that sounds far-fetched, but…"

"Far-fetched? How about impossible? Things that go bump in the night are just that. Things. Tangibles. Not ghosts or spooks or poltergeists—or 'haints'—or whatever else we've called them. You had a brief waking-dream because of your exhaustion that seemed very real. You picked up a complimentary copy of the newspaper that had been delivered earlier when you came home with the dog, threw it on your table and forgot about it. Maybe you stayed up a little too late last night. Or were in one of your creative fogs. Hey, you could even be making all this up so that when you eventually write that book of fiction you've been threatening us with, everyone—including your old pal Mitch Landry—can swear that it really happened and that it wasn't fiction. That ought to be worth another $150,000 in book sales."

Landry glanced at her and regretted immediately what he had said. Mara first looked hurt. It smoldered into anger within a few seconds. She turned from him, slumped against the back of the bench and crossed her arms.

At that moment, Mitch Landry realized again why he was so enamored with Mara McKay. As she glared across the park, he could barely see her hazel eyes with their orange streaks shot through them. One dark eyebrow was lifted in anger. Her straight brunette hair hung past her ears to her chin and a few strands of bronze blew across her face. She had the looks to have been a model, or at least an actress, except her nose was just a tad too long. Her lips were full and naturally pouted. It was after several months of knowing her that he realized where the sexual attraction came from: the way her lips pouted made it look like she always wanted you to kiss her.

And although they had gone out a number of times as drinking pals when they both lived in Cleveland, and even nearly made drunken love one night under the influence of Dom Perignon before she left his apartment in a hurry, Landry knew, in spite of his attraction to her, they would probably remain just close friends. She had her writing, so she said, and men were a nice part of her life…but only a part. *And there had been that Rex guy….*

"Hey," he said. "I'm sorry. I didn't mean to insult your integrity as a.…"

"Knucklehead."

"Hey…"

"Shut up."

"You shut up." I remember this, Mitch thought.

"*You* shut up!"

"*You* shut up!"

"*You* shut the bleep up!"

She started to snicker then laugh, then jumped in his lap, and pushed the last bite of her sandwich in his face.

She popped up, scattering pigeons. "I gotta go," she said, glancing back over her shoulder at the mess on his face. "I've got a date with a guy from the Other World. See you later."

He sat on the bench with chicken salad from nose to chin, watching her brunette hair sway and her lovely butt move just below her casually slung backpack. Somehow, Mitch Landry found himself curiously jealous of this hallucination who had garnered so much attention from Mara McKay.

CHAPTER 20

Ghosts, huh? Mara thought as she sat down at her laptop with her third cup of coffee for the morning. That security guard was probably right and Mitch seemed to agree: that she had dozed off briefly in the elevator and dreamed that crazy scene of the Civil War hospital. What else could it have been, since ghosts don't exist?

She put the cursor in the search bar, typed in "Civil War Ghosts," and hit "enter." Within seconds she clicked on a YouTube video of a so-called paranormal investigator talking in what looked like his basement studio. She looked at the length. Eight minutes. I need a break anyway.

Fortunately he was a handsome well-spoken man in his forties, looking a little like a college professor. "Why would the American Civil War be such a fertile source for ghost stories? Possibly the huge death toll of approximately 850,000 in a war that lasted about four years. That's more dead American soldiers than in all other American wars combined."

What? Mara thought, and jotted down a note to fact check this guy's stats.

"Perhaps," he went on, "analyzing why spirits are thought to linger at certain places will help us understand."

Spirits *lingering*? Mara thought. *Like they're on vacation or at a bus stop?*

"First, an abrupt death is thought to cause spirit energy to remain at the place of its body's demise. Death comes so quickly that the surviving mental faculties don't even know that the body is dead. There is just no transition, no preparation for death, and the vital spark within continues operating like nothing has changed. Which leads us to a second reason thought to entrap spirits at a certain place.

"An unexpected death. Once again, a soldier, for one reason or another—perhaps his personal experience in previous combat situations—feels that he will once again come through unscathed. This time he's wrong. So he doesn't believe he's actually dead.

"Fear of judgment may also be a reason why the spirit refuses to move on. The Civil War was known for its numerous Christian revivals. They all knew they were violating one of the Ten Commandments when they shot and killed each other. They refuse to go to the final judgment for fear that it will not turn out well for them."

Man, Mara thought. *This is all presupposing that there actually are ghosts, that we retain some of our personality when we die.* She took another sip of coffee, relaxing a little and letting the guy continue knowing that at any moment one rude mouse-click could send him into Internet oblivion and her back to her writing.

"But from the anecdotal data collected over the centuries, what is it that ghost lore can teach us about the afterlife? Let's look at the classifications of hauntings that paranormalists have observed.

"First there is the Intelligent or Interactive haunting, where the ghost actually acknowledges the living percipient's presence, by talking to him or looking directly at her. Many, many examples of this type of haunting have been documented."

Kind of like when that orderly with the armful of amputated limbs looked directly at me from outside the elevator, Mara thought. *Stop it! That was a dream!*

"So an intelligent haunting means that the dead can still see, recognize and communicate with us."

Mara grabbed the mouse. *I'm going to click this guy just because he's...scaring me? Come on, Mara.*

"A residual haunting is one that repeats over and over, with no change, like a DVD."

"More like a GIF," Mara said out loud, "since the encounters are so short." Reynolds lifted his sleepy head for a second to look at her.

"Residual hauntings indicate that there seems to be no linear time involved in death; or perhaps time does strange things like loops back around upon itself. According to what we know about ghosts, death may also be timeless. They appear the same every time; they do not age."

Mara was reminded of something the actor James Dean once said: "Live fast, die young and leave a good-looking corpse." Or a good-looking ghost, she thought.

"Warps are another ghostly phenomenon. They are like a tear in time, like a portal opening up before our eyes to give us a glimpse into the past or possibly another dimension."

Mara sat up. He was describing what happened to her in the elevator.

"Warps indicate that reality may not be as solid as we think, that there may be portals to other dimensions or through time."

She looked almost sheepishly at the clock and clicked the pause button on the video. She clicked the minimize button and brought the file for the Fisher biography back on the screen. She started to type, but couldn't concentrate.

"It was just a stupid video," she said loudly. Reynolds stood this time. Mara took him out the back door into the yard. The warm autumn day helped her re-focus.

The video was over half done when she paused it. How often had she traipsed down Internet rabbit holes to avoid writing something she didn't want to write.

Now I'm writing to avoid that video. What? Are you afraid of where he's going to lead you?

She got Reynolds back into the house. At the top of her lungs she shouted: "There are no such things as ghosts!"

Reynolds ran into the living room and hopped on the couch. Mara sat back down and began typing again.

CHAPTER 21

I know we're in big trouble. The commanders. Goddamn commanders must all be insane. The enemy, not three hundred yards away, crouched down behind a solid stone wall. Behind them, artillery starts to limber up. Are they going to ride away...or toward us? That will make all the difference.

One cannon puffs smoke and fire. Sounds like a low cough. In a second a shell bursts overhead and pounds two men to the ground like they're driven with sledgehammers. Another two in front and behind them stagger. One hit on his arm, which suddenly goes loose. Starts to make his way to the rear but is stopped and examined by one of the damned file closers. The other has his rifle blown off his shoulder and begins to walk toward the enemy not knowing where he is. Blood streaming from his nose and ears. The stupidest smile on his face. Two pards go out, wheel him around, send him to the rear, a happy idiot. Maybe I'll do that as a dodge next time.

A few of the enemy were already popping off rounds. Hear the minie balls hiss as they pass the line. Hit one of those Goddamn officers. Hit the jackass who ordered this charge.

We're called to attention. Officers shout orders, the orders relayed down the line. A sudden knife of fear right through my gut. Move when the man next to me and in front of me move. Be finding a big rock to hide behind and play out as soon as I can.

But there are no big rocks in the field we cross. No trees, no swales to hide in. My gut is really tearing in me. We're so out in the open, so exposed. Start running now I still won't make it to the trees before we reach the enemy at this slow walk. Heaven help me. The Devil help me. Anyone. I don't want to die.

Artillery pieces I saw are not going away. They're riding down the hill behind the infantry. Infantry behind the wall stands, aiming a line of rifles, like some spiked animal angry at us crossing its territory. They stand and stand, rifles wavering in the sunlight. When are they going to fire? Stomach churns and I'm wild to find shelter. Goddamn them. They're taunting us.

Look down the line and there is Malachai marching along. Still has that look about him, like he's going to kill the first officer he sees then steal his haversack.

The entire line explodes in yellow fire. A dozen men around me are whipped to the ground. They shriek, moan, humph like they'd been struck by a fist in the gut. Thumping of lead into their flesh sounds like they were all kicked by mules at the same time.

Smoke from their rifles drifts slowly into our lines, it's hard to see. We keep moving forward. Look over, but Malachai isn't there anymore. Did he dodge? Lying on the ground somewhere? Can't tell. Got to find a way out of this.

CHAPTER 22

On her way to the police station Mara drove past some of the larger sandstone and brick mansions of restored downtown. She thought again of her grandfather, who had driven her when she was only twelve to Shaker Heights, a ritzy Cleveland suburb.

He knew I wanted to be a writer. He stopped in front of one of the huge Victorians and made me get out of the car. He sat me down beneath a tree at curbside, gave me a pen and a pad of paper, and told me to write about the house. "There's nothing to write about, Pop-pop; I don't know who lives there; I don't know anything about it."
"Just start writing. Start describing it. It will work, you'll see." I watched him drive away.
He parked just down the street and when he saw me lay the pen down he drove up. I had filled nine pages. I described the house, then what I imagined to be the history, then the imaginary generations of families who had lived there with the layered memories.
He asked to see it. I saw his gray face crack and his watery eyes tear up when he read the last sentence. "...somewhere in our little hearts, in our little families, in our little houses, in our little towns, on this little, little earth, we'll find what we all seek so desperately: a way home."
"Yes," he had said, pulling out his ragged handkerchief, stained permanently with his sweat from years in the mills. "Thank God, you'll be a writer some day."

It was the best writing exercise she'd ever done, including anything in college. But his encouragement was his greatest gift to her.

He lived another five years, and died one summer as a result of emphysema—complications from spending his entire life as a smoker in the steel mills of Northern Ohio. Mara was heartbroken.

He was the only one in the family who had continued to encourage me to be a writer. Everyone else said I was wasting my intelligence or begging to be a starving artist, or just plain dumb. Since his death, I wished a thousand times I could talk to him again, to receive his special brand of encouragement.

I thought I might hear from him again, or at least be aware of his presence even after his death. In spite of my trying to be sensitive to any spiritual incident or to be aware of even the tiniest feeling that he was near me, it didn't work.

Then, after years, she was convinced. There's nothing after we die. Nothing.

Because, if there was anything to this heaven or nirvana or life after death, surely, surely, if there was a way, Pop-pop would have let me know, would have come to me.

And my recent dream in the elevator and forgetfulness bringing in the paper were simply taunting me. Mitch was right. There were rational explanations for both events. There is no such thing as an afterlife, or the other world.

She almost passed the turn into the police station.

She parked in the reporters' space and jogged up the stairs to the detective section. There was Oscar Fosster with his feet up on his desk reading a *Smith and Wesson* gun catalog.

"Getting ready to re-arm, Detective?"

"New back-up weapon, Mac. Look at this one. Holds ten rounds and one chambered. Eleven rounds of .45 caliber mayhem small enough to fit in the palm of your hand"

"Now, why is an eleven round gun better than one that holds ten?"

The sergeant looked up from the catalog and Mara could see the experience in his swimming-pool-blue eyes. She knew about—hell, she'd written about—the one-on-one wild west shoot-out he had won against a nut-case terrorist in a Branfield Heights schoolyard three years ago. He'd taken two bullets from a TEC-9 and just stood there, broad as a wall, as a shield for the screaming kids, calmly squeezing off rounds until one hit the bearded maniac in the forehead.

They both said the mantra at the same time: "Because eleven rounds is one more than ten."

She just shook her head, smiled admiringly at Oscar Fosster, and sat down in the chair in front of his desk. She had met him doing research for an earlier Internet series on Branston Sheely, the serial killer, had actually gotten embroiled in the court case and was called in to reveal a source for some incriminating evidence. That's when she'd been cited for contempt for not revealing her source. Her source, of course, had been Fosster.

"What's with the interest in the computer geek Mac? The guy sounds pretty boring to me."

"The life *you* live, O, bailing out of the space shuttle would seem boring. Actually, some people thought the guy was on the cutting edge of a lot of iconoclastic theories about physics. Stuff that went right to the core, the definition of reality, and such. He was brilliant, and so young. Had he lived he would have changed a lot of thinking about the way we all look at the world. It's like Einstein dying at 35."

She got an over-the-reading-glasses look from Fosster.

"Okay, let me try this again," she said. "It's like Cal Ripken dying at 21. Get it now?"

"Wrong team." Mara forgot Fosster was a rabid Red Sox fan. "But I get your drift. Come on." He stood slowly, apparently still feeling the effects of his old wounds. He certainly deserved—but turned down flat—disability. "Let's go to the file room."

They left the detectives' area and strolled down the brightly-lit white hall. This was no Hollywood police station: no dusty sepia photos of old, long-dead lawmen on the walls, but pastel colors and modern art.

"Actually," Mara began absent-mindedly, "he—Fisher—could write on two different levels: one for the intelligentsia and another for us poor slobs who had trouble with 10th grade math. So a fairly large number of people were followers."

"Keep talkin'." Fosster was obviously not convinced. "What else is there about him? I know you McKay. You're not going to put in a couple years of research if there's not a…what the hell do you writers call it…a handle?"

"A hook. You're right, O. He had a little bit of charisma, too. He had appeared on *Rosie* and *Oprah* and a couple of other daytime programs. He had a walk-on in *The Young and the Restless*, and was kind of cute in an angular sort of way. I just thought…"

"What else?"

"Damn you, O. Will you quit reading my mind. Can't I just research the guy without you needing to know my deepest, darkest, inner secrets?"

Fosster raised his hands in mock surrender. "I know, I know. 'Read the book.' Here."

They turned into the files room and opened the drawer marked "F". "Here's where I'll be someday," Oscar joked darkly. "I can just see you reading through my obit."

"Or writing it. Now, *you'd* make a great bio."

Fosster tossed the file so that it made a slapping noise on the long wooden table. "Help yourself. Stop by before you leave."

He started to turn but she grabbed his big arm and swung him around. She threw her arms around him. "You know," she said. "If you weren't such a big dork cop…"

"Yeah, and if you weren't such a big ho…maybe we could…"

They looked at each other and sneered simultaneously, "Naaaa." Laughing as he walked out the door, he left her alone with the file on the dead theoretical physicist.

Mara couldn't help but smile. For all the blatant, insouciant flirting she did with him, she knew that Oscar Fosster was the real thing, one of the last of the breed that tamed the American west or stormed beaches under fire.

He had often spoken—bragged, actually—about how, after the Civil War, thousands of African Americans went west, and that there were as many black cowboys as there were white. He once traced his ancestry back to a black cowboy from Montana—and then to a white slaveholder from Alabama—whose names escaped her at the moment. In homage to his great-great grandfather—the black one—he wore his closely cropped beard. Plus, he always added, "babes dig it." Oscar was an original, and she appreciated that.

She sat down and opened the file. A chill rolled up her spine from tailbone to neck, like someone had run an icy hand there. She looked behind her, but the door was closed and the air conditioning vent was across the room. The chill was so intense that the hairs on her arms stood. She shivered, rubbed her arms, pulled out a pen and some note cards, opened her laptop, and lifted the first document from the file.

It was the autopsy report. She started jotting down the technical terms she needed definitions for, then ran through a list in her head of physician friends she could call for the information.

She had finished going through the autopsy report in less than twenty minutes. No alcohol or drugs in his system, no diseases, no cancer, or something he had been hiding from the world. Everything seemed normal, except the shocking way he died.

She read of the large caliber bullet wound that killed him. A *huge* caliber bullet wound, like .58 caliber. Mara wasn't even sure they made bullets that big anymore. It seemed more like a hideous sadistic murder. It was, without a doubt, the strangest case of suicide she'd ever encountered. In fact, she was surprised the coroner had classified it as such.

"Hey, this ain't working, O." Mara had popped her head into Fosster's office and surprised him. His back to the door, startled, he jolted, glanced quickly over his shoulder, and took a deep breath. She swore she saw his hand go to his gun then relax. "Oops," she said.

"Mara. Don't..."

"I know, I know. Don't ever sneak up on a cop. My bad." She remembered when they had gone to dinner after Sheely had been convicted. He specifically had their table changed to one against the wall and made her sit facing the wall while he sat with his back to it. At first she thought it was because he wanted to watch the women, and she teased him about it. He carefully explained the built-in paranoia of every cop then told her that she really *wanted* him to be the first one to know when the bad guys came into the room, rather than her or anyone else. She asked how he knew just who the "bad guys" were. He answered without hesitation that he just knew. She scoffed then, but it was true.

"You done with the reports already?"

"There isn't anything in them."

"No 'handle', huh?

"Hook."

"Whatever."

"Detective Fosster, now I need a really big favor."

"Oh, shit. Here it comes. The one that brings in Internal Affairs."

"I need to get into his apartment."

"Wups. There it is. Sorry, Mara. It's still under lock and key. Besides, only the next of kin are allowed in there. Legally, it's their stuff now."

"I know all that. I just need something more personal than the autopsy reports. They give me a little, but not enough."

"I can't Mara."

"Come on, O. Even if you got caught—which you never do—what are they going to do to their hero-cop?"

"You'd be surprised. Besides, that was a while ago. Everybody's forgotten."

"Fat chance they have. Hey, you can come along. Watch every move I make. I'll even leave the bathroom door open."

He chuckled. "You *did* learn something in your 45 minutes in the box."

"It was an hour!" She faux-pouted. "You're lucky I didn't come out a hardened criminal-type, with a girlfriend, a 'tude and tattoos."

Fosster had to laugh. "You already *have* a tattoo."

He could swear he saw her blush and fluster.

"Oscar. Shit. How did you know about that?"

"We cops know everything."

"Are we going?"

Fosster shook his head in resignation. How does she do it? he wondered as he found himself walking out with her, the keys to Fisher's apartment palmed from the holding cabinet.

This girl's good.

CHAPTER 23

The man in front of me continues to walk, but there's something funny about him. His kepi sits at a funny angle on his head. He turns to look down the line and I see a quarter of his head, from right eyebrow up is a bloody gray pulp and the hairy, bloody skull flaps down over his ear. Still he walks, doing the last thing his now-scrambled brain had told him to do.

I'm going to throw up. Fall to my knees. That volley was as good an excuse, now with all the confusion, to drop out of this fight. Look for shelter. Nothing in the flat field but the bodies of the dead and the squirming wounded.

There was a sharp prick in my spine.

"What the hell?..." I turn. It's the file closer, bayonet at my back.

"Where ye hurt, sonny? Show me red or I'll show ye some."

Goddamn Irishman. I look up into dull gray eyes above a full red beard. The Irishman had taken a bullet from the last volley across the shoulder, ripping his sleeve but drawing little blood.

"Then, by God, if yer not hurted, git up and be a man or I'll kill ye where ye lays like the shittin' dog ye are."

No choice. The sergeant saw right through my dodge. Stand and jog back to the line. The men had stopped to return a volley and temporarily disappeared in the foul-smelling smoke. Look back, but the sergeant has his eye on me.

A few rebels had fallen across the wall, but both sides are reloading. See that the enemy will be ready to fire before our line, so I place myself behind a large farm lad. The enemy fire and men scream. At the same time I turn and put a ball into the chest of the file closer, not ten feet away. He falls to his knees, then onto his face. Watch the blood spit from his mouth.

Look to the rebel line as I re-load. In the smoke, nobody noticed that I fired in the wrong direction. Doesn't matter. We have something more important to worry about. The rebel infantry at the wall has parted. See mouths of cannon line up one by one at the wall. A young officer on a white horse panics and starts shouting orders that make no sense. An older officer rides over to him and relieves him of command and he starts to ride to the rear. The graying officer orders our line to advance. He must be insane.

CHAPTER 24

Apartment was the wrong word for where Dr. Ricard Fisher had lived in Harrison, a restored artsy section of town. Penthouse was more like it. If this guy was the king of the nerds, Mara thought, he certainly had exquisite taste when it came to decorating. Sculpture seemed to be his thing. The female figure seemed to be his thing. The female *buttocks* seemed to be his thing, Mara realized as she scanned the room. There were nude sculptures scattered around, all done in white marble on white pedestals against white backgrounds, like dozens of naked materializing specters.

In concordance with the elaborate and expensive decorations was a sophisticated security system that consisted of numerous interior locks. While one key could get you in, a half-dozen deadbolts, chains and locks would keep you safe inside.

Oscar had wandered over to a magnificent leather couch with a console imbedded in the middle. "Watch this," he called across the room and bent to flip switches.

One by one, the figures were illuminated by an intense spotlight. Then the light would shift to another angle and dim as Fosster played with the switches. The effect was dramatic. The figures seemed in motion, like spirits moving through the night, a *danse macabre* performed for Dr. Ricard Fisher's own personal pleasure by naked, pale, cold wraiths.

"Quite a show, huh Mac?"

"Kinda weird, if you ask me. What else is there?"

"Over here is his in-house lab."

Fosster led the way to a step-up platform covered with redwood parquet. The walls were banked with a dozen computer screens. Three keyboards were spaced evenly about the room on large executive-style desks. A single secretary's wheeled chair was placed at the middle console. On each side of each keyboard were spread graph-style lined papers, most of which were covered with pencil jottings of formulae. Some were savagely scratched out. Many were covered with three-dimensional drawings and mathematical equations scrawled next to them.

One whole wall was covered, floor-to-ceiling with books: textbooks, mostly, and bound scientific journals. Virtually every book was full of yellow post-it notes, upon which he had scribbled a reference note indicating that he had read nearly every one of them.

In one corner near a surround-sound speaker set-up there was a CD collection of classical music: Bach, Rimsky-Korsakov, Vivaldi, Beethoven, Addinsell, Handel, Liszt, Grieg, Mozart, DeBussy. Mara understood. Classical was the only music she could write to.

But there was a solid collection of blues too: Clapton, Muddy Waters, Lightnin' Hopkins, Kenny Wayne Shepherd, B.B. King, Howlin' Wolf, Stevie Ray Vaughan, Jonny Lang.

On a smaller set of bookshelves to one side of the room was a small grouping of military books: titles spanning the period from the earliest of wars to the Middle East wars, but concentrating mostly on the American Civil War and World War II, mostly Pacific Theater. World War II made sense to her, with his interest in physics and the atomic bomb. *But why the Civil War?*

"Looks like you could press a button," she mused out loud, "and have one of these bookshelves spin around to reveal a hidden cellar with Dracula in it."

"I wouldn't have pegged him as the mad scientist type, except for the way he offed himself," Fosster said.

"So, O. Where did he do it?"

"Sorry, Mara. That's off limits."

"If I promise not to touch anything…?"

"No."

"Just a peek? Just to make sure you guys didn't miss anything? You know how I need to get a 'feel' for someone I'm going to write about. I can't do that without your help, O. How about two minutes? Just one? Just let me look in the room, or just set foot in it. Please? I won't tell anyone, I promise. Remember the time you needed that confidential information to make the Seeley arrest? We work well together, don't we, Oscar?"

There was the silence she knew her fusillade of questions would cause. Mara also knew Fosster would eventually cave. In spite of her obvious, campy regression to adolescent attempts at manipulation, theirs was a special relationship, and he knew that if anything went wrong, she *would* go to jail rather than reveal him as a source. And Mara knew how far Oscar Fosster would go for her.

At least as far as he did for the kids in the schoolyard.

Fosster walked silently over to the front door, locked it and slid one deadbolt into place.

"So we can have a little privacy," he said. He walked over to her, paused a second, hunching his massive body over hers, and untied the yellow "crime scene" tape at the door of the death room. Mara opened the door.

She stepped across the threshold into frozen bedlam: an overturned chair, papers scattered, a bedspread clumped together on the floor like a miniature mountain range.

Blood was spattered and dripped and thrown across the room and the walls and ceiling looked like one of those paintings done by that elephant, only in one color: rust. She moved closer to a wall, lit her tiny high-intensity light and almost gagged as she saw that some of the blood matted on the wall still held hunks of flesh, artery, and flecks of bone within it. She could smell the iron from the clotted blood pooled on the carpet.

She unconsciously flinched as her thoughts flashed back to the hospital scene she saw in the basement of the university library.

"They're calling this a suicide?" Mara said as she turned her eyes to the sculpture garden outside the room for a little break from the mayhem. "Looks like a Mafia torture scene from the thirties, like the St. Valentine's Day massacre, for cryin' out loud."

"He shot himself with a Civil War rifle firing a .58 caliber Civil War bullet. That's over half an inch in diameter. Made out of soft lead and expands when it hits flesh and bone. Bigger and more inhumane than any jacketed bullet we have today. Goes in the size of your thumb, comes out the size of your fist. You okay, Mac?"

Mara had to take a few deep breaths with her head outside the door. This guy was pretty far out, she thought. The autopsy report didn't do this shooting justice at all. She finally pulled herself together to look back in the room.

"Was there a note?" she asked.

"Yes and no."

"What's that mean, O?"

"Off the record, that means the note they thought they found was just a bunch of equations. Probably just a scrap from his work that fell out of a notebook."

"No explanation for all this?"

"Pretty nutty, huh?"

"Hey, O. This makes no sense. This guy had everything to live for. Yeah, he was a science nerd, but he was the king of science nerds. He was the crossover geek, making the pop shows with Oprah and Rosie and stuff. Plus, he was brilliant. He knew he had a fabulous future. He was working on some groundbreaking theories. He was as dedicated a scientist as you could imagine. This is the work of some self-hating sicko."

"Maybe it got to him." Oscar hovered around Mara like he was ready to catch her when she finally passed out. "I mean, being ostracized all his life. Like the kids in the high schools who flip out and gun down their fellow students because they were never athletes."

"This guy was no high school kid. Hey, what's this?"

She bent and lifted a small piece of paper that was peeking out from under a nightstand.

"Mara! Don't.... Oh, man! There you go. Disturbing a death scene. Now, why did you do that?"

"Easy, O. Your guys have already been through this. This is something they missed."

The paper was blank. But when she turned it over she saw some of Ricard Fisher's scientific handwriting including a date, several calculations, half a dozen three-dimensional sketches, one with an exclamation point behind it, and what seemed to be a footnote or reference phrase and number. Also, in tight tiny printing the words, "See you later."

"What is it?"

"Nothing, Oscar. Some more of the mumbo-jumbo." She folded it and put it in her coat pocket.

"Mara..."

"Come on, O. Your guys took everything they wanted. You said there was no note. This probably blew in here from the other room. I need it to write about the guy. Something of his. It helps, honest.

I'm kind of like a bloodhound. Give me something to sniff and I'll track down my man."

Detective Fosster just shook his head. "You're a real piece of work, girl."

They left the death room. As they walked to the door to leave the apartment, Mara stopped and looked back. "Hey, O. Ever wonder what it's like to die?"

If anyone has, she thought, it would be Oscar.

"Nah. Not really."

"What do you think it's like?"

Oscar twisted his neck to get out a kink. "I've seen a lot of dead people over the years. There's not a lot to see. They're just dead. So, I think death is just a whole lotta nothing."

"Yeah. Me too, I guess."

CHAPTER 25

Our line moves forward and I'm close enough to see the cannoneers load canister. Seen it before in the artillery camps. Dozens of lead balls packed into a tin can. It makes a giant shotgun of the cannon, tears holes in packed ranks like ours....

They're priming now, lanyards are stretched taut. Close enough to hear a scream, "Fire!"

Fake a stumble and go to ground like an animal. Roll on my back, look up and see pieces of men—arms, legs, bodies, heads—fly in the air above. Smell shit from the soldier in front whose guts had been blown on my chest. Move but feel a sharp pain in my hip. I look and see an arm and hand protruding from below my coat. Pull on the hand and the arm comes loose from where it was driven into my waist. It's still warm. Can't tell whose blood drips from my wound.

"Up, up you men. Into line before they can re-load." Commander rides along the line, eyes mad, sword like a whirly-gig, like he's going to cut off his horse's head at any second. "Guide center, on the double-quick, forward! For God's sake, forward!"

I'm happy to lie right here, but a goddamn sergeant on foot beats me on the shoulder with the flat of his sword. If only I had loaded my rifle, this baby-faced son-of-a-bitch would be dead.

"I'm wounded, let me lie. I'm hurt."

Sergeant is thrown aside. There's Malachai, huge, a crazy look on his face.

"Malachai! Thank the devil it's you. Help me dodge, will you?"

He grins like a fiend.

"No, Laddie," he rasps. "It's your turn. Time to join us. And I'm here to help." Grabs me by the collar, lifts me up, shoves me back into line. It moves quickly toward the enemy. Look back, but the smoke is so thick, can't see anything beyond ten feet. Jog a few steps, smoke clears and I see the gunners reloading.

Shouting, "On the run, men! Before they can prime the pieces! Faster men! Run!" Then, "Oh, Mother of God, help us."

Look up to see we're thirty yards from the muzzles of the guns. A young gunner pulls the lanyard tight. His face becomes a red explosion, he goes down. Fifteen yards, now, and some old bastard picks up the lanyard. Someone shoot him. Someone shoot the son of a....

Flash of white heat hits my face with the loudest noise I ever heard. All is whirling till the rolling stops. Can't blink, can't take a breath, suffocating. Can see, but things are upside down. See my uniform crumpled there with pieces missing, arm, leg, gushing blood...from my neck...headless body...no wonder I can't draw a brea...Malachai...goddamn Malachai...it...fading...gray...white.

CHAPTER 26

Even in her own home, with Reynolds warm at her feet, writing up her mental notes, she still shuddered at the apparent ferocity of the suicide scene. This guy virtually tortured himself to death, she thought. Why the hell would anyone put themselves through that?

She paused at her laptop. There must be some connection between his life and the way he died, some mental aberration that caused him to inflict so much pain upon himself before he ended it. Something that never showed in her face-to-face with him.

It almost seemed that this was becoming the main story of his nascent biography: not his award-winning work in physics, but what it was that caused him to choose such a morbid method of death. It was sort of like Marines jumping on hand grenades, or kamikaze pilots in World War II.

But what was it in Dr. Ricard Fisher that made him choose to die the way he did? What mattered more to him than life?

She picked up the phone book to look up his next of kin. No luck. There were dozens of Fishers in the book. She tried a search on the net, but still, with no hometown, she was at a loss. Finally she called the funeral home that was taking care of the service and found out the time of the funeral. Today at six. At the university chapel.

Driving to the funeral her phone rang. A quick check showed it was her friend and former roommate Amanda in Cleveland.

"Mander! S'up, roomie?"

"Hey, Mara. Just calling to see how you're doing. At least you're still functional after your going away party."

"Yeah. Thanks for the headache for half the drive here. Oh, and for hiring Jack the Stripper. But I'm all moved in. Got a nice office in the kitchen all set up right next to the coffee. What's going on with you?"

"Not a lot. Just wanted to check in. What are you doing right now?"

"Well, I'm driving to a funeral."

"Get out! You just got there. Who died?"

"Believe it or not, the subject of my book. Ricard Fisher."

"Oh, no. Does that mean you're not going to do the book? Honey, you've been waiting so long for this."

"My publisher is way too mercenary for that. My editor said the guy just made himself more interesting."

"Whoa, that is cold."

There was a longer than usual silence from Amanda.

"You okay? Still there?"

"Yeah. I was just thinking about the last funeral you went to."

"My grandfather?"

"Yeah. He was the sweetest guy...."

And, Mara thought, the most horrible day of my life, to that point.

Dear, dear Pop-pop. After her parent's divorce—which hit her hard like most children—he became more than a mainstay, more than the one family member she could trust. She would run to him at his shop—a little shed in his back yard where he worked on his projects—whenever her parents would begin arguing. He would read her fear of the most beloved beings in her life fighting, and would find something for her to do—not just busy work, but something useful. When he found out that she wanted to write, he seemed to understand that there was no holding down the stories and the people that grew within her and her desire to share them. She read him some of the first stories she had written when she was only eight or nine. He later told her he had secretly watched her as she carefully formed the letters into sentences and sentences into paragraphs. While the stories were childish—with mismatched analogies and overly dramatic endings—he still encouraged her, because he figured being a writer was so much better than how he had to make a living.

In the family, he was the only one.

Mara heard Amanda's voice through her thoughts: "Now, are *you* still there?"

"Yeah. You just got me thinking about him."

A couple of years after he died, she found among the papers he kept in his business desk, her stories, each and every one, from the first silly shipwreck story to her last high school newspaper editorial.

"I'm sorry. I didn't mean to bring back sad memories."

"Oh, no, Mander. They are wonderful memories. You have no idea how many times I have wished I could talk to him, lean on him again."

His encouragement offset the random, often drunken slams from her father, who told her "there are a lot of writers out there unemployed," and that she should concentrate her studies on a business degree. It seemed that, every chance he got, her father would discourage her for having her nose in a notebook, writing. "You're wasting your time."

"The divorce wasn't fair for you." She heard Amanda sigh.

"Who's to say what's fair in this crazy world? Hey, I'm at the funeral now. Just found a parking space. How about if I call you sometime in the next week?"

"You just take care of yourself. Love ya!"

"Love you too, sweetie."

Mara sat in her car watching the black-clad and blue-jeaned crowd queue up to the doors of the chapel. She really didn't know Ricard Fisher that well. She was here just for the contacts she might make. *And Amanda thought my editor was cold.*

So, it was even more ironic that her much-loved, gentle, caring grandfather's death was what gave Mara her writer's skepticism and doubt about so-called life after death.

Dressing in black made it all come painfully back.

CHAPTER 27

"Where am I? Who are you? Why can't I recognize you? Why can't I even see your features clearly? What has happened to my eyes?"

Hovering creature floated, shimmering a few feet from me. Distance is skewed: there is no distance. No time either. Can't tell if the thing had been there a few minutes, a day, or ten years. Can't tell how long I've been here, staring. As if time didn't move.

"Speak, damn you!" I try to say. Thinking it, but can't hear myself or my words outside me.

Same is true of the response: aware of it, but can't hear it.

"Don't be afraid," it seemed to say. The fact that I understand it, but not hear it, scares me.

"Who are you?" I ask. Why do I assume it is alive? Don't even know what it is. But it moves, floats before my face.

My entire body—or where my body should be—tingles with millions of pinpricks. My senses seem so alive. But, all around there is nothing to be alive to. Around me seems a void, but not a black void; more of a lighted gray, almost a foggy morning on a body of water. Now comes the noise: thunder, was it? Sometimes distant, sometimes right at my shoulder. Or a long ominous low roar. Now a heavy thumping bang, like I'm standing next to a bass drum when it is struck. What is that infernal whistling, like a hard wind through the rigging of a ship?

Now I'm aware of speed, feel acceleration, like on the back of a racehorse, only so much faster: ten, twenty, a hundred times faster, faster than I've ever gone before. Going through a narrow tunnel, so narrow at such great speed I know I'm going to crash into the sides. But the tunnel is made of light.

People appear off in the mist.

Recognize some of them. Some of them are familiar, but cannot place them. All around now: above, below, to all the sides of where

I am. Reach out, but no matter how close they look, I can never quite touch them.

My hands are made of the same misty shining substance they are. Feel no pressure pulling me down, as if I'm floating. Feel my feet upon something, like the thickest velvety moss I had ever touched. It gives way as I touch it. Confusing, understandable at the same time, as if I'd been here before.

Approach beings made of the same shining, glowing, blue-white light as I, they begin to reach out. I recoil; then realize I know them. Not recognize them, but know them on an intimate basis. Feel they are all related, and related to me. Features on their faces clear a little. Look like people in my family. Brothers and sisters and uncles.

Moving toward me is grandmother, ten years dead now. The others I recognize—they had been dead too, for years

I scream, nothing emerges, except a mass of fear from deep inside. Forms grow translucent, vanish as I pass the spot where they had been. Feel relief, but only for a moment.

Misty light tunnel begins to darken, break up along its edges. There are things, shapes, outside the tube of light, as it begins to mist away. What I see horrifies.

Me, or my body, or what was left of my body, in bits and pieces below, as if I were hovering above it. Men pulling the pieces together, tossing them into a wheelbarrow with other pieces of other men. There...what was that? My God, it is my own face on the bloody ball of meat that soldier just picked up. Holding it by the hair, laughing...so are the others! Throws it into the wheelbarrow, it sloughs hard against other body parts. But I feel no pain. What is this?

Now where are we? Keep moving from one place to another. In a house now, in a...a...funeral parlor. Going downstairs though, not to the finely finished parlor but into the cellar. No! Soldiers are shoveling the pieces into a hole in the wall. They toss the bloody ball with my face on it into the hole. Toss a muddy, bloody kepi on top. Smell musty earth. I am in there, and here watching, at the same time. See it getting dark. They're closing the hole with boards, dirt. No. No.

In panic, fear, I turn toward the light tunnel, feel myself move along it. It begins to change colors. A figure near the end. It seems so real, but I'm confused as to what is real and what isn't. See features on the figure, begin to recognize the features. My God, I know it.

Malachai.

CHAPTER 28

This is some kind of a geek's carnival, Mara thought as she walked toward the university chapel. Teaching colleagues, the university president and his administration, admirers from other institutions both home and abroad, many carrying their holy laptop computers to the funeral like others carry Bibles, filed into the sanctuary and sat. Fisher's casket was open, in spite of the fact that his method of suicide, it was finally revealed, was extremely violent. The newspapers had made something about it. They said that it was almost as if he were trying to make some sort of point, or perhaps create something—an impression—so that he would never be forgotten. Just why, at the upswing of his career and nearing the apex of his intellectual powers and energy he would choose to kill himself, was an enigma. And why he would dramatize his death in such a violent way just to be remembered didn't make sense to Mara.

But, on a purely professional level, that was just the kind of senseless death and mystery that made for a good book. So she needed to be here. As well, she needed a contact, someone to interview on a personal level, a family member whom she might meet at the funeral. That, and the weird coincidence of her dream of the hospital scene with him in it—since Mitch had convinced her it must have been a dream—was why she was here.

As she sat through the service and listened to the eulogists drone on about wasted talent and youth and a troubled mind and soul that no one had detected or appreciated, she wasn't buying it. They listed his achievements, from his first publications at eleven years old, to his Ph.D. at seventeen, to his whirlwind double career of professor to the intellectually elite to celebrity theoretical physicist. Some pop singer, it was revealed, had featured him in her last music video for God's sake, and Springer was looking to book him. He had an agent who sat weeping at the front of the church, no doubt more for the lost future revenues than for the person lying in the casket before him.

Everything in Fisher's life to this point had been calculated. He would not have ended it on a whim, or because he was depressed. From what Mara had read, he was the pure intellectual, the calculator, the orchestrator of his and other's lives. What was still a nagging, underlying question for Mara, of course, was: *was it really suicide?*

One by one the rows stood and began to file past the casket. As she drew closer, she saw computer chips and thumb drives strewn upon Fisher's dead chest, some kind of wonks' offering. She thought of how proto-humans one hundred thousand years ago, foolishly began to bury their dead with food and implements to help them get started in the other world. Thus the myth began.

A Bach Oratorio vibrated deeply from the huge pipe organ. The sickly-sweet, heavy scent of orchids swept past her nose as if animated. Someone, apparently, had started burning some incense at the head of the casket: there was a column of bluish smoke rising from there. The closer she got to it, the thicker and more distinct it became.

The smoke grew ropy. It seemed to be coalescing around a point. Mara squinted her eyes shut, then opened them again to remove what she thought was a haze under her contact lenses. But the column continued to grow and solidify. She wondered if someone had accidentally tipped over a candle and if she should call their attention to the growing fire. But there was no fire.

The only light source came from within the bluish column, a tall, thin strand of opalescence. She had seen it once before, through a microscope watching cells divide: it was the glowing luminescence of life she saw within the bluish gray column. She watched it form a mirror image of the body she saw lying in the casket. *It was Dr. Ricard Fisher, standing at the head of his coffin, watching the mourners at his own funeral.*

Did anyone else see it? Mara spun her head around. There were people with depressed looks on their faces, some crying, all sad, but no one surprised or even noticing the bizarre specter brooding over his casket. She looked back at it; to her horror, its eyes moved and locked level with hers.

Then she heard two words in her head, echoing like his death knell: *Help me!*

"Please," she jumped at a voice behind her. "Keep the line moving." There was a bump to her back, and when she turned back to the casket, the column was gone. She had to step out of line.

For a moment she thought her mind was going. Two times now she had apparently seen some sort of apparition of this Dr. Ricard Fisher. Or had she…? Halfway down the aisle she turned back to look at the casket. The blue smoke had vanished. The queue continued to pass the dead body of Fisher. No one else had seemed to notice the macabre phenomenon.

It must be me, Mara thought, beginning to panic.

CHAPTER 29

"Laddie. Laddie! Come with me."
From the brown, swirling muck Malachai's raspy voice. Sounds like he's in a hurry. Feel like I'm moving. Or the brown sludge is moving past me. A shining in the distance. I know it's Malachai.
"Here."
In a darkened room. The living are moving around efficiently. I know they're surgeons and nurses and orderlies, but it doesn't look anything like any hospital I remember. There are women. It fades in and out. I follow Malachai. We're hovering over a blonde woman.
"She's yours, Lad. She's helpless as can be, just out of the care of the sawbones. Still under the laudanum. Take her. Enter her. Be her."
"No." I hear myself say.
"This is one way to live again. Enter her. Become her."
"I want a dark-haired one." My voice is a faint echo.
"Suit yourself. There will be others. This one will be easy though. The first of many for us all. For we are Legion, an army. And I lead."
Malachai floats over the woman. She moves. He thrusts hard into her, then disappears in her. She screams. Orderlies come, calm her, fuss over her. She wakes, yells at them to leave her.

CHAPTER 30

As shaken as she was, the one thing Mara did at Fisher's funeral as the weird throngs exited the cemetery, was talk with his sister Eleanor. Though nearly overcome with emotion, Eleanor agreed to meet with her the next day.

To speak with the meek college professor, she drove to Eleanor's home on tree-lined Beech Street on the outskirts of town. Her house was a Victorian-style, two-turreted half-manse with a carriage house in the back and an arbored back yard patio. As she was led through the house, Mara noticed a large dark library filled to the ceiling with leather-bound books, and longed to spend an afternoon browsing. They sat under hanging wisteria in the yard while Eleanor served iced peach tea in a glass pitcher.

Eleanor was a plain woman with light, blonde hair. Mara noticed a hospital band still on her wrist. She had to look especially hard to see the resemblance to her brother. Perhaps around the eyes....

"It's obvious that the quest for knowledge must run in the family," she commented as she took her first sip of tea.

"Our father was a great man. A college professor, who became president of a university. He worked his way up through academia. He became president of the university because he cared about education and the students, not because he was a professional administrator bent on making the school a multi-million dollar business." There was a particular bite in Eleanor's voice that made it clear how she felt about the current crop of college administrators.

"So Ricard and I were never intimidated by intellectuals, or administrators. I think that showed in his books, especially *Einstein Schmeinstein*. Hideous title, don't you think? Ricard was never happy with it, but the editors insisted. Iconoclasty must have a shocking title they said. Perhaps they were right." She paused and looked out through the kaleidoscope dapple made by the sun through the wind-blown wisteria. "How sad," she sighed, obviously thinking again about the circumstances of her brother's death. "How very sad."

Mara paused long enough to give Eleanor her space, then began: "As I mentioned at the funeral, I've been working on Ricard's biography. I don't want to concentrate only upon his work, but it will become an important part of the book eventually. But for now, I'm more interested in his life." Mara fiddled with her recorder—a tiny digital model using microchips instead of tape—and nearly upset her tea with the cord to the mike.

"Of course," Eleanor began, then paused while Mara moved the microphone closer. "Of course, but his life and his work were intertwined inextricably. From childhood he seemed aloof, thoughtful, contemplative. But then, we didn't have the normal childhood. I had to help him with so much. Father was in his forties when he and Mother had us, and so there was little horseplay. Reading, dinner discussions, the theater on weekends. Ricard loved the symphony, the classics. And he would spend hours wandering the halls of an art gallery." She paused to sip her tea.

This is good stuff, thought Mara. "So he wasn't just an egghead?" Eleanor whipped her head towards Mara who recovered quickly: "Like others have called him?"

Eleanor relaxed. "Well, he certainly *was* that. Fortunately he was a speed reader, and had uncanny powers of concentration. Even though he criticized Einstein in his book, he utilized Einstein's techniques for sharpening his concentration. He kept three computers going at one time, each with a different subject on it. He would spend a few minutes at one, then, while working on one subject, his mind would fill with ideas for the other subject. He would move his wheeled chair to that computer and work some on that subject."

So, Mara thought, that explains the three computer consoles and the wheeled desk chair.

"He eschewed sports and games; thought them a waste of time. Except for game theory, of course. He seemed to avoid anything he couldn't learn from. It was almost from the beginning that he seemed to be driven, that he seemed to know he was going to die young and not have enough time to complete everything."

"But wait a minute." Mara rarely interrupted an interviewee's comments. This she couldn't let go. "He was the one who chose an early death. Doesn't that seem antithetical to that philosophy, that he was limited on time?"

"Yes," said Eleanor, pondering the statement herself. "It does seem curious."

"Did he have any problems that you know of? Financial, mental?"

"Heavens, no. He had been financially secure since Father's death. As well, everyone was always trying to give him money for research purposes, if for nothing else than to list his name on their stationery as an honorary director. He had received a research grant a year or so ago and hadn't yet needed the money. Every time he set foot on one of those disgusting talk shows he got forty or fifty thousand dollars—and that price kept going up thanks to his greedy agent—abhorrent little man. And his lifestyle was not that extravagant. Other than research books and equipment—and those were all paid for by universities and foundations—he had no other expenditures, and virtually no expensive vices. No, he was more than comfortable financially."

And now you—we—have inherited it all my Lassie.

Eleanor shook her head. There's that voice again, she thought. I've been hearing it since the surgery. Strange….

She continued: "And from the time he was a child he had been studied, poked and prodded by some of the finest psychologists in the world, who were writing their theses on his remarkable abilities. If there had been a psychological or mental problem, don't you think they would have picked up on it?"

"It would certainly seem so." Mara paused for a second to peek at the recorder and make sure it was still running. When she looked back at Eleanor, she had her eyes closed. "Eleanor, tell me more about Ricard as an individual. What was he like as a boy? Did he date or have any girlfriends I could talk to? How about hobbies? You said he didn't like sports. Was there anything else?"

"Well," Eleanor sipped her tea and the ice cubes rang like bell clappers against the fine glassware. "As I said, he was quite precocious, so it seemed that he was grown up already as a little boy. Have you heard the term, 'Old Soul'? Those who believe in reincarnation say that some of us are inhabited by souls who have been around for eons, who have endured countless reincarnations; others of us are inhabited by souls who have only spent one lifetime or perhaps two on earth, or perhaps by souls of children who died young and never got the chance to grow up. I would say—if I believed in reincarnation—that Ricard was inhabited by an old soul. Myself as well." Eleanor paused for a sip of tea. "And you are inhabited by a young soul."

Mara did an inadvertent double take. "Excuse me? How can you tell?" Mara was intrigued, actually skeptical of the theory.

"You are a writer because you are curious as to how others have managed in this life. If you were a teacher or perhaps a writer of fiction, I would say that you were probably a beneficent old soul, attempting to help the rest of us along, interpreting this world to others as opposed to scrutinizing others' views of it."

Mara was about to say that this was her first book and just happened to be a biography, but her mind got sidetracked. She wanted to ask more about the young soul that had, according to Eleanor, somehow inhabited her body. The thought that something or someone dead would be able to invade her body frightened her. Even if it happened at birth, it would seem like an invasion. It gave her the creeps, like finding out a weird neighbor had been watching you shower.

Just as frightening—or at least unbelievable—it meant that there was something that went on after death, an utter impossibility. She took a sip of tea to regain her focus and returned to her subject.

"Was his precociousness the only reason you think Ricard was an old soul?"

"No. You could see it in his eyes. As a young man he had those sad weary eyes, like some overworked beast of burden. And he had his voices."

"Voices?" Now we're getting into something, Mara thought. "He heard voices?"

"Well, not exactly like some psychopath would. No one was telling him to go out and become an axe murderer. And certainly no voices told him to kill himself."

"How do you know?"

"I know," Eleanor said forcefully. "Those weren't the kind of voices Ricci heard."

It was the first time Mara had heard anyone refer to Dr. Ricard Fisher by a nickname. "What 'voices' did he hear then?"

"The voice of pure scientific logic. The voice of reason, of thoughtful analysis. He called them by names, sometimes. 'Logos is talking to me,' he'd say. You could actually see him stop, tilt his head and listen. It was his own brain, of course, reasoning things out and coming to a conclusion." Eleanor paused and turned her face toward Mara. "At least I think it was his own brain that spoke to him."

Mara started to chuckle, suppressed it into a smile because Eleanor was dead serious. "But I suppose in your research you may find something else."

"How about girlfriends?"

Eleanor elegantly brushed off a petal that had fallen on her dress. "Ricard was strange about women. Actually, I suppose, not any stranger about women than anyone else who's a dedicated professional nowadays. He was always keeping them at arm's length. There was one recently, a former researcher or professor who worked with him. Oh, I've quite forgotten her name. Not very important. They spent quite a bit of time together. But I wouldn't be able to tell you if the time was social or professional. I believe she still works at the university. Physics Department, of course. What was her name? I'll remember it in a second."

"Can we get back to the voices?"

"Actually, I don't think it's very significant. The world might think that some of Ricard's actions were weird, but the world does not know genius. Most people haven't the slightest clue where inspired ideas come from—that's why the shrinks wrote their papers and got their Ph.D.'s studying Ricci. Most don't hear voices because most are imbeciles compared to Ricci."

Mara looked at Eleanor who was clearly a genius, herself. You could practically hear the correct punctuation in her sentences and Mara had a sense that she was holding back on some words, actually talking down to a professional writer.

There was a long silence. Apparently Eleanor was through with the interview. Staring out across the garden, tears began to form in her eyes.

"You must forgive me," Eleanor said. "I'm recovering from minor surgery, so I'm not quite myself."

"That's fine," Mara said.

Mara began to shuffle her notes and reach for the recorder. "Thank you, Eleanor. I've probably taken up enough of your time. May I call on you again sometime?"

"Oh, probably not."

The answer shocked Mara. Most people agreed to a second interview.

"You see," Eleanor said, "Ricard was a brilliant enigma. There were so many things going on inside his head. No one will ever be able to explain what a complex man he was. He had one driving force and that was the quest for knowledge. Sometimes I wonder if *that's* the reason he killed himself: merely to find out what was on the other side."

"That's quite a price to pay for knowledge."

"He had a favorite poem by Charles Baudelaire. Let us see if I can remember it…"

Malachai. Malachai! Where are you? It is Will. I'm lost.

"*Here, Laddie. You can't recognize me. I'm here. This is how you do it. How you can live again.*"

I want to, Malachai. And there she is. That's the one. The beautiful, dark-haired one with the pretty eyes. Give me her, Malachai. Deliver her to me like you did Private MacGillicuddy.

"*We'll see, Laddie. We'll see what I can do.*"

Eleanor paused for a second, her lips moving, then began reciting dramatically out loud:

> "*O Death, old captain, it is time! Set Sail!*
> *This land palls on us, Death! Let's put to sea!*
> *If sky and ocean are black as coal,*
> *You know our hearts are full of brilliancy!*
>
> *Pour forth your poison, our deliverance!*
> *This fire consumes our minds, let's bid adieu,*
> *Plumb Hell or Heaven, what's the difference?*
> *Plumb the Unknown, to find out something new!*

Does that shed any light upon his driving thirst for understanding?"

Mara wasn't sure what to say. Was Eleanor just rationalizing the unexplainable death of a loved one? Or was this true insight from one who had seen Ricard in his most formative years; a child but already forced into intellectual manhood by the quirk of nature that gave him superior intelligence?

"Well, Eleanor. Thank you for what you've given me. I appreciate your time. I'll send you a copy of the book when it's published."

"Oh, don't bother," Eleanor managed a half-smile with tearing eyes. "I already know the subject intimately. And, sadly, I also know how it ends."

She was right, of course, but Mara still felt a little insulted. Most people are pleased to have an autographed copy of a book they helped create. She slipped her papers and recorder into her backpack and slung it over her shoulder.

"Well, thank you again. It was nice meeting you."

There was no answer from Eleanor, twirling her hospital band absentmindedly, already back in her own dark world of mourning and memory.

CHAPTER 31

Driving back to her house, Mara suddenly realized why Ricard Fisher was so intense about knowledge: she was the same way about writing.

>   There was that time she had crawled out on the ledge of the observation deck of the Terminal Tower Building in downtown Cleveland to talk to the suicidal woman. Analyzing the whole thing later, Mara realized that it wasn't the headlines or even the story that drove her to risk her life, but the curiosity of the whole event. She wondered about this woman: what brought her here? What random matrix of events made her choose utter extinction over life? Was she serious about ending her own life or pleading for help? Which was it? Mara had to know. Kate Peterson was her name. She was eventually talked down by the police. Mara was "detained" for violating a police line. Actually, she got there before the police, so the charge, technically, couldn't stick. The story, with Mara's own unique twist, was called "Working Without a Net." Her use of the woman's plight as analogy to millions of other working women won her a "Sinclair Lewis Prize" in journalism.

When she got back to her rented house that was once a funeral home, Reynolds was stretched out on the kitchen floor by her chair. Mara sat at the kitchen table to transcribe her recorded notes. Part way through the tape, she realized something strange had happened to her recorder. After some of the questions, especially when Eleanor paused, there seemed to be some sort of interference.

"Oh, great," she said to herself as she looked for the instructions to the new digital recorder. "Way to go." Reynolds whined. "I should have taken my old, trusty, cassette recorder instead of this fancy-schmancy thing." She was rummaging through her bag for the instructions when she heard Eleanor casting about for the name of Ricard's one lady friend: "Oh, I've quite forgotten her name." she heard Eleanor say. "Not very important."

"Katherine."

The voice was raspy, intertwined with some strange interference, but the name, in answer to Eleanor's question was unmistakable: Katherine.

And Mara knew instinctively, that it was a male voice.

She turned back to the kitchen table as she heard her own voice on the recorder: "Can we get back to the voices?"

Then Eleanor: "Actually, I don't think it's very...." She stopped the digital device and twirled the little wheel that moved the recording back to before Eleanor's lost memory: "...quite forgotten her name" she heard Eleanor's voice repeat. "Not very important."

"Katherine." It hissed from the small speaker on the recorder. Undoubtedly male. In fact, vaguely familiar. Then a raspy, intensifying roar from the recorder.

Mara forced herself to try and remember if she'd heard anything in the background while she was recording, a neighbor, perhaps, calling his wife. No. There had been nothing. It was so quiet in Eleanor's garden, she remembered hearing bees buzzing at the roses fifteen feet away.

Where had she heard that voice before? And how in the world did it get on the recorder?

Mara suddenly realized how exhausted she was. She had always had a tendency to work until she dropped, so to speak, to run the engine until the tank was dry. And when she got tired she would "hit the wall," like a long distance runner.

She locked up the house and climbed the stairs to her bedroom, Reynolds following dutifully. Within minutes after crawling into bed, she was asleep.

She bolted upright in her bed, gazing in panic into the dark in her bedroom. She fumbled for the light and knocked her alarm clock off the stand before she found it and turned it on.

The voice that said, *"Katherine."* She remembered where she had heard it before. She had heard it the day before.

It was the same voice she heard say, *"Help me,"* at the head of Ricard Fisher's coffin.

CHAPTER 32

It was the strangest research Mara had ever done: tracking down an individual from a name left on a digital recorder in some unknown fashion. In fact, she thought that she was way off course with this one, but it was either this, or hope that Eleanor would remember the name of Fisher's girlfriend and concede to speak with her again.

She called the university's Physics Department and asked the secretary if there were any Katherines working there. Sure enough, there were two.

"Did either work with Dr. Fisher?"

"That would be Ms. Bircham. She was the late Dr. Fisher's assistant. Tragic, what happened to him, wasn't it?"

"Absolutely. Can you connect me with Ms. Bircham's extension?"

While she waited for "Katherine" to pick up her extension, Mara shook her head. I've done some investigative journalism before, she thought, and got clues from some strange sources, but this is....

Katherine Bircham actually answered her own extension and Mara made an appointment to meet with her later that afternoon, hoping that she wouldn't ask how she got her name.

"The one passion that grew in Ricard that no one, and certainly not his family, ever knew about, was his interest in the military. Especially the American Civil War."

Since Mara had called her to set up an interview, Katherine's schedule had filled with an appointment with the head of the department. As it worked out, Katherine was unavailable all the other times Mara had free, so she agreed to talk for a few minutes between class and lab time. Bircham was plain and wore large, red-framed glasses. She stood—as Mara reckoned—about 5' 11" and seemed even taller in her white lab coat. Mara vaguely remembered seeing her at the funeral. She carried several books in one arm and a large briefcase as they walked from her classroom to the laboratory. Mara juggled her notebook and recorder to take advantage of whichever side Katherine walked on at the moment.

"The Civil War?" Mara asked. "Yes." Katherine's voice echoed in the hall. "He studied it on two levels: He enjoyed the tactical side of the battles; as well he marveled at the immense social ramifications the loss of an entire generation of young men had upon America in the 19th century."

"An entire generation? What do you mean? Allegorically?"

"No. An entire generation. Eight hundred-some thousand young men died because of the Civil War. At least, that's the number I remember him using. All those deaths in a country with one-tenth the population of today. In this day and age, it would be like losing eight million young men between the ages of nineteen and twenty-six in just four years. An American Holocaust, if you will. Can you imagine it? The figures are so stunning that I memorized them from Ricard's notes."

Mara remembered the YouTube video and the speaker's figures, now confirmed by Ricard Fisher.

"He postulated that the incredible death toll was one of the reasons for the upsurge in Spiritualism and religion in the mid-19th century. Mothers were trying to contact their sons, and wives their husbands, after their deaths in battle. He made a relatively serious study of the Civil War period."

"Where did his interest initiate?"

"Actually, it was his sister, Eleanor, who got him interested. Talk about a brilliant scholar. Sometimes I think she was even brighter than he was."

"She was a Civil War buff? Isn't that more the male thing?"

"Unsung scholar is more the term. If I recall, it became her passion quite suddenly. She was recently in the hospital for a surgical procedure. Her interest in history seemed to have begun right after the operation. I mean, she really dove into it. She loaned many of her books to Ricard. I believe they're in his library now."

"He sounds like quite a renaissance man."

"You should see his apartment."

Mara started a little at the comment, but couldn't pass up an opportunity to perhaps see it again, this time with a guide.

"I'd love to. Could you meet me there and walk around with me?"

"I'm afraid the police have sealed it off. I have some papers in there that I'd love to get, but I can't get in. Not yet, anyway."

"Anything that might help me with my biography?"

"Perhaps."

"Now, it was my impression that you and Dr. Fisher dated?"

"Well, if you could call it that. A date with Ricard was spending a Friday night in the lab, as well as your weekdays, then maybe going over to his place to listen to some Bach or some Kenny Wayne Shepherd."

"Bach to Blues, huh?"

"Oh, yeah. Ricard's taste in music was broad, but focused on classical and blues. He had quite a collection."

"I get the picture of him watching *Gone with the Wind*, while listening to Beethoven."

"Actually, Wagner. You know, 'Ride of the Valkyries.' That was about the only time he would relax."

"So you tired of your work dates?"

"No, not really. I'm pretty driven myself. I gained a great deal from his vast knowledge and facile mind. He could really 'bend a thought,' as he liked to call it."

"Was the relationship going anywhere?"

"You mean marriage? No. Neither of us wanted that. It wasn't a relationship in the usual sense, but not a whole lot about Ricard was usual or ordinary."

"Did you ever go anywhere except the lab?"

"He took me to some art museums. But you certainly couldn't call those dates. He would clam up as soon as we walked in the door and something caught his attention. I remember walking into the National Gallery just a few months before he died. His attention was caught by a carved ivory statue—actually a tableau—of Joseph of Arimathea and the Marys removing Christ from the cross, on loan from another museum. He stopped talking as soon as he saw it—in mid-sentence. I had to walk away after about fifteen minutes of him circling the pedestal upon which it sat. I recall seeing him later on that afternoon, pondering the Matisses or Renoirs or something, and again later at the tableau of Christ. He kept coming back to that sculpture. He seemed obsessed. 'He was really dead,' he kept saying and commented upon how realistically the sculptor had portrayed his body in death. Then he said, 'but he was seen again. Was it a ghost? Impossible. But how did it happen?' Ricard was like that. He would think about things forever to come up with an answer."

"Even miracles?"

"Yes. He needed some kind of positive evidence as to the 'why' things happened. It was his scientific mind, I guess."

"Was he overly religious?"

"No. Not 'born again' or anything like that. We never talked about it, and he certainly didn't proselytize or try to convert me. Once again, it was a mental challenge to him to determine how Christ appeared again to his disciples. For that matter, how anyone could appear after their death."

"You mean as in ghosts?"

"He may have been doing some research on the subject."

"What? An eminent scholar like Dr. Ricard Fisher doing research on ghosts?"

What a weird coincidence, Mara thought. I could use his input now. Suddenly, her thought turned macabre: Or maybe that's what I was getting the first morning in my house....

"Actually, paranormal phenomena to prove life after death. Immortality. Which, for the greatest scientific mind of our generation, I think is appropriate. No one knows about it, not even his family. In fact he really only mentioned it to me in the last year or so. I'm not sure when he first started thinking about it. But no doubt it had something to do with physics and his thought experiments."

Katherine stopped in front of the lab. "I think his main interests were in the contradictory nature of reality. He had mentioned once that there was a conundrum in the argument that there is a finality that comes along with death. His theory was based completely on quantum physics. Scientists know that electromagnetic energy is the basis for all physical reality. Every high school science student knows that, according to the laws of thermodynamics, energy cannot be created or destroyed in the universe. That would seem to indicate that, if we cannot detect paranormal activity, it's not because it is not there—it is because we are sensory-deprived. We just don't have the ability to perceive it...yet." she said with a finality that indicated the interview was coming to a close.

"May I call you back for a follow-up interview?"

"Certainly. You may want to give me some lead-time. My schedule is fairly busy this time of year." Katherine turned and started into the lab.

"Did you ever dream about Ricard?" Mara asked it, but had no idea where the question had come from.

Katherine stopped short, her face twisted with a quizzical expression.

Slowly Katherine turned and moved towards her, then stopped short. "What a *non sequitur*. Why in the world would you ask that?"

"I don't know. Did you?"

"Yes, as a matter of fact. The night of his funeral."

"Would you like to share it with me?"

"No. I mean, maybe, some day." She started to turn.

"Can you tell me anything about it?"

Katherine got a curious smile on her face, turned, and moved to close the gap between herself and Mara. "This is a little embarrassing," she said, lowering her voice. "Don't think I'm crazy or perverted or anything but it was kind of an erotic dream."

Mara couldn't say anything as she digested this information. *Sex with the dead?*

"You see, Ricard and I never had sex during our relationship. Then, the night he was buried, I had this dream." Katherine moved from the lab door to allow a few students to enter, then started into the classroom, stopped, and turned back to Mara. "It was like he came back to consummate the relationship. It was kind of touching...but now it seems sort of...well, strange."

Mara paused for a second too long. "Yes, thanks, Katherine. I'll be in touch."

Sex with a ghost, thought Mara. I'm not sure my curiosity extends quite *that* far.

CHAPTER 33

Mara thought the restored Victorian era house she had rented would have been truly charming if it hadn't once been used as a mortuary. According to the real estate agent, a family named Clinton ran their funeral business out of it in the 19th century. She said the Clintons made their money because of the Civil War and were able to move out. After the battle, nearly in their own back yard, they hauled boys' moldering bodies off the battlefield by the score, to crudely embalm them and send them to their families.

"Rumor had it that he had dug out a cellar in the carriage house and other outbuildings on the property," the real estate agent had told her. "They possibly even scraped out catacombs in the cellar of the main house."

Mara remembered seeing vague indentations in the cellar wall on her walk-through. "The legend still floats around town that the temporary morgue spaces were too small and he had to break collarbones and ribs to make some of the men fit. So," the real estate agent had told Mara laughingly, "if you hear anything strange in the house, don't say I didn't warn you!"

Other than the two weird dreams and the newspaper showing up on the kitchen table—which were all strange enough—nothing else out of the ordinary had happened in the house since.

As she stood naked in front of the mirror after her shower Mara ran her fingers through her damp hair. The morning sun angled gently through the slatted mini-blind, but the effect put her in mind of freshly washed sheets hanging in her mother's back yard. As a child, she would let the breeze blow the icy sheets into her until they clung to her face. She could breathe in the soap and Clorox and ozone smell of fresh laundry drying in the sun.

She was always an early riser, but autumn mornings were especially her favorites. Reynolds was still conked out on her bed, even though his food was in his bowl. The early walks must be getting to him, she thought. Her comb snagged a couple of times while it slid down her scalp. Suddenly, there was the smell of fresh roses pressing against the back of her nose, a smell so strong she had to look out into the hallway to see if anyone had entered her house wearing the scent. There was no one. Yet the smell lingered, overpowering even her shampoo and rinse, for at least a couple of minutes.

That was strange, she thought. Now whom did she know who wore the scent. Mitch? No. Oscar? No. In fact, she didn't currently know anyone who wore it. The last time she smelled it was several years ago, when Rex had taken her to St. Croix and they had shopped for a special "scent" for him as a Christmas present. "Each man has his own," she had told him, "that blends with his natural odors. Keep trying," she said, as they sprayed testers on paper strips, inhaled, then sniffed the jars of coffee beans to cleanse their olfactory senses. The scent that smelled vaguely of rosewater was the one, in spite of its usual feminine connection, that smelled the best with his scent. She remembered it because of the erotic connection—still smelling it on him that night when they made love—two powerful sensations blending into one unforgettable memory.

She shook her head violently, angry for letting him get into her head once more.

Since Rex she had begun to notice a pattern in her relationships: it almost seemed as if, as the boyfriend grew closer, she would do things to wreck the relationship. Be late for a date, or simply not show up; get caught out for a drink with another guy. Little things, but events fatal to any serious relationship. She finished brushing her hair, closing her eyes, pushing the thought of Rex and how he had changed her, into the back of her mind, like an unfinished manuscript she didn't want anyone to see yet.

When she looked back into the mirror, as if peering from the inside of a foggy glass, was the reflection of a dark face. She sucked in her breath, spun around while trying to cover her nakedness, to see...nothing.

She looked again at the mirror. Then to the window. Was it a shadow hitting the mirror? She moved her hand in front of the light from the window trying to recreate it. She couldn't. Damn! What is going on? Am I losing it?

"*Ah, Laddie. I see why you wanted this one. How lovely her skin is, how dark the hair where we once were not allowed to look. So much better than those smelly Irish girls you always got. Can you smell her?"*

Floating up through the floor. Following the sound of Malachai's voice. Feel a wave of damp heat and see the gentle curve of her calf then thigh then the swell of her backside, still wet, droplets running down. Looking over her shoulder, seeing her in the mirror, watching her touch her hair and waist, I feel like me again, warm, alive.

She spins around, looks straight through me, and I get a glimpse of her breasts with perfectly round brown buttons in their centers and the dark fluff of hair between her legs glistening with drops of water, shining triangle she covers quickly. Start to move away, but I realize she cannot see me, so I stay and watch her turn back to the mirror, drying with a towel, her hair, her buttocks, the triangle, until she puts on her robe.

Floating again, downward, dropping with no feeling of fear. Smelling Mrs. McGillis's rosewater.

She half-finished towel-drying her hair, slipped on a robe, went downstairs and poured a bowl of cereal and milk and sat.

Her phone rang.

"Mara?" It was Katherine.

"I hate to impose. I know you're busy, but I have a group you might be interested in meeting. It's an organization that Ricard started."

Mumbling through a mouthful of cereal, Mara said, "Tell me more."

"The information—even the existence of the group, at least for now—has to be, what's the journalism term? Off the record?"

"Yeah, Katherine. In other words, you don't want this to end up in my book. That's okay. Where and when?"

"ASAP. They're meeting now in the lab here and they're going to be doing some experiments I think you'll be interested in watching."

"How ASAP? I'm sure they won't want to see me in my ragged old robe. I can be there in a half-hour. That okay?"

"You bet. I'll meet you at the security entrance."

"Okay, I'll see you...."

"Wait, Mara. There's one more thing I wanted to tell you about an experiment I...someone set up in my lab."

"Sure. Go ahead."

"Well, you would not have noticed, but my lab is sort of a lab within a lab. You just saw the outer lab. Only two other scientists are allowed in there with me. Scientists are notorious for borrowing other scientists' work and running to a publisher with it."

"Kind of like writers."

"So, I worked a little late last night after you left, stopped when I hit a snag, and decided to sleep on it. When I came in this morning, the project was partially finished."

"What do you mean?"

"Things were moved. Measurements were changed, a digital spectroscope was turned on, two of the gauss meters were re-calibrated."

Come on, Mara thought. This is not exactly a mystery. "Perhaps someone else had access to the lab? A student? A cleaning lady or janitor maybe?"

"They're not allowed in this section of the lab. It is for faculty only. There are only three keys and we make sure that only scholars working on completely different projects are given them at the same time. Ricard was adamant about that. I've already spoken with Dr. Powell; he was speaking at Princeton last night. Dr. Christ is out of the country for two weeks. Mine is the third key."

"Who do you think it was, Katherine?"

"I don't know. But someone got in here and set up an experiment. Or tried to help me with *my* experiment."

"What was the experiment?"

"Whoever set this up was attempting to create wormholes in the lab."

"Time out," Mara said. "The little mouse in my head just fell off his wheel. Give him a second to get back on. Wormholes? You mean the physics kind, right? And these have to do with...come on Katherine, work with me. I'm a little rusty on my theoretical physics."

"Actually, it's quantum physics, and the theory is that wormholes, the tubes through which one is supposed to be able to visit other universes—and travel backwards in time—can be replicated in a lab."

"Wait a minute. I thought wormholes were a part of black holes, and that they were humongous, far, far out in space." Mara put a spoonful of soggy flakes into her mouth.

"Not necessarily. That's what everyone had thought. But some physicists think that they might also exist on an incredibly tiny scale, once again referring to the quantum world of particle and sub-particle physics. One devised a theory—and actually described an invention—that would allow travel between parallel universes."

"The ultimate physicist's vacation, huh?"

"Yes," Katherine said. Mara made an attempt at humor; Katherine took it seriously. "Just substitute 'doorway' for 'wormhole,' and it's less intimidating.

"The first theoretical design consisted of a tube made up of what was imagined to be 'exotic matter,' material from the interior of a wormhole. The 'exotic matter' is so powerful that it twists space and time around it and a wormhole is born, leading whoever happens to be in the center of the tube to a faraway place in the universe in a different time. The term 'faraway,' of course, being just an understandable metaphor for somewhere we don't understand yet.

"A second design was of two parallel metal plates aligned with two other parallel plates. When enough electrical energy is applied, a rip in the fabric of Einstein's 'space-time' is created—a wormhole opens. It's called the Casimir Effect. There are two problems, however: first, there is not enough energy in the world to power it; second, one of the set of plates has to be accelerated to near the speed of light.

"It wasn't the time travel—as fascinating as that might sound— that was so interesting. It was that one could go to a different place in the universe. Ricard mentioned it once, but he felt that it could be a place, a plane of existence, another universe or dimension that might co-exist with this one: a pure energy field that suffuses everything, from the cosmos to the space between the parts of the atom, a matrix of some kind. Of course, these are all theories based upon things that can't happen, like finding 'exotic matter' or accelerating to the speed of light.

"But these changes in my experiment…these calculations…this can't be right…they allow it to happen by calculating how to boost energy levels briefly in the last nanosecond high enough on a small enough scale to…allow a wormhole to be created. And the energy comes from the matrix field."

Katherine was silent.

"Okay, Katherine. You still want me to come down and meet?" Mara dumped her cereal into the sink.

"Oh, absolutely."

"See you in a little."

Mara had to make a big step over Reynolds to get to the stairs. "Sorry, boy. I'm leaving you in charge this morning."

CHAPTER 34

Katherine, in her red-framed glasses and lab coat, met Mara at the door, got her a visitor's tag, and started toward the elevator. She began the conversation as they walked, clicking heels echoing through the large hall.

"I had the sense after our conversation you had an interest in Ricard that went a little deeper than just the regular 'who, what, when, why, how' biographer. I thought that you needed to see the other side of Ricard, the side that was interested in the occult."

Mara shook her head. "The occult? I thought you said he was interested in the afterlife?"

"'Occult' merely means 'hidden.' The word has gotten a bad rap. Ricard was interested in the hidden part of our world and the scientific explanations for it."

"You're sure I can't use this in the book?"

"You can probably mention his interest in the subject, but you can't mention the group, the university, or the individuals."

"That's pretty much everything. Are you sure you want me to see this?"

The elevator began to go down instead of up to Katherine's lab. "I think you *need* to see it."

The doors opened and Katherine took a left. She began again in quieter tones.

"Ricard started this group about a year ago. No one at the university knows about it. The members meet once a week. They decided to continue the experiments even without Ricard. Actually, they're hoping he will still be able to help them."

Mara stopped in the hall.

"Ricard is dead. How can he help?"

Katherine just looked at her through her red glasses. She pointed to a door at the end of the hall.

"We're almost there."

The door opened and Mara was met by the uneasy gazes of three lab-coated individuals.

"Mara, I'd like you to meet Dr. Torres, from the Physics Department, Dr. Coleman, a neuro-biologist, and Dr. Ross, from the Psychology Department. Including myself, we comprise the Institute for the Study of Anomalous Phenomena—'ISAP.' Gentlemen, Mara McKay."

Three men mumbled a greeting from their lab tables where several experiments were set up. At least, from the electronics she saw, Mara was convinced they had been working on something that was about to be explained to her.

"The only one missing," Katherine continued, "is Dr. Fisher."

"It's obvious you were about to begin some sort of experiment," Mara said more as a question. "I've been sworn to secrecy by Katherine," she said lightheartedly, "so you can let me in on what's going on."

Convinced that things would not go beyond the lab, the scientists looked around at each other until Dr. Ross began.

"Dr. Fisher came to us about a year ago. I'm sure by now that you know of his interest in the paranormal. Since the field of parapsychology had pretty much run its course, he was convinced that two new sciences should be introduced to study the phenomena: neurobiology to determine what was occurring in the percipient, and quantum physics to understand what was going on outside the percipient."

Mara shrugged. "Makes sense."

"So we've gathered together to scientifically prove—or debunk—some of the observations and postulates on the paranormal."

Mara pulled out her notebook and digital recorder. "I'm a note junkie. I have to take notes on everything. Do you mind?"

"As long as it's off the record—at least for now."

"You got it." She flipped on her recorder and folded the notepad so she could write on it. "If you ever decide to release your findings, I'll have the early notes."

"Miss McKay." Dr. Torres began. "Let's start simply. I'm sure you've heard of the phenomenon of auras."

Mara nodded her head. *Some kind of hippie thing from the 60s*, she thought. *A glow, or light, or something, that hovers around us.*

"Sensitives, yogis, psychics, clairvoyants have claimed for centuries to see them around all living things. It wasn't until the late 1930s that Kirlian discovered that he could photograph this strange aura when a high frequency current field is brought near the subject. You don't even need a camera. Just photo paper. And the technique has worked on all living things: leaves, animals, human body parts. In fact, when a leaf is torn, or a limb is amputated from an animal, the aura remains intact, outlining where the missing piece should be."

"I think I remember reading about this. The point is...?"

"Is that there apparently are energy fields in layers around the bodies of living things."

"Layers? With an 's'?"

"Eastern religions have touted for centuries that several astral bodies surround living things, especially humans," Dr. Coleman said. "It seems they've been correct all along."

"Do I see skepticism in your face, Ms. McKay?" Dr. Torres said.

"You would see less if I could witness an aura in action."

Torres smiled, opened a drawer and pulled out a pair of glasses with indigo lenses. "Here. Put these on."

Mara looked at Katherine who nodded. She slipped the glasses on.

"Okay. Stand here. I want you to look at that wall. Focus your eyes on that wall."

Mara turned to the dull, beige wall of the lab about six feet from her.

"Just relax and soften your focus on the wall. Dr. Bircham—Katherine—would you please step into her line of view."

Katherine moved in front of Mara's gaze.

"Now, continuing your focus on the wall behind her, center your gaze on her nose. Wait a little bit."

Several seconds passed. Finally Mara said, "You know, I'm not the most patient person in the world. In fact, for me, immediate gratification takes way too long. How long...holy crap!"

It began with a shimmering, like heat waves, around Katherine's head. Within seconds Mara could see the waves outlining the rest of her body.

"Wow. Okay, I'm impressed."

"That's just the first of seven—some say eight—layers of aura," said Dr. Coleman. "With some practice, you won't need the glasses anymore. What this indicates, however, is that all things are more than just physical. There is energy that radiates, like a force-field, virtually invisibly, from everything."

Mara was just beginning to see what she thought was another layer when Katherine moved. Mara took off the glasses and handed them back to Dr. Torres.

Dr. Ross rolled two lab chairs over to a computer screen. He sat down and gestured for Mara to join him. "The old Soviet Union was doing death studies back in the 60s. Although you're too young to remember the communist regime, its tenets designated that religion was the so-called opiate of the masses. Whether we agree with that or not, it meant that their studies into the supernatural, the paranormal, life after death were completely devoid of any religious over- or under-tones. Their experiments were completely, coldly scientific."

Ross moved the computer mouse and the screen lit. Mara could see a frozen image of a flower that looked like a white starburst. It was attached to a cactus. The filming was being done at night.

"This is the kadupul flower of Sri Lanka, one of the rarest, most delicate flowers in the world. It only blooms at night. Once it is picked, it dies within an hour or so. This is a time-lapsed video."

Ross started the video. The minute counter in the corner zoomed. Mara saw the flower dying before her eyes. As the counter rolled and the flower slowly collapsed, sparks and flares flew from it. The flares seemed to have a life of their own, moving in an undulating motion as if through a liquid.

She could see the counter slow to regular time. By the time the flower was dead, the flashes and flares had ceased emanating from the plant. But in the background, some meters continued to register.

"What are those meters in the background?" Mara asked.

Dr. Coleman spoke up. "Those are Sergeyev biological field detectors. They continued to pick up biological—life—energy emanating from the plant even after it was dead."

"Energy was still coming from a dead plant?"

"Yes. From the DNA unraveling, we surmise. As it does from other life forms as well."

There was an awkward silence in the lab. Mara looked toward Katherine, who had a knowing look on her face.

Mara broke the silence. "That means...."

"Let's continue." Dr. Ross moved the mouse and clicked it on another file.

"The Soviets, in their pursuit of their so-called 'Godless' science had few—if any—restrictions on experimenting with living creatures, including humans. I hope you're not squeamish, Ms. McKay."

"I've seen my share of dying people and corpses while I was with the newspaper," Mara said. "I'm not so sure I could take watching people in pain, though."

"No. You'll see." He clicked on a video.

It showed a person in a hospital bed, unconscious, with technicians and doctors in lab coats and masks and instruments across the room. Mara could clearly hear the person's labored breathing stopping and starting intermittently. He was obviously dying.

"You're about to witness what happens at the moment of death. It has been described for centuries, but only been scientifically recorded in the last few decades with the help of special recording techniques and devices. Although, some mediums claim to have seen it with the naked eye. The famous psychic Eileen Garrett claimed to have seen spirals of energy leaving the bodies of the dead for up to three days after clinical death. One Polish scientist actually measured what you are about to see and named it a 'light shout,' a burst of photons a thousand times stronger than what humans normally emit. Other researchers found that photons can bi-locate as well."

Mara could see that the lights in the patient's room were dim giving the video a grainy effect. The instrument measuring the heartbeat began to whine indicating the organ had stopped beating. Within a minute, green and blue lights began to flash from the body making weird spirals as they left. Mara watched as a large orb-shaped mass of mist emerged from the patient's mouth, ascended, and began to slowly dissipate. Across the room, at least ten or twelve feet away, instruments were indicating they were picking up something.

Just as Mara was about to ask, Dr. Torres spoke up: "Those meters across the room are not connected to the patient. They have their own sensors picking up fields emanating from the patient. The meters will continue to register long after he is dead. Some have recorded it as long as three days after death, verifying Garrett's observations."

"The energy field is picked up by electromagnetic field meters," Dr. Coleman said, "it may indeed be energy, not necessarily electromagnetic, but that can be detected by EMF meters."

"A new type of energy?" Mara looked up from her notebook at Dr. Coleman, who smiled.

"A bio-plasmic energy, unique to all things living."

"But the meters going off across the room after the person is dead? You said for days after death. What does that mean?"

Katherine moved into the little group gathered around the computed monitor. "It means that the bio-plasmic energy removes itself from the body and goes somewhere else. Since energy cannot be created or destroyed, it continues on."

Again, uncharacteristically from Mara, more silence.

She finally spoke up. "In other words…you've just shown me…scientific proof of…."

Katherine said what Mara wouldn't allow herself to:

"Life after death."

"But how do you know this wasn't faked? You're showing me an experiment that was done fifty years ago in the old Soviet Union. This could be like some of the videos of alien autopsies."

The scientists looked from one to another. Finally their eyes rested upon Katherine who spoke up.

"These experiments weren't done fifty years ago. They were done just a couple of months ago.

"And they weren't done in the old Soviet Union.

"They were done right here."

CHAPTER 35

Mara stared at the monitor and let what she'd seen sink in. Blue and green wisps were still coiling from the body, but at a slower rate. The meters across the room were still registering and the clock in the corner of the computer screen was still rolling. *Could this be? Scientific evidence of the afterlife? And is Ricard Fisher's ISAP group proving it?*

"There's more." Dr. Coleman moved the mouse over another file and clicked.

"Ms. McKay, have you ever heard of psychometry?"

"Yes. Psychometry. Isn't that where...um. Okay, refresh my memory."

"Psychometry is where an object is handled and information is gained psychically from that object."

"Okay. I think I've seen it used by psychics when they're trying to help police solve a case. Kind of like psychic bloodhounds picking up a scent."

"Very good analogy. The interesting part about psychometry is that, while all objects retain energy, the more traumatic the event the object is associated with, the easier it is for someone to read."

Katherine interjected. "In other words, something associated with a death is more 'charged,' for lack of a better word, than something associated with a normal, everyday event—like a coffee cup."

"Actually," Dr. Torres said, "'charged' is exactly the appropriate word for the explanation of psychometry. The object is charged with bio-energy. It's also been called psychotronic energy, but regardless of what you call it, it's an unseen energy that emanates from all living things and can apparently be imbedded in non-living things permanently."

Mara gave her best skeptical look at the Ph.D.'s gathered around her. "You mean there is an invisible, heretofore unknown and normally undetectable force, coming off of living things that can attach itself to inanimate objects and provide information from the living things?"

"Exactly," Dr. Coleman said. "Except that this knowledge was available millennia ago and was lost, so it's not exactly unknown. And, they don't necessarily have to be living things. They can be *formerly* living things."

"As you can see," said Dr. Torres, "we have methods to detect these bio-energies. We are also working on methods to gather the information in a format that will be understandable to all."

"And,"—Dr. Ross, set down his coffee cup—"there are other methods to detect this human energy that's imbedded in inanimate objects. And you don't even have to be psychic."

"Okay," Mara said, curiosity piqued. "I'll suspend my disbelief. Show me."

Dr. Ross reached into the drawer again and pulled out a pair of copper rods bent at right angles. The short ends were enclosed in copper tubes so that they rotated freely. He handed them to Mara. She recognized them right away.

"Dowsing rods?"

"You're familiar with their use?"

"Yeah. Don't you use these to find water?"

"Actually, what they indicate it the *energy* from the water. Water is one of the most mysterious—and energetic—of all substances. But dowsing can pick up all kinds of energy."

Dr. Ross rolled his chair closer to Mara. "This technique for finding things from water to buried treasure to different ores has been around for at least seven thousand years. Ancient Egyptian artists portrayed dowsers, as did the Chinese, some four thousand years ago. U.S. Marines dowsed in Vietnam for booby traps and enemy tunnels. Some military units still utilize dowsing rods to locate underground antipersonnel mines. Law enforcement has used the rods or even pendulums to track down criminals. They can tell where the bodies had lain and follow the tracks of the fugitives, like your bloodhound. They've been used in archaeology for many years. We have videos of dowsers finding missing graves on battlefields. They've even found empty graves in abandoned churchyard cemeteries—the remnant energy from the once living humans now removed."

"You can communicate with them, too," Dr. Coleman said.

Mara tilted her head, skeptical at the statement. "How?"

Dr. Ross clicked the computer mouse a couple of times and a video popped up on the screen. "Here. Let's say you think you've contacted someone, but want confirmation. Watch."

Contacted someone? Mara thought. *Is he talking about contacting....*

The computer video showed a woman holding some rods identical to the ones Mara was holding. Mara heard her say, to an empty room, "If you are here with me now, please cross the rods." Seemingly without the woman moving, the rods slowly crossed. "Thank you. Now uncross the rods." Mara stared hard this time, trying to pick up any motion from the woman's hands. There was no movement, but the rods began to uncross.

"Thank you," she said politely to no one. "Now, if your first name starts with a letter from A to M, please cross the rods." Nothing happened; the rods remained straight. "Okay. Does your name start with a letter from N to Z?" The rods crossed.

"Crap," said Mara, not wanting to believe what she was seeing. The scientists looked at her. "Sorry."

The woman on the video said, "Does your name start with N?" No movement from the rods. "Does it start with O?" Again no movement. "Does it start with P?" The rods crossed and the woman straightened them. "Is the second letter in your name A?" The rods crossed. "Is your name Patrick?" The rods remained still. "Are you a woman?" The rods crossed and she straightened them. "Is your name Patricia?" The rods crossed.

Dr. Ross stopped the video. "It's a binary method—yes or no. You need a little patience, but you can gain a lot of information with the dowsing method."

Mara shook her head. "How do you know she wasn't faking?"

The four scientists looked at each other. Dr. Coleman spoke for the group. "Ms. McKay, the video you just saw is number one hundred and twenty-seven in the series. They were all controlled experiments. We used laser levels on the first fifty to verify the subject wasn't moving the rods. I assure you...."

Mara apologized. "Of course. I didn't mean to insinuate...."

Katherine broke in, "That's all right, Mara. Skepticism is a good thing. Believe it or not, we're happy to hear it."

Mara fiddled with the rods in her hands. "But what is it that moves them, that crosses the rods?"

"We believe," Dr. Torres began, "In fact, it was suggested by Dr. Fisher that it's the bio-energies you just saw on the previous videos that moves the rods."

"You mean the energy that showed up across the room on Sergie...whatever, meters?"

"Sergeyev biological field meters," Dr. Coleman said.

Mara looked at the rods and mumbled, "And the energy comes from...." She really didn't want to say it.

So Dr. Ross did: "The dead."

"Take those with you, Mara" Katherine said. "Give them a try. I'll walk you out."

CHAPTER 36

"Hey! I think it's time we visited Dr. Fisher's house again."

Oscar Fosster jumped, spilling half of the toppings of his hot dog onto the street. For a second Mara thought he was going for his gun again. In fact, if his hands hadn't been full of hot dog and coffee, he would have, until he saw who it was.

"Jesus, Mac! There goes half my lunch."

"That was the half that was bad for you. Look at all that crap. Do you know how much sugar there is in ketchup? And those onions? And what was that brown stuff?"

"Lettuce, tomatoes and onions," he said as he looked mournfully at the glob on the street. "That was my salad."

"That was lettuce? Hey, O, why don't you let me buy you a decent meal? Come on." She grabbed the hot dog from his hand and threw it into a convenient trash can. She hooked his arm with hers and dragged him down the street, away from the protesting street vendor.

Fifteen steps and they turned into Delmonico's, a once exclusive, high-priced steak house. Now, after renovations and improvements to the downtown, it was a glass, brass, and fern bar with light fare catering to the grown-up, health-conscious, millennials. "Two, please." Mara said to the hostess.

Grabbing two menus, she nodded. "This way, please."

"Mara, I don't have time for this. I gotta be back on the west side by one."

"They never give you guys enough time for lunch. No wonder you are all so trigger-happy." They were seated at a table overlooking a lush public park.

Oscar moved around to get comfortable in the bentwood seat. Mara saw him grimace once and remembered his battle for the school children. She had never heard him say word one about it. It was as if he just accepted the pain as a toll for helping others to live. Mara knew she would have to write something more about Oscar Fosster one day. He was such an exceptional, average man who, in a split second, took the matter of his own death in his large, cinnamon-colored hands, weighed it against the lives of others, realized that there was no choice, that it was what he had reckoned with long ago—that this day would come—and did what he knew he would do all along. One day, she swore, as she saw him wince again—the pain must be getting worse as he ages, she thought—she would write that tribute.

He was looking reluctantly at the menu when it suddenly dawned on him what she had said in the street. He looked up at her. "What did you say about going back to Fisher's place?"

"We've got to go. I'd like to take someone along."

"Whoa, Nellie. You really *do* want to see me sweeping up at the station. Or maybe I can buy Pee Wee's mobile dog stand and work *that* for a living. Lots of fresh air in that job. Especially in December."

"You'd eat up all the profits in a week. And kill yourself doing it. Really, Oscar. I've got to get in to the apartment again. I want to take Fisher's old girlfriend with us. I'm sure she'll be discrete."

"Man, Mac, you're killin' me."

"Nah, I just saved your life." Oscar winced as Mara ordered two salads with raspberry vinaigrette dressing from the waitress. "Street vendor hotdogs. Honestly O. You don't need a wife, you need a keeper."

CHAPTER 37

Ricard Fisher's apartment was beginning to smell of rotten meat. It was blood and flesh from the death room that needed to be cleaned up. Something else was amiss to Mara as well. She couldn't put her finger on it, but something just wasn't right. Katherine took a handkerchief from her purse and held it over her nose.

"When are they going to clean up in here?" Mara asked Fosster.

"That's up to the next of kin. His sister, I guess. This belongs to her, now." He turned to Katherine. "You are *not* going to tell anyone you were here, right?"

Katherine nodded.

"Now," Mara said. "What more can you tell me from this apartment about Ricard Fisher's life?"

"Well," Katherine began. "First of all, you are seeing less than half of it."

"What do you mean?"

Katherine moved to a wall next to the bookshelves and touched a wall switch that looked like a regular light switch.

A low whirring of machinery began. Half the bookshelves moved back a foot; the other half slid across in front of them exposing sets of hidden bookshelves around another large room.

"Shit," Oscar said. "We never even saw that when we did our investigation. I wonder what else there is in this place."

"Remember, O. I said I thought there should be a hidden passageway or something." Mara turned to Katherine. "Why would he hide this from anyone?"

"Well, as you can see, it's not exactly hidden. A flip of one of the light switches did it. I think he did this just to save room. Originally there were closets behind the bookshelves. Ricard never had that many clothes, but books…that's another thing."

Mara had already started browsing through titles. There were literally hundreds of books on the Civil War, and dozens on various other wars, in particular, the Pacific Theater of World War II, and some on the bloody trench warfare of World War I.

Hanging over one of the bookshelves was a longer-than-usual rifle, obviously from an earlier era. "O?" Mara asked tentatively. "Is that the gun he shot himself with?"

Katherine froze, not wanting to hear the answer.

"No," Oscar said. "That's in evidence at the station. This is a different one we hadn't seen because it was back here. A Springfield from the looks of it. I'm very familiar with it from reenactments."

"Here was one of the most brilliant men in the world—perhaps the most brilliant physicist ever—and his pastime was reading about the bloodiest battles in history and collecting weapons. What was the connection?" Mara wondered out loud.

"Actually, most of these books are Eleanor's. On loan to Ricard for his studies."

"Katherine, would it be right for me to assume that Ricard had a fascination with death and killing?" Mara ran her finger across the spine of Michael Shaara's *The Killer Angels*, a Pulitzer Prize-winning novel she herself once read about the great Battle of Gettysburg. She glanced again at the rifle.

"No. Not necessarily. At least he never dwelled upon any of this while we were together. I think he was genuinely interested in the whole panoply of war. How little things change great battles and thus alter history; how the poor common man gets caught up in—as Ricard used to call it—the 'great, cosmic whirligig of events' and can end up a hero or simply dead. And he wondered, since we all will end up dead anyway—as a species, I think he meant—what good is being a hero when there is no history, no one to remember? I recall him pondering that. With his incredible memory and facile mind, I think Ricard thought he might have made a good military commander. I couldn't see past the scientist, of course."

"Here's something else," Katherine motioned for Mara to follow her to a wall of file folders, much like the ones in a doctor's office. The files were color-coded. In black magic marker she could read some of the topics they covered: *Quantum Theory—Mistakes*; *Blunders—Einstein, Bohr, Feynman, Hawking*; *Energy and Time's Meaninglessness*; *Gravity—Faster than Light*; *Subatomics and*

Reality. But those were just a tame sampling compared to other topics that apparently roiled through the mind of Ricard Fisher.

Again, Katherine flipped another light switch in plain view. The vertical files filled with colored folders began to rotate behind the wall and were replaced by others. Each file folder was filled almost to overflowing with typed and handwritten notes. The titles on those folders bordered on illogical: *Zero-Point Field Studies* was the heading of an entire row of folders. In that row were titles like, *The Cosmic Hum, Jung, the Z. P. Field and Collective Subconsciousness on the Psychic Level, Tenth Dimension Studies,* and *Psychic Phenomena and Zero-Point Fields.*

Mara tried to run her eyes across the folders quickly, but there were too many. She wanted to linger on some with especially provocative titles that seemed to touch a cord within her. She reached for one: *Electromagnetic Studies and Otherworld Entrypoints.*

"Mac!" It was Oscar. "Look but don't touch. That doesn't belong to you."

"Oscar." Mara smiled. "That's my line from one of our dates!"

"Yeah. A future date. From another life. C'mon. Let's go before *we* get *me* in trouble."

Mara turned to Katherine. "These folders—they represent some sort of research on Ricard's part?"

"Yes. I suppose. Or perhaps some of his 'mind experiments.' He could run experiments in his mind—I'm sure you're aware of that phenomenon."

"I had read that he could do it. He and Einstein."

"Yes. I would think you could get a great deal out of some of these folders in terms of Ricard's mind. From the way he thought to how he conducted his experiments."

"Actually, I'm interested in the topics. *Tenth Dimension Studies? Electromagnetic Studies and Otherworld Entrypoints*? Those sound pretty fascinating to me. Do you know what he meant by those?"

"Actually, I don't. At least not the last topic. I was aware of his studies into several dimensions other than the three or four we acknowledge. He hadn't published anything on it yet; he was still 'experimenting' as far as I could tell from our conversations. I knew about his studies on electromagnetics. That's where he realized that since all matter is made up of energy, and all energy is electromagnetic in nature, electromagnetism must be the key to all reality. You've heard about that, haven't you?"

Mara recalled the article she had read when she was doing her initial research in the *Sun* archives. She was about to mention it when Katherine resumed her comments.

"But this 'otherworld entrypoints.' I'm completely baffled by that one. What 'otherworld' is he talking about?" She reached to pull the folder from its file.

"Hold it, Ladies." Oscar had stepped over to the files. "Do I have to remind you again that this material does not belong to you."

"Oscar!" Mara suddenly turned toward the door. "Was that someone at…."

Fosster was already moving with Mara towards the door. His hand was on his pistol. Mara gave a quick look to Katherine who pulled the folder from the file and slid it into her bag. Fosster had his ear to the door and a look of hard concentration on his handsome face.

"No," he said and relaxed.

Katherine had already flipped the switch to rotate the files.

"Who do I have to get permission from again, to look through these?" Mara asked the visibly nervous detective.

"Next of kin. Let's get out of here. I'm getting that feeling again."

"What feeling?"

"That feeling I always get when you're about to stick me with the check."

CHAPTER 38

Mara found Eleanor Fisher's number on a scrap of paper in one of her notebooks after a half-hour search. For the millionth time she swore she would get a better organizing system one day.

Eleanor picked up. "Eleanor, this is Mara McKay. We spoke the other day at your house."

"Who?"

"Mara McKay. Ricard's biographer." Sheesh, thought Mara.

"Oh, yes. I'm sorry. How are you?"

"Fine, thank you. I was wondering. Would you have any objections if I visited Ricard's apartment? With you accompanying me, of course. That is if you wish to."

No, Lassie, no. You don't want to talk to her again. She's trouble.

"No, Ms. McKay. I don't think that is possible."

Silence.

"Oh?" Mara prompted.

More silence.

"Would you like to explain why not?"

Like I said, nothing but trouble.

"No."

Throw me a friggin' bone lady, Mara thought.

"Don't you want me to gain better insight into Ricard's life?"

"I think you'll have to do this on your own."

"So you won't help me at all?"

"No. No more than I have."

Well done, Lassie. Don't give her anything more.

Silence.

Mara: "Well…."

Eleanor interrupted, "Goodbye, Ms. McKay."

She hung up.

Mara would have thought her a complete bitch if it hadn't been for her utterly unemotional responses. She wasn't being hostile. It didn't even seem as if she had a purpose for being uncooperative. It seemed she just didn't want to be involved anymore.

You would think his sister—his only surviving relative—would want a full and accurate picture of her brother for posterity's sake, Mara thought. Could she be hiding something she knew was in the apartment? Mara remembered the smell growing in the apartment. No. She certainly wasn't in a hurry to get in there. Why the uncooperativeness then?

Mara's mind started to wander. She had been up early and now the effects were beginning to show. Reynolds was already collapsed on her bed. She removed her contacts, brushed her teeth, stripped and crawled into bed. Sleep rolled over her like a warm ocean wave.

In her Victorian half-manse on Beech Street, Eleanor Fisher smiled to herself. "Ricard," she said out loud in the empty library as she ran her fingertips across the spines of some books.

"You, my dear brother, weren't the only one who had voices. Now I have one, too."

That's right, Lassie. And I'll take care of you.

Reynolds growled low in his chest.

Mara's mind rose slowly from the thick depths of unconsciousness. Something was wrong in the room. There was a heavy presence, almost a suffocating feeling, like a strangulating gas. She thought she had opened her eyes, but the total darkness of the room made her unsure. But there was a glow at the foot of her bed, a shimmering. She thought she had reached for her glasses, but in her sleepiness couldn't even find her nightstand. She squinted at the luminescence. It was a tall blue column. There, standing at the foot of her bed within the column was a vague, shimmering image of Dr. Ricard Fisher.

She thought she tried to sit up in bed, but felt as if she were pinned to it. She couldn't move her arms. Her legs felt as if someone were sitting on them. The bed at her feet appeared to depress.

The specter floated closer.

Panic began to rise as she struggled against whatever it was holding her to the bed. It felt like the sheets weighed a ton. And the glowing image began to bend down toward her face.

She tried to scream but nothing would come out. It was as if her lips had been sealed shut. So she screamed inside her head at the phosphorescent face that was lowering itself like it wanted to present her with an unworldly kiss from the dead.

The lips were just a few inches from hers. The mouth opened and she began to smell the same odor she smelled at Fisher's apartment, the same odor that had assaulted her when the elevator doors opened.

It was the smell of death.

"*Laboratory....*" hissed from the unclean mouth.

Oh, God, she thought. It speaks!

She tried to cry out again, but with her mouth paralyzed it was just a muffled noise.

"*Laboratory...Key.*"

Now it was a low moaning she heard.

She wanted to wake up. If this was a nightmare she wanted out.

Louder now. Raspier. As if the death rattle were taking effect:

"*Laboratory...Key...Home.*"

She squeezed her eyes shut—or thought she had—and when she opened them again, it was gone.

Reynolds was at her feet now, sniffing and sneezing, and the foul odor immediately gone. She could move her arms and legs, but was now trembling uncontrollably.

Was that a dream? God, what a horrible nightmare!

She sat up and stretched out her arm, waving it tentatively through the dark space formerly occupied by the vision. The air was cold and the hair on the back of her arm stood. A chill ran through her gut. She put her hands to her face. Her one hand was actually colder than the other.

What kind of a dream was that? And what was it that it said?

But it didn't *say* anything. It opened its mouth—with its horrid odor—but didn't actually form words with its lips. But Mara got the message: "Key," it had communicated. "Home." "Laboratory."

She rose from the bed, still shaky. She turned on the bedside lamp and found a pen and paper on the small roll-top desk near her bed. She wrote the words down: *Key. Home. Lab.*

She looked at the clock. Five A.M. There would be no more sleep this night, except for Reynolds who had collapsed onto his side on the bed and was already snoring softly.

Katherine had slipped the file she had palmed from Fisher's apartment into Mara's backpack as it sat on the back seat of Oscar's car on the ride home. With no more prospect of sleep for the morning, Mara ripped open the zipper on her pack and pulled the file marked "Electromagnetic Studies and Otherworld Entrypoints."

It was disappointingly slim. Inside the file were three sheets of paper with nothing but equations and calculations on them. On the back cover of the file was scrawled, "See file #2."

File number two? Mara thought.

She closed the file. On the tab was written "Electromagnetic Studies and Otherworld Entrypoints: File 1 of 2."

Shit.

Mara's heartbeat quickened.

She took a deep breath and squeezed her eyes closed. "Damn," she said.

I've got to go back to Fisher's apartment.

CHAPTER 39

After they had left Fisher's apartment, Mara made an appointment with Katherine to visit the lab again at 8:00 A.M.

Once again they passed through levels of security to reach the inner sanctum of the faculty lab. There was another faculty member working, obviously the Dr. Powell Katherine had told her was the only other faculty member in the country at that time who had a key to the facility. He scowled at her through protective goggles.

Mara clicked on her digital recorder by habit.

"What can I do for you, Mara?"

"Just a question or two. Do you know if Dr. Fisher kept any personal belongings here in the lab?"

Katherine looked to the left and squinted, thinking. She shook her head. "No. I can't recall him ever bringing anything of a personal nature into the lab. At least not while we were working together. What sort of personal item did you mean?"

"An extra key. A key to his apartment."

Katherine thought again for a few seconds and shook her head again. "No. Not that I recall. I don't remember him bringing a key in here."

"Did he have a special place where he may have kept personal items?"

"Not in here. In his office he had a small locker like we all have, for lab coats and toiletries and the like."

"Could we go see that?"

"I'm afraid it's been cleaned out."

Mara gave a quizzical tilt to her head.

"Eleanor, Ricard's sister, had someone come in and remove everything. She's as practical and prosaic as he was, I'm afraid."

Well, thought Mara, there goes my last chance to get into his apartment before it's cleaned out.

"Why did I get that message from him?" Mara caught herself thinking out loud.

"What did you say?" Katherine asked.

"Nothing. I'm just confused. It's just that this time the confusion came from an odd source. Well, I'm sorry to have troubled you again. I guess I'm at a dead end."

They turned to go out the door. There was a loud crash at the end of the lab. Both Katherine and Mara jumped. At first Mara thought Dr. Powell had dropped something, but he was at the other side of the room. The three of them converged upon the shards of a shattered beaker that had fallen from atop a cabinet. There, in the broken glass, was a key.

Mara stooped to pick it up and recognized it as the twin to the one Oscar Fosster had used to let them into Fisher's apartment.

"All those trucks rumbling by," mumbled Dr. Powell. "Must have shaken it from the cabinet. I knew this would happen one day." He turned and walked back to his experiment.

Katherine looked at the silver object in Mara's hand.

"A key. That's the key to... How?"

Mara felt another cold breeze blow up the back of her sweater and tickle the hairs on her nape. She involuntarily shivered and looked at Katherine. "Don't ask," she said.

On the ride home Mara realized that she had left her recorder on. Voice-activated, it had picked up inadvertent snippets of conversation and background noise. A couple of things popped through the white noise.

She turned the car radio down and held the device up to her ear. She heard her conversation with Katherine in the lab as they discussed the possible location of an additional key to Ricard's home:

"No. I can't recall him ever bringing anything of a personal nature into the lab. At least not while we were working together. What sort of personal item did you mean?"

"An extra key. A key to his apartment."

"No. Not that I recall. I don't remember him bringing a key in here."

See the beaker.

Mara almost drove into a ditch. She slowed and pulled over to the side of the highway. What the hell was that? She backed the recorder up a few seconds.

"...ever bringing anything of a personal nature into the lab. At least not while we were working together. What sort of personal item did you mean?"

"An extra key. A key to his apartment."

"No. Not that I recall. I don't remember him bringing a key in here."

See the beaker.

There it was again! A voice imbedded in a hiss on the recorder answering a question. She stopped the recorder. She ran through those few seconds in the lab in her head again. Had anyone said anything in the background? No. All she could remember was silence while Katherine answered the question. She started the recorder again.

"Did he have a special place where he may have kept personal items?"

The beaker!

The words came through in a guttural, crescendo of a roar, so loud it hurt Mara's ear. She quickly pressed the button to rewind, and listened again:

"Did he have a special place where he may have kept personal items?"

The beaker! Again the roar. It was almost unintelligible, but the roar was definitely human—or at least had human qualities to it.

This was the second...or third time now that something unheard was recorded on her digital recorder. How could that be? The roar was very loud; so loud that Mara had to pull her ear away from the recorder when she heard it. But how could something not heard, that obviously did not produce sound waves, be impressed upon her recorder? Mara promised herself to listen to the rest of the recording when she got home.

The most frightening part about it was that the voice sounded very angry...or at least supremely frustrated.

No, Mara thought. That's not the most frightening part.

The most frightening part is that the voice sounded so familiar.

CHAPTER 40

Earlier in the week Mitch Landry had called and invited Mara out for dinner. She felt she was busy enough, but before their brief lunch meeting she hadn't really seen Mitch since he had moved from Cleveland. It would be a relaxing evening, away from research and deadlines.

She knew that Mitch would have liked their relationship to be more serious than it had been up to now. There was that time when they'd gone out a few times as friends, and had almost made drunken love, years ago. Then he moved and the relationship cooled. But he continued to call and e-mail and keep her updated on his life and to be interested in hers.

Mitch had been educated at MIT, a laser-leap from his small-town Georgia upbringing. While remarkably bright, he was no intellectual geek. He could speak as easily on quasars or quarks as he could about a specific ballplayer's batting average against left-handers, or the latest cheap novel. As he pointed out to Mara when she realized his broad panoply of interests, "Mara, the great mathematician-philosopher Blaise Pascal once said that 'greatness is not achieved by reaching one extreme nor the other…but by touching both at once.'"

"And the women you date actually buy that Pascal stuff?" she had teased.

She had pulled out the tiny silver recorder from her writer's pack and was about to listen to the recording she'd gotten earlier at the lab when the doorbell rang. She dropped the recorder in her coat pocket, opened the door, and there was Mitch with a handful of half-wilted flowers.

"What the hell are these?" she said half-laughing.

Mitch shook his head. "They were the last the street vendor had. I guess after sitting out all day they sort of drooped."

"Drooped? You can say that again. But thanks anyway for the thought. You're cute!"

Mara took them and placed them in a vase of water. Mitch just shook his head. "Hope springs eternal, eh?"

"They may come back. Ready to go?"

Mitch had arranged for dinner at Umbro's, a chic Italian restaurant in town. They sat at the bar for two drinks waiting for their table. "Normally, I'd complain that our reservation wasn't ready," Mitch commented. "But I don't like to be rushed either. That's part of the charm of this place."

"Besides, when do we get this much time to talk?"

"I think the last time was when you smashed a sandwich into my face. You're not going to do that tonight are you?"

Mara laughed, reminded of their lunch *al fresco* a week before. "But you looked so cute with chicken salad all over your mush."

"Yeah. Well, I found some in my collar later that day. You do know that chicken salad is supposed to be refrigerated, or else..."

"Did it start to smell?"

"How do you think I found it?"

When their table was finally ready, Mara ordered the chicken Marsala. Mitch ordered the blackened salmon Alfredo with calamari for an appetizer.

"Alfredo? Calamari? I can hear your arteries closing down as we speak."

"Cholesterol was low last time I had it checked."

"So you're trying to bring it up to the national average?"

And back and forth it went, most of the evening. There were a few moments of serious talk: What Mitch was working on at the think-tank; Mara's last free-lance job. She purposefully avoided any talk on her Ricard Fisher project until Mitch asked, "So, see any more ghosts?"

He was chuckling, sipping his Margaux, but stopped when he saw the serious look on her face.

"Mara? Did I strike a nerve?"

"Forget it. You'll just laugh."

"Actually, I may have something to add to your paranormal studies."

"I swear, Mitch, if you're going to make fun...."

"No. I was doing some research. About the newspaper that turned up in your kitchen the other morning...if you have run out of normal explanations, I think I may have a paranormal one."

"I'm still suspicious. Go on."

"There's a phenomenon called an apport. It's when something just appears out of nowhere. Usually it is something small, but newspapers, especially from the past, have appeared, even under bell jars, during controlled experiments. If you want a supernatural explanation for what happened, there you go."

"Thanks, Mitch. I just about had myself convinced that I was crazy. Now you've given me hope."

"So, did this supernatural aspect turn into something big? Want to tell me? I promise I'll take you seriously."

"You'll bust my chops like always."

"Pax, Mara. I promise. If you can take seriously my ruminations when we were in Cleveland on how time began, I can certainly be sensitive to your work. Please, Mara. I'd like to know how the book is progressing. And I'd love to help—from a scientific point of view—if I can."

She shook her head. "I'm really not sure where to start."

"Ask a question. That's the way you always seem to start these things."

Mara smiled. Mitch knew her better than she thought.

"Okay. Since you're a scientist. You've had some background in sound propagation, right?"

"Yeah. In 10th grade."

"Well, can sound travel without being heard? I mean a loud sound?"

"Well, you've already lost me, Mara."

"I mean, what if I had a digital recorder, and I was there while it was running, and I heard nothing but silence, then, when I played the recorder back, there was a loud roar on the recorder, or words discernible in the roar. What would that mean?"

"Well, if it was loud enough to be recorded, and you were there while it was being recorded, you would have heard it."

"But I didn't."

"That's impossible. Unless you were distracted and just didn't hear it."

"No. I'm 99 percent positive that what I heard on the recorder I didn't hear when I was recording."

Mara suddenly remembered that she had slipped the recorder in her pocket before they left for dinner.

"Wait. Here. Listen. I was in the lab at the university. The inner lab. There were two other people with me. You'll hear the one. The other was across the room working on his own experiment. Listen."

Mara pressed the replay button and held the recorder to Mitch's ear.

Katherine's voice: "...ever bringing anything of a personal nature into the lab. At least not while we were working together. What sort of personal item did you mean?"

Mara's voice: "An extra key. A key to his apartment."

"No. Not that I recall. I don't remember him bringing a key in here."

See the beaker.

"There," Mara said, excited again at the sound that wasn't supposed to be there. "Did you hear that?"

"Wait a minute. Play that again."

She replayed the segment for Mitch.

"See the what?" he asked.

" 'See the beaker.' Listen again."

Again she replayed the recording.

"Are you sure the other scientist wasn't anywhere near the recorder when you turned it on?"

"He was across the room. Now, listen to this."

She pressed a button on the tiny recorder: "Did he have a special place where he may have kept personal items?" It was obviously Mara's voice. Then the guttural, angry, frustrated roar:

The beaker!

Mitch had to pull his ear away from the speaker on the recorder.

"Wow! And you say you didn't hear that? That hurt my ear, it was so loud."

"Never heard it."

"Well, it's got to be an anomaly on the tape. Wait a minute. That's a digital recorder."

"Right. No tape."

Mitch put on his readers to look more closely at the tiny recorder.

"That's not all. Right after that was recorded, a beaker fell off a top shelf and shattered on the floor. Want to know what was in it? A key."

Mitch looked at Mara over the top of his reading glasses.

"You know this is scientifically impossible," he finally said.

"But it happened."

Mitch rubbed his forehead hard. The waiter came and asked if they would like anything else. "Just the check," Mitch said and continued to rub his head.

"There is an explanation," he said. "Or sort of an explanation."

"Shoot."

"Scientifically, the only way anything could have gotten on the microchip that does the recording is by electromagnetic surge. That's how the microphone works. You talk and a diaphragm vibrates creating electrical impulses which are captured by the chip. Somehow, that noise bypassed the microphone—since you didn't hear it—and went directly into the chip by electromagnetic means. I've heard of this before."

"Oh yeah? Where?"

"You're not going to like this, Mara."

"I'm a big girl. I can take it." She wanted Mitch to bring it up first.

"It's a phenomenon called 'EVP'—electronic voice phenomena. I went down an Internet rabbit hole when I was researching apports. It seems that ever since the invention of electromagnetic tape, people have been getting spikes or surges at certain points on the tape. They claim it is unheard and therefore does not rely upon air molecules for propagation. Instead, it is propagated by an electromagnetic wave. Like a radio wave. Some people have claimed to hear human voices. Like on your recording."

There it is, she thought. A scientist's conclusion to what she recorded.

"Electromagnetic waves?" Mara prodded. "People's voice boxes don't vibrate because of electromagnetism. Like you said, voice propagation is strictly physical: air pushed against vocal cords. Where do these voices come from?"

"Well, there are theories…"

"Yeah. Go on."

"Possibly from rogue radio waves in the air. Static, maybe."

"But it *said* something in response to a question. What are the chances of a deejay a hundred miles away just happening to say a word—and my little recorder just happening to pick it up—that answers a question? And predict the fall of a beaker. And for it to happen twice? Wait. Three times."

"What?"

"I just remembered. There was another time I picked up this EVP stuff. Wait."

She fumbled with the recorder, setting it back to previous recordings. Finally she found it. It was the interview with Eleanor that she had recorded. "Listen," she said to herself, as much as to Mitch, since she hadn't heard the recording in a week or so.

It was Eleanor, Ricard Fisher's sister's voice as she tried to remember Katherine's name: "What was her name? I'll remember it in a second."

Katherine. A male voice, then a raspy, intensifying roar from the recorder.

"Listen!" She practically shouted to Mitch. "Did you hear it?"

"A little hard to miss. And the voice. I'm not sure, but it sounded like the voice you played me before.

"I know."

"Look, Mara. Let's take that into the sound lab at the university. No, hell, we don't need the university. I have the software to analyze that on my computer at the 'Tank.' We can run a voiceprint and see if they're the same. We'll have it on tape and visually, so that we can compare it with other's and find out…"

"I already know who it is," Mara said. She was staring, almost catatonic, at the tiny recorder.

"How could you know? Who is it then?" Mitch was distracted by the arrival of the check and trying to find a credit card.

Mara knew because she had heard the voice come from a face and body. It was the glowing face and body that had hovered over her the other night as she lay unable to move in her own bed. It was the voice she heard come from the apparition standing beside the coffin.

It was Ricard Fisher's voice, dead now for nearly a week.

CHAPTER 41

Mara's phone rang as she was doing her dinner dishes.

"Hey, Girlfriend! You forget about me?"

"Mander! Damn, I was gonna call you back, wasn't I?" From the background noise, Amanda was obviously calling from her car.

"Yeah. But I figured you got lost in your writing. Or finally fell off some window ledge you'd crawled out on for a story."

"My suicide-chasing days are over...I hope. I really apologize for not getting back, but there are some strange things going on in this little town—hell, in this house—that have been keeping me busy."

"Small towns, Mara. I came from one. That's why I moved to Cleveland. I can get lost when I have to. So, how's the dating scene there?"

Mara laughed out loud. "Well, first, if I had the time to go out, the dating scene would be non-existent. I went to dinner the other night with...wait for it...Mitch Landry."

"Whaaaat? Yeah, I heard that he'd moved out east. Hey, I always thought he was cute."

"Cute he is. And brilliant almost to a fault. And making a ton of money at this think tank here."

Silence from Amanda. Finally, "So, what's the prob?"

"Ah, I don't know. Scared, I guess."

More silence from Amanda's end. "Oh, honey. You've got to get over him."

"Yeah. But every time I get a mental break, bingo, a flashback. But it's not just him. My parents, Pop-pop. It just seems like I have the reverse-Midas touch when it comes to loving someone."

"Reverse-Midas touch?"

"Yeah. Every loving relationship I touch turns to crap."

"Now look, Mara. You've got to get out of this funk. You're sounding like you're having, what the psychologists where I work would call, abandonment issues."

"Next step is what? I become a mad bomber or ax murderer?"

"No. Just extremely unhappy. Look, if it makes you feel any better, the good news is that Rex just got traded."

"What's the bad news? He's been traded to a team closer to me?"

"No. He's going to San Diego."

"And the bad news?"

Silence again from Amanda.

Mara had to prompt: "Mander?"

"Well, apparently he's taking Ramona with him."

"Fuck."

"Well put. You must be a writer. Look at the bright side. He's her problem now."

And there's that flashback again.

"Look Mara honey, I didn't call to plunge you into the depths of remorse. I just wanted to see how you're doing and remind you that periodically it's nice to hear from you."

Mara could hear the phone switch from car speaker and Amanda's car door slam.

"Where are you?"

"The gym."

"Rockin' those yoga pants, huh, Mander?"

"Not exactly. That's why I'm spinning three times a week. Goin' in now, as a matter of fact. Call me when you can."

"You got it. Love ya, roomie."

"Back atcha!"

So, that should slam the door on Rex the Ex, thought Mara. *So, how come I don't feel any better?*

Mara finished drying the dishes—one plate, one glass, one fork, one knife—and put them away. She looked at Reynolds who was lying asleep, flat on his side on the floor, then at the kitchen table, her computer, her stack of notes and papers.

"Abandonment issues," she said aloud.

CHAPTER 42

It was after dark when Mara entered Dr. Ricard Fisher's apartment, alone. She took her tiny flashlight, her digital camera, and her digital recorder to take notes on instead of notepaper—although by habit she still carried a small notebook, a replacement for the one she had lost in the library. She wanted to go through as many of Fisher's files as she could.

But she had promised herself that she would not enter the death room. That room—she was tempted to say "something in that room," but there was nothing animate in it—absolutely gave her the creeps. On an inner level she couldn't comprehend, the room disrupted her cold writer's objectivity, like static jams a radio. The files around the living room and in the hidden room should be enough to satisfy her curiosity and provide information on what she was after. Or so she hoped.

She moved through the statue room, which was frightening enough. Her flashlight played on the sculptures making weird shadows dance on the walls, like some ballet of the dead. Once or twice, catching them out of the corner of her eye, she swore she saw them move on their own.

She touched the wall switch and the bookcase silently twirled to reveal folders with their edges neatly color-coded and indexed. She found the row of folders marked *Zero-Point Field Studies*. From that row she thumbed through *The Cosmic Hum, Jung, the Z. P. Field and Collective Subconsciousness on the Psychic Level, The Tenth Dimension Studies*, and *Psychic Phenomena and Z. P. Fields*.

Mara tried to run her eyes across the other folders quickly but there were too many. She wanted to linger on some with especially provocative titles that seemed to touch a chord within her, particularly one that was marked *Entity use of the Ether Medium*. But she found and quickly reached for the one marked *Electromagnetic Studies and Otherworld Entrypoints: File 2 of 2,* the continuation of the file she had at home.

She pulled a sheaf of notes curiously labeled "*Inter-dimensional Contacts: Field Notes,*" and began to leaf through it.

There were dates and times in the left margin with descriptive paragraphs accompanying them:

1/14—Photographed energy globe at Hope Cemetery for the first time. Located with thermal scanner. 400 Fuji film. One mist photo. 4 successful photos out of 24 exposures. Weather: clear. Temps 35–37 degrees F. Humidity normal. Began about 8 pm. T. scanner dropped to minus 12F then photos taken. One mist column, bluish white, floating.

What the hell was he writing about? Mara wondered. *What are these "globes" and "mists"—that was something out of science fiction. She continued to read,*

1/21—Attempt at photographing with thermal scanner in yard north of apartment. No results. Thermal scanner indicated nothing. Can I consider this a "control" area for experiments with equipment?

She remembered from her cousin Harry, who owned a construction company, that a thermal scanner was a long distance thermometer. Shaped like a pistol, Harry would point it at different corners of a room or at windows and be able to tell where cold air was leaking in during the winter, and where cool air was leaking out in the summer. Fisher's using a thermal scanner to locate cold spots, she concluded.

2/1—Used digital camera for first time at Our Lady of the Resurrection Cemetery. Remarkable results. Numerous globes/orbs, mists/ecto. Probably took 50 shots, 25 successful. Thermal scanner indicates orbs rise and perhaps move laterally as well. Rising impossible if just cold air. Used mental persuasion for first time and thanks afterwards.

After this entry was a computer generated photo. It showed a cemetery at night, with tombstones fading off into the darkness, and what appeared to be a stone fence at the farthest distance from the camera. The strangest thing about it was the white-blue spots—orbs or globes he called them—that seemed to be floating above the stones at various heights and distances from the photographer. Indeed they looked like what one might dismiss as water spots, but having been taken with a digital camera, as Fisher had written, would mean they couldn't be water since liquid is not a part of the development of digital images. *I've seen this before,* Mara thought. *In the ISAP video. In Katherine's lab.* The last part of the entry confused her. What's up with "mental persuasion," and "thanks," as if he were communicating with…whatever?

2/3—Attempted photos in apartment using thermal scanner. Again no results, no drops in temp, no photos taken. Apparently there is no activity here. This place is clean.

2/5—Resurrection Cemetery. More energy globes than before. 35 of 45 shots. Ectoplasm in 5–6 shots.

There were some more computer-generated photos, again taken in the same cemetery from about the same area as was the last photo she had seen. Indeed there were more of the "orbs" Fisher kept mentioning, but there were other things as well: forms, smoky, misty images with ropey tendrils that seemed to reach out, then reconnect with the main body. At first she thought that someone had been smoking a cigar or cigarette and blowing smoke, or perhaps some fog had floated in front of the lens and someone had taken a picture of it. But the more she looked, the more she realized that there was a certain glow that emanated from inside the mist. Unless the computer and printer had malfunctioned, there was a bluish glow that was appearing within the misty smoke—like what she saw before Fisher's casket at his funeral. Some of the other pictures were even more remarkable.

As she shuffled through the pictures she recognized more of the "orbs," and more of what Dr. Fisher had called "ectoplasm." As she gazed at the last picture, suddenly her breath caught.

There, in the corner of the picture, apparently emerging from the smoky, ropey mist was a human arm. She could make out what appeared to be the top of a military uniform leading down a dark sleeve with buttons attached to the cuff. Emerging from the sleeve was part of a forearm, leading to a long-fingered, graceful hand. It was unmistakable. Unless someone had tampered with the computer-generated picture—or unless her eyes were playing tricks with her—something definitely human was emerging from—or forming out of—Ricard Fisher's photograph of "ectoplasm."

She placed the folder in her backpack and returned to the file.

She stopped cold. There was someone in the room with her, behind her, staring at her. She glanced over her shoulder, but no one was there. She shook her head, turned back to the filing cabinet, thumbed through a few more files and found one entitled, *Creation of Other World Beings*.

Now a chill—no, it was an actual breeze of moving air—fanned across her cheek. She involuntarily gave a small grunt as she passed her hand up to the cold spot.

She forced herself back to the files. She pulled the one on *Creation of Other World Beings* and placed it in her pack.

She thumbed several more tabs, all marked with provocative titles, and stopped at one marked, *Spirit Guides*. She pulled the file.

What the hell was that?

Something dark moved through her peripheral vision.

At first she thought *intruder*, but there was something strange about it.

It was black, shadow-like, moving at a steady pace between what little reflected light there was on the statues and Mara.

That's it, Mara thought. I'm out of here.

She gathered up the folder, grabbed some others, and put them quickly into her backpack, then checked to make sure everything else was there. She couldn't afford to leave anything else behind. Key or no key, she didn't want to have to come back to this place again.

She was passing through the statue room and heading toward the door as quickly as she could, trying not to see anything out of the corner of her eye. But there was something she couldn't avoid seeing.

It was right in front of her.

The door to the death room was open.

Her mind flashed back to when she had entered the apartment.

Jesus, she thought. I know that door was closed when I came in. At least, I think it was. No. *I know it was!*

She stopped. She turned toward the open room. The little voice in her head warned her again, *don't do this. Don't let the curiosity get to you.*

She walked to the door and pushed it open just a little more.

Something tugged the back of her sweater.

She jumped and turned expecting to see Oscar or Eleanor: someone, anyone who had a key.

But there was no one behind her.

It was like reason set off a hand grenade in her head.

This can't be. What touched me? There's nothing there. Am I in danger? Am I going nuts? Is something trying to scare me? I've got to get out of here....

Something pushed her shoulder from behind.

She stumbled into the death room.

She gagged. The smell of rotted meat was overpowering. A quick spin around revealed that no one had been in to clean up, and the closed windows and door guaranteed a rancid vapor that seeped into her pores. And there was no one behind her who could have pushed her. Her only thought was to get the hell out of this room and its hideous, greasy, penetrating odor. She turned to walk back through the door and froze.

Crumpled before the door was a decaying corpse.

Flesh sloughed from the nearly skeletonized face and the hair had fallen to the floor in clumps. Great patches of dried blood had spread across his tattered, dark blue clothing and the head seemed to hang by a thread of sinew. Mara involuntarily gagged and put her hand to her mouth.

The tangled form appeared to be wearing a uniform of some kind, but it was stained with earth, as if he had been buried unceremoniously, without a coffin, in a makeshift, hasty grave. She was trying not to breathe the fetid air in the room, but what she recognized next made her gasp.

The blue, tattered sleeve had brass buttons attached to the cuff.

Like the one in Ricard Fisher's photograph.

She had to get out. She knew she had to step over the body to do it. She took a step towards the body lying before the door.

Oh, God! She thought. *It's moving.*

The body in its moldy, tattered uniform began to rise.

Mara summoned will she never thought she had. She sprinted two steps and leapt over the half sitting, moving form, stumbling into the statue room and crab-crawled toward the exit.

She never looked back. She rushed out the door, slamming it behind her. She got to the elevator, but it was on another floor and she didn't want to wait. She ran to the stairs and rushed down them. She got to her car on the street and sped home.

Even with the wind rushing in through the car windows, as if emanating from her skin, she could still smell the rotting meat.

Back at her house, Reynolds greeted her with his usual enthusiasm. She let him out to pee, grabbed a soda from the refrigerator, and sat at her kitchen table. Her hand shook visibly.

Reynolds wanted to come back in. Returning from the door, she realized her legs were shaky too, and so sat down again to drink her soda.

Reynolds was acting funny, sniffing her up and down.

It's that damn smell from that room. It's all over me.

He was focusing his attention on her ankle. She looked down at the white sock above her Nike.

There, smeared on it, was dried, coagulated blood, and bits of flesh.

Mara leapt to her feet and rushed into the laundry room, stripping off clothing as she moved. It all went into the washer except for the stained sock, which she tossed out onto the concrete step to the back door. She impulsively kicked the cloth behind the garbage can. She closed and locked the back door and rushed upstairs to the shower.

She washed her hair three times and nearly scrubbed the skin off her ankle where the sock had been. Standing there, letting the warm water stream down her body she realized why she had stumbled coming out of the death room.

She stumbled because a rotting hand had grabbed her ankle.

CHAPTER 43

For the first time in her life Mara had the feeling that something else was taking control. She felt that she was being herded—or goaded—into an area about which she didn't have enough knowledge. And she didn't like it at all.

Of course, the simple way out was to say that everything she had experienced could be logically explained: The vision in the elevator was a vivid daydream brought on by overwork; the haze at Ricard Fisher's casket could be written off as a piece of dust under her contact and her imagination getting the better of her; the experiment that was created in Fisher's lab a set up—either on purpose or as a prank; the bizarre noises that sounded like voices on the recorder just interference; the experiences at Fisher's apartment, just a set of hallucinations brought on by the nervousness of participating in a break-in.

Mara, ghosts don't exist, she reminded herself. Or they're not supposed to.

But then there was ISAP's evidence. And Mitch's confirmation of what EVP is. And apports. And Katherine's poltergeist activity in her lab. And my vivid dreams.

But, damn it, the bottom line of all this was to write a biography of Ricard Fisher, whose major accomplishments were in science and physics—not in the field of paranormal research.

Still it bothered her: his *other* accomplishments—unknown scientific studies which may have an even greater impact on the way humans perceive life and death—were in paranormal research.

And, in spite of all his accolades and endowments and awards, the world didn't know this. She and a few intimate associates of Fisher's were the only ones. And she was the only one to know the depth into which he explored the field. To release this information to the world in such a respected intellect's biography could change everything, not the least of which was her career. She could draw rave reviews, or abject ridicule for exposing this side of the world's most promising, and now most tragic, scientist. It could make or break her career; it could make or break Dr. Ricard Fisher's legacy.

It was a biographer's dream...and nightmare.

From everything she had experienced so far, she knew one thing: she had to know more.

Sitting at her kitchen table sipping her fourth cup of coffee, she ran through her mind the people who might be able to help her. Oscar, of course, but more as a supportive friend—and the vehicle to get her into forbidden areas—than to help her understand what was now going on.

Mitch, though she appreciated his healthy skepticism, was limited by his strictly scientific approach.

She did a web search for paranormal investigators in the area. Along with the county, state and local "Ghost Hunters' Societies" which popped up, she found a couple of profiles.

There was one person who might be able to help.

Bradley Knowles's profile said that he had been researching the paranormal since he had been in college. Incredibly, he had gone to Mara's college and had relocated to this area. In fact, she vaguely remembered him from one of her classes.

She also remembered him from some stories she had read about him in the *Plain Dealer*. Now that her memory cells were in full gear, she remembered the first time she spoke with him, although the state he was in, he probably wouldn't have remembered much of the conversation.

They were in one of the local watering holes where students drank. She just happened to be standing next to him ordering a drink. It was near Halloween, and several people in the bar were dressed in costumes. Two of the football players had dressed in drag and were stumbling around on high heels. The sight of a hairy bellybutton beneath a lace midriff top struck Mara as so funny she laughed out loud, turned to a handsome fellow student and said, "Looks like they're getting ready for Halloween."

"Or using it as an excuse."

She laughed again at the comment and introduced herself to Brad, then realized he was the good-looking guy in her sociology class who had caught her eye the first day. From then on they had little more than a passing acquaintance.

According to his Internet bio, after college Knowles had published several serious articles on various aspects of the paranormal and had collected enough stories on ghostly sightings in the area to publish a book, *Cleveland's Other World.*

She found him on Facebook and sent him a quick message mentioning that she was doing research in the area of the paranormal.

Mara made some chai tea for a change, took Reynolds out, and by the time she got back found that Brad had answered her message.

He left his number. What the hell, Mara thought, and dialed it.

"Mara McKay?" Brad's voice was deeper than Mara had remembered from college. "The writer Mara McKay? There was a Mara McKay where I went to school. Is that you?"

"One and the same."

Surprisingly, Brad remembered a number of things about her from college and said he had read some of her articles in the paper. She was obscure about the reasons for the call, but he said that he'd be glad to get together with her over a couple of drinks. Should he bring the hearse?

"You have a hearse?"

"Bought it in Cleveland after I wrote the book. Thought it would help promotions."

"Did it?"

"You know that old saying that there's no such thing as bad publicity?"

"Yeah?"

"It's wrong."

Mara laughed. "So you brought the thing from Cleveland? Sure, Brad. Why not? There are a number of people who think I'm headed straight for Hell anyway; I might as well show them I'm going in style. See you at seven."

The hearse, she found, was surprisingly normal inside. Contrary to what she had anticipated, there was no weird odor of formaldehyde or dead rats. Brad tried coaxing her into riding in the back, but she insisted that she ride next to him in the passenger's seat. When they pulled up to Don Diego's, a trendy, upscale bar and restaurant, heads inside the picture windows turned. Although it had been in mothballs for a while, the "Hearse to Hell" with its painted flames along the sides was still an eye-catcher. Everyone wanted to know who was going to get out of it.

They had drinks and a light dinner, catching up on old times and college memories. Some mutual friends had become incredibly successful. Some had died. She realized that Brad was a lot of laughs and even found herself beginning to be attracted to him—his personality and his good looks, which he had kept despite a slightly receding hairline that didn't seem to matter as much as when she was in college. She decided quickly that he wasn't a psycho after all.

They caught up on their personal lives. He had been married for a while, but divorced two years ago. No children. The hearse had lasted longer than the wife. "Then again," he added, "maybe my keeping the hearse is why she left. It's almost a cliché for failed marriages that so many people get married expecting to change the other person. Of course, in my case, it might have been a good thing!"

He said he had heard from mutual friends that she was seeing some pro athlete.

"Ancient history," she said.

Silence from Brad.

"That bad, huh?"

She flagged down a waiter and ordered another drink. Mara figured she'd better cut right to the point: "Brad, can I ask you some questions about your studies into the paranormal?"

"Sure. Did my book on spooks finally get to you?"

"Well, actually, I haven't even read it, I'm embarrassed to say."

"That's okay. You and about a million other Clevelanders. Good thing I don't depend on my royalties for a living."

"You seem to be the one person I know who has done a lot of research on the paranormal. And I seem to be—inadvertently—running into some very strange happenings while working on this book."

"Strange happenings? Things that are actually happening to you?"

"Yeah. Actual happenings."

"Go on," Brad suddenly turned serious. "I need to hear this."

It took her about twenty minutes to sum up the several odd events that, to her mind, had no logical explanation, including the newspaper appearing, the dreams, and the vision in the elevator that she had experienced. At each event, Brad seemed to become more and more interested, asking numerous questions, some of them seemingly hostile to Mara's observations. She had thought Mitch was difficult to explain the events to; Brad seemed downright mean.

"Look, if you don't want to believe me just say so."

"No. Mara," Brad smiled under his blonde moustache. "No, you misunderstand. I'm playing the devil's advocate here." He nodded semi-seriously towards the hearse. "No pun intended." Mara rolled her eyes. "I'm raking you over the coals for a reason. I believe you, but I'm trying to get every morsel of detail out of you because sometimes even the subtlest action on their part is indicative of intent."

"Intent?"

"Yes. You want to know why the entities are bothering you, right?"

Mara sat back. Yes indeed, "they" were bothering her. But the way Brad said it, it was as if "they" were after her for some reason. She still wasn't even sure "they" existed.

"Brad, do you think 'they' want something from me?"

"That's what I'm trying to determine."

"But wait. If 'they' want something from me, that would mean they have some sort of intelligence. You're saying the dead retain some essence of a human after they're gone?"

"Well, that's one pretty common aspect of a spirit entity, or ghost, if you prefer: They try to communicate in sometimes unconventional ways, often to someone they believe is able to help them, and who is susceptible—I mean physically able to receive their communication—or sympathetic to the existence of life after death.

Mara took a deep breath after Brad's explanation. Going through her head was the last thing she read in Ricard Fisher's notes about finally communicating with the spirits. She fingered the rim of her glass.

"Brad, what do you mean, susceptible? Do you mean weak?"

"What I meant was that some people have the physiological make-up to be receptive to what seem to be very subtle communications from beyond this life. It's sort of like a radio receiver. First the radio has to be tuned to the right frequency; then you can learn to fine-tune it. Not all people can receive spirit communications because many don't even own a radio, if you get my metaphor. Or if they do, they don't know how to tune it. Or maybe the batteries are weak. I think the radio is a pretty good analogy for inter-plane communications."

Brad continued. "Thomas Edison was working on a machine to communicate with the dead when he died. Apparently, he hadn't succeeded or he'd still be telling us what to invent next. Marconi, one of the inventors of radio, also felt we could communicate with the dead. Psychics, apparently, are individuals who are naturally susceptible to whatever emanations the dead send out and have been doing it for millennia. Some believe that psychics may have a different brain pattern than the rest of us. Others think that because of a different chemical makeup, they can receive the electromagnetic waves some believe the dead use to communicate with us. I suspect that's not what you were asking. Mara, are you afraid?"

Her mind was still whirling over the concepts of electromagnetic communications from the dead, the strange voices on her digital recorder, Brad's phrase "inter-plane" communications, and Mitch's comments on electromagnetics, when Brad's question brought her back down. She blurted out, "Yes."

"You get the feeling that you are in danger?"

"No, Brad. I mean, yes, I get a subtle feeling that there is some danger involved, but there is no real reason to be afraid…of the dead. Is there?"

He paused and was about to answer when Mara spoke.

"Wait. I'm not sure I want to hear the answer to that one. Not yet, at least."

"Well," Brad said, looking down into his drink with a broad smile on his face.

"Yes?" Mara encouraged.

"Well, maybe you don't realize it, but this could turn into one of the biggest and most important projects of your life. Bigger than a bio on some weirdo physicist. This is one of your projects that you just cannot get away from, you just can't drop because you're getting bored with it, or because no publisher will buy it. You're going to get as deeply into this as I am and I'll tell you why." He took a long sip of his drink and paused.

"Go on, Brad. I'm waiting."

"You're going to get hooked on this because this is the ultimate question before mankind: What happens to the dead? Where do we go when we die? It is the greatest theme any writer can write about. It is the final question in life: what is death?"

Brad's comment struck a nerve that sent a knot into Mara's stomach. Immediately she wished he hadn't said it.

"If you put it that way, I may not be able to let this go. Jesus, Brad. Thanks a lot."

Brad smiled a disarming smile and toasted Mara. "Welcome to the world of paranormal research."

"What about the mainstream scientists though?" She thought about her conversation with Mitch. "To them, paranormal research is akin to alchemy or voodoo. Didn't Carl Sagan publish a book about this subject? And I have a friend who is a scientist working at a think tank who thinks I'm nuts just talking about the paranormal. Could they be right? Is all we're—you're—doing is chasing something that doesn't exist?"

Brad took a deep breath and smiled.

"Well, Mara. I guess you have to decide for yourself. Your own experiences: were they real or not? Before you answer, pull all the rationalizations out of your mind; leave only the experience. Did you or did you not see something or hear something?"

"Of course I did."

"Now ask yourself, why would a scientist deny something that was experienced? You do realize that observation used to be the basis for all science—still is, as a matter of fact. One of the biggest problems for scientists is that they cannot replicate a paranormal experience in a lab. That, of course, is how they study things: by reproducing the event, then analyzing the results to make sure they are consistent.

"And speaking of Carl Sagan: he dismissed ghosts, but believed that there were extra-terrestrials—aliens, if you will. And I wonder if he'd seen either."

Mara jumped in. "And, it's impossible to reproduce everything in a lab. The big bang for example. And certainly you cannot reproduce how a human will react to certain stimuli. Sure, he's going to back away from pain—most humans that is—but the subtleties of a human are non-reproducible. I can't even predict how *I'm* going to react to certain stimuli from day to day. That doesn't mean that the big bang didn't happen...or that my varied reactions to things don't exist."

"Exactly. The other problem for scientists is that they—like all other established disciplines—live in a house of cards. It's like any other profession: people get to the top by falling into line with other's established ideas."

"Kissing up?"

"Exactly. Some incredibly high-powered people have staked their reputations, their tenure, their salaries, their futures on a particular idea. Einstein must have truly blown some minds with his theories. Ricard Fisher must have ruffled some feathers too, with his scientific arguments against Einstein."

"And paranormal studies…" Mara stopped. She wasn't sure she wanted Brad to know about Fisher's experiments in the paranormal.

"Paranormal studies," Brad continued her thought, "has them all 'shuckin' and jivin',' so to speak. First by allowing normal individuals—not Ph.D.'s or grad students or published scientists—to do the observing and field research. With the proliferation of digital cameras and recorders and computer programs to help the average individual to analyze their data, you have a whole segment of the population out there gathering an immense amount of raw data, and you have scientists in their ivory towers looking down and wondering what's going on. The only thing for them to do is pooh-pooh it as 'junk science' and turn away.

"What I'm saying is, when there's noise in the henhouse, whom do you call? The fox? Scientists would be the last people you'd call to verify or debunk paranormal studies. First, they have the most to lose if the paranormal becomes normal; second, in their ivory tower egotism, it really would be tough for paranormal science to break through into 'mainstream' science."

"So you and I are stuck gathering data and confirming results, with nowhere to put it," Mara observed.

"So far. But that may change."

"How?"

"Well, with a little book that should be coming out within the next year or so."

"You're writing a book on the data you've collected?"

"No, silly. You will be. You won't be able to help yourself."

Mara smiled uncomfortably. "Well, I don't even have a proposal or…."

There was a long silence as Mara digested what had just passed between Brad and her. *Scientists living in a house of cards...reputations and tenures on the line...the sudden weight of responsibility I feel...the strange circumstances of Fisher's death...*

"You know Brad, the way Fisher died...." Mara looked up to see Brad smiling patiently at her, giving her space to digest everything.

"Yes?"

"Some of the cops even said that it looked more like a torture/murder than a suicide. Do you think someone in the academic community could have killed him?"

"It's a thought, Mara. Certainly there would be the motive. How many scientists have built their reputations on spin-offs from Einstein?"

Brad took a sip. Mara took advantage of the pause.

"Or would be outraged at some of Fisher's delving into..." Mara had to stop herself again. Brad was so easy to talk to. "I mean, some of the stuff he was getting into could have been really ground-breaking. Some of it could have tipped the adherents to the scientific method on their heads. Could have brought down that house of cards you spoke of. But would that be enough for someone to murder him?"

"If you had staked your entire reputation upon a single theory or a spin-off from it and received your salary, retirement package, numerous publications, and professional security from it, I suppose someone—or some people—would feel it in their best interests to kill off someone threatening all that."

Mara sat and stared thoughtfully at her glass. Something was bothering her and she couldn't put her finger on it.

They both took a long drink. The waitress came by and Brad motioned for two more drinks and the check. Mara found herself feeling a little disappointed that their evening was going to end so soon.

"Wait a minute," Mara said. "My being fearful of what could happen to me. This is all presupposing that there is something that goes on after death. If you don't accept that original presumption—and I'm still not sure I do—the rest falls apart."

Brad answered. "For centuries scientists and philosophers have been debating whether the mind continues on after the brain dies. They're about evenly split. Also, where do all the reports come from? Where do all the sightings come from? I mean historically. Do billions of people have over-active imaginations? It's called anecdotal evidence, Mara.

It's how we first learned about the world before the scientific method was developed. We observed. Then individuals compared their observations and drew data down from the commonality of their experiences. Hell, it's how we discovered sex."

"Huh?" Mara almost choked on her last sip of cocktail.

"That sex made babies, at any rate. People had sex, then, for some reason, nine months later they had a baby. Lots of people compared notes and, lo and behold, the connection was made."

Mara gave Brad one of her "where did *that* come from" looks.

"Simplified," he said.

"Over-simplified," she said.

The drinks came and while Brad was sipping, Mara decided to throw the hand-grenade.

"Did I tell you that I was picking up unheard voices on my digital recorder?"

Brad stopped drinking in mid-sip. "What? Really? Now that's significant. I have been experimenting with that as well. I've had only limited success and I'm trying to figure out why, whether it's the questions I'm asking, or the place, or the equipment. What have you been using?"

"Just my regular digital recorder." She reached in her pack and pulled out the tiny silver device she used to record snippets of conversation and interviews. It was the size of a credit card and just a little thicker.

"This little thing? You've picked up EVP on this?"

"Well, let's just say I've picked up voices that were not audible in the room. I'm still not sure they were communications from the dead." Mara paused and thought about the information relayed by the voice: *the beaker, Katherine.* "Then again, the words did make sense in their context."

Brad twirled the little recorder around in his hand.

It was completely opposed to her nature, but looking at his handsome face and thinking about his boyish, playful nature, Mara suddenly felt like she could share something vital with Brad.

"Hey, Brad. Are you up for a little adventure?"

He smiled and showed long vertical lines that formed a strong parenthesis on either side of his mouth.

"What do you have in mind?"

CHAPTER 44

Standing in the yellow half-cone of her porch light, Brad said, "Mara, this place is delightful. Where did you find this house?"

"A friend found it for me. It's a little old," she said as she struggled with the skeleton key, "but it will do for the short time I'm here."

The door finally popped open with an authentic horror-film creak.

"Nice touch," Brad said. "This place has character."

"That it certainly has. Did you want a beer?" she shouted over Reynolds's din as he barked his way from the living room couch to the slippery kitchen floor.

"Sure. Is he gentle?" Brad said as he tried to avoid the twirling Reynolds's slapping tail.

"What do you think? He'll calm down in a second. Here you go, boy."

Mara scooped the dog food out of the can and sprinkled it with some green beans from the refrigerator. Reynolds gobbled the first few bites, pausing briefly to give a thank-you look to Mara.

"A vegetarian dog?"

"He likes it and it can't hurt him. Here. A lite beer okay?"

"Sure."

"Have a seat while I let him out."

Between letting the dog in and out, Mara got herself a beer and retrieved the folders from her backpack. She pulled a chair up next to Brad and opened the folder marked *Electromagnetic Studies and Otherworld Entrypoints: File 2 of 2*. She leafed to a page that she had marked with a post-it note and picked up where she left off in Fisher's apartment, with his notes labeled *Inter-dimensional Contacts: Field Notes*.

"Check this out," she said to Brad, and started reading aloud from Ricard Fisher's notes.

"2/10—Orbs (energy globes) set off motion detector for the first time in Columbiana Tunnel site of 1903 disaster. Therefore they move about and are not stationary. Temp. constant 55 degrees from being underground. Slightly higher humidity. Photo of huge bright orb and ecto. Later picked up vortices. Must get digital camcorder to capture motion. Confirms my motion theory.

"2/14—Still experimenting with digital camcorder. Bring tripod next time. Sent for digital recorder. Received gauss meter today for electromagnetic field detection. Something about "digital" equipment: seems to be more sensitive.

"2/16—Mount of Olives Cemetery near State Prison, burial site of executed criminals from Death Row. Many unmarked graves, stones overturned, moved. Gauss meter spiked numerous times at about 6"–12" over graves; after several minutes of connective meditation, began taking photos with digital still camera. Numerous orbs, some emergent ectoplasm. Could they have electromagnetic properties as well? Is that why digital equipment is affected so strongly?"

"A gauss meter is used to detect electromagnetic fields around electrical wires," Brad said. "This, evidently, is someone doing a paranormal investigation?"

"Just listen." Mara took a sip of beer and read on.

"2/18—Camcorder worked in conjunction with still camera. Experiment: Set up camcorder on tripod at Mount of Olives Cemetery. Walked to farthest edge of cemetery and began photographing. "Chased" orbs towards camcorder, it seemed. Flash of camera seems to bother them…or activate them. Orbs rushing towards camcorder and seemingly dodging it at last moment. Got 3-D image, so they're not flat disks but true orbs. Begin EVP experiments next week.'"

"EVP? Electronic Voice Phenomena? Mara, are these your notes? Have you been experimenting?"

Mara gave Brad a blank look. She was reading this for the first time herself. She thought, EVP. Now he's getting into something I can relate to, remembering her conversation with Mitch. But what's this about them dodging the camera? What? Chased orbs towards the camera? She looked up at Brad.

"Mara, this is some fine work you've done. These 'orbs' and 'ectoplasm' you're talking about are some kind of energy or they wouldn't be setting off the gauss meter. The gauss meter just tells you what kind of energy they are, or at least one of the types of energy they contain: electromagnetic. Obviously, they have light energy associated with them as well, since they show up in photos on light sensitive film or monitor in the case of a digital camera.

"They must have thermal energy too, because they can be detected with a thermal scanner—a thermometer. There must be some sort of kinetic energy too, since they move—or appear to move. That they 'dodged' an object though; that means they must have some sort of..."

Mara could hardly bring herself to think the word.

Brad said it: "They must have some sort of...intelligence."

Mara continued reading:

" 2/25—Indian Field, 11:55 pm. 38 degrees; humidity normal; barometer dropping; storm front moving in. Full moon (any effect upon results???) Camcorder, while on auto focus, continually goes in and out of focus, even when there is something solid (me!) to focus on. Coincides with E's still photos of numerous orbs between me and camcorder taken at the same time. Even when orbs cannot be seen they seem to set off infrared focusing on camcorder. Indian Field is extremely active. Numerous orbs, ectoplasm, unseen entities mucking up focus on camcorder. On purpose or are they doing it accidentally? Asked to leave area by armed night watchman.

"(Historical note: Indian Field was the site of a massacre of Native Americans. Christian Indians, ca 1699, in an effort to convert local tribe, killed some 230 men, women and children. Tribal animosity was the real reason behind the massacre. Mass burials in a mound the shape of a serpent eating an egg. Mound barely discernable now. Scheduled for destruction by developers to build a shopping mall complex. Local historian's efforts to save site swept aside. Rumors of increased activity in the area when backhoes and bulldozers began their work: Foreman knocked to his knees walking to toilet at north end of field; said it felt like a tree branch fell and hit him across the shoulders; no trees in area and no tree branch on ground around him. Backhoe operator fell from machine; claimed he was "knocked off;" machine tore into a shed destroying some equipment; operator fired for "drinking on job;" I suspect a cover-up—he's a Mormon and doesn't even drink caffeine. Reports from locals of strange lights seen in area, possibly investigators, possibly ectoplasm. Sightings of "mists"—upright, in motion.)"

"Who's this 'E,' Mara?"

"I don't know."

"What do you mean? You were there in Indian Field with 'E'...wait a minute. These aren't your notes, are they?"

Mara shook her head.

"These are Fisher's notes, aren't they? The most prominent physicist in modern times and he's doing experiments with the paranormal? Oh, brother, Mara, will this ever lend credence to the cause!"

"Listen, Brad. You've got to swear that you won't say a thing to anyone about this. It changes everything in my bio of Fisher. If it's not handled right, it could create a disaster and end my career."

"No, Mara. I won't say anything to anyone. I mean, you're the one doing the biography. This will all come out in it, right?"

Mara paused.

"It has got to come out in his bio, Mara. You agree, don't you?"

"Brad, I'm not sure. I don't know what my editor will say when I tell her this. I mean, this changes everything, the whole thrust of the book is altered now. I'm really not sure. Plus, there may not even be enough on the paranormal to use."

The last part was a lie, and Brad seemed to see right through it.

"There are more folders, aren't there Mara?"

Sheesh, Mara thought. Am I that obvious?

"Yes. But you've got to respect my wishes on this. Honestly, Brad, it could ruin my career."

Brad paused an uncomfortably long time.

"All right, Mara. But I'll tell you what. I want you to finish reading me Fisher's notes. And if you're not going to publish anything about his investigations into the paranormal, I'm going to personally replicate his experiments. I'll do it and publish my own results. Fair deal?" He stuck out his hand.

Mara paused. Brad continued:

"The world has to know about this, Mara. If there is absolute, scientific proof of life after death, the world should know, so that they may have hope."

Hope, thought Mara. Hope for a world wanting to believe that there is something that goes on after death. Death is not a closing door but one that is opening. Hope for a grief-stricken world that they will see their loved ones again and that we all are not thrown into the black bottomless hole of nothingness at the hour of our death.

Mara took a deep breath, reached out and took Brad Knowles's hand. She hoped it wasn't a pact she would later regret.

CHAPTER 45

Brad finished his beer and left after giving Mara his e-mail address.

"Please," he said, "Please, Mara. We absolutely have to do something together on this. Keep me in the loop or I'll keep bugging you."

Mara promised to call Brad as soon as she was finished reviewing Fisher's notes. But she was torn.

First, there was the obvious physical attraction she felt for Brad. He was handsome and passionate. He had a delightful, maybe a little goofy sense of humor, but Mara liked that offbeat stuff. And until she had shared Ricard Fisher's notes with him, she felt she just might like to spend time with him.

But his laser-like intensity about revealing to the world the existence of an afterlife that the great theoretical physicist Ricard Fisher believed in—and seemed to be proving—frightened her. It was as if he'd only thought it part way through, saw only the end results and not the twisted corollaries.

What if it *were* true? What if there were an afterlife, and we go on and on throughout time? More frightening than that was the possibility that there may be *just* that: surviving on some plane of existence without the threat of retribution or punishment for what evil we have done in this life.

That there will be retribution by God or karma or whatever seems to keep most people from indulging their every whim, keeps us from becoming selfish, self-centered takers, and threatens us if we do not behave morally.

The world knowing with absolute, scientific certainty there is life after death—with no punishment, not even extinction—may be more sinister than just giving them hope. Murderers realizing there is no real threat in execution; radical suicide bombers knowing that they *will* go on to their 72 virgins, or, if not the virgin part, at least go on; teenage suicide pacts losing their stigma; murder/suicides going ultimately unpunished.

She remembered her Bible: *Death, where is thy sting?*

Just beyond hope, she thought, there lies terror.

She pressed her temples with her knuckles, then gave Reynolds a good rub on his back to make both of them feel good and to break the mood she was descending into. Time to get back to work.

She picked up Fisher's book *Einstein Schmeinstein* and began paging through it. She had read it when it first came out and found it simple, almost elegant in its explanations of his theories. Now she wanted to look through it again, since it would be the closest she could get to interviewing its dead author.

Now, for some reason, everything in the book had a different meaning. Instead of looking at it as an explanation for the physical world, she saw it as an explanation for the metaphysical world. She found herself in the middle of a page with her eyes scanning the sentences, but her mind thinking about other things—like life after death.

Damn it! she thought after having to go back to the top of the page and re-read what she'd already read twice before.

Finally she gave up. I'll have to go at this from the back door, she thought. I'll go through his silly ghost stuff first, then go back and do the rest.

She picked up one of Fisher's folders—the one she had been reading to Brad— opened it and started.

> *3/2—While still camera took numerous orbs—a shower of them—mine showed nothing. Possible reason: we were at a battlefield, place called Widow's Ridge, site of confused fighting. I have studied the area well. Experiment for tomorrow night: Read off list of names from Co. C, 5th Texas Infantry Regiment as if reading off muster for pay. Read into digital recorder and pause to see if there is an answer. Answer should be simple: 'Yes,' or 'Here.' We'll see!*

Apparently Fisher had gone to a battlefield to do some research. Perhaps that's the Civil War connection? Which came first, his interest in the Civil War or his interest in the paranormal? She continued reading.

> *3/3—Unbelievable! This is incredibly exciting. I need to get everything down so there is a complete record of all factors that may give variance to results and so that the experiment may be able to be reproduced. Weather: Temp—balmy 66 degrees, unseasonable. Thunderstorms in the area. Slightly higher than normal humidity. Moon was on the wane. Barometer falling. Little wind. Began experiments at 9 pm. Near Widow's Ridge at place called the Slaughter Pen, lower end.*
>
> *History; Civil War battle around 5–7 pm several assaults up the field by Texas troops and Georgia troops; repulsed by New York troops and Pennsylvania troops. Eventually rebels took the high ground at top of Slaughter Pen and swept up Widow's Ridge.*
>
> *Set up digital camcorder on stationary tripod to record field of experimentation. Plan to take still photos from various angles. Used "OM" tuning fork for the first time to prepare area/self for ease of entry. Held quartz pyramid for ether focus. Placed gauss meter on adjacent log after getting generalized local readings for control.*
>
> *Started digital camcorder and recorder and began with orders from Civil War era Confederate drill manual. Used regular magnetic tape of Civil War music with original instrumentation. Songs "Lorena" followed by drum cadence for "assembly." Next began reading muster list of 5th Texas Regiment name by name, pausing 45 seconds between each name.*
>
> *Observation: The recorder is "voice activated" and so should only record when I speak the name. As I watched, however, the digital LED numbers that indicated that the machine was recording, ticked off in sequence, as if something unheard was being recorded! There was no audible sound, however, at the bottom of the Slaughter Pen as indicated by the recording on the digital camcorder, which was running the entire time.*

Results: I read off forty-seven names. After the names of the men who were ill during the battle and on sick leave (5) there was nothing and the recorder moved immediately on to my voice reciting the next name; After the names of men who were in the battle and survived (18), there was no sound and the recorder moved immediately on to my voice pronouncing the next name; After the names of men who were wounded in the fighting but survived the battle (12) there was nothing but my voice going on to the next name; But after reading the names of the men who were killed in action in the fighting in the Slaughter Pen (12), there was something recorded.

In five of the "answers" there was a definite "roar" or loud, raspy interference that lasted approximately one half second. The strange thing about the "roar" is that it had a definitely human quality about it. It seemed as if it had a tone of frustration to it. (In explaining this, I can only refer to the various sounds animals make—we don't understand exactly what they are saying, but we know when they are angry or pleased or content. Same idea with the "roar." And yet, discernible within the roar are one or two words—a muffled "yes" with intonations, or "no." It remains to be seen whether longer sentences can be heard or even coaxed from...whatever it is that is making the odd noises.)

Mara had to consciously close her jaw. What Fisher wrote, more than any of the photographs she had seen, gave her the proverbial chills up her spine. The roars and voices. Were they the same as she had been getting inadvertently on her recorder?

3/4—This is either supremely complicated or extremely simple. If I am right, we are delving into the greatest question facing mankind: where do we go when we die? Is this what we are doing? Are the "orbs" and "ectoplasms" and "EVP" actually images and voices of the energy we become after we die? Or are they just some electromagnetic anomaly mucking up our instruments?

Or, perhaps more significantly, have we inadvertently tapped into a brand new energy source that is actually independent of any others? Is this energy source linked to the human soul or spirit? Is it of another world? If it is a new energy source, does it act and react the same way as the old energy sources—heat, light, electromagnetic, atomic—do? Does it play by the same rules as all the others that mankind has been familiar with over his existence such as the Laws of Thermodynamics? Certainly atomic energy didn't play by all the rules and Einstein had to virtually create new rules for it.

I will begin introducing into the experiments an eliminator factor to weed out any possible known interference.

Typical of Dr. Ricard Fisher, Mara thought. He's beginning to apply his physics and scientific mind to the problem. This should get interesting now.

3/5—Time 9 pm. Location: Field of Marin's Charge. Temp 42 degrees. Some thunderstorms in the distance to the west. Humidity, slightly higher than normal. Repeated protocol of 3/3. More orbs surrounding me. Perhaps from other regiments or units? Anyone famous? Dozens floating, moving, being attracted by my voice. Recording on a digital recorder that can be downloaded into a computer for voice analysis. Though we cannot compare with original "live" voice, we can compare with other recordings extant to match if possible. Perhaps we keep contacting the same individuals?

Request they return with me.

What? Mara thought. Return with him? What the hell is he talking about? Bringing them back…to his apartment? She looked up from the manuscript and pictured his apartment as the light moved among the statues and their shadows danced weirdly upon the white walls. And the body she had to jump over to get out. A chill like a cold hand pressed against her chest and she felt it right down to her heart. Her chest got even colder when she read the next sentence:

Dream sequence and discussion during the night. Learning new things constantly from them re: objectives, desires, plans. All cogent.

He was communicating with them.

CHAPTER 46

Just start typing you moron.
 Crap, Mara thought. Writer's block. Typing. Reading. Backspacing. This is no way to start off a day I need to fill with words.
 After an hour and two cups of coffee, her eye was caught by the little YouTube symbol in the bottom bar of her computer screen. It was the video of the ghost hunter explaining what ghosts have to teach us about death. Before thinking about it, Mara clicked it and the screen filled with the guy, mouth frozen since the last time she watched him a week or so ago.
 "...Ghost lights," he was saying. A PowerPoint screen behind him flashed on showing orbs of light. "The fact that we can periodically see ghosts means that they have enough substance—matter—that they reflect ambient light, although this matter seems to come and go, since they can vanish as quickly as they appear. Or, does it mean they produce the light energy themselves, like bioluminescence, even after death?"
 Bio, meaning some kind of life, applied to the dead? That's right. This guy was trying to explain what the dead have to teach us about the afterlife. Once again, this stretches all credibility. *But there was that body I saw in Fisher's apartment, and the lights coming from dying organisms, like in the ISAP videos....*
 "How ghosts manifest to us may also give us some clues as to what happens to us after we die.
 "Chills are commonly reported during a so-called ghostly encounter."
 Yeah, Mara thought. I've gotten those chills.
 "They are often tested by using quick-read, non-contact thermometers to make sure they're not just the researcher's imagination. Does that mean we can change the surrounding

temperature by our presence after we die? At the very least it means that there is some sort of energy—in this case, heat energy—exchange going on in the vicinity of a haunting.

"Feelings. You know, 'the willies' as some would call them. It is a scientifically proven fact that, more often than not, statistically we can tell when someone is watching us from behind. What happens when we get exactly that same feeling, turn around, and find there is no one there—no one visible, that is?"

He found the water bottle under the podium and took a swig.

"Auditory manifestations seemed to be the most common of all. We will hear a ghost before we will ever see one. The most common noise is footsteps, so somehow we can still make noise in the afterlife, hard shoes upon a wooden floor or gravel or pavement.

"Seeing a ghost is relatively rare, but everyone's first question is, 'have you ever seen a ghost?' Most have to say no and so they think they've never had a ghostly experience. But all the human senses are involved, not just sight, in ghostly manifestations."

Once again, Mara thought. *This all presupposes that the spirit lives on in another dimension. And just because I've had a few weird experiences, which could have been my imagination.... Except, of course, the recordings. Those would have to be classified about as objective as anything can be. It was a machine that heard the voices. But still, personally, I remain unconvinced. I* have *to remain unconvinced....*

"Oh, I almost forgot," Mr. YouTube Ghost Hunter said. "Touches. People have actually been touched by ghosts."

Or grabbed? Like I was in Fisher's apartment by that visual manifestation?

"Which brings up poltergeist activity, poltergeist meaning 'noisy ghost.' This type of activity is characterized by doors slamming, lights flickering on and off, objects being thrown across the room, or levitated, or moved, by some unseen force. The reason evidence of poltergeist activity is important is because of some work done and conclusions drawn in the study of Psychokinesis.

"Psychokinesis is the physical movement of matter by energy coming from the mind. Though rare, it also has been proven scientifically, in the old Soviet Union and in the Rhine Institute at Duke University where Dr. J. B. Rhine worked with people affecting random number generators with their thoughts."

Once again, Mara thought, machines, completely objective, being affected. "But what does this have to do with ghosts?" she said out loud.

"Rhine reasoned that since the results from psychokinesis and poltergeist activity were so similar, it could mean the survival of the mind, or consciousness beyond death."

Mara clicked the pause button. Once again, Mr. YouTube Ghost Hunter touched a nerve. Or several nerves.

CHAPTER 47

The hearse seemed apropos as they rolled silently up to Laurel Grove, one of the oldest cemeteries in the city. Fall was settling in and the chill was also appropriate for the darkened graveyard. Mara had given in and called Brad to ask if she could work with him on some of his paranormal research.

Yes it's unprofessional, she reminded herself. Yes, it's not on track with Fisher's bio, but it might lead to another book someday. Plus, the research fascinates me—the old writer's curiosity kicking in again.

And there was one other reason that she would hardly admit to herself. She was attracted to Brad on an other-than-professional basis.

Everyone from the town's 19th century past was buried in Laurel Grove, from newspaper publishers to sea captains to army generals. The site was once an old Indian battle and burial ground, and the Native American bones got displaced and scattered when the white settlers began using it. Their ashes too were said to have been disturbed when the dead from Civil War regiments began to overflow the small plot designated for them. During her research into local paranormal groups, Mara read the Internet rumors that the place was haunted; had even driven by it a couple of times, but never had the desire—or maybe the guts—to stop and go in.

Now, here she was, a grown woman, sneaking into a darkened cemetery at night to hunt for ghosts.

Brad turned the hearse off. The silence seemed loud.

"So, leetle missy" Brad said, trying out what he thought was his best southern accent. "Air you a-skeered?"

Mara tried to match his humor, but had to admit to herself that she was having a bad feeling about the place. "Let's just get this over with. What's the procedure?"

Brad smiled and Mara noticed again the long, sexy creases next to his mouth. "Your recorder is voice-activated, right Mara? So, what we want to do is go out into the cemetery and ask some questions, pause twenty or thirty seconds, then ask another. We want to give the spirits time to answer."

Mara thought: Sounds like the same technique Fisher had used at...where was that battlefield?

"Can you get the same results with a regular recorder?" Mara asked

"Actually, you can. I have, in fact, but you have to listen to the whole recording to try and hear anything. It's really pretty boring, especially if you don't get anything. Older models seem to get better results than the newer ones with noise cancellation. That's why I asked to borrow yours. With this little gem, we'll optimize our chances and be able to see if we've picked anything up right away. Ready?"

"Ready."

They left the hearse and walked to the large, cast iron gate. Of course it groaned as they opened it. Brad flashed a sinister smile at Mara. She just rolled her eyes and pushed him into the cemetery.

"Hey, Mara. All kidding aside, I want to thank you again for calling me to do this with you."

"Are you kidding? After hearing what Fisher was doing with this EVP technique, I figured you'd go ahead and do it yourself anyway. I'm just here to take notes."

"For the book?"

Mara paused for what she thought might have been a little too long. "Okay. Where are we going, hotshot?"

"Well, I figured we'd stop at a couple of the older graves, then go back to the Civil War section. I've done a little research on the unit the men were fighting with and I might be able to ask them some pertinent questions."

"That matters?"

"Well, think about it. Suppose you are in a room and all of a sudden you start hearing a voice. The voice out of nowhere starts saying, 'Is there anybody here with us now?' What would you think? You'd ignore it like a caller ID name that you don't recognize. Instead, a voice calls your name, says the names of other people that you might know, or talks about the military unit you were in and the places you fought at or visited. You might be a little more amenable to answering that strange voice out of nowhere. Right?"

The same technique Ricard Fisher tried with success, Mara thought.

"Brad, you're making this all sound so logical, as if the *ghosts* are out there thinking or something."

"Who says they're not? What are the rules for the spirit world? Nobody knows. I'm just going along with what makes sense to me. Wait. Here we are. All right, we'll try it."

Brad stopped and suddenly stepped off the macadam onto a grassy side path, then stopped in front of a grouping of gravestones, several of which were smaller than the others. Brad pulled out a small flashlight and held it down to the stones. Two of the smaller ones were illegible, but two others, Mara could read. One read, "Beloved son, William. Aged 6 yrs 4 mos 12 dys." The other read, "Beloved daughter, Rebekkah, gone home to God, Aged 10 yrs 7 mos 2 dys."

Shadows danced eerily as Brad's light moved to the larger gravestone.

The stone had an ornate carved design of angels descending across the top. Mara read the names of those upon whose sepulture they stood: "Ephraim Squires, 1814–1858; Sephrina Squires, his wife 1824–1883."

Brad turned the light off.

"Are you ready?"

Mara pulled the small recorder from her pocket, slid off the "Hold" button, pressed record and handed it to Brad.

Brad fumbled with it for a second, then brought the tiny machine to his mouth.

"Hello Sephrina. We're here to visit with you."

Brad paused for about twenty seconds, then continued.

"Sephrina, we see you lost some children. Did you miss William?"

Mara felt a wave of profound sadness when Brad asked the question. But it was strange, as if the feeling came from outside rather than from within.

Brad paused another twenty seconds: "Sephrina, did you love Rebekkah?"

Mara was looking over her shoulder when Brad elbowed her. She almost punched him back when she saw that he was pointing at her recorder. The LED light that was supposed to be pulsing rhythmically was glowing steadily. In the total silence of the graveyard, something was being recorded.

The light stopped glowing and began pulsing, indicating that nothing more was being recorded. She wanted Brad to stop and play back what they had just recorded, but he continued.

"Ephraim Squires, did you miss your family when you died?"

Again, Brad paused. Again the LED went from flickering to a steady glow. Something else was being recorded. Mara strained to hear something, anything, coming from outside the graveyard that might cause the recorder to activate. But there was nothing. She had to smile at herself when she thought, it's quiet as a tomb.

"Ephraim, are you in pain?"

More steady glowing from the light. Mara moved closer to Brad and saw that the numbers on the recorder's miniature readout were rolling. More of something she could not hear was being recorded.

Brad pushed the button to stop the recording.

"Well, Mara, what do you think?"

"What am I supposed to think? Something was being recorded on the recorder, something that wasn't being propagated through the air."

"Or at a frequency that human ears couldn't detect."

"Whatever it was, I couldn't hear it."

"Well, let's find out. How do you play this back."

Mara took the recorder and pressed the play button. By all rights there should only be Brad's voice on the machine, and being voice activated, the questions should come one on top of the other.

Sure enough, after Brad's first question, "Hello Sephrina. We're here to visit with you," there was virtually no pause where Brad had been silent; the next question came right on the heels of the first.

"Sephrina, we see you lost some children. Did you miss William?"

Mara had her ear pressed up against the recorder. There was a second of silence, then a loud, agonized roar drove a pinprick of pain into her eardrum. Where there should have been total silence was a noise so loud that anyone standing within twenty feet could have heard it. And yet, at the time Brad recorded it, Mara heard nothing.

She heard Brad's voice ask the next question, "Sephrina, did you love Rebekkah?" On the machine she heard four distinct syllables, the first two slow and the last two in staccato. She decided she'd have to listen to them a second time, but realized one quality about the voice that was unmistakable: it was female.

"Ephraim Squires, did you miss your family when you died?" Again Brad had asked a very personal question.

This time Mara heard another roar—or was it more of a growl? Whatever it was, it was distinctly male, and sounded angry. She also thought she had heard a hissing sound, perhaps a "yesss."

"Ephraim, are you in pain?"

There were three distinct syllables, then one. Mara strained to hear words, and finally shook her head.

She looked up at Brad. A smile began to spread across his face.

"I couldn't make out the words," Mara said. "I think I heard them say words, but I just couldn't make them out completely."

"Mara, we'll take this home, run it through your computer, and you can listen more closely with earphones. Maybe you can figure out what they are saying. But don't lose the forest for the trees. You stood right here in the silence. By all rights, there shouldn't have been anything recorded on the machine. The fact that something was recorded in silence is important."

"How could that be?" Mara paused in thought. "How could something be recorded when we couldn't hear anything?" Maybe Brad could add something to what Mitch had already told her.

"Well, reasoning it out, it could be that the sounds are above or below the frequency that our ears can hear. Or, it could be some sort of electromagnetic means of communication. EVP was discovered when magnetic tape was invented. Back in the 1950s, a man was recording bird songs on a reel-to-reel recorder and inadvertently recorded what he identified as his dead father's voice. The word got out, and psychics and mediums began using tapes to try to record their communications with the dead. They were successful, but the laymen who tried it often were not.

"But with new technology, digital recorders and the like, the computer chips are apparently so sensitive that they are picking up even the smallest of vibrations, whether those vibrations are of the audible variety or the electromagnetic type."

A rustle behind them made Mara jump, but it was only a small breeze that had blown up some leaves.

"Come on," Brad said. "Let's go to the soldiers' plot."

They cut crossways through the older section of the cemetery, Brad plodding along ignorant of the graves upon which he was treading. It made Mara unexplainably uneasy and she did a hop step now and again, attempting not to step directly upon the darkened sepulchres of long dead humans. Some of the graves were sunken. Mara had the uneasy feeling they were ready to collapse and swallow her up.

She could see in the dim-lighted distance row upon row of similar gravestones: the knee-high, half-rounded stones meant to make all soldiers—generals to privates—alike in death as they had never been in life, a thin concession, she thought, now that they were beyond knowing.

Brad stopped at the head of the section, like he was about to review the army represented by their standing gravestones. Their number was staggering to Mara; they didn't end so much as they stretched out until they seemed to fade into eternal blackness.

"Now, don't laugh at me," Brad said to Mara. "I've been wanting to try this."

Brad hitched himself up into a military position of "attention," chest puffed out, arms straight down his sides.

"Company B, First Regiment, attention!" he said in an official voice. "Muster for pay call."

Mara saw him reach into his pocket and pull out a small piece of paper upon which she could barely make out several names. He held up the recorder and began to call out the names, pausing the requisite twenty seconds between each, performing a roll call of the dead:

"Ackerman…
Adolphson…
Allman…
Atkinson…
Ball…
Beatty…
Bigelow…"

Mara watched over his shoulder. Incredibly, after several of the names, the tiny led light on the recorder glowed steadily. This is the same technique Fisher had developed, Mara thought.

"Bond…
Booker…
Bulger…

Charney...."

And on and on it went. She wanted Brad to stop for a second to hear what he was obviously recording, but she didn't want to break the spell.

"Deaver...

Dodge...

Dunnigan..."

He turned the paper over and began to read the names of some places Mara was vaguely aware of.

"Brave men of Bull Run...of Antietam...of Fredericksburg...of Chancellorsville...of Gettysburg...of Mine Run...of Petersburg. Remember where you fought and fell and answer me now.

He then continued to read the names of the men.

Evans...

Fields...

Folk...

Gardner...

Gibbs...."

Mara heard another rustle behind them and unconsciously moved a little closer to Brad. She could smell him.

"Hunter...

Jackson...

Martin...

McGillis..."

Brad paused longer than ever after the last name. A full 45 seconds later he repeated, "McGillis. William McGillis."

Okay, Mara thought, this is enough.

"Whoa!"

Brad's exclamation made Mara grab his arm. "What?"

"Did you see that? The last name. It must have recorded for a full minute! Somebody had something to say!"

Now Mara was truly growing apprehensive. She began to feel a cold chill spread down her spine and the hairs on her arms began to stand. It didn't help when she remembered a sentence in Fisher's notes that one psychic had called the hairs on your body standing up an "affirmation" that the spirits were nearby and passing among the living.

Mara heard the rustle behind them again and ignored it.

Suddenly a flash of white light blinded her and she jumped as a cracked voice came out of the darkness:

"What's going on, you two?"

It was a local police officer and his partner who had silently made their way into the cemetery after seeing Brad's hearse.

Brad squinted against the officer's flashlight.

"Nothing, sir. We're just...uh...we're simply...uh...."

"Doing some research," Mara blurted out, sticking her open hand nearly into the officer's face for him to shake. He took it awkwardly. "I'm Mara McKay, you know, the writer. The one who's good friends with Oscar Fosster. You know Oscar...or, 'the Big O', as I like to call him, don't you? The detective who took the bullets for the kids in the schoolyard? Sure, you know him. I'll tell you, Oscar has nothing but superlatives for all you beat cops—that is what you call yourselves, right? Well, he just has nothing but good things to say about you beat cops. In fact, just the other day, over lunch as a matter of fact, he was saying there are a couple of you guys he's almost sure should make detective as soon as the slots...or spots...or whatever you guys call them, open up. And you are officer...I'm sorry, I can't read the name, but I'm sure, 'the Big O' would recognize it if I were to...."

"Uh, ma'am."

"Yes, officer?"

"Just leave. The cemetery is closed after dark. We thought you might be vandals. You can go now."

Mara and Brad found themselves closer to the macadam road as the officer sort of herded them there as he talked. Mara began her nervous babble again as they walked through the light spots made by the officers' flashlights. She was still talking as they got into their patrol car and waited as Mara and Brad drove off in the hearse.

"Mara, that was pretty quick thinking to keep babbling until they got sick of you."

"I hate to admit it but I was getting the willies in there. Was I babbling?"

"Like a brook."

"Did you get anything on the recorder?"

"Didn't you see the light? It was steady almost the entire time. Are you ready to hear what we got?"

"Do you mind if I take the recorder and listen to it first?"

Brad looked a little disappointed.

"No problem," he said. "But promise me we'll get together real soon. So that I can listen."

"I think I can e-mail it from my computer. You can listen to that."

"So, you're saying we can't get together?"

"No. No! That's not what I'm saying. Yes, it'll be fun to get together. I mean to listen to the recording."

Listen to me, Mara thought. I'm sounding like a tenth-grader.

"How about tomorrow night? For dinner?"

"Uh, I have to write." *Really I do. Please understand I have to get these notes in the computer.*

"Oh."

"No, really."

"How about Thursday?"

"Uh, Thursday. Sure. No. I have an interview."

Brad was silent as they pulled up in front of Mara's house.

"You know, from here your house…" he said "looks haunted."

"Yeah."

Invite him in, you blockhead!

Brad spoke up first. "Well, I gotta go."

Mara got out of the hearse.

"I'll call you, Brad, when we can get together."

"Sure."

He grinned through his blond moustache and Mara noticed once more the vertical smile lines that put parenthesis around his flawless teeth. He turned a nearly perfect profile to her and stepped on the gas.

The first thing Mara thought as the hearse pulled out of sight was Sheesh, Mac, you're such a dope.

The second thing she thought was: I hope I didn't blow it. This Brad guy's hot.

CHAPTER 48

Of living: last I remember is after cannons puked their fire and lead. Men piling pieces into the wheelbarrow. Damp, earthy hole in the cellar, sealing of the grave. When was that? A second ago? Ten, twenty, a hundred years ago?

Malachai motions for me to come near. Feels like swimming against a tide and getting nowhere. Want to get closer, but I can't move. Malachai speaks: "Come. If you want to live. Come."

Oh, yes. I want to live. Anything to be alive.

Turn away from the tube of light, other familiar beings of light. Now, movement is possible. Floating toward Malachai, we move together, things darken.

Below me, around me, above me the scene is frightening, also familiar like from a lost memory.

Dark brown moving sludge. Not light, airy mist anymore, but thick fog to cover everything with gloom. Hear a noise growing outside the tunnel, a slow moving scream coming from both sides, meets in the middle. Heard that kind of scream before: battlefield, when I watch men torn open by a piece of shell, when they saw their own guts ripped out and knew there were a few moments to live, to get everything done and taken care of before...whatever came next. Now the screams are so much more horrifying, because there is going to be no end to it, the pain and fear.

Through the sludge and misty muck in the distance: long poles—pikes—with ball-like forms stuck on top. Like cavalry drills I saw, where the men rode with sabers, struck at balls of straw atop poles on the parade ground. Something here is different, I look harder through the brown haze. God. They're human heads, stuck like rotten cabbages, brown hunks sloughed off hanging by threads.

There is more. The thick fog begins to vanish, replaced by brownish, ropey, hazy material floating past my face. Pieces of men, women—legs, torsos, arms, guts—strewn about like a battlefield, but much larger than any field I'd ever seen before. Individual fires, huge bonfires, far but near, roaring, leaping upward. No end to this awful land. Far as I see it is the same thing: desolation. Another thing I see: all the body parts are moving, or quivering with a desperation, all looking for one another to piece up: all wanting to get back together again—and in vain.

There's a smell. Smelled it before, on the battlefield. Men's and horses' guts sliced open, shit everywhere. Soldiers splattered with it, mixing brains and blood of comrades, horses, the strange enemy. Stink is appalling. Ripe, penetrating, wretched smell of iron in blood and shit.

Beings made of light, somewhere—in time or distance—behind me, trying to call me back. I no longer see them, just never-ending landscape of crawling body parts and the forest of pikes. From inside comes the notion: if I wait long enough, this will pass, I'll find the light, and will move on to something else. But know from somewhere that this is it. There are only two places. Already passed through the one I would have wanted to be in.

Pick out images: human body, naked, in a caged metal ball—a shining, shimmering metal unlike any I'd seen before—being poked at with a sharp pike by a man on top of the ball; another, tied hand and foot to a staff, being roasted over a roaring fire still alive; another man's naked body bent backwards over a red hot stone about to have his back broken; ugly people jammed into a large vat or barrel, arms pinned, only their heads visible and a huge, red-eyed vulture pecking out their eyes and black muck running down their cheeks; an entire row of men hanging from a beam by their wrists, privates sliced off, lying below their dangling feet; a group of blind, naked women being poked and burned with sharp flaming sticks in the hands of dark, animal fiends; devil-like, dark creatures riding, whipping naked humans like some infernal cavalry; bodies skewered with swords; faces with mouths open, screaming, fire belching from some; sanctums and inner sanctums, curtained and covered with oil on fire; bodies within burned to ash, each rebirthing itself back into a body to begin to burn in agony again and again; naked women fondled and raped by dark demons; foul, strangely shaped birds eating humans whole and defecating them into a pit filled with more humans; flaming, red hot swords held to women's breasts, genitals. And always, constantly the smell of shit and decay and booming noises.

The pain begins. Like pinpricks in my groin where my balls were...once. Hot, sharp, searing pain, a razor cutting along my crotch and up my stomach. Look down but cannot see myself, my stomach. Just thick, muddy fog. And the pain.

Then in what were once my eyes, stabbing needles. Try to scream, but I have no throat or mouth or lips to form and release the cry. Then heat, like a branding iron, to the tips of my fingers, to my buttocks, to my face: the heat, the pain. "Malachai!" I scream inside. "Help me!"

My senses are ripping, like sod before a cannon ball, tearing apart with pain. One image floats to the top, like scum on a pond's surface. Instead of bringing comfort, it drives a scalding spike of fear into my chest. The message is clear, ominous, like the voice of the sergeant ordering us into battle: "We don't die. It will go on forever."

Then a voice: hissing, ragged at first, then becoming clearer.
"McGillis."

What in hell is this? How does anyone here know who I am, who I was, know my name? But the voice was not coming from anywhere near. It was distant. But...

"McGillis...William McGillis.
Will, are you here with us?"

Oh, God yes. Wherever you are is better than where I am. Yes. Yes!

"Are you in pain?"

What did they mean by that? Oh, God yes!

"Will you talk to us? We have so many questions."

Oh yes, I want to talk to you.

I try to speak, but all that comes out is a roaring hiss: Yessss!

There is Malachai, lording over, hovering, motioning for me to come.

"Will? Can you say something?"

I will do more than talk to you. I will be with you. I will be with you. I will be with you.

I will be you....

CHAPTER 49

After the warm greeting from Reynolds and a quick bowl of food for him, Mara sat down in front of her laptop computer, plugged the hand-held digital recorder into it as Brad had recommended, and began to listen through earphones to the recordings they had made in the cemetery as she recorded them on her computer's sound recording software.

She turned the volume down for the first loud roar, which she knew was coming. She then heard Brad's voice ask the second question: "Sephrina, did you love Rebekkah?" Again she heard four syllables in a distinctly female voice, the first two slow and the last two in rapid succession. Still, they were frustratingly elusive to her comprehension.

She adjusted the volume to as high as she could stand it, and replayed it again. And again. She adjusted out some of the background hiss from the recorder and played it again, moving the cursor back time after time. Brad: "Sephrina, did you love Rebekkah?"

"Oh Lord, I did."

Mara ripped the earphones off her head. She heard the words clearly. It was like trying to listen to someone with a thick accent; after a while you got used to it and the words suddenly became understandable. But it wasn't so much the content that bothered Mara; it was the agony in the voice that tore at her. And the fact that it was undoubtedly female.

The emotion in the recording told her one frightening thing: the voice on the tape was definitely human. And yet, Mara thought, there was no human nearby to create it.

Mara clicked the play button again. Again she heard Brad's voice: "Ephraim Squires, did you miss your family when you died?"

Mara heard the angry, frustrated growl she had heard coming from the recorder when they were in the cemetery. But on the earphones she heard more clearly the drawn-out hiss embedded in the growl: "Yessss."

Mara's shoulders gave an involuntary shiver. But she continued to listen.

"Ephraim, are you in pain?"

She could make out three quick syllables, a low moan or groan and one more syllable. Again she moved the cursor back along the sound line on the computer display and replayed the answer. Once, twice, a half dozen times until the words became clear: "Terrible…heart."

What did that mean? Mara wondered: Did the pain in his heart come from the loss of his children? Mara made a mental note to do more research on Mr. Ephraim Squires and his family.

She heard Brad's voice on the recorder: "Company B, First Regiment, attention! Muster for pay call."

Several of the names came in rapid succession, even though Brad had paused at least twenty seconds between each. Then, after the name, "Ball," she heard two rough syllables. She moved the cursor back to before the noise and replayed it. Several times. She was having trouble with this one; there was what seemed to be a thick, backwoods accent. Suddenly, she heard the words, "Here, Sir."

A male voice. Answering to his name. Mustering to receive his pay as a soldier. *From his grave!*

Then another, one syllable answer after the name "Bigelow": "Sir!"

After several of the names there were one and two syllable answers that sounded like "Yes, Sir," or "Here, Sir." There was even one angry roar that sounded like a man answering, "Present."

She made her way down the list until she got to "Jackson, Martin, McGillis," and stopped. It was late and she knew there was a lot of EVP at the end of the recording. She wanted to give it her full attention, and that wasn't going to happen at this hour.

Reynolds was more than happy to head for bed.

It was a feeling of floating, like she had been underwater and was slowly rising to the surface. Except that there were noises.

She heard a low growling. That was the dog. As she became more aware she heard voices: tinny, raspy voices, straining as if through labored breath, frustrated in tone for not being able to say what they wanted.

She was awake now. The voices were only one voice.

It came from downstairs.

"Reynolds. Go see! Go on. Go see!"

It was her command to the dog to check something out, whether it was a bird in a field or someone at the door. Normally, he would rush enthusiastically to where she pointed. Now, he hesitated.

Mara found the baseball bat behind her bedroom door. She threw on some jeans and a sweatshirt and started downstairs. Reynolds moved ahead of her. She stepped on Reynolds's tennis ball on the darkened stairs and clutched at the railing.

As she descended, the voice became more discernible. There was more heavy strangled breathing than actual words. She got to the bottom of the stairs, entered the kitchen and threw on the light. There she saw the source of the breathing.

"I'm wounded."

"I'm hurt!"

Her digital recorder was on. It was playing back the last few minutes of Brad's queries in the cemetery. How the recorder could have started by itself was a mystery; it was in the same position Mara had left it in when she'd gone to bed. Listening to the labored breathing and muffled words she began to understand some of them.

"Help me dodge!"

"White…it's all…."

Mara grabbed the recorder and shut it off. She was startled by a liquid sound behind her and spun to see Reynolds lapping water from his bowl. She closed her eyes and took a deep breath trying to calm herself. Reynolds had finished and was dribbling his way over to the cellar door. He began to sniff tentatively at the darkness of the cellar stairway, and Mara noticed something that she hadn't noticed when she went to bed.

The door was open.

She rushed the door almost slamming poor Reynolds's nose in it. She slid the lock into place. She grabbed the oak kitchen table, wrestled it to the door and jammed it against it. If someone had broken a window in the basement to get in, they would have to exit the same way. Superman couldn't open the door with the table in front of it. She'd have moved the refrigerator in front of the door if she could have handled it. Instead, she put the tiny recorder in the refrigerator and slammed the door. If whatever wanted the recorder on came back, at least she wouldn't have to hear it the rest of the night.

She ran back upstairs leaving the light on in the kitchen and the hall and almost tripped over the dog. She crawled back into bed with her clothes on and the baseball bat next to her. She didn't sleep until the early morning light drew horizontal slashes across the walls of her room.

CHAPTER 50

"Hey, Mara, it's Brad." Halfway through putting a thought into her laptop, her phone almost switched to answer mode.

"Yeah. Hi, Brad. S'up, good-lookin'?"

He paused a second. Whoops, too forward? she thought.

"Listen. There's a video on the net you might want to see. It's a brief history of paranormal studies by Dr. Robert Ammons, someone I consider the modern expert on the history of EVP. It's only about a half-hour long and I think you'll get a lot out of it."

Here's your chance, dummy, Mara thought. Make up for the other night.

"You want to come over and watch it with me?"

"Ah, I'd love to...."

Yes, Mara....

"...but I've sort of made plans."

Crap!

"No problem. I've always got Reynolds. Except he doesn't drink."

"I'll make it up to you. Watch the video and it will give us something to talk about next time we get together."

He gave her the web address. "See you soon."

Well, thought Mara. This is good.

Mara made herself a cup of tea then found the online video.

On the screen stood a very professorial-looking, middle-aged man in a bow tie and jacket. The setting seemed to be some kind of conference. Behind the speaker at the lectern was the first slide with the title "What is EVP?" The speaker began.

"For the last half century, individuals have been hearing odd voices recorded on magnetic audio tape, when there were no voices to be heard by the human ear.

"Parapsychologists named the phenomena EVP for Electronic Voice Phenomena. While clairaudience—clear hearing of voices without artificial augmentation—is probably as old as mankind, EVP began with the advent of electronic recording devices. Skeptics have claimed that the sounds are merely errant radio or television broadcasts being picked up on the sensitive tape or internal circuits of the digital recorders. But recordings have been made in tombs, deep in caves, in bank vaults and Faraday cages, ruling out the possibility of radio waves."

Mara took a sip of tea. *This seems to be a little more detailed than what Mitch talked about.*

"The sounds are often a definite, but indistinct background clutter—sort of like what you hear at a party—indistinguishable mutters going on underneath the understandable conversation nearby. Then, out of nowhere, comes a loud, sometimes ear-splitting roar, occasionally multi-syllabic, often with a sentence-like rhythm, nearly always discernible as male, female, or child."

Holy crap, thought Mara. This guy's been reading my mail. That's exactly what I've been hearing.

The slide changed to, "A Brief History." Dr. Ammons continued.

"Human attempts at communicating with the dead are as old as death itself. Seventy thousand years ago, proto-humans laid tools, weapons, and food in the graves of their relatives, indicating a belief in some sort of afterlife. The dead communicating with the living has been a part of literature for ages. Ancient Greeks had ghosts in their literature and drama. Hamlet, the Danish Prince, communicated with his dead father the King in Shakespeare's play. Since it was written in the early 1600s, audiences apparently accepted communication with the dead with little question. Modern grieving mourners will attempt to talk to the freshly deceased, not believing they could have died. People will discuss current family events at gravesites with long dead relatives. Over the centuries, individuals have recruited psychics—some legitimate, some bogus—to help them talk to dead loved ones.

"In the 19th century an entire industry grew out of relatives' desire to communicate with the generation slaughtered during the Civil War. Spiritualism resulted in séances, often faked. The hopeful relatives of the deceased heard rapping on a table, bells ringing, voices echoing from special trumpets, and witnessed a bizarre substance, called ectoplasm, emanating from various orifices of mediums."

Mara thought: Mitch should hear this, since he was the one who first identified my EVP recordings. The speaker stopped, took a swig from a water bottle below the lectern, and switched slides. There was a photo of Thomas Edison and another man Mara did not recognize.

"While the antics of fake mediums made headlines when exposed, renowned and esteemed inventors Thomas Edison and Guglielmo Marconi reportedly worked on machines to attempt to communicate with the dead."

Another black and white photo of a man popped up on the screen.

"As early as 1936, Attila von Szalay worked at receiving EVP with a device used to cut phonograph records. Two years later he claimed to have heard his dead son's voice, various rapping noises, whistles, and random voices of both sexes recorded on the records. By 1956 he was working with paranormal pioneer D. Scott Rogo.

"Some of the most consistent EVP was recorded in 1959, on regular magnetic tape by Friedrich Jürgenson. Alone in an open field recording birds, he inadvertently recorded a male voice expertly discussing, in Norwegian, nocturnal bird songs. Repeated experiments produced more voices on the tape, although unheard by Jürgenson while he was recording. Eventually he ruled out extraneous sources such as radio or television broadcasts—the voices relayed personal information and even began giving Jürgenson instructions on how to more effectively record the bird songs. Later he successfully communicated with spirits via radio frequency 1485 kHz, which is now known in paranormal circles, as the Jürgenson frequency.

"A Latvian researcher named Konstantin Raudive worked with Jürgenson and eventually recorded over 100,000 voices, finally publishing his results in 1971 in his book *Breakthrough*."

A hundred thousand voices? All on magnetic tape? Mara remembered her father's reel-to-reel tape recorder from when she was growing up. She thought: Why hasn't more been made of this communication with the dead? Why hadn't I heard of it before now?

Another slide flashed onto the screen behind the lecturer. It was a kindly-faced woman in her sixties. Mara leaned closer to the screen.

"Since the early experiments, literally thousands of individuals, worldwide, have captured hundreds of thousands of examples of EVP. Sarah Estep established the American Association of Electronic Voice Phenomena in 1982. Estep, and others, use a rating system for the differing quality of the recordings. Class C voices are barely audible and beyond understanding; Class B voices can be heard without using headphones and are clearer; Class A voices are clear and understandable and are able to be duplicated upon other tapes."

You can easily understand the voices on my recordings, thought Mara. They must be class A.

Another slide popped onto the screen with the title, "How Does EVP Happen?" Dr. Ammons began.

"How are voices recorded on the electronic devices or magnetic tapes when nothing can be heard during the time the recording is being made? And, the most important question of all, are these really communications from the dead?"

"Same question I asked Mitch," Mara said out loud to a sleeping Reynolds.

"Generally three theories have evolved about the nature of the paranormal voices from the evidence gathered."

"That's a couple more than Mitch had." Reynolds finally woke looking annoyed.

The slide showed standard sine waves of different frequencies undulating across the screen. Dr. Ammons continued.

"The first theory is that the voices are carried as vibrations through the air—the same way all other noises are created and heard—except that they are either too high or too low in pitch to be heard by the human ear. However, if indeed these are communications from the dead, the flesh and blood vocal cords of the communicators have long ago decomposed, ruling out, it would seem, their ability to communicate via sound waves propagated through the air and into the microphone of the recorder."

Mara shuddered at the thought of decomposing vocal cords.

"As well, this theory begs the question, if the noises are of a frequency that cannot be heard by the human ear in real time, what makes them audible when they are played back on the recorder?

"A second theory is that the voices are the remnants of the electromagnetic energy all living beings possess and that this energy remains in existence after the living being dies. It can be manipulated into a frequency by the "spirit" of the dead and can produce an electromagnetic signature directly on the magnetic tape or a digital chip.

"Since magnetic tape and digital recorders can be affected by magnetic or electromagnetic surges, it makes sense that the entities are communicating via electromagnetic surges on a particular wave length."

Mara took a sip of her now cold tea and remembered the Sergeyev meters in the ISAP lab spiking. She watched the slides change. Now there was the photograph of an attractive dark haired woman.

"In addition, research done by Dr. Renato Orso of Turin, Italy, appears to verify the fact that vocal apparatus is not the source of entity voices she supplied to technicians.

"The technicians subjected Dr. Orso's paranormal voices to a sonograph used in speech identification, a machine so reliable it is recognized in court proceedings. The acoustical structure of the paranormal voices was similar to human voices. By analyzing the vowels, consonants, and speech rhythm, the technicians determined that the paranormal voices are an objective reality and not what they called a 'psychoacoustic illusion.'"

Mara remembered her linguistics classes from college: diphthongs, fricatives, palatals, all referring to the sound-making physical parts of the mouth that must be intact and not decomposed to work.

"In other words," Dr Ammons continued, "the sounds were not the product of the human brain imagining words and phrases out of garble, like an auditory ink-blot test.

"The other thing they discovered from the spectrograms produced by the sonograph tests was the absence of the main frequency produced by human vocal cords."

Okay, Mara thought. Here's something a former English major can sink her teeth into. Mara and Dr. Ammons both took a sip of liquid together. He continued.

"Examination of the nature of the consonants in the paranormal voices was also enlightening. Consonants in human speech are produced by the interruption of air flowing from the lungs or by obstructing the air flow by passing it over or through biological, physical obstacles along the vocal tract. Presi Paolo, renowned Italian EVP researcher wrote that 'the lack of fundamental frequency coupled with the lack of consonants that, in humans is given by the vocal tract, suggest that the paranormal producer of these linguistic events does not have a production speech apparatus.'"

Mara caught the simple mistake. "Speech production apparatus," must be what he meant.

"There is a third theory as to how voices come from 'out of thin air' and embed themselves on recording devices: Perhaps there is yet another type of energy, as yet undiscovered, that is either associated with electromagnetism or can, at least occasionally, be detected by electromagnetic field detection devices. Perhaps this energy is the essence of our being that survives death. Could this afterlife, remnant energy be what ghosts use to manipulate the local electromagnetic field in order to communicate with us?"

Dr. Ammons now opened the floor to questions. She listened to one or two, and decided she needed to get back to work.

CHAPTER 51

Mara was researching on the Internet when Reynolds went nuts at the arrival of the mail. Earlier, she had dragged the heavy kitchen table away from the basement door and, buoyed with the courage daylight bore, had searched the cellar for any signs of an intruder.

With every light on in the cellar and her huge cop-style flashlight beaming into the corners, she realized that there had been no one in the cellar the night before. No window was broken, nothing moved, no indication whatsoever that it had been occupied. With the exception of some dirt that had fallen from one of the creepy indentations in the wall, nothing had changed from the day she moved in. Apparently, somehow, the recorder went on by itself and, coincidentally, the door blew open. *It could happen,* Mara thought. She had to admit she wasn't all that familiar with the new recorder. *Thank God,* she thought as she hurried up the cellar stairs, *I don't need to use this place for storage.*

She finished printing off what she needed then went to the mailbox at the front door. There was a small package from Brad. She happened to look at the date. He had mailed it just yesterday.

She undid the wrapping and there was a note stuck to another lightly wrapped package. Before she opened the inner package, she began to read the note.

"Mara—Had the strangest experience the other evening. Was researching at the college. Took the elevator in the college library to the first floor to leave the building. Went right by the first floor and into the basement..."

What the hell? Mara thought. *Where is he going with this? I didn't tell him about my experience. Did he talk to the security guy? Is he making fun of me? I'll kill him if he is....*

"...The doors opened and it was as if I was having a '70s acid flashback, except I was too young in the '70s to take acid. It was like a cold, swirling breeze came through the doors. The hairs on the back of my neck stood. When I looked through the doors, there was a scene forming before my very eyes. Things were materializing out of nothing. Actually, I shouldn't say 'nothing' because there was a misty ropy substance that seemed to be swirling, coagulating into different forms and shapes. I think it was actually ectoplasm. They were pretty indistinct. I could see partially formed objects, and what appeared to be forms of human bodies, but they were all jumbled, rushing together, then moving apart, then coming together again. I couldn't quite make out what was going on. Suddenly, the elevator doors closed and I came up to the first floor. I tried to make the thing go down again, but it seemed frozen at the first floor. I got off and it went up.

"I did manage to pick this up. Imagine my surprise when I saw whose it was! Wasn't sure when I'd see you again so I dropped it in the mail."

Mara peeled away the tissue paper. What she saw made her catch her breath. There was her own small notebook, the one she had dropped into the Civil War hospital nearly a week before.

Brad's note went on.

"I'm going back to the elevator sometime soon. Want to come? Don't know if I'll get the same ride, but it's worth a try. Call."

She grabbed her phone and touched Brad's number. As the phone rang a fourth time, she realized she was probably going to have to leave a message and began composing one. *Brad, don't go into that elevator again. Something's not right. I can just feel it. I can't put my finger on it, but I don't want you to….*

Brad answered, "Hello?"

"Brad?"

"Mara? Hi! Sorry it took so long to answer. I just stepped out of the shower. What's up?"

"I just got your package. Thanks for sending my notebook back. I knew I'd dropped it. I'm just surprised that no one had seen it in the elevator, as much as it is used."

"Well, I didn't exactly find it *in* the elevator."

"Where was it?"

"Actually, it was just outside the door, in the basement. It was kind of spooky, reaching into the strange scene that seemed to be…for lack of a better word…materializing before me. And you're right. I can't figure out why someone hadn't seen it before. It was right in front of the door."

Mara's mind spun. It was there in the basement, then it apparently was gone for a week. Surely someone—a janitor, an electrician, a maintenance man, someone—had stepped off that elevator to go to work in the last week. They had to have seen the notebook. Unless, it had become a part of that weird scene she...and now Brad...had witnessed.

"Uh, Mara? You still there? I'm getting a little chilly and making a swimming pool out of my bedroom."

"Brad! I'm sorry. That's right. You need to dry off. Hey, you're naked, aren't you?"

"Uh, well, yes."

He doesn't even sound embarrassed, thought Mara. That's good.

"Well. These are the times I'm so glad I've been blessed with a writer's imagination."

There was silence on the other end of the line, but Mara swore she could hear Brad smile. She waited a few more seconds for her comment to have its full effect.

"Not to change the subject," she said, "but, when are you planning to go back to the elevator?

" I'm not sure. Why? You want to go?"

"Sure." Mara hesitated: *Do I really want to go back?* "Pick a day."

"I have a friend who works there. I'll check with her as to what night she can let us in."

"Sounds good," Mara said, not really wanting to go at night.

Well, Mara thought, remembering her Shakespeare, *Once more unto the breach.*

And, she thought, it sounds like Brad is still interested.

She sat down at her computer again, began to scroll through some sites and stopped to click on one. As she waited for the site to come up, she picked up the small notebook Brad had returned and absentmindedly began to leaf through it.

She stopped turning pages at the middle of the notebook. A page was partially crumbled. Smeared across it was a dried brownish stain. Mara knew what it was immediately.

Blood. Old blood. A lot of blood.

And beneath the blood were some words scrawled in a dull pencil. She unconsciously stood as she read the words,

I want you.

CHAPTER 52

"*Okay, Laddie. Come with me.*"

Following Malachai's voice. Can't see him through the brown mist, but hear him and feel his presence. Not sure exactly how I'm moving, but I am.

"*Where are we going? Where <u>can</u> we go?*"

"*You'll be surprised.*"

"*How do you know all this? How do you know how to move?*"

"*I've done this a time or two. Now look, Laddie, where we are.*"

It's the sod hole dug in the cellar wall where I had been placed. Other bodies are stuffed in other holes in the earthen and stone wall. This is a mortuary, I think. My body had been brought here instead of buried on the battlefield. Then the bodies are gone, vanish in the brown mist. Just the holes are left. Begin to rise, through the ceiling and into the room above.

"*Come on, Laddie. Keep comin'*"

Pass into the room through the floor and continue to rise as if I am weightless. Duck my head as I rise through the ceiling from the first to the second floor, but pass through effortlessly. Then my rising stops at the foot of a bed.

In the bed under the covers is the young woman with the dark hair and beautiful eyes. I have to look twice since she's asleep. She is lying on her back.

"*Go ahead.*" *I hear Malachai rasp.* "*Touch her.*"

I know what Malachai means. But it wasn't accompanied with the lustful heat feeling I remember. I feel nothing.

"*It's the first step. Touch her.*"

Feel a part of me—my hand—go through the covers and float to her breasts. The woman moves and moans.

"*Keep going.*"

Move my hand and she moans again. Feel like Malachai is pushing me. Moving toward the form in the bed until I'm over her. She moans even louder. And I feel that old feeling, that urge, that steam engine with the valve tied down like I'm alive again with her.
"This," I hear Malachai say, "is one way."

It started with a disembodied feeling: She was on her back floating like she was lying suspended in a warm liquid. Her breasts were being harshly rubbed then lifted by some unidentifiable object in the sensitive area, just next to her arm. It was crude, like a hand in a work glove, or a reptilian appendage, and her nipples felt like a dozen needles were poking them. She kept her eyes closed, a little fearful: what's next? Is this a dream?

Rough hands were moving along her sides now, lifting her breasts from behind. The hands began to touch her nipples, circled the areolas, making the blood flow faster into them. Then the painful, hard pinches.

Now she was standing, leaning, straight-armed, against the footboard of her bed, legs pushed apart. Strong hands were grasping her hips hard and rotating them from side to side and forward and backward, forcing her to move. Still she was afraid to open her eyes.

Something was sliding roughly into her, and she jerked away from the entry. Her hips twisted to avoid the sudden pain, but it now started happening too quickly. She wasn't ready and….

From somewhere outside a siren wailed. She was sitting up now and realized she was alone in bed. Reynolds was on the floor and the police car was passing the house, the siren sound lowering in pitch as it zoomed down the road. Mara looked at the clock and it was 4:30.

CHAPTER 53

It was late. Reynolds was conked out against her feet on the kitchen floor and Mara had dumped the contents of her backpack on the solid oak table. This is probably not the thing I should be getting into now, she thought, but started to rummage through the cards and papers and notes that had accumulated since she had moved into the house.

"A writer in search of an organizational system," she said out loud. Reynolds lifted his furry head and glared sleepily at her. "Sorry," she said. His chin hit the floor with a clink of vaccine medals.

She began to make piles of the scraps of notes: some were for the current Fisher bio; others for future works; still others mere notes on her life: *pick up cereal; check tapes; pick up TP.* Now, was that toilet paper or toothpaste? She had enough toothpaste. Must be toilet paper.

Sliding most of it aside she found the folders from Fisher's apartment at the bottom of the slurry of notes. Don't Mara, she thought. Don't do this now. You're tired. Go to bed. Do not open the file.

Her curiosity ignored her, as usual, and she opened the file marked *Electromagnetic Studies and Otherworld Entrypoints.*

Inside there were several paper-clipped packets of papers with headings. Mara had seen some of them before. "Contacts with the Otherworld: Field notes." That one she had already begun reading. Two more caught her eye: "Parallel Universe as a Microcosmic Otherworld," and "Guides to the Beyond."

She pulled the sheaf marked "Guides to the Beyond," assuming it would be a bibliography of source books Fisher used in his work.

Instead she found a list of names, and dates.

Names of people and dates when they had died.

What the hell? she thought.

"*Alexander Rankin....b. 1828, d. April, 1862. No contact.*"

"Truman Smith....b. 1833, d. July 2, 1863. No contact."
"William Conkling....b. 1840, d. March 29, 1865. No contact."
"Hardesty McGee....b. 1841, d. July 3, 1863. No contact."
"James Nance, aka Seamus, aka Will aka Will McGillis...b. 1839, d. 1863. Contact!"

The list stopped with the name James Nance also known as Will McGillis. Mara had to read the entry twice. What did Ricard Fisher mean putting in several names? Apparently they were aliases, indicating they were all the same person.

And one sounded familiar.

Confusing as the naming system was, there was no confusion about what "contact" meant. Indeed, as she had realized before, Fisher was—or thought he was—in contact with the dead. In particular, this Will McGillis.

All the men on the list were contemporaries, all of the same generation. All died between 1862 and 1865. The years rang a bell with Mara.

The Civil War. All these men died in—or were killed in—the Civil War.

Mara began wondering if they were buried in the cemetery Brad and she had just visited. She wondered if any of them might have been killed in the battle just outside town or, worse, if any of them were brought here—to the house she had rented—to die?

Or were they still buried…in that cellar just below her feet?

CHAPTER 54

"I can't believe you brought me here."
"I can't believe you finally took a night off from writing."
"For you, Brad, anything."
"Somehow, Mara, I'm not sure I completely believe that."
After just a few minutes, Mara knew the atmosphere at Delvigne's was exactly what she needed to take her mind off the pressure her editor had been applying. Upscale but not too, the restaurant had enough whitenoise chatter from the bar and tables for Brad and Mara to have their own conversation without anyone listening or interrupting. Except, Mara thought, for that one loudmouth behind me.
"So," Brad began. "Any more notes on the paranormal from the esteemed Dr. Fisher you'd like to share?"
"No. And you can stop right there. I decided after you invited me to dinner that the supernatural was *not* going to be a topic of conversation tonight. I think we need to expand this relationship beyond that mutual subject." *Crap. Did I just say that?*
"Thanks, Mara. I was hoping one of us would say that. Here's something simple, just conversation. Tell me about your life *before* college. Parents, siblings, old flames, the night you lost your virginity...."
"Huh?"
"Just kidding."
Over the appetizer Mara told him about her parents' fighting and divorce and her grandfather stepping in to soothe her childish fears with encouragement. "If it wasn't for him, I don't think I would have continued writing."
There were four battles all around this town...one hundred thousand casualties...General such-and-such shot right in the eye....

Mara rolled her eyes to Brad at the guy behind her who seemed bent on showing the five surrounding tables what an expert he was on the local history.

"And what about you? Other than the one class in college, I have no idea about your past. Tell, tell!"

"Let's see, where do I start? Boy scouts, stripper, or male whore?"

Mara gave him a scowl, which turned into a smile. "You can skip the boy scout part."

"How do you think I got the stripper gig?"

Brad told her about his days growing up in a perfectly normal household: no parental divorce, no fights—at least none that he heard—one brother, Jerry, who had moved from Cleveland and owned an antique shop on the main street in town, and had endured his own short marriage and divorce.

Yeah. They fought in the pouring rain for twenty-some hours straight...trampled the wounded into the mud still alive...pieces of men just shot to mush...

The guy behind her, Mara decided, just had one of those voices that carried. The fact that he was talking about something he was passionate about, and wanted everyone to know that he was an expert, did nothing to alleviate the fact that he was intruding upon Mara and Brad's date.

"I can't believe that someone as pretty and personable as you never got married. Ever close?"

Mara flashed to Rex, then tossed that thought out of her mind just as quickly. No. He wasn't the marrying-type, just the heart-breaker-type. "Not really. Trying to make it as a writer takes up a lot of time. What made you decide to get married?"

"Protocol."

"What?"

"Well, I was out of college, had gotten a job, and it was what we do. I mean, us non-writers of the world. But neither one of us was quite ready, and when the inevitable affair reared its ugly head, we weren't mature enough—or maybe didn't care enough—to work it out."

"Whose affair?"

"Hers. A guy from work. They eventually got married, had a couple of kids, and also broke up."

So General Lee was way too aggressive...cost him dearly...Now Grant, there was a general....

The beers taking hold, he was practically shouting, now.

"Sometimes living in this little, dinky historic town is what makes a person," Brad said under his breath so the loudmouth couldn't hear. "It's like a psychological crutch. They couldn't make it anywhere else. It's sort of comforting to them being here because they always know how this particular story of the battle is going to end. All wrapped up nicely. No surprises. It never changes."

"And you like surprises?"

"Sometimes. I like new twists. I like change."

"I think I knew that about you already."

The entrées came and the waiter poured more wine. Conversation continued with small talk, about life in a small town, places to go to drink after a hard day, his career, her career, friends. The entrées were consumed and the waiter poured more wine.

"I should be slowing down on the wine. Tomorrow is a writing day and a hangover doesn't help."

"The food will help absorb it. So, what's next?"

Mara smiled and looked at him sideways. "You mean with us?"

His smile lines made those parentheses around his mouth. "I meant, what are you writing next?"

Mara shook her head. "How embarrassing. I didn't mean...."

"I'm okay with us right now. This is going just fine for me, in case you're wondering, and you apparently are. Just the right speed. You intrigue me, Mara McKay. I think you did in college, too, but we just didn't make the connection."

"Well, I have to admit, I sort of had...."

Nah. Ya can't piss out a window in this town without getting something historic wet.

Mara and Brad looked at each other and laughed.

Brad raised his hand to the waiter. "Check, please."

They went up to the bar for a nightcap, far enough away from the loudmouthed historian so they could barely hear him.

McClellan was an asshole...Burnside was a bigger asshole....

By the time they'd finished their drinks, Mara had told him about losing her virginity.

When he dropped her off, he gave her a long kiss. The whole time she was thinking, *invite him in or not?*

His comment about her intriguing him remained in her head.

For the sake of a little intrigue, she thought, *not yet.*

CHAPTER 55

Mara had just gotten out of the shower when she heard her phone ringing.

Undecided where to wrap the towel, she turbaned it around her head, whisked past the bedroom window, and picked up her phone.

Mara took the offensive: "Oh, no you don't. What is this, payback for last week?"

"In the shower?"

"Yeah."

"Naked?"

"Uh, yeah."

"Now it's my turn to imagine."

She paused just long enough for the image to sink in. "What did you call for? Before I catch pneumonia."

"I have some people who want to meet you. It's a group, actually. They call themselves 'ghost hunters,' but I think they may be a little more into it than that. They want to come over and interview you, and maybe do a little looking around."

"When and where?"

"Boy, you really cut to the chase. Your house. Tomorrow night. Say 7 o'clock."

"Sounds good. I'll be here."

There was a pause on Brad's end of the line.

"Hello?" Mara said.

"Yeah. Just imagining."

"Good bye." Mara laughed, hung up her phone and continued to dry off. At least it's another chance to get together with Brad, she thought.

She was finishing sorting the papers on the kitchen table when her phone rang again. It was her editor.

"How's the bio coming, kiddo?"

She hated the condescending terms her editor used for her writers, but had decided that she would live with it to be able to write for a living. Now she *had* to take the condescension, since she had run into a quagmire of extraneous information her editor didn't even know about.

"Pretty well," she lied.

"Good. 'Cause your book just got bumped up the list. I need it in two weeks. Three, max."

"What? I'm not sure…I mean I have to get another interview…interviews…with his colleagues, and some more background on…."

"Forget it, sweetheart. Wrap it up. The guy offed himself. Story over. He's hot now, but won't be in two months. Get the manuscript to us in a couple of weeks, we can do a rush job on the printing, and have it out before someone more famous does a murder/suicide."

"But…."

"Mara. I gotta go, hon. I've got Harriet Potter, the porn star, doing her autobiography on line two and Simon Delany—the book on Churchill I told you about—on three. Love you, dear. Two weeks. Bubye!"

Mara slumped into the kitchen chair and fired up her laptop. She jammed all the papers into their file folders while her machine booted. The folders all went into her backpack, except for one: "Early years: Ricard Fisher." She pulled her handwritten notes and mini-tape from the folder, spread the notes out and began to type.

CHAPTER 56

Mara had just finished the third chapter in Fisher's biography, taken from her recorded notes of the interview with Eleanor. She really wasn't happy with the way it was turning out. It was as if she were holding something back from her readers—which she was—and it was apparent in the writing. *Never write down to your audience* was one of the rules she never broke, but with the utterly fascinating yet explosive revelations she had about Fisher's life and death, it felt as if she were trying to keep a secret from God.

Brad's group wanted to do their investigation at her house and she wondered why. Had they heard something about the things that have been happening to me here? That's impossible. I haven't told anyone but Mitch and he doesn't know Brad. Then she thought: Maybe they heard something about this place from before I moved in....

She unconsciously jumped when the doorbell rang and Reynolds, startled awake, spun his wheels on the linoleum floor in the kitchen. It was Brad at the door with three individuals—two men and a woman—who carried several large bags, a backpack each, and two tripods.

Brad leaned into her and gave her a surprisingly affectionate hug. The thought went through her head: Could this be Brad ratcheting the relationship up a notch? Then: Yeah, right, Mara. Hope springs eternal.

"Mara, here are the folks I spoke to you about on the phone. This is Bob Neruda. Booth Blackwell. And this is Sage."

Bob was thin and tall and looked more like he would have been a basketball player. Booth was shorter and had adorned his face with a broad mustache and the area beneath his lower lip with a dark tuft of beard—a soul patch. Mara thought he looked like one of those photographs of some Civil War general. Sage was actually quite beautiful: thin under her flowing shift, her long, honey-blond hair swaying halfway down her back. They looked to be in their early thirties, except for Sage whose face had a sort of timeless, ethereal look to it.

"Nice to meet you. How did you all get interested in ghost hunting? Are you members of a local group?"

Mara watched as the three of them looked back and forth at each other. Finally, the one Brad introduced as Booth answered.

"No, Ms. McKay. We don't belong to any of the 'ghost hunter' groups. We are paranormal investigators. We don't go looking for photos of 'orbs' or 'ectoplasm.' We go much deeper than that, as you will witness during this particular session."

The way he said "particular session," Mara got the impression that this might not be the last time she would see these people in her home. As the three lowered their bags to the floor, Brad spoke up.

"Bob, Sage, and Booth do this all a little differently than any of the investigators I've seen. They use a technique they call 'intuition forward,' relying on Sage. The instruments are for backup documentation, to assure others of the validity of Sage's findings. Also, just a warning: Some of what you see and hear tonight might be a little frightening."

Mara believed him when she saw some of the things they pulled out of the bags: Standard digital cameras, camcorders, reel-to-reel tape recorders and digital recorders. Sage brought out several glass-clear crystals in different shapes and sizes ranging from the length of her little finger to a balled-up fist. From the bags came a tuning fork, incense, candles, and a mirror with an ancient gilded frame, which she attached to one of the tripods. Finally she pulled a folded leather pouch tied with a string of leather. She untied it carefully and drew out a crumpled folded piece of worn paper-thin cardboard, and a small triangular chip of wood with a hole through the center. As she slowly unfolded the cardboard, Mara realized that it was some sort of Ouija board.

"Aren't those things supposed to be dangerous?" she asked.

"Only in the hands of amateurs," Bob said.

Mara recalled her childhood. "My girlfriends and I used to play with one of those things. Tried to talk to JFK and witches and ghosts. Scared the living be-jeebers out of ourselves a couple of...." Sage's somber stare made Mara stop talking.

"This is one of the earliest boards we've ever found," Sage said. "It may, in fact, be an original, hand-made board from eastern Europe. But its origins are unknown. A board-type device was used in pre-Confucian China to communicate with the dead. The Greeks used one about the same time, as did the Romans. Wars always make the Ouija more popular since there are so many loved ones to reach in the other world."

Mara paused to make sure Sage was through and asked in a professional tone, "Don't some people say that its results are merely the subconscious of the users moving the little triangular plate?"

"Planchette," Sage corrected. "Yes, but the subconscious is merely the vehicle through which the dead communicate with us. In this case it's like automatic writing. With psychics they communicate through the medium's words; with a trance medium, they literally kidnap—take possession of their consciousness—and use the medium's voicebox, sometimes altering the way they sound."

The way Sage said the words "kidnap" and "possession" made Mara shudder.

"Do you really believe that you can tap into the other world with the Ouija?" she asked.

"Absolutely. Perhaps we will get to show you tonight." Sage's statement rang ominously in Mara's ears.

"Where do we start?" Mara asked.

Everyone scanned everyone else as if looking for a leader. Bob piped up. "Can we just look around a little?"

"Help yourself," Mara offered.

Sage selected one of the larger, ball-shaped crystals, closed her eyes for a few seconds, and started up the stairs. Halfway up she stopped and Mara almost ran into her. Her eyes were closed again and she seemed to be hearing something no one else could hear. Mara could see rapid eye movements beneath her lids. She opened her eyes and continued up the stairs.

The group followed her as far as the narrow hallway. She went first into the small bathroom, then partway into the spare bedroom, which was empty save for a few books in boxes Mara stashed there. Sage backed out, went back to the bathroom for a moment, and emerged with a raised-eyebrow expression and a cryptic "hmmm."

She walked into Mara's bedroom, to the window, along one wall to the foot of Mara's bed and froze. "Oh!" she said.

Mara looked at Bob and Brad. Brad shrugged his shoulders. Bob continued to stare at Sage. Booth was filming it all with a camcorder.

"What is it?" Mara asked. She wasn't sure what protocol was in effect at this time, but it was her bedroom, and she wanted to know what Sage thought she had found.

Sage seemed to sway in a little dance-like circular motion around a spot until she stopped in the center. "Oh, wow!" she said.

"What is it?" Mara was getting restless now.

"It's an energy center," Bob said.

"It's more than that," Sage said. "It's a vortex. It's a column of energy. Wait." She stepped two feet to the left. "Bob, could you hand me the tuning fork?"

Bob reached into his back pocket and pulled out a purple felt bag. From it he removed what appeared to be a regular musical tuning fork. Mara must have had a confused look on her face; Bob smiled at her and said, "It's tuned to the pitch of *om*, the universal vibration of the earth."

"Uh, okay," Mara said, her inner writer's skeptic piquing.

Bob slapped it against his knee and handed the vibrating fork to Sage. Mara could barely hear the tone.

Sage walked to the end of the bed again, into what she had identified as the energy vortex. The sound from the pitchfork began to intensify. Within five seconds it had grown to fill the room. Mara covered her ears, but she actually felt the vibrations in her heart. Sage dropped the violently moving fork to the carpeted floor like it was red hot. Like some dying animal, it slowly pulsed to silence. Mara had never seen anything like it.

"My God," Sage said. "This is incredibly powerful." She paused and closed her eyes again, then shook her head as if to remove some uncomfortable thought. "I wonder…what's below this room?" She opened her eyes and looked at Mara.

Mara had to think. "My kitchen. My kitchen table as a matter of fact."

"Have you had any activity here, at this spot at the foot of your bed, or at the table below?"

"Activity?"

"Paranormal activity."

Mara thought about the dream of being buried alive the first night in the house, and the visions of Ricard Fisher she'd had just nights before and the cold spot in the bed next to her. And the other dreams. She hoped no one would ask too many details. "Yes. Right at the foot of my bed."

Sage smiled as if she knew what had been in Mara's dreams. Mara felt her cheeks go red.

"How about at the table below us?"

"I use that for writing sometimes."

"I'm surprised you can write in that space."

"Nothing's happened there. Wait!" Mara suddenly remembered the paper that mysteriously appeared just after she's moved in, the tape recorder that turned itself on, and the cellar door that apparently had opened by itself just a few feet from the table. "Yes," she said. "A couple of things did happen there, but on the opposite side of the table from where I write."

"Okay," Sage said. "Let's check it out."

"Sage, wait," Booth said from behind the camera. Look. Look at your legs."

"Oh my God."

Sage lifted up her shift exposing solid, sleek thighs. For a second it seemed very sensuous, but her legs were vibrating rapidly, far too rapidly for her to be doing it. She started to step forward, but instead was propelled backward, like some bizarre version of Michael Jackson's moonwalk. She almost stumbled as her heels caught on the carpet behind her.

"Did you see that?" She said, astonished. She dropped her shift, which fell to her ankles. "It's time to go downstairs."

"What the hell just happened?" Mara asked. Sage just shook her head as she preceded Mara down the stairs. Mara could smell the faint odor of rosewater coming from Sage's hair. Once they entered the kitchen, she stopped and turned.

"Didn't you see me?"

"Yes, it looked like you were stepping forward and went backward. How did that happen?"

"It happened because I was floating. I was levitating on that spot. You've got some powerful forces in this house, Miss McKay."

CHAPTER 57

"Where do we go next?" Mara asked.

Sage spoke up: "I want to see the kitchen again."

As the group descended the stairs, Mara thought she heard some thunder rumble in the distance. The storm they had predicted? The group stopped in the kitchen.

"Let me check out the table," Sage said. "This is right below where I was standing in the bedroom?"

"That side of the table." Mara pointed to the side of the table closest to the cellar door.

"Mmmm." Sage rotated the crystal in her palm. "I'm not feeling that much right here. It's like something is blocking it right now."

Mara was intrigued. "You mean something has the power to block the energy?"

"Certainly. Or to turn it off. It's never a steady energy, but fluctuating all the time. Otherwise we wouldn't be able to take it. How about the cellar? It seems that would be a likely source for this energy vortex."

Oh, great, Mara thought. The cellar.

"Well, I really haven't been down there much since I moved in."

"Good," said Booth. "Maybe we'll really stir something up."

"Yeah," said Mara, trying to sound enthusiastic. "Maybe we will."

Mara opened the board and batten door that led to the cellar. Sage turned to Booth and Bob. "Could you bring the mirror, the candles and incense, the tuning fork...oh, and the board."

Mara stood beside the door. "Aren't you going down?" Brad asked.

"Yeah. Sure," Mara said trying to convince herself she really wanted to go into the dank subterranean space below the old house. She twisted the circular switch, which appeared to have been installed when the house was first electrified. A dim light barely lit the narrow, rickety board stairs. "Be careful," she cautioned to those behind.

When they gathered in the damp cellar, the light bulb was virtually no use at all. "Light the candles, please Bob," Sage requested. Squinching up her nose at the dead-rat smell in the cellar, she added, "and could we get some incense lit?"

Mara took the incense sticks from Bob, placed them around on several stone shelves built into the walls for some architectural reason she still didn't fathom, and lit them. She never ventured outside the sense of safety the group gave her, except for once when she went to place a stick in a corner of the cellar, just behind a supporting pillar, farthest from them. She hit an icy wall. She backed away from the darkened corner like she had been physically struck, and lit the stick closer to the group. She laid it on a nearby cement block.

In the meantime, Sage directed the placement of other instruments: the reel-to-reel recorder was activated and set on one of the odd stone shelves behind them; Booth ran the microphone cord along some rusty nails imbedded in the rafters and hung the mike above their heads. He set the camcorder on the spare tripod, and walked the other tripod with the mirror into the area from which Mara had just retreated. He returned with an odd half-smile on his face, shivering, rubbing his hands. *So it isn't just me*, Mara thought.

"Let's just get tuned with the psychic venue," Sage said in a quiet monotone. She took a deep breath, let her head fall back, and spread her arms out wide to her sides. Bob and Booth repeated the action. Brad looked at Mara, shrugged and began the same exercise. Sage lowered her head as she exhaled. Her arms lowered, moving in a circular motion before her with the palms to the floor, fingers delicately splayed.

They all repeated this same motion for three or four minutes. Mara actually found it relaxing in spite of the natural apprehension she'd always felt in this dungeon. She slowly felt her fear slide away, like a veil being drawn upward. *I'll have to try this alone sometime*, she thought.

"*Yes.*"

She opened her eyes to smile at Brad, who seemed to be reading her thoughts and answering them. But his eyes were still closed. She took another deep breath and began to let it out. *Now I'm talking to myself in my head*, she thought.

She heard a low hum, opened her eyes to see Bob holding the tuning fork at arm's length, eyes wide with astonishment.

"Did you strike it on anything?" Mara whispered. Bob, wide-eyed, simply shook his head, no. The fork was vibrating on its own.

"I'm shown as though there was a crowd down here." Sage began, her eyes still closed and her arms spread wide. "I'm shown as though there still are a lot of people down here." She moved her arms in front of herself, hands motioning from the wrists as if beckoning someone unseen.

She was silent for a good thirty seconds, her hands moving in a gathering motion. Suddenly she uttered, "Oh!" opened her eyes and turned to Mara.

"What's the matter?" Mara asked.

It was almost as if Sage was in a trance: her eyes were slit and her voice was monotoned. She said, matter-of-factly, "Oh. They can't come to you."

"Why not?" asked Mara.

"They're all dead," said Sage.

Booth spoke. "Sage, do you want the board?"

That seemed to draw her slightly back to reality, although she still acted and talked as if heavily doped. "Yes. Bring it to me."

Booth drew the ancient, fragile board from the corner where he had set it. Bob found a couple of old wooden kitchen chairs sitting against one of the walls and a small wooden table with its legs sawed off. He set the chairs around the table and opened the board upon it. The planchette he placed in the center. Sage sat slowly. She looked drowsily about the dim room. Her eyes stopped at Mara. "Sit," she commanded, gesturing with one delicate hand.

What? Me? How about Bob or Brad. They're much braver at this stuff than I am.

"*No. You.*"

There's my mind talking to me again, she thought. *Screw up your writer's false courage. Do it,* she ordered herself.

She sat on the rickety chair, which felt more like cold iron than wood. Following Sage's lead she reached toward the planchette and lightly placed her fingertips upon it. She closed her eyes.

Sage began speaking almost like it was a chant. "Hello. We are here to visit with you. We just want to know about you. Can you hear us?"

At first there was nothing. Mara glanced at Sage. She had her eyes closed and was breathing deeply.

The slight movement of the planchette almost went unnoticed. Mara didn't think it was moving until she looked down at it. The piece move so slightly toward "Yes" then stopped abruptly.

"It's all right. We can be your friends. I'm Sage. This is Mara. We want to find out about you."

Again, seemingly without touching it, the planchette moved so slightly toward "Yes."

If I wasn't doing this, Mara thought, I wouldn't believe it. But I'm barely touching it.

"Can you tell us your name?"

There was no movement of the planchette for a good thirty seconds. Mara was about to move her hands back to her lap; in fact, she thought she had already lifted them from the planchette when it moved.

Slowly, almost imperceptibly, the planchette began to slide toward the "C." There it stopped briefly. It began to move toward the "A." Then "R." Then in rapid succession, "TER."

"Carter," whispered Brad. Booth began to move the camcorder and tripod closer to record the session.

"Are you alone?" asked Sage.

Mara was determined to pay special attention to see if Sage was moving the planchette. She kept her own fingers glued to the piece, consciously trying to feel if Sage applied any pressure on it. She felt nothing as the planchette began to slide across the cardboard toward "No."

"Are you with your wife?"

The planchette didn't move. Aha, thought Mara. It's not working.

Sage lifted her hand from the piece, picked it up and placed it in the middle of the board.

"Are you with your wife?" she asked again.

The planchette slid back to "No." Sage looked up at Mara knowingly.

"Are you in pain?" The planchette took off and went immediately to "O."

Mara gave Sage a confused look. Concern shadowed Sage's face.

"Is there anything we can do to help you?"

As if driven, the planchette rushed to the edge of the board. Mara felt as if she physically had to press on it to stop it from falling off the edge, but she couldn't stop it. Sage pulled back her hands like she had touched a hot stove. The planchette bounced once on the earthen floor and rolled on its edge three feet from the table.

"Damn!" Booth said. He had been looking through the viewfinder of the camcorder. "The batteries just died. Just like that," he snapped his fingers. "The indicator said I had twenty-five minutes left, and they just gave out."

Bob leaned over the reel-to-reel recorder. "Huh! This is gone too."

"What? That can't be," said Booth. "I bought those batteries on the way over."

"Mara, where are we in this cellar?" Sage asked.

"What do you mean?"

"In relation to your kitchen table."

Mara looked around to the stairs. "It would be right…" She paused for a moment. She found herself reluctantly pointing to the spot where the planchette had been pulled.

Sage stood and began to back away from the table. She no longer had the wispy, ethereal look to her. She suddenly took on an aura of seriousness. She turned to Bob and Booth.

"We need to leave," she said suddenly. "Now."

Bob and Booth immediately began gathering the equipment.

"What's the matter?" Mara asked, confused yet curious. "Why did the batteries die? Why did the planchette fly…."

Sage's face was frantic. "Now!" she practically shouted.

They hustled up the rickety stairs, grabbing gear and snuffing candles. They burst into the kitchen, all breathing hard. Mara was getting upset. She looked at Brad as if to say, is this part of some act? Brad's face betrayed no emotion.

"Miss Mara," Sage began. She stopped and took a deep breath as if to compose herself. "Mara, you've got several powerful forces in this house. Some are just pathetic weaklings, slave spirits, as they are known. Others are master spirits. Still others are even more powerful…they seem to be masters over the masters, enslaving even them." She paused again. "We need to go."

The men had loaded everything into the bags and headed out the door.

Mara was more confused than ever. What was this woman talking about? Slave spirits, masters of the masters?

"What? You can't go now, Sage. Please, explain this to me."

The three were already out the kitchen door. Brad turned to Mara. "I'll find out what happened. I'll call." And suddenly Mara was alone in the house.

She looked around. The first thing she did was call for Reynolds. When he didn't come, she went looking for him and found him curled up in a far corner of the dining room, his ears pinned back and his tail wagging sheepishly.

"What? Did you get scared too?" He got up and followed her back into the kitchen. She walked purposely close to the side of the table Sage had said was in "the vortex." She felt nothing. What the hell did I just witness? Was that an act?

She noticed that in their hurry to exit the place, they had left the cellar door open. She began to close it when she noticed the light was still on. She touched the switch, but it was in the off position. "Shit," she said out loud. "We must have left one of the candles burning."

She started down the creaking stairs but pulled up short. For a moment she thought, should I be doing this? She felt a small chill creep up her back to the nape of her neck and shivered.

I can't leave a candle burning all night. Come on, Mara.

She got to the bottom of the stairs and saw the light coming from behind the pillar where she had tried to put the incense.

I don't remember lighting a candle there.

She walked toward the light. Again, it was as if she'd hit an icy wall. As she rounded the corner, she involuntarily gasped.

There, in a white, glowing haze was a man dressed in a rotting military uniform of the last century. Although the image was unmistakable, Mara could see through him to the wall behind. More frightening than that was his head: most of it was blown away, gone, with one fleshy cheek dangling above a vacant eye-socket, and broken teeth in a mangled jaw. Mara wanted to run but she was transfixed in horror. Suddenly the one good eye, turned to look directly into hers. As she watched, the apparition levitated, moved backward, and vanished into one of the niches dug into the cellar wall. As if someone had flipped a switch, the light in the cellar went out, and Mara was in total darkness.

She spun in the direction she thought the stairs stood and stumbled over one of the chairs they had set up for the séance. Her legs got tangled and she crashed to the dirt floor. She felt her hands slide along the slimy mud and the back of the chair poked hard into her gut. She could barely make out the light from the kitchen at the top of the stairs. She could see that it was growing dimmer. The door was closing.

She rushed to the stairs and raced up them using her hands to help her climb. The door had half a foot to go before she would be in total darkness again. She sprung up the last six feet of stairs and landed on her belly on the sharp edge of the top of the stairs, jamming her arm into the crack. The door stopped against it.

She stood in the kitchen and shut the cellar door, panting from her fall, her leap up the stairs, and from fright.

She caught her breath. "Okay," she said, still breathing deeply. She took a few more deep breaths and thought about what she was about to say.

"Okay. Okay. What is it you want?"

CHAPTER 58

To calm her nerves, Mara took a short walk without the frenetic Reynolds. Once home, she made herself some chai tea and was attempting to settle back into writing Fisher's bio. She'd gotten a few sentences into the computer, but the crazy events of earlier that evening still dominated her mind, intruding like Muzak, resisting all efforts to push them aside.

She didn't want to think about it anymore. She thought: There's just too much to do, damn it! Not only that, but I have to live in this house, to sleep in it, and sleep with whatever's in the cellar that seems to have a direct connection, through my kitchen, to my bedroom!

She decided tomorrow, first thing, she would go out and buy some sleeping pills.

She had just put the teacup in the sink when her phone rang.

"Miss McKay. It's Sage. After we left, I felt bad. I felt as if I needed to give you an explanation for my abrupt departure earlier."

"Yeah, Sage. Actually it sort of scared me. In fact, I had another experience after you guys left."

"No. What happened?"

Mara told her of the light in the cellar, and of the apparitional 19th century soldier she saw disappear into the niche in the wall.

"Oh my God," said Sage. "I knew it! I saw...actually felt something of death in that cellar. And something more ominous as well."

"According to what I was told," Mara informed her, "this house was used as a morgue for the battle that took place outside of town."

"Yes. That explains the first spirits I encountered, the slave spirits. But the others? Listen: There is something potentially dangerous in that house. You must protect yourself from it."

"What is it?"

"I want you to know that I don't normally counsel clients on this type of thing, but it felt as if something very powerful was trying to take over."

"Take over the house?"

"Take over me. And possibly you, as well."

"Take over? What do you mean?"

"It's called a walk-in. It's a type of possession. A discarnate human spirit normally attaches itself to the psyche and manifests itself in benign ways, through dreams or sometimes visions. Past life therapists claim that some seventy percent of all patients have at least one or more discarnate spirit attached to them. They are deceased humans who have not—or cannot—leave this plane and move on to a higher plane."

"You say 'normally.' None of this sounds very normal at all."

"Yes. But if the spirit is undetectable, a person just continues to live his or her life never knowing that a spirit is attached to them. People around them don't know it because the attached spirit merely incorporates itself into the living person's daily life. Yet they can manifest themselves in various ways."

"Such as?"

"Mental illness, physical illness, mood swings, chronic pain, dependency problems, even suicidal tendencies. All of which are, if not normal in our modern world, at least common enough to accept in a person."

"And all of which can be treated."

"Yes. Except for elementals and evil entities. And especially in a walk-in."

"Okay. Now you have to explain a few things. Elementals, first please."

Mara jotted the word *elementals* down in her notebook for future reference.

"Elementals are spirits that exist free in nature. According to legend, they can take on various appearances: animals, half-animal, half-human, or all human. In history they have been recognized as a lower order of spirit. In the past people thought they have manifested themselves to humans as elves, water babies, trolls, and gnomes. But of course, much of that was merely unsubstantiated folklore. More recently people have attributed the strange lights seen in fields or forests—some call them "fairy-lights"—and within structures. Some people have taken pictures of them—the 'orbs' they catch on cameras. They appear to psychics and are said to understand our speech, music, and enjoy our company."

Sage paused. This chick is completely off the wall, thought Mara.

"Go ahead, Sage."

"I know this sounds crazy, but you must realize that although some of this is ancient mythology—trolls, fairies and the like—modern scientific methods have been used to study these lights and have come up with no explanation for them. I'm just giving you the background."

"So far, elementals seem pretty harmless."

"Most, according to legend, are. But there is another type of elemental, extremely malevolent, deceitful, evil that will do anything to harm humans. They can attack you psychically; they drain your aura of its energy; they drive you crazy—literally—and can wreak havoc in your interpersonal relationships. They're vile and exist only to create chaos and deceit, evil's greatest tool."

"Come on, Sage. You're talking like there is some unknown evil force loose in this world that can take over human minds and hearts."

Sage's long pause on the other end of the line made Mara realize that, yes, sometimes it seemed like there was a universal evil power which, when directed at particular individuals, made them malevolent beyond their control and deceitfully ordinary to the rest of us. Ted Bundy, the charmer, came immediately to mind. Or John Wayne Gacy, the killer clown. Or priests who were later exposed as child molesters. Crime TV shows were full of them, and those are just the ones they've caught.

Sage continued: "There are dozens of ways this evil can attach to humans. Psychic attack, thought forms, by psychokinesis where it does things to your physical body. But the worst is the walk-in. An entity actually enters your body. It replaces your spirit, your very soul, and takes over. It lives as you, your very self, deceiving all your friends and relatives until it can do harm."

"That's a possession, right? I saw *The Exorcist*. Same thing? Get rid of it with a priest?"

"No. A demonic possession merely displaces, pushes aside, the person's psyche, their soul. Later, when the demonic presence is removed by exorcism, the individual's soul remains to begin functioning again. A walk-in—as benign as it sounds—is when the entire spirit, or psyche, or soul, if you will, is completely removed and replaced by another. Some say they kill a person's soul so that it can never even move on to the other plane."

Sage paused again, piquing Mara's interest. "There's more, isn't there?"

"Yes. Sometimes they regenerate. They become part of the reincarnation cycle."

"First, that assumes that one believes in reincarnation."

"Believing in something has nothing to do with whether it exists or not. You don't have to believe in an apple for it to be on the table in front of you. It exists. Period."

It made perfect sense. How many times had Mara heard it: There are no such things as ghosts—or the paranormal, or the afterlife—because I just don't believe in them. Mara realized that it was like saying there was no such thing as the Vietnam War—or World War II, or anything in the past—just because "I" wasn't there. If something exists, it exists.

"Okay, so assuming reincarnation exists, that means they can come back after death?"

"Yes. Again and again. For them, there is no death."

Sage paused again. It sunk in to Mara.

"For evil, there is no death?" But, Mara thought back to her Sunday school teachings, isn't that what Christ said about the righteous?

"Miss McKay, I think we should talk sometime, face to face."

"Sage, I am so busy writing...I've got this deadline and...." But which is it that can live forever? Mara wondered. Is it Good or is it Evil that can live on after bodily death?

"Wait, Sage. You're right. I need to talk to you. I need to talk to somebody. This all is a little...frightening."

"I know. It has me worried, too. I don't know if you're safe in that house. Not from what I felt. Not from what I was shown."

Mara was quiet.

"Miss McKay, I'm sorry. I probably shouldn't have said anything. You have to live there. I hope you'll be all right."

"Well, at least I'll be aware." Mara smiled nervously to herself. "You don't have any magic incantations or anything, to protect me...do you?"

"Just keep positive. It seems like these things can walk-in when we're weak, or ill. You know, when our physical and psychic defenses are down. Don't get too tired. Try to stay healthy. Don't work too hard."

Fat chance of that, thought Mara. I'll be up most nights working until the deadline.

"I'll be in touch."

"Thanks, Sage."

Her phone beeped, dead in Mara's ear.

CHAPTER 59

Mara realized that the rest of the house was dark. She stood and walked cautiously to the living room and turned on a light. Out of the corner of her eye she thought she saw a movement near her couch. When she looked directly at it, she realized it was nothing. Damn! Now I'm getting spooked.

Spirits that walk in to your body and kill your soul. Kill your soul so that it cannot move on to a higher plane. A soul that just ceases to exist precludes going to heaven or another dimension, or reincarnating or meeting again with friends and loved ones on that higher plane. If there is anything after physical death, it would be preferable to experience it rather than suffer complete extinction.

Mara shivered at the thought of total extinction of the body and soul. She jumped when her phone rang again. It was Brad.

"Hey, Mara. How are you doing?"

"Not too well." She thought: Why do I feel like I'm going to start crying?

"Did that shake you up this afternoon?"

"Yeah. That and the call I just got from Sage."

"She called?"

"Have you ever heard of 'elementals' and 'walk-ins?'"

"Oh. She's associating what is in your house with an invading entity?"

"Yeah. I take it you know about these things?"

"I did some research into them, yes."

"Am I in danger?"

Brad was uncomfortably silent on the other end.

"Say something," Mara demanded.

"I'd be careful."

"Could you come over tonight?"

"Could use a roommate, could you?"

"Yeah."

"I'll be right over."

Sitting on the couch with Brad next to her and Reynolds warm against her feet made Mara feel more comfortable than she had in a long time, maybe since the early days with Rex. Comfortable enough to tell him about her experience in the elevator.

"Okay," he said. "I'm not going to get all cerebral on you, or try to cross-examine you for data or grill you for details. What you've been through since you got here has been pretty intense. How about if I just hold you?"

If circumstances had been any different…if Mara hadn't been so exhausted from writing, if Brad had not been so understanding, if she hadn't been so frightened earlier that day, for God's sake, if she wasn't afraid of her own house… she never would have slept with him that night.

But suddenly the kidding and teasing and false bravado that Mara used as a defense fell away like children's masks the night of All Hallow's Eve. She realized that Brad was beginning to care for her. And that she was starting to care for him—needed him, as a matter of fact—to help put some fragmented pieces of her life together. Maybe there was more to life than writing. No, of course there's more to life than writing, she thought as she was falling asleep curled in his arms. Writing was a mask, too. I've been using it to protect myself. From pain. From fear of failing. From life. No more. Hopefully, cautiously, tentatively she thought, maybe never again.

CHAPTER 60

Mara sat at her kitchen table waiting for Sage to show up. They had scheduled a get-together to talk about "supernatural stuff"—Mara really didn't know what else to call it—the morning after Brad stayed. She smiled. It was great to connect with a man. It was even better to commit instead of holding him at arm's length. Opening up about her frightening elevator experience helped. He seemed to change a little after her confession, become more understanding about the fact that she was treading new ground—in more ways than one. Before he left that morning, he did have one question she thought strange.

"Did you ever wonder what would have happened if you had stepped off the elevator?"

She couldn't answer because it had never crossed her mind.

"By the way," he said. "Cute tattoo. A soccer ball and the number one?"

"I'll explain…someday."

He left with a quizzical, handsome half-smile.

Within a few minutes, Sage was sitting at Mara's kitchen table in her yellow and green flowered shift sipping chamomile tea. With her long, straight, blonde hair and sweet face, she looked to Mara like a throwback to the '60s, some ditzy, hippy chick. A photograph right out of her father's scrapbook of Woodstock. As she reached to place the mug back on the table, Mara saw her breasts flutter gently beneath her shift. Braless, thought Mara. The perfect touch.

"Sage, tell me more about your psychic powers." Mara couldn't help but smile; it sounded a little corny to her. Or, it would have sounded corny if she hadn't experienced what she had in the last few weeks.

Sage put down her mug of tea. "They started when I was a teenager. I had what most parents call imaginary friends. Except that I was too old for imaginary friends and they weren't imaginary friends; they were the spirits of dead relatives that were all around the house. A couple. My grandparents. No one else saw them.

"Then I started seeing them in other places. I've been called in, by the police, to crime scenes to help identify the victims and the perpetrators. I've been pretty successful at that. Maybe four or five convictions."

"Anyone I've heard of?"

"Murderers. I don't tell anyone their names. You know, many criminals are psychic and use their powers to tap into the evil forces that permeate the earth plane."

"So evil is a palpable presence in this world?"

"Yes. A palpable force. It's all around us. All we have to do is tap into it."

"Anyone can tap into it?"

"Of course."

"Do you have any other powers?"

"I also found that I could listen in on other people's thoughts, especially when their energy is running at a high level."

"Can you read my mind?" Mara tested Sage. "What am I thinking now?"

"Well, it doesn't work quite like that. First of all you either have to learn to focus and concentrate on a higher level, or the energy levels must already be up in your body. That's how I can find clues for the police. Everybody's energy levels are extremely high: criminal, police and victims."

"You discover a victim's whereabouts by reading their mind? Their dead mind?"

"Mind never dies. Just the brain. The mind—or what we call the mind or consciousness or soul—has a personality and existence all its own. Aristotle was the one who tried to lodge the mind in the brain and declared that they were inseparable; when the body dies so does the soul. Common wisdom and observation through the centuries has changed people's thoughts about that. Modern physics is contemplating consciousness."

"Sage, is that why a walk-in that kills the soul is so abhorrent?"

Sage paused for an uncomfortably long time, took a long sip of tea. Finally she answered. "I can't think of anything more horrible than for the last existing bit of you to become extinct. At least, if we know the soul survives death, we can hope for its betterment, it's moving on to a higher plane or perhaps returning to earth in another entity to try again to be better. If the soul is killed, that's it. No more. No hope. No redemption. No forgiveness. Nothing. Nada, nada, nada...." Sage's voice trailed off as she stared at the floor. She shook her head as if she were coming out of a trance and looked at Mara.

"I'm sorry. It's truly depressing to think about. To get down to why I called. I had to come over and talk to you about this. I'm sorry for bothering you last night, but the experience yesterday afternoon was pretty overpowering."

Mara felt she needed something explained. "What I can't figure out, Sage, is why you're not experiencing anything now. You're sitting right in the 'vortex' as you called it, right at the table."

"Well, energy comes and goes. I've seen it before. They apparently have to rest some times, too. Or they need to steal energy from some other source. That's why the batteries in the camcorder and tape recorder died. I've seen it happen hundreds of times."

"And now the energy is resting?"

"Apparently."

"Why was it so active before?"

"We upset them."

"How?"

"Just by being in their space. By upsetting their routine. It's as if someone came into your house and started moving all your furniture around. We all have a comfort 'arrangement.' The way we like things, 'just so.' Asians call it *feng shui* and it refers to setting up your furniture arrangement to facilitate the energy flow through your living space. I'm certain that there is a particular arrangement that facilitates spirit energy flow. I am also certain that, after a brief period, the spirit energies will adapt."

"Suppose one doesn't want them around. Is there any way you can chase them away?"

"Certainly. Most of them will go away if you simply yell at them, show your displeasure at the way they are acting, or explain to them why they shouldn't move things around in your house or make things disappear."

"Just shout at them?"

"Often."

Mara paused at the way Sage said it, as if there were other times when they could not be chased away. Before Mara could ask about it, Sage spoke again.

"There are ways you can call them down, too."

"Call them down?"

"Yes. If you want them to appear, to answer questions or reveal something about themselves. Or help."

"You mean like with EVP?"

"Electronic Voice Phenomena. Yes. But that is so tedious. You have to ask the question and then wait for the recorder to give you the answer. What I'm referring to is actually talking to them, one-on-one, in real time."

"Have you been successful at 'calling them down'?"

"Yes, a few times. The ability comes from a technique developed by a prominent researcher who studied the ancients and how they would be able to see those that had gone on before them."

"To Heaven?"

"To the spiritual plane. Heaven is a religiously loaded term, like hell or purgatory. The spiritual plane can be represented by any concept of time or space you want. I'm just now beginning to understand what a thin veil it is between these planes of existence, but I'm also astounded at the number of main-stream scientists who are beginning to explain just how an entire other world can co-exist alongside this world, and never be seen or heard except for an occasional, random sighting or auditory sign."

Mitch ought to be here for this, thought Mara. And Ricard Fisher too. "How much reading have you done on this, Sage? Can you give me a general idea of what scientists say about these occasional 'blips' in reality—as we define it, of course."

"Well, there are several authors you need to read if you really want to get into this. I'll get you a list, if you want."

"Sure. I'll take it."

Mara poured another mug of tea for Sage, who sipped thoughtfully and formed her next question. "Did you have a lot of paranormal activity when you first moved in?"

"Yes. But not just in this house. I mean, I had some experiences in this community. Maybe it was because I was working on Ricard Fisher's biography—the scientist at the university who killed himself."

Sage seemed to perk up a little at the mention of Fisher's name. "Have you had a sighting of Fisher?"

"Well, yes."

Sage nodded and cleared her throat.

"No," Sage said. She lifted her eyes dramatically to the ceiling and shook her head. "There's something missing, some connection that isn't connecting. If you were working on something from the catastrophic battle that occurred here, that would explain why you would have experiences that were related to that—sightings of soldiers and the like."

Mara remembered her first experience, witnessing the phantom, bloody hospital, and the two decomposing soldiers she saw—or the *apparitions* of soldiers she saw.

"There's always a connection, no matter how tenuous it may seem, between the site, them, and you. Always."

Sage played with the handle of the mug and paused. Mara wished she would get on with the conversation: good news or bad, Mara had to get back to her writing.

Sage turned her head to one side and brushed a strand of hair from her face to behind her ear, exposing a breathtaking silhouette. "You said there was a connection between the house and the dying that was done here?"

"Yes," Mara answered. "Remember, it was used as a mortuary, before and after—especially after—the battle."

"And they kept the bodies...?"

"In the cellar."

"Ahh. Well, that explains the activity there. And perhaps why they remain. You see, one theory why spirits linger is that there has been no consecration of their gravesite."

"Sage. Consecrating a gravesite just means saying some words over it."

"No, Mara. It's deeper than that. It's like spiritual protection, a psychic wall to keep evil from the dead as they make their way from one world to the next. It goes back millennia."

"How's that?"

"Well, there are numerous myths about the dead. Romans considered dead men as a shadow empty of substance. Ceremony involving human sacrifice in the ancient world was practiced for the purpose of nourishing the dead with the blood of the dying victim. Gladiatorial combat later took the place of human sacrifice on an altar, blood flowing from their bodies, once again to appease the spirits of the dead.

"The Romans, who got their ideas of the afterlife from the Greeks, respected and were frightened of the powers of the dead. Virtually all ancient peoples feared the dead. They also thought that on occasions the dead could force entry to the realm of the living and perform evil deeds, including dragging people back with them to the other world. Hence the numerous, scheduled ceremonies to circumscribe the powers of the spirits, often confining their return to Earth only to certain days coinciding with natural events: full or new moon or harvest time. That's where we get Halloween: from the conquered peoples of Rome.

"The dead's anger was only aroused if the ceremonies—like consecration of their resting place—were not performed properly. The consecration builds a psychic barrier against evil, a protective wall for the spirits. If the ceremonies were not properly taken care of, appeasing was accomplished only with the spilling of human blood, the very fluid of life itself. Then the dead could be presented with a reality, albeit transitory."

"Bloodthirsty spirits of the dead?" Mara asked.

"According to the ancients."

Mara took a deep breath. This little visit of Sage's was taking a turn more fascinating than the cold biography of Ricard Fisher. Cold, that is, as long as she was forbidden by her editor, to include the paranormal aspects of Fisher. But something Sage had said earlier still had Mara intrigued.

"You mentioned something about 'calling down the ghosts.' How can that happen?"

"It's like using polarized sunglasses, or a diving mask, to look below the surface of the water. You need something to break through the thin surface to see into the depths."

In spite of her frightening experiences with the paranormal, Mara's interest was piqued.

"What sort of environment do you need? Can you teach me how to call them down?"

"I can try."

"What do we need?"

"A quiet, dark space; an hour or so for preparation; a comfortable chair, and…. In fact, I think one of the items we need is here already. In our rush to leave the other day, we left my mirror in your cellar. Is it still there, or did you move it?"

Mara didn't even remember seeing it when she went down and confronted the soldier's spirit the night they had the séance.

"I'm not sure."

"Let's go look." Sage stood and started walking toward the cellar door. Mara hesitated.

"It's all right for me to go into your cellar, isn't it?"

Mara stood quickly, a little embarrassed at her sudden, unreasonable fear.

"Sure. I'm sorry. Let's go."

CHAPTER 61

The stairs creaked ominously. Just like some B-movie horror flick, Mara thought. The cellar still smelled moldy and damp. Mara hesitated as Sage walked directly over to the wall of the cellar where Mara had seen her ghostly, mutilated soldier. There, right where he had stood, was the large mirror on its tripod. *Could I have merely seen my own reflection in the mirror and let my imagination run away with me?* Mara was attempting to conjure up the memory of that horrible vision to convince herself that it had been a reflection, but as the picture of the torn and bloodied soldier materialized in her mind's eye, she knew how utterly impossible it would have been to have mistaken her own reflected image for it.

Sage picked up the mirror and tripod and moved them slightly, looking at the ceiling of the cellar, the walls, the floor. "I don't know," she said. "This may not work."

"What's wrong?" Mara asked.

"There should be a sort of darkened chamber around you to serve as a necrotorium—a place dedicated to communicating directly with the dead. You need a comfortable chair. The mirror should be a little above your head so that you're looking up and not at your own reflection."

"What should happen then?"

"In the mirror. You should see the spirits appear, the spirits that you call down."

"How do you call them down?"

"Mentally. Just call their names, or open your mind to whatever name comes in. Be relaxed. Some say if your brain is in the alpha state—near sleep—they come more easily."

"It's not a dream?"

"No. You're not asleep."

"Sage, I think I may have already experienced a vision from this mirror."

"Oh, that's terrific!"

"Uh, I'm not so sure of that. It was a mutilated soldier. I can't be sure if he was in the mirror, but he was in this area of the cellar. Hey, can we try something?"

"What's that?"

"I'll be right back." Mara was back down the stairs in a few seconds with the dowsing rods from ISAP in her hands.

"Ah." Sage nodded. "Do you know how to use these?"

"Is it complicated?"

"Here, hold them like this, pointed downward just a little so they stay parallel. There."

The rods lined up with one another, pointing straight out from Mara's body. Suddenly they swiveled to her right and stood straight out.

"No," Sage said. "Don't move. Don't tilt your hands. Keep them pointed slightly downward in front of you."

Mara tilted the rods so they pointed away from her again. She thought: I don't think I moved them. She held them at an even more acute angle in front of her body. Just as quickly as before, they swiveled again to the right.

Sage stared. "You're not doing that, are you?"

"No. I'm not moving my hands at all. Sage, what's going on?"

Sage looked beyond the rods. Mara followed her gaze. The rods were pointing directly at the depressions in the cellar wall. Mara turned to face them and the rods moved to point at the dark pits in the wall.

Sage began to sway, much like she did when she found herself in the vortex in Mara's bedroom. She closed her eyes.

"Sage. Are you okay? Do you want to go?"

"Yes."

Sage swerved into Mara's arms and Mara had to lead her to the stairs. For just an instant Mara thought she saw something out of the corner of her eye, in the mirror. My reflection, she thought, our reflection, the reflection of something on the other side of the cellar. Anything, but.... Sage stumbled once on the lower stairs and Mara started to hold her tighter, but she seemed suddenly to grow light. Once they were in the kitchen, she seemed to regain her composure.

"I'm sorry," Sage said sitting at the kitchen table. "Sometimes I think I'm *too* sensitive."

"Did you feel their energy return?"

"Yes. Stronger than ever. I'm not sure what happened in that cellar years ago, but it's bad. And it's residual. I'm not sure it will go away."

There was a full minute of silence between them as Sage began to breathe deeply, appearing to regain more of her composure with each breath. Finally she stood and smiled weakly. Mara helped Sage with her coat. "I'll be in touch, Sage. Maybe we can try this again."

Sage looked at Mara. Without speaking, she opened the door and raised her hand in farewell. Mara watched her walk to her car and wondered just what it was in the house that wouldn't go away.

Mara was relieved when Brad called and asked to come over. He stayed again that night and in the morning, just after he left, as Mara was still in the sleepy warmth of his memory, her phone rang.

"Mara, I really think I need to teach you to call down the ghosts."

"What?" It was Sage. Mara was still pushing the sleep out of her head.

"Call down the ghosts. To query them, to find out what they want."

"Can't you do it, Sage?"

"For some reason, they are interested in you. More than anyone else that was in the house the other night. More than me. It came to me in the middle of the night."

Then Sage said something that brought Mara's senses to full pique.

"I'm not sure that I emphasized enough the danger and the importance of what is going on in your life right now. It's not the town; it's not the house."

There was an uneasy silence. Finally Sage continued.

"They want you."

CHAPTER 62

Sage was due at Mara's house any minute. Mara knew that she had to see if she could "call down the ghosts," as Sage put it. In reality, what she was talking about was contacting the dead, and Mara began to wonder if she was about to become the victim of what was nothing but an old parlor trick. She began to boil some water for tea, but turned it off again, wondering just what the tone of their meeting should be.

Mara's phone rang. It was her editor.

"So, Babe. How's the manuscript coming? I need it by the end of this week, you know."

Okay, Mara, she thought to herself. Time to do some tap dancing.

"Look, Lillian. I've run into some additional information I'd like to use in the bio. Can you give me an extension on the deadline?"

There was silence on the other end of the line.

"Lillian?"

"Look, kiddo. You know it's a six-month lead time on the presses. If you want more time we'll have to skip one of the editorial processes. Or put severe pressure on one of them, and you know how copy editors are when they're pressed. I don't have to remind you of the old saying in this business: it's the deadline or the breadline."

"I'm really serious, Lillian. Some more information on Fisher just came up and I want to work it in."

More silence.

"Okay. But if I don't have something from you by the end of next week, forget the project. And you know you'll have to return the advance. And you probably shouldn't try this publishing house again. Okay?"

Mara could feel Lillian's voice grow colder as she finished her last sentence.

"Great. I'll have something for you by then. Thanks."

"Yeah, Babe. Bubye."

As soon as she hung up, her phone rang again.

"Hey, gorgeous!"

She smiled at the sound of Brad's voice.

"You know, there was a time when I would get all anxious if a guy called me after I'd slept with him. You must be something special, Mr. Brad." Mara chuckled at herself, starting to use the local idiom of putting 'mister' in front of first names.

"I hope so. Can we get together again tonight? Dinner maybe? I'm in the mood for Italian and there's this great place just down the road...."

She cut him off. "Listen, Brad. I just got a call from my editor and she is on a serious rampage. I've got to get some writing done tonight. Plus Sage is coming over to...we're going to do some research together. So, I'm not sure I'll have the time tonight."

"Sage, huh? You guys have been putting in the time together."

For a second, it sounded as if Brad were jealous.

"How about tomorrow?" Mara figured she'd have to at least eat, even though she had the deadline.

"Okay. I'll call you tomorrow. Work hard."

"I will."

The doorbell rang just as she hung up.

Mara let Sage in and was shocked at her appearance. As little-girlish as she appeared the day before with her flowered dress, today she had taken on a completely different look. She was dressed in a black, long-sleeved, flowing dress with a V-neck and ragged-cut hem. She had put on make-up and looked at least ten years older than the woman just pushing thirty of the day before. Despite the apparent aging, she was still remarkably attractive.

"Sage, did you want some tea before we start?"

"No. That's all right. We need to get started."

Apparently we're all business today, thought Mara.

"Okay, what do we do?"

"Well, let's go downstairs. Did you fix the place up the way I asked?"

"I think it's what you wanted. Let's look."

As they descended into the cellar, the light bulb began flickering again. Sage looked at it suspiciously, as if it were more than the ancient wiring animating it.

Mara had tacked some black cloth to the rafters forming a small room around the mirror and had placed a comfortable sling chair, half reclined, in the center facing the mirror. Over the yellow cloth of the chair she had placed a dark blue comforter and a pillow. Sage looked pleased with the setup. She pulled one side of the cloth back.

"You've created a pretty good necrotorium here. Normally, this would be an all day affair. We'd start by getting you accustomed to the fact that you'll be speaking to the dead. But I get the feeling that you're pretty much ready for that right now."

Mara wasn't so sure. "Whatever you say."

"Why don't you just sit down in the chair and relax."

Mara did what she was told. Sage closed the curtain. Her muffled voice came softly to Mara.

"Can you see anything other than the dark curtain behind you in the mirror?"

"Not from this angle." The chair was lower than the mirror. Mara couldn't even see the top of her own head. "What am I supposed to do?"

"In a minute, you're going to try to think of nothing."

It sounded easy, but when Mara tried to blank her mind just to try it, Brad popped into her thoughts. When she pushed him out, Lillian's voice rasped at her. Then the Fisher bio crowded in. When she dispelled that, an idea for another book started to form. This is not going to be easy, she thought.

"First I want you to loosen your belt and the top button of your blouse. You must feel unconstricted and comfortable."

Mara loosened her garments.

"Close your eyes. Concentrate on your breathing. Breathe in openness; breathe out all your thoughts." Sage paused for the concept to register in Mara's mind and for her to inhale and exhale slowly half a dozen times.

"Breathe in the energy of the cosmos; breathe out your own personal energy." Again a long pause. Mara could feel her heart beat and began to concentrate on that.

"Breathe in receptivity; breathe out doubt."

Mara became aware of a low tone in the room and wasn't sure what it was. It was soothing and seemed to harmonize with everything around her and she forgot about trying to determine what it was or where it came from. She could barely hear Sage now: "You're relaxed. Your breathing has become everything. You will begin to make the whole universe available to yourself through your breathing in. You will breathe out all impurities."

Mara felt like she was floating. For the first time, it felt like her mind was empty of thought and was like a clear crystal decanter ready to be filled. She opened her eyes, but the blackness was so total that she could not tell if she was looking into the mirror or not. She could hardly tell if her eyes were open. It was as if she were floating in nothingness, not knowing up or down.

Then she began to see something.

It began as a tiny, light blue pinpoint. It seemed as if it were growing or coming nearer, but very, very slowly. At first it seemed like smoke, wispy and moving. Then it appeared to congeal. The edges became ragged and began to form a shape. It would start to come into view, then fade. Mara wasn't sure if she was seeing this image in her mind or in the mirror, since it seemed to be moving with no boundaries, like a hologram. She put the thought of trying to determine what it was out of her mind. It expanded and seemed amorphous, its shape shifting from wide to narrow, growing appendages and losing them again, as they receded back into the main form. Mara realized that without being able to see anything else as a reference point, she couldn't tell if the thing was close to her or far away and large. She tried to touch it when it appeared to be closer, but her invisible hand grasped nothing. It began to fade back into the distance, back into what she thought was the mirror. The tone began to fade. Mara called out.

"Sage. Sage. I can't see."

The curtain was pulled back and Sage stood smiling. "Well?"

Mara suddenly realized that she had experienced something she'd never experienced before.

"Sage! That was marvelous!"

"What happened?"

"I don't know. I saw…something. Bluish. It had no shape, but it was there for…I don't know how long. How long was I in there?"

Sage looked at her watch. "About an hour."

"No. That's impossible. It went so quickly, like there was no time at all."

"That's what happens. Let's rest a little bit and we'll try it again."

Mara was more than eager to try again, but reality dropped into her lap. She started to buckle the belt on her jeans and button her blouse. "Sage, I can't. I'd like to, but I have this deadline. I have to write."

"Oh. That's too bad. You seem to be in a very receptive mood this morning. Maybe we can do this again later today or tonight?"

"I'll have to call you. That seemed easy. Is relaxation the key?"

"Pretty much. Clearing your mind of everything is the most important. Some say that we enter the Alpha state of brain waves. Then we are able to use our most receptive powers."

"That's funny," Mara said. "That's where the writing comes from. I mean the creativity. What else can I do to enhance this experience?"

"Do whatever you need to relax. Some take drugs, but I don't recommend that. Mushrooms are the main drug used to enhance visions. That comes, of course, from the Native American customs. Teas, decaffeinated, of course. Maybe a warm bath before we try this again. Make sure you're not hungry, but don't overeat so as to be distracted. You get the picture."

"Sage, let me get some writing done and I'll call you." Mara started to usher Sage up the stairs and into the kitchen.

"Next time we'll talk about calling down the ghosts in pairs."

"You mean more than one ghost?"

"No. More than one caller."

CHAPTER 63

Later that day Mara called Oscar Fosster.

"Hey, O. How are you doing?"

"Mara. That you? Long time no hear from. What's up? You sound upset. Not your usual ball-bustin'."

"Yeah, Oscar. I'm kinda stressed out over this deadline for the Fisher bio. Hey, here's a wild question for you. Are you guys sure that Fisher wasn't murdered?"

"Hell, that was the first thing we assumed. And it really looked like someone had taken him out. But we were missing some prime elements. We couldn't find anyone with a motive. The means were available—those wicked Civil War rifles he had around—but how many murderers actually know how to load one? You need special powder and bullets for the thing, and some kind of weird percussion cap ignition system. You really have to have some insight into how they fought in the Civil War just to load and fire the thing. So the perp had to take a lot of time to shoot him. Almost like someone would have had free access to him. And you saw how secure the place was. No one could have broken in without being noticed. So that sort of rules out opportunity."

Even though I got in without any problem, Mara thought. Of course, no one was inside to bolt the place up. And I did have a little paranormal help.

"Our forensic team figured he'd used some things we found around the room—a loose-leaf notebook, a backscratcher, a slide rule, for God's sake—to activate the trigger once he'd loaded the thing. Why? Have you uncovered something?"

"No. Not really." At least not in the traditional sense, she thought. "But murder just crossed my mind again."

"Better handle if he'd gotten murdered?"

"Hook. It's hook! And no. I'm not trying to sell more books off of this."

I'll be lucky to get this damn one finished at this rate.

"Sorry for bothering you, Oscar."

"No prob Mara. Lunch sometime soon?"

"Well, I'll be done with the manuscript—one way or another—in a week. How about then?"

"You know where to find me."

Mara spent the rest of the afternoon typing. She couldn't even call it writing. At this point I feel like I'm just a stenographer, she thought.

She took a break from typing and pulled out Fisher's files again. She realized she hadn't read them through completely. Even though they dealt with something that was never going to get into the biography, she felt compelled to skim them anyway.

She thumbed through the files and pulled the one marked *Electromagnetic Studies & Otherworld Entrypoints: File 2 of 2*. For some reason, it seemed more sparse than the last time she'd read it with Brad.

She skipped over the several pages of *Inter-dimensional Contacts: Field Notes*. She pulled a file labeled *Spirit Guides* and realized it was empty. Why would Fisher have a file folder and no information in it? She flipped through several other folders whose titles were intriguing: *The Creation of Otherworld Beings; Light and the Z.P.F.* apparently meaning the Zero-Point Field; and one that particularly caught Mara's attention.

She pulled the file with the heading that reminded her of something Sage had said: *Heaven, aka the Spiritual Plane and the Z.P.F.*

She began to read Ricard Fisher's scrawled notes. These, obviously, were the ruminations of an absolutely brilliant mind. Based upon virtually no scientific data except the accumulated *gestalt* of data floating around in his fertile brain, he was jotting down the whisperings—the voices—inside his head concerning the afterlife. Along the margins were his trademark mathematical calculations: long series of letters and numbers, calculus and physics equations.

She continued to read through the second page of obviously extemporaneous notes, sometimes enthralled, often confused, by the technical scientific explanations. Mara stretched and yawned and was about to set the notes aside when her eye was caught by a single paragraph.

Humans are constantly being taken from the earth; perhaps the same occurs in the spirit plane. Where is it they go? Perhaps this explains re-incarnation as a continual exchanging of souls, spirit energy, always in obeyance to the laws of thermodynamics—that energy is a constant in the universe and cannot be destroyed—from earth to the Z.P.F and back again.

The more she read in his notes—the thought that the mind outlives the body in opposition to Aristotle's maxim; the realization that communication *should* be achievable between living minds and "dead" minds; that we are on the cusp of discovering the answer to the greatest question mankind faces—the more she wished she could have talked to him while he was still alive.

Wait, she thought. The mirror in the cellar. I can still talk to him. Even though he's dead, I can still talk to him.

CHAPTER 64

Mara waited until 9:00 P.M., but Sage never showed for a 7:30 get together. Although she was happy about the extra time it had given her to write, she wondered when she was going to get some additional information on whether they could—or even should—contact Fisher again. Mara was about to pick up her phone when it rang.

She heard the deep, reassuring voice of Oscar Fosster on the other end of the line.

"Mara. I've got some interesting news. Maybe something that has to do with your bio. Maybe not."

"What's that, O?"

"I got a message from someone I think was Eleanor Fisher, the next of kin. She didn't leave a name but she said that someone else has been in Ricard Fisher's apartment besides us."

Uh oh, thought Mara. *I just got caught.*

"What do you mean, Oscar?"

"She said some files are missing."

Should I confess now or wait until Oscar finds out...which he certainly will. Or is he baiting me?

"Lots of files," Oscar continued. "Like someone carried out boxfuls."

Whew. I just snagged a few.

Mara tried her best to be stunned.

"Oscar. I can see why some of Fisher's colleagues—or competitors—would want some of his files. He was always on the cutting edge of theoretical physics."

"Mara, they weren't files on physics. All the missing files had to do with some weird occult stuff: communicating with the spirit world, ghosts, the afterlife and stuff like that."

"Lots of files? Not just one or two?"

"According to the caller's message, five bankers' boxes full. Fisher had a strange hobby and apparently documented all of it. And someone passed up all his physics files to pull out the ones on the occult. I'm re-canvassing some of Fisher's friends to find out if he was some cult member or something."

"He wasn't a cult member. I mean, I'm the one doing the bio and I haven't gotten any information on that aspect of Fisher."

"Yeah, I guess you would know. Nevertheless, I've got to go back to the apartment. I'll check it for anything else. Mara, if you come up with something give me a buzz."

"Likewise, O. I'll be in touch."

Mara finished feeding the dog, preoccupied with Oscar's call. She sat down in front of her computer to write some more. She couldn't help but wonder who else was so interested in Fisher that they would break into his apartment to gather information. They would have to at least be as interested as she was. But they were interested in the paranormal aspect of his research.

The phone rang again. It was Brad.

"Hey, Babe. Would you like some company tonight?"

Mara smiled at the sound of his voice. "Only if you are *extremely* horny and want to satisfy my every sick whim."

Brad laughed. "One of the things I like about you is your subtlety. Give me a half-hour and I'll be over."

"Twenty minutes or the deal's off."

Brad made it in fifteen.

Mara remembered thinking that she was dreaming that Brad left in the middle of the night, while she lay in bed. She was horribly groggy, as if she'd taken one too many sleeping pills. She got out of bed with a deep, growing unspecified panic in her gut. It was 5:30 in the morning. As tired as she felt, the fear wouldn't let her sleep any more. Her mind felt like it was floating six inches above her head as she walked into the bathroom and turned on the water in the shower. As she washed herself she felt soreness. When she looked down and saw the bruises between her legs and more on her shoulders she vaguely, slowly began to recall the tumultuous, violent sex she and Brad engaged in the night before. Then she winced. It was rough, but she didn't think it was anything to leave bruises. It was when he came back.... It was *mean*, what he did, so unlike how he was. *Or how I thought he was, or how he made me think he was....* Is this another side of him?

She remembered fading in and out of realizing what was going on. It was like a sexual blackout, or like she took drugs or had too much to drink, but that wasn't the case. She vaguely recalled asking him to go easy, but he just went harder, more frenzied.

Her wrists hurt and there was a bruise in the shape of a handprint on her upper arm. She reached down between her legs and felt a sting. He was going down on her sometime in the night and she felt a sharp pain. She looked down and saw a red, semi-circular impression of teeth where he had bitten her. She tried to protest, but by that time he was inside her again, using his penis like a club, ramming hard, over and over.

She quickly rinsed and got out of the shower. For some reason, Rex and the emotional pain he had caused blew into her head. She dried and dressed as rapidly as she could. Her head was still not right, but she had to do some work, had to start writing again.

She sat down at her laptop, pulled up the latest chapter on Ricard Fisher, stopped and began to cry.

CHAPTER 65

Hear his evil laugh, a cackle, come from the brown sludge that slowly moves past me.

"So, how was that, Laddie? The dark-haired one, the one you wanted. Bring back some memories?"

Malachai. Was he here with me? Did he watch? Still can't see him but I get the feeling he helped somehow.

"Do you remember it? The feeling? The gush through you?"

He's talking about that old feeling I used to get. Like a steam engine with the valve tied down. Yes. Yes, I got that feeling again because of the dark-haired girl.

No, I didn't take my time. She was asleep. It was like the contraband or the smelly Irish girls. Or...what was her name? In and out. Do anything I want with her. Fast and hard and the valve blows. And I'm gone.

But I'll be back. Because Malachai told me this is one way to live again.

He was right.

CHAPTER 66

She had just finished a chapter in the bio when her phone rang. Mara picked up her phone before seeing who was calling. It was Brad.

"Hey, beautiful!"

Mara was silent. What could she say? After the other night, how could she talk to him?

"You there?"

"Yeah. Hi."

More silence.

"Is it something I said?"

More silence.

"Look, Brad. You caught me at a bad time. I'm right in the middle of a chapter," she lied. "I'm sorry. My head is just not into a conversation right now."

"Oh. Okay. I'll give you a call later."

"Yeah. Sounds good."

She put her phone down and promised herself to check to see who's calling before she answered it again.

And if it's Brad, she wouldn't.

CHAPTER 67

Sage had called and apologized for missing her appointment and Mara told her she could make it up by meeting someone.

"Just tell me when you're available, Mitch, and I'll make it work. I really need for you to talk to this person."

A review of his calendar, a return call, and Mara and Sage were at Mitch's office at the think tank. A very young-looking man, apparently Mitch's student-assistant, let them in.

His office was sparse. The walls held talismans to his god: photographs of the first atomic pile underneath the stadium at the University of Chicago; the image of the earth taken by the astronauts from the moon; Einstein riding a bicycle; the photo of an atomic explosion taken a nano-second after ignition looking like a giant disembodied eyeball peering into the soul of man.

Mitch entered a minute later and caught Mara staring into the atomic eyeball.

"Who would believe an atomic blast would look so human?" Mitch's southern drawl always put Mara at ease.

"If the eyes are the window to the soul," Mara said, transfixed by the image, "what does this say about us?"

Mara introduced Sage to Mitch. Today she looked like a throwback to the '60s: flowered mini-shift, sandals, blonde hair down her back, and appearing young enough to still be an undergrad. Mitch perked up, obviously impressed with Sage's natural beauty. Then he glanced at Mara, dark-haired and stunning in her own right. *Both in my office at the same time. You done somethin' right this week, Georgia-boy*, he thought.

"So, Mara," Mitch said, sliding his way past a stack of file folders on the edge of his desk. "To what do I owe the pleasure of this visit?"

"Sage and I have been working together at my house. As you know, there seems to be something strange going on there, maybe even something that has to do with science and physics. Sage knows more about the spiritual side of things and you know the science side." Mara pulled out her digital recorder and notebook. "I think there's a point where there is some kind of fusion between science and spirit. I thought it might be good for the two of you to talk."

Mitch dragged two chairs from the wall and pulled his own from behind the desk. "Well, as my granddaddy used to say, 'let's get to shuckin'.'"

Mara looked at Sage. "I told you. Cute as a pile of fried grits."

There was a discussion about definitions. Sage and Mitch agreed that her word "transregions" was another word for his "dimensions." She mentioned that in her world there were actually many "planes" of reality, at least seven, and according to some, many others.

"Interesting," said Mitch. "Scientists—especially physicists—like to refer to a multi-dimensioned universe, or 'multi-verse' as some have called it. Virtually all now believe in more than three or four dimensions of reality. Some say as many as a dozen."

"How does one travel from one of your dimensions to the other?" Sage asked.

"Well, one doesn't, actually," Mitch said. "At least not other than theoretically. Wormholes, which are mini-subways between, and are also theoretical. One eminent scientist has suggested that the dimensions are set up like membranes."

"Membranes? Sage asked. "Like in the body?"

"No. Metaphorically. It's just a way to imagine the reality, the dimension in which we live."

Mitch walked to his white board, picked up some markers and drew two vertical, parallel lines. "Imagine rubbery malleable sheets upon which reality—matter, energy—resides."

He took a green marker and put little dots along the two lines.

"Neither of these realities is aware of the other, until...."

He drew another blue line with a bulge in it. Then another parallel red line that crossed into the blue line. He dotted them both with green.

"In terms of interplay between the dimensions, now imagine them intersecting, actually crossing over each other and carrying information into the other brane's space. What would that mean to our detection devices, say, our eyes or ears?"

"Well." Mara paused at the implication. "It would mean that we would have direct knowledge of what was in that other dimension."

"Yes," Mitch said. "Perhaps we would even get a glimpse into that dimension. But it appears to be pretty rare. And, as I mentioned before, all theoretical"

"In my world," Sage said, "it's a little easier. Meditation. Altering states of consciousness. Slowing down of one's vibrational state. Yogis, in a deep brain-wave altering trance, have been known to bilocate—be in two places at one time. They become one with the universe."

Mitch said, "That kind of reminds me of a physics term: non-locality, which opens up a whole new can of worms. Quantum physics predicts some pretty strange things, like events even Einstein called 'spooky action at a distance.'"

"And that is?" Mara prompted.

"Two particles are separated. When one is acted upon, the other acts like it has been acted upon as well, no matter what the distance between them. The kicker is, no matter how far apart they are, the action is instantaneous."

Mara thought about the "light-shout," the burst of photons from the dying and asked, "Mitch, does this apply to photons, this bilocating?"

"You mean non-locality? As far as I know, yes. The particles appear to be, what they call, entangled."

"Fascinating," Sage said. "Two famous parapsychologists coined the term 'psi-entanglement' to explain some supernatural phenomena."

"After all that I've seen and read, Mitch," Mara said, "I've come to the conclusion that we have two 'bodies.' A physical body and a bio-plasmic body. You know the aura that people talk about? I've seen it using special glasses. Apparently, there are a number of layers to that body, like the different planes or dimensions. And it all has to do with energy—subtle energy, of course, but energy nonetheless."

"Makes sense," Mitch said, "since, according to Einstein, everything, including matter, is energy."

"And," Sage said, "speaking of energy. The brain produces electromagnetic energy. Not a lot, perhaps enough to light a small electric bulb, but enough to be detected by EEG machines. And if the human brain creates electromagnetic energy fields, billions of human brains over millions of years have created trillions of watts of electromagnetic energy.

"Where has it all gone?" Sage continued like a good lawyer, already knowing the answer.

Mitch sat, frowning, not wanting to acknowledge the obvious answer.

"It has to be somewhere," Sage continued, "because of…oh, what was that silly law of thermo…something or other."

"Thermodynamics," Mitch said with a half-smile. "The first law of thermodynamics, specifically, the conservation of energy which states that energy can be neither created nor destroyed, but can change forms, and can flow from one place to another."

"May I suggest a place this energy has gone?"

"Sage, you certainly may," Mitch said, his interest piqued.

"Some paranormalists think there is a field—the Akashic field—holding all the records of everything that has occurred on earth. A recording of sorts. Is there anything in your science that corresponds to this?"

"As a matter of fact, some scientists theorize about an energy matrix, a sea of energy, which would be able to hold great quantities of energy," Mitch said.

"The Zero-Point Field," Mara interjected, recalling Ricard Fisher's files.

"Carl Jung," Sage said, "the eminent psychologist, felt that there are what he called 'ancestral memories,' stored in his famous Collective Unconscious, many of which appear as symbols or archetypes, accessible during the alpha state of sleep—in other words, through dreams during a particular brain wave frequency. His Collective Unconscious transcended individuals as well as time, sounding a lot like Mara's Zero-Point Field.

"Now the alpha state is one of several vibratory levels of brain waves, all corresponding to various states of consciousness, as I'm sure you know. And that waves appear almost everywhere in various theories of physics, am I right?"

"You certainly are. Especially quantum physics."

"And waves spread out virtually everywhere unless they are acted upon by an object to stop them?"

"Yes again."

"And waves can synch in frequency during certain times?"

"Also correct."

"So, could the electromagnetic energy that comes from the brain possibly find its way into another dimension if the frequency were the same or at least complementary—harmonic or resonant?"

Again, Mitch frowned deep in thought, trying to analyze Sage's science.

She went on: "Is it true that science has confirmed that only about ten percent of the universe is visible while the other ninety percent consists of dark matter, dark energy, and possibly some other unknowns, invisible but detectable through instrumentation?"

"Yes," Mitch answered, starting to feel like he was on the witness stand and needed a good defense lawyer.

"Dr. Landry," Sage paused. "Mitch?"

Mara swore she could hear Mitch gulp, like in a cartoon.

"Yes, Sage?"

"Would your colleagues agree that ninety percent unknown energy and matter in the universe gives a lot of wiggle room for numerous alternative theories, as well as lots of room into which waves—whatever kind they may be—may propagate?"

"I can't speak for my colleagues, but you're doing a pretty good job of convincing me. Of course, this all needs mathematical proof to convince them."

Mara spoke up. "Since when is nine to one not pretty good mathematical proof? I'll take those odds any day."

"Speaking of waves," said Sage, "I was at the lake the other day thinking about what we can detect of things in the other dimensions. I was struck by the notion that it's kind of like seeing them as reflections in water. When the waves are at a minimum, you can see the reflections of things like pilings and docks and someone standing on the dock clearly, almost like in a mirror. But have a boat go by and change the frequency of the waves, altering the matrix of the liquid, and your vision gets distorted to the point of not being able to even tell what you're seeing. Since we're talking waves in quantum, is that an appropriate analogy?"

Mitch moved his fingertips from in front of his mouth where they had gone in a gesture of deep thought while Sage spoke. "Well, sort of. By the way, there is the existence of matter waves."

"Tell me more, Doctor." Sage casually pulled a bottle of water from her bag and took a sip.

Mitch smiled at Sage's insistence on addressing him by his hard-earned title. "It's not just liquid or gases that can be involved in waves. Even matter can display wave-like behavior. In fact, they were first proposed back in the 1920s."

Sage took another sip, capped her bottle and replaced it in her bag. "What would you say if I told you that some parapsychologists have theorized what they call 'consciousness waves.' If they acted like all other waves, wouldn't they propagate far and wide?"

Mitch leaned back in his chair and tilted his head up, letting what Sage said sink in. And I'm the one with the Ph.D., he thought.

"I have another question." Sage paused, drawing looks from Mara and Mitch. "If matter and energy are made up of waves, what happens to their frequency when the material body and bio-plasmic, or 'astral' bodies, separate? In other words, when a person dies? Does the physical body's frequency slow to a stop and the astral body's frequency take over? Is it the astral bodies that we see, in my analogy, as reflections in the consciousness matrix?"

Both Mara and Mitch paused, not knowing what to say. Sage finally spoke.

"As in…." She and Mitch said it at the same time: "Ghosts?"

"And death," Sage said, "is a transforming, a separating of mind from body, setting astral energy free through a portal, across dimensions into the sea of consciousness."

Mitch picked it up: "And so you're thinking these astral bodies reserve or take over some of the physical body's energy in the form of waves, to not only manifest themselves, but alter—affect—matter and energy—things—in this dimension?"

"By temporarily altering their frequency and moving from the dimension they are residing in, to our dimension." Mara finished the thought.

There was a long silence in Mitch's office, until Mara finally broke the spell, picking up her recorder from his desk.

"Mitch, this was great. I knew you guys would give me some fabulous ideas. I knew that you would also see these two disciplines as closer rather than farther apart."

"You know, Mara," Mitch started to say as he stood to see them out. "I have to admit, I'm not quite the skeptic I was when you two first walked in." He opened the door for Sage and Mara, who turned and looked at Mitch. "This sound like sow slop to you?"

Sage got a confused look on her face.

Mitch just smiled at her.

"Not at all."

CHAPTER 68

She had absolutely had it with the Fisher biography. She had to finish the damn thing and get out of this little town. Enough was enough.

By seven, Mara had packed her laptop, notebooks, recorder and bottled water. She sat and waited impatiently to time her drive so that she would get to the university library the moment it opened. Too many distractions here, she thought. Several twelve hour days in the library and I can rid myself of this bitch and leave.

It was overcast and raining. She parked a block from the library, but when she turned the corner she saw that the building had been cordoned off with yellow police tape. Some officers stood guard at the tape while others moved around inside it, going in and out of the building in their POLICE raincoats. There was an ambulance and a hearse parked on the lawn outside the doors to the building. She walked up to a policeman at the tape.

"What's going on?"

"Can't say, Ma'am."

Mara rolled her eyes. This guy's way too camp. "Is Detective Fosster here? May I speak with him?"

The cop turned to look just as Oscar emerged from behind the ambulance under a black umbrella, flipping through his notebook.

"Oscar!" Mara called.

Oscar turned toward her and nodded. "It's okay, John," he said to the cop. "She's family."

Mara ducked under the tape. "What's going on, O?"

"They've found some bodies in the basement of this place."

"What? Some people got killed in here?"

"No. They'd been buried."

"Buried? Under the tiles and concrete?"

"Nope. There was a section in the cellar that had never been modernized. It had a dirt floor. The bodies were buried there."

"Murdered?"

"That's what I'm here to determine. So far, I think they were buried a long time ago."

Over Oscar's shoulder Mara saw a priest with a Bible walking toward the front doors.

"Can I get in, O?"

Oscar turned and Mara followed. He spoke out of the side of his mouth to Mara.

"Catch up. Thank God you wore nice clothes today under your raincoat. Pull your hood a little farther down and they may not recognize you. And can you carry the pack like a briefcase? I can get you by as a visiting investigator."

They dodged their way through the crowd. They got a few looks from some of Oscar's colleagues, but moved swiftly to the elevator. Mara felt a familiar lump of apprehension in her chest as they descended and the doors opened.

Just as she remembered it—at least the second time she'd descended—there was the concrete block wall with electrical panels mounted on it directly in front of the elevator. But she could see that there was some activity to the right and behind the wall.

Oscar walked around the wall to an opening in the cinder block and ducked to enter. Mara followed and caught her breath as she nearly crashed into two men carrying a partially opened body bag. A quick glance into the bag showed Mara several bleached bones. There was also a human skull rolling back and forth in the hollow at the bottom of the bag.

She looked up into a low-ceilinged, unfinished room—probably the original cellar to the ancient building—into which some of the trash and fill from its remodeling had gone. It was brightly lit by high intensity construction lamps. Four or five more men in white lab coats were picking away with trowels at a couple of sites not far from the wall. Mara could see white bone poking from the excavated earth. And some bits of faded blue cloth.

"Oscar, is this a burial site from the battle?"

"We think so, but we're not sure. That's why they called us. We think that these bodies were buried here temporarily, when this was an aide station—field hospital, I guess they called it back then—during the battle. If so, then it's a job for the archaeologists from here on out. But whenever they find bones buried, they have to call us in to make sure there was no foul play. So far, it looks pretty routine."

"But why would they bury bodies here?"

Oscar shrugged.

"Convenience." One of the men in a lab coat answered the question for him. "Or possibly the bodies were left down here when the hospital was abandoned after the battle, and some worker from the building just began burying them rather than trying to haul them out in stages of decomposition. It would have been easier. So far this looks like a job for the archaeologists and historians."

"Looks like my work here is done," Oscar said. "I'm going over to Fisher's apartment to investigate the possible break-in complaint."

"Well, so much for my writing here today" Mara mumbled.

"You were going to work here, Mara?"

"Yeah. I guess I'll go home."

Mara raised her hand in a quick little wave to Oscar and made her way out, past the priest who was ducking his way into the cellar, up the elevator and across campus.

Well, that's just one more thing to screw up my writing of this bio, Mara thought with a cynical smile on her face. She shook her head, wondering what it would take to get this damn book finished.

That's it, Mara thought as she tossed her soggy bag on the kitchen table, bent down and rubbed Reynolds's ears. I'm not going out. I'm not answering the phone. I'm not taking walks— "Sorry, boy," she said to the happy dog. "I'm going to finish this damn thing and mail it off by the end of the week."

In ten minutes she had everything set up just the way she liked it: huge coffee cup next to her computer, notes splayed like autumn leaves around the table, her laptop warm underneath her palms.

It was well into the evening before Mara even realized how long she had been working without a break. Deep into the state that writers enter when they are creating, time has no significance or even existence; the world a mere shadow outside the bright cone of creation, things moving in darkness in the periphery of the writer's vision; she being sustained and fed and nourished by the glory of the creative act. It was like that when Mara sat before the house her grandfather had taken her to for her first writing lesson. It must be like death or sainthood, she had often thought, to be of this world but not in it; to be a part and apart.

She had inadvertently answered her ringing phone before she realized what she was doing. Damn! And I was going to ignore it!

"Mara," it was Sage. "Can we possibly schedule another meeting at your place very soon? It's vital."

Mara was ready to blow her off instantaneously—she certainly had reasons to—but Sage's use of the word 'vital' was curious.

"Sage, I'm really busy with my book. I'm not sure if I can spend the time...."

Sage interrupted: "Mara, this is the most important thing you'll ever write about. I think we can conduct a breakthrough, if we can spend a little time together; if we can pair up and do a call-down. We can double the energy. I have some new information."

Mara looked at the clock and was surprised to see it was nearly 10:00 P.M. "When do you want to do this, Sage?"

"Tonight. At midnight. Everything's perfect."

"All right. I'll wait up."

Mara took a deep sigh as she hung up the phone. She forced herself to sit down again at her computer and begin to type. After her great afternoon, the words came to her tortuously.

She was thinking about what Sage had said.

CHAPTER 69

Mara knew that she would barely make the deadline, even if she started writing now and continued right up to it. Sage would be there shortly. Still, she sat down and re-read some of her notes. She forced herself to begin typing into her laptop.

She stopped. The thought of doing the bio of Ricard Fisher without the paranormal aspect really began to bother her. It seemed utterly untruthful to her readers. She also knew that she'd never get a second chance to resurrect Fisher in a follow-up bio. She might be blackballed by her publisher if she didn't get *something* in, and by the publishing industry if she got a reputation as not being able to hit her deadlines. Then there was the advance she would have to return—which was already spent on rent for this strange house. But this cold, analytical biography was turning out like Fisher's mathematical calculations. Even his death, as bizarre as it was, had a sort of precision to it, the way he shot himself with some ancient Civil War rifle. While horrific and weird, still, it was calculated. And yet, by merely describing his manner of death and not telling about his interest in the paranormal, her readers would never know Ricard Fisher.

She had to admit, at this stage of the writing, thanks to Fisher's sister Eleanor's reticence to talk, she'd probably never find out any more about him and his interest in the afterlife. Unless….

She rose from the computer and put two mugs of water and teabags in the microwave.

While it steeped, she went upstairs to her bathroom and drew a warm bath. She got her mug of chamomile tea, stripped off her clothes, lay back in the comforting water, and drank her tea. After ten minutes, she rose and put her nightgown on. The doorbell rang.

"Hi, Sage."

"Mara."

Mara noticed that Sage wore a flowing shift that came to mid-thigh, again reminiscent of a by-gone era, yet looking amazingly fresh and modern on her.

Mara looked down at her nightgown.

"Sorry, Sage. I'll go change."

"No. That's fine. Do I smell chamomile tea?"

Mara retrieved the mug from the microwave and Sage sipped.

"What do I have to look forward to, calling down the ghosts with you?"

"It will be about the same as last time, as far as preparation, attitude, intent. We're just doubling the energy available to the entities. Some say we're actually squaring the energy with two of us. Suffice it to say, if any spirits we call on want to communicate, they'll have the energy to do it."

"I think I'm prepared."

"You took a warm bath to mellow out?"

"Did you pick that up psychically?"

Sage smiled. "No. I smelled the soap on you."

She put the mug down on the kitchen table. "Are you ready?"

"I guess."

Sage opened the cellar door and they descended the creaky stairs. At the bottom Sage lit one of the candles on the stone ledge, pulled a chair from the shadows and placed it inside the curtained-off area with the mirror.

They stepped inside of the makeshift room and sat on the chairs, Mara in the sling and Sage on the chair she had brought in. Once inside the mirror room, the light from the candle faded to black.

Inside the room with its soft cloth walls, Mara felt even more relaxed than the first time. In the utter darkness, she began to breathe deeply and to follow the mantra she heard from Sage:

Breathe in openness; breathe out all your thoughts.

Breathe in the energy of the cosmos; breathe out your own personal energy.

Mara once again could feel her heart beat and began concentrating on it.

She heard Sage:

Breathe in receptivity; breathe out doubt.

Mara again became aware of the low tone in the room. Again it soothed and harmonized things around her.

Again Sage's soothing mantra:

You're totally relaxed. Breathing has become everything. The whole universe available to you by breathing in. You will breathe out all impurities.

She tried to relax since she knew that not thinking about anything was the way to make it appear, but she wanted so badly to see....

Mara felt Sage's hand clasp hers and lift it from her bare thigh. She couldn't see in the darkness, but she knew Sage was holding her own hand, palm-to-palm, near Mara's. She felt a tingling sensation, a connection without touching of the two.

She thought she heard Sage stand and move behind her. The sensation in her hand was gone, replaced by the same tingling at the back of her head which moved over and around to her forehead and stopped. Then she felt the tingling descend to her throat and pause. Unconsciously Mara lifted her chin.

How long Sage's hands remained at her throat, Mara couldn't guess. Time was irrelevant. Only the energy mattered.

She felt the tingling from Sage's hands move over her chest pause at her heart. More energy passed between them. Then down to her solar plexus.

Apparently, Sage had moved to her front. Again Mara felt the tingling energy move. It was centered now between her legs and Mara felt a rush from her sexual parts. But it was not sexual. The energy began to build until there was a rush in Mara's head. It was like some kind of a non-sexual orgasm, Mara thought.

Then the tingling moved to between her ankles, like a beach ball of energy. Again, for how long, Mara had no clue.

She was aware that Sage had moved again, perhaps behind her, because her entire backside was being caressed by the same energy that Sage had concentrated on certain centers along her front. Then she heard Sage's muted voice.

Who is it you want to speak with? Name the entity.

Mara heard herself say, "Dr. Ricard Fisher."

Again?

"Dr. Ricard Fisher."

Mara opened her eyes...or she thought she opened her eyes. It was so dark she couldn't tell. But the floating feeling was back. As was the tiny pinprick of blue light in the distance. Slowly, sometimes fading in, sometimes fading out, it grew. Again, the image formed a translucent, undulating mist. The way it moved, Mara thought she could almost see arms stretching out…and the wispy tendrils at the end of those arms became fingers forming.

The mist began to coalesce into a circle…no, a sphere. Mara could see there was depth to it. From top to bottom: a flat area, a bulge, another flat area. Now a hole in the bottom flat area and two holes above the bulge. *A face!*

Mara began to squirm, like in a bad dream when you cannot get away from a pursuer. Would this be the decomposed faces of the soldiers she'd seen? She felt her face begin to distort into a grimace as more of the image became clear. No. There was no sloughing flesh. It was…it was Ricard Fisher.

"Fisher," Mara heard herself say. "Dr. Fisher?"

The bluish face tilted back. Its eyes closed.

"Dr. Fisher. I know it's you. I need your help. You once asked me to help you. I'm trying. Now I need your help to finish your biogra…."

The face lowered. She tried to see its eyes, but they seemed to be rolled back into its head.

Its mouth began to open and its lips twisted in an anguished curl as if it were trying to say something. Mara tried to read its lips. It was repeating the same word over again. Finally it began to make sense. Suddenly the room grew icy. The word was….

Mara leapt to her feet upsetting the chair. She nearly tore down the curtain trying to find the gap in it. She rushed to the stairs, almost fainting from the sudden flow of blood from her head. She burst into her kitchen, startling the dog. She leaned on the table to catch her breath and looked at the clock. Ninety minutes had passed since she had gone into the cellar.

Sage came into the kitchen.

"I think you got what you wanted," Sage said.

"Did you hear it, too?"

Sage nodded.

Rather than remembering, Mara felt the word she had seen formed by the twisted dead lips and shuddered. Sage and Mara said the word together.

Murdered!

CHAPTER 70

It was an oasis of calm Mara was in, before she had her morning coffee, after Reynolds was fed and was lying at her feet. The breathing exercises she had learned at the relaxation seminar she'd covered for the paper were paying off. She imagined the bubble of stress from her looming deadline begin to shimmer in rainbow colors and, in slow motion, pop around her. She thought: even some of her calling down experiences with Sage might help. *Breathe in good energy...breathe out the bad.* Over and over the mantra.

She wasn't sure how long she had sat cross-legged on the carpeted living room floor, but it was the image of Oscar floating in her mind that brought her out of the semi-trance. As she rose, she remembered she needed to call him.

His cell phone rolled over to voicemail.

She dialed the Department's main number and was put on hold to wait for the Detective Squad.

A long three minutes later: "Yeah. Can I help you?"

Not Oscar's voice. After all that wait.

"May I speak to Detective Fosster, please?"

"Uh. Are you next-of-kin?"

What is this, some kind of a joke?

"Yeah, I'm his sister."

"Hang on." *What the hell...?*

Another strange voice: "Ms. Fosster. First of all, let me say that, on behalf of the entire Department, we are so sorry for your loss."

"What are you talking about?"

"Oh. You hadn't....Oh, I thought someone had called....Well, there's no easy way to break this. Detective Fosster was killed last night."

Mara was silent, slowly coming to the realization that this wasn't some sort of mix-up or weird sick joke someone was playing on her. It settled like a lump of lead in her gut.

"How?" she said, fighting the burning behind her eyes. "Where?"

"He was doing a follow-up at the apartment of the college professor who committed suicide last week. He had logged in that he wasn't so sure anymore that it was a suicide and wanted to pursue a murder theory. He was shot."

"Do they know who did it?" Mara began to choke up.

"It was an accident. Apparently one of the old fashioned rifles went off while he was handling it. It was loaded and he didn't realize it. The sad part is, he radioed that there had been no break-in and that nothing was actually missing. It was a false report. Again, on behalf of the Department, let me convey my condolences to...."

Mara barely had the energy to gasp, "Thank you," before she hung up and collapsed—melted—into the sofa, crying uncontrollably.

CHAPTER 71

Reynolds's bark startled Mara, deep in concentration working on the Fisher book. It was followed by a knock on the door. Mara looked at the clock. Ten. She'd worked through breakfast. Scattered around the table were balled-up tissues, reminders of the news of Oscar's death.

Sage was standing outside, once again seemingly shape-shifting her look. Now she was a dark wraith in a flowing indigo caftan. "Mara. May I come in? I know you're busy, but...."

"Sure, Sage. I needed a break anyway. Come on in. Tea?"

"No. I can't stay long. I got something this morning that may be of importance to you and your book." She sat at the kitchen table, the loose folds of the caftan moving in the breeze from the open kitchen window. Mara gathered up the tissues and threw them in the trash. She slumped back into her chair.

"My book? Okay. What is it?"

"I was doing some remote viewing, and I saw something that was very disturbing. I..."

"Wait, Sage. Remote viewing? I need some more on that."

Sage tucked a strand of hair behind her ear. "Remote viewing is being able to see things at a distance, psychically. Basically you travel—or should I say your spirit travels—to see something out of your physical realm. It was developed by two scientists during the Cold War and was funded by the government as a method of spying. The Carter administration used it to try and locate the Iranian hostages. The government claims it defunded it years ago, but those remote viewers still living say it's a disinformation ploy."

"So, where did you view that has something to do with my book?"

"Ricard Fisher's apartment. The day of his murder."

"So, we're calling it murder now?"

"No. *He* called it murder."

"Wait. This remote viewing. I thought you could travel distances to view things."

"Yes, but you can travel back in time, as well. Especially to places that have a lot of emotion associated with them. Like a battleground. Or the scene of a murder."

"The police have the case solved as a suicide. I—I mean, they—even found a suicide note. It was a twisted, almost impossible suicide, but no one else could have been involved."

"Not according to what I saw."

"Sage, are you sure this isn't just your imagination running wild? I've never heard you mention remote viewing before. Did you just start this method? I mean, I might take information from a dream before I could from a person who claimed they travelled to visit another place and time."

"Well, it's really not all that far off from dreaming. You have to put yourself in a relaxed state, like in the necrotorium, and concentrate only on the remote target. I used his address from the university directory."

"What? You used an address?"

"Yes. That's the preferred method. Remote viewers will sometimes be given an address, or even just GPS coordinates."

"So, what did you see?"

"Well, here are the sketches I made of impressions."

She handed several scraps of paper to Mara who began to shuffle through them. The first one showed a series of curved lines, a possible allusion to Fisher's nude statues. There was a half-wall of squares: his computer screen bank. Then a sketch of a wall of small lines—books packed on a shelf. In the middle was a blank area—a door. *The* door to the second room behind the book shelves. Mara was astounded. "You've never been to his apartment?"

"No."

Mara thought: *Either I'm talking with a woman with yet another incredible gift, or...*

"So, what did you see of the murder?"

"I got the image of the murderer."

"What did he look like?"

"Not he. She."

It was easy—and now frightening—for Mara to finish her thought: *Or I'm standing in front of Ricard Fisher's murderer.*

CHAPTER 72

Sage had gone. Mara hammered down her new sudden suspicion of Sage. There were so many things bothering Mara. She couldn't quite put her finger on one. Remote viewing. The necrotorium below her. Her shattered feelings for Brad. Oscar. Her mind spun.

She *wanted* to believe that some of the things that happened to her were because of some sort of life after death. Introducing Mitch to Sage helped to somewhat fuse science and spirit.

Who can I talk to?

Other than Mitch, who Mara felt she had probably bothered enough already, and Eleanor, who may or may not want to talk to her ever again depending upon her mood. Katherine was the only person who seemed open to some questions stretching from the supernatural into the scientific. Katherine, who filled her in on her gifted colleague, boyfriend Ricard Fisher, who introduced her to his group ISAP. Mara called her number.

Luckily, Katherine had just finished her time slot in the lab and was free that afternoon. After a quick lunch, Mara met her at the university.

Instead of having to go through security checkpoints, Katherine got her a visitor's tag and they went to Katherine's office where she took a salad and a bottle of water. "Mind if I catch some lunch?" Mara smiled and shook her head.

Katherine's office was sparsely decorated. Two large file cabinets dominated one wall. There were framed photos on top and a couple of old "Far Side" cartoons stuck under magnets to the drawers. On another wall was a large white board. Two large framed prints hung in the room—both by Marc Chagall. Mara wandered closer to the brightly colored "Blue Circus" and marveled at the creativity of the artist. Katherine sat behind her desk in a chair on rollers that creaked.

"So, Mara. What's up?" She popped open her salad container and began to add dressing.

Mara sat in the chair in front of Katherine's desk, started her recorder and placed it next to some books sitting there. "Just a couple of questions, Katherine. After what I saw with your ISAP group, the wormhole experiment set up in your lab, and some other things that have happened to me lately, I'm confused. Apparently there are other worlds that exist alongside the one we're living in now. Is that a scientifically accepted fact?" She'd heard it from Mitch, but she'd see if it's common knowledge among all scientists.

"Well, it's a scientifically accepted *theory* or set of theories still being argued about."

"Some insight, please?"

"Hang on." Katherine picked up her office phone and punched a button.

"Yeah, Tom. Hey, Mara's here. You remember, the writer from the other day? Can you come over for a minute? She's got some questions I think you'll find interesting."

Mara gave Katherine a quizzical tilt of the head. Katherine answered her unspoken question.

"Dr. Torres. You met him in the ISAP lab. This question is right up his alley."

Katherine barely had enough time to swallow her first bite of salad when Mara heard a light knock on the door.

Dr. Torres entered in his white lab coat, nodded hello, reached out and shook Mara's hand. He pulled a chair over from the wall and sat.

"Tom, Mara had a question about parallel dimensions. At least, I *think* that's what she has a question about. I thought you might like to share some of your knowledge."

Mara saw Dr. Torres's face light up as if she'd offered him Super Bowl tickets. Okay, she thought, maybe super-*collider* tickets.

"Well," said Torres. "What can I try to answer for you?"

In the ISAP session he had given her a lot to think about during the experiments, about energy leaving the body after death, and living on. She still had the dowsing rods the group had given her—which she promised herself to use again some day.

"Okay. Apparently, from what I've been reading and hearing, there seems to be consensus that there are other dimensions besides the three in which we exist. True?"

"Well, Mara. Like much in science, there is little consensus about it. However, there are some theories that suggest there are. In fact, you missed one that I'm sure you're familiar with."

"Height, width, and depth. Which did I miss?"

"Time. Nothing can exist without occupying some time."

Mara smiled. "Got me. But beyond those, are there other dimensions, other—for lack of a better word—worlds that can be occupied?"

"Certainly, there are hypotheses about other dimensions, even other worlds. Some scientists who adhere to the famous string theory have postulated there are ten or more additional dimensions. Some have suggested since we can detect only about four percent of matter, but see the effects of the rest, perhaps these dimensions lie somewhere in that ninety-six percent we cannot detect. This also goes for energy. They are called dark matter and dark energy, and may be the place where bio-plasmic energy migrates and resides."

Now, thought Mara, we're getting to the point.

Torres continued, lecturing to a classroom of two. "Still others have postulated that this is not a universe we occupy—"uni" meaning one—but a multi-verse—meaning many." So far, thought Mara, the same things I learned from Mitch.

Katherine said, "Don't forget the meta-verse."

"Ah, yes. The significance of this theory, as far as our studies into death are concerned, is that time, as we know it, seems to be meaningless, seems to vanish for the dead, in their space."

"Unlike the dimensions we're used to," Mara added, a little surprised at her own conclusion.

"Correct," said Torres. "So, if time dissolves upon death, it means it leaves everything open to a future-verse as well as non-spatial other-verses yet to be imagined. Perhaps this is why we see and hear things from the distant past—Civil War soldiers or deceased relatives or ancient kings and queens. We may also be able to witness things from the future, if that is one of the multi-verses."

"Also," Katherine began, her salad momentarily forgotten, "there's this little thing about non-locality. It seems to confirm the pliability of time." Again, Mara was reminded of Mitch.

"Wait," Mara broke in. "That time thing. Wasn't that one of Dr. Fisher's bugaboos about Einstein's work? That it was all predicated upon the speed of light—the *time* it takes for light to travel—and that it was a constant, and if it isn't, it messes up his equations?"

"*Einstein, Schmeinstein.*" Katherine and Torres said it simultaneously and laughed.

"Now, let's talk a little bit about consciousness, since it is the essence of the afterlife."

Torres looked at the ceiling, continuing his lecture.

"Just what is consciousness?"

He paused long enough to make Mara think she was back in class.

"Rhetorical?" she asked.

"Oh, yes. Sorry. Now, materialists believe consciousness resides in the brain. Therefore no brain activity, no consciousness. But recent studies into near death experiences, and people in surgery who have been placed in a clinically dead state, suggest that even with flat line brain activity, we still experience things like floating above our bodies and observing visually what is happening. Auditory stimuli, as well. In addition there are other experiences we have and remember when brought back from death. This brings us to one of the more ancient beliefs about consciousness.

"Call it a higher consciousness, or Prana, or God, but some ancient civilizations—mainly eastern—thought there was a universal energy, a consciousness that surrounds us. In more recent times it has been called the Akashic field, perhaps because of the chic of field studies."

Sage's Akashic field, Mara thought. It seems like I've had this conversation—or parts of it—before.

Katherine chimed in. "Basically it states that consciousness is all around us. Everything, every thought, every action on earth has been recorded in this field."

"Yeah," Mara said. "I'm familiar with the Akashic field."

"Well," Katherine continued, "the other part of the theory is that, when it comes to learning and memory, our brains are more like radio receivers than libraries. In other words, we don't so much store thoughts as we retrieve them from the great universal consciousness."

Carl Jung's Collective Unconscious, Mara remembered from Sage.

"Now," Torres said, "what does this mean when it comes to other dimensions?"

Again he paused. He's still in the classroom, Mara thought. "It means...." she prompted.

"Oh, yes. It means that the consciousness energy of the dead has a place to go, which is occasionally accessible to us."

"It confirms," Katherine interjected, "the so-called survival of the personality, which is one of the key questions in afterlife studies."

Mara added: "As does psychokinesis—moving of matter via disembodied thought energy. At least that's what Dr. Rhine from Duke thought. Speaking of where the dead go, are you suggesting that is where the energy I saw on the video the other day went?"

Katherine smiled and Torres nodded.

"And that some of the personality of the dead person went along with the energy?"

"Precisely," Torres began. "Scientific studies show us that transmigration of energy can happen—transmigration to a different dimension, plane, or world, if you will."

Katherine finished the thought. "Paranormal studies—simple ghost stories, apocryphal as they may be—have given us the raw data to show that personality traits such as humor, mischievous behavior, playfulness, repetition, even stubbornness, are also traits of ghost activity."

"But wait," Mara said. "You said that time is not a factor for the dead. That for them, an instant can be a decade or century?" *Just like Dr. Ammons's Podcast about what ghosts can teach us about death.*

"Yes." Katherine stopped eating.

"If their existence is timeless, what difference does it make where they are? If they are only there for a nano-second or less, then move to a future-verse from the past, *where* doesn't matter. The time thing is more important than the location-dimension thing. That the dead can travel into the future or that the passage of time is meaningless is more important than where they are staying. Like Dr. Torres pointed out at the beginning: the three dimensions don't matter much without the fourth, time. Location doesn't matter if you aren't there for any time at all."

Both Katherine and Torres said nothing, looking back and forth between each other and Mara for a good half-minute. Finally, Katherine began to smile.

Mara panicked. Now I've proven what an idiot I am.

"Nice," Katherine said, drawing out the single word. "We've been concentrating so much on the place-space thing that we forgot about the time thing."

Torres quickly gathered his papers and started toward the door. "I've got some calculations to do."

Katherine shouted after him, "I don't know what there is to calculate." Then she turned to Mara. "You've brought it down to its most common denominator. The time thing."

And, Mara thought, that tied Ricard Fisher's phenomenal genius in theoretical physics to his studies in the paranormal.

That time thing.

Walking down the hall from Katherine's office, looking at the trappings of academia and the acclaim—in fact, the very edifice—funded by the brilliant ideas and groundbreaking and award-winning concepts of professors, Mara understood what Brad had said about why some of Fisher's colleagues might want him dead for upsetting the proverbial apple cart.

She wondered how Katherine always seemed aloof when Mara asked her about Fisher—for better or worse her love interest—and his sudden death. Then something else popped into her mind: Sage's comment on her remote viewing Fisher's apartment and his murderer.

Not he. She.

Mara stopped at the exit and turned to look back down the hall.

From the door to her office Katherine waved.

This is getting complicated.

CHAPTER 73

"This damn kitchen table."

Reynolds lifted his head and cocked it in canine expectation, then resumed his position on the floor. Mara picked up a stack of note cards that had fallen to the floor when she slid her laptop to one side, which moved a couple of stacked books, which hit the note cards.

Cards re-stacked, she put her hands to her eyes and almost screamed, "I need more! Ricard Fisher, I wish you could talk to me! Tell me what happened!"

She stood to pour yet another cup of coffee. When she turned back, her small, silver, digital recorder was right behind her laptop in the middle of the table.

"So, that's where it was." Under some papers? I've sort of been looking for it. Why hadn't I noticed it before?

She absent-mindedly picked it up. She slid the hold switch and pressed the record button. Feeling almost foolish, she said to the empty room, "Ricard. You asked me to help you at your funeral. I'm confused. What did you mean?"

She watched as the tiny red LED flashed, indicating nothing was being recorded.

"Ricard," she repeated. "Did you put this recorder there so I could talk to you?"

Again, the LED flashed. She had her finger on the stop button when the light started to glow steadily. It was recording something.

She stopped it and played it back. She heard her voice ask, "Ricard, did you put this recorder there so I could talk to you?"

She heard a raspy voice respond, "Yessss."

It's happening, she thought. I'm doing it. I'm getting EVP. She hit record again. "I'm going to ask you again. You requested my help at your funeral. What did you mean?"

She waited. There! The LED was glowing again, indicating a longer recording than before.

She hit the play button and heard herself ask, "What did you mean?" and the answer came in a rough, stilted growl: "Don't…me…die…n…vain."

Mara said what she thought she heard out loud: "Don't let me die in vain."

She punched the record button again and said, "You said 'murdered.' I thought you killed yourself." One, two seconds passed. Mara worried that Fisher was done talking. The LED glowed again.

Mara played it back. As clearly as if Fisher had been whispering into the tiny microphone on the recorder, his voice came through: "Misunderstood me."

She stopped the machine to digest what she'd heard, then hit the record button again. "Is there anything else?" she asked. The LED flashed rhythmically. She waited a good minute. Nothing was being recorded.

"'Misunderstood me,'" Mara said out loud, wondering who misunderstood Ricard Fisher in his last moments alive.

CHAPTER 74

Time to make a decision.

I'm going to finish this book the way Lillian wants it, on time and advance my career; or I'm going to finish the book with Fisher's breakthrough in the supernatural, miss my deadline, perhaps never find another publisher, and end up the world's youngest greeter at a big box store.

She knew in her heart it was way more serious than that.

I'm either going to write a book or write a lie.

Regardless, I've got to find out more. The EVP was a tease but there seems to be a communication connection with Fisher right below my feet in the cellar—in the necrotorium we set up. Maybe just one more bit of information from Fisher and I can convince Lillian to give me a little more time.

Mara rose from the kitchen table, looked wistfully at her laptop, and began her ritual.

The chamomile tea was brewed, the bath drawn. Ten minutes of soaking in lavender-scented water and she made her way down to the necrotorium.

She parted the curtain, pulled at her short nightgown to loosen it, sat in the sling chair and began the mantra softly.

Breathe in openness; breathe out all your thoughts.

Breathe in the energy of the cosmos; breathe out your own personal energy.

Mara once again could feel her heartbeat slow and mellow out and began concentrating on it.

Breathe in receptivity; breathe out doubt.

She imagined she felt Sage's hand palm-to-palm with hers and felt the energy flow. Then Sage's hands at the back of her neck and moving across her head. The subtle tingle of energy exchange continued in the center of her forehead—the so-called third eye she'd read about.

Again time vanished, became meaningless. Only the energy mattered.

Her throat was next. Like before she felt her chin unconsciously raise to allow the energy easy access to her throat center—the chakra in Eastern terms.

Then down her chest to her heart. She could feel that more energy than before was flowing from the heart chakra. How long she concentrated on her heart she couldn't tell.

Then her solar plexus. That felt warm and good. She began to open her eyes and saw the pinprick of blue light forming in what she thought in the darkness was the mirror. The light grew into a pale column, and split, one azure light on each side of where she thought the mirror was located.

Then she realized, the columns were too far apart. They couldn't be inside the mirror. They had grown as well, and appeared as two cobalt pillars almost beside her in the necrotorium.

Mara closed her eyes and they disappeared. She concentrated on her energy again. This time it floated down to her groin where she felt the exchange. This time it felt like it was moving in a circular motion. She spread her legs to facilitate the energy movement and began to think Ricard Fisher's name.

"Dr. Fisher," she murmured.

The moving energy seemed to circle more rapidly. She thought, this is almost erotic, and began to move her ankles apart for the energy to float down there. But it wasn't moving.

She opened her eyes and saw the two columns, now about the height of a man, converge before her.

"Dr. Fisher?" softly again.

No, she heard in her head.

"Dr. Fisher," in a whisper. "I want to talk to you."

Again, *no*.

The columns had melded, moved between her legs, and the energy there made her tense up.

"Who is this?" she said out loud.

I am James. I am Will.

Now it was outside her head, coming from somewhere inside the necrotorium.

She tried to stand up but felt the energy, like a hand, push her down by the shoulder back into the chair. The swirling between her thighs increased. She would have felt the rush of sexual gratification if she hadn't felt the fear.

CHAPTER 75

"That's it, Laddie. Take your time. You're always in such a rush. Move in circles. Seduce her and this time it will work. Can you feel it?"

I hear Malachai's voice, but once again I can't see him through the brown sludge. But I feel her, her energy, her sex. And I feel like I'm beginning to enter her again, only not just her bottom. I'm feeling points of connection from her forehead, her chest, her stomach and her loins. It's all coming together. I'll soon be in her, soon be her.

"That's right. Slowly. I have so many to teach. But they're all watching. Watching you for instruction. So do it right, Laddie, just like I tell you. Now a little closer, a little deeper. Deeper.

"She's moving now, because it's not what she wants. Yet. But soon she will be gone and you will be there, inside, living again. That's what you want, isn't it?"

More than anything Malachai. More than you know. I want this body and its pleasures. I'm beginning to feel it now. Now....

CHAPTER 76

It feels so good, Mara thought. Hot, sexual, but more than that. Like she was wanted, needed.

There was also something wrong.

She was feeling crowded, being pushed, being moved out of her shell. He—she realized that whatever was touching her, making her feel this way—was a male, and that's why she fought it. But the energy was insistent, muscling its way, like big shoulders, invasive fingers, hurried thrusts and bumps. He's too far in, she thought, and began to panic. I'm losing, I'm being squeezed out of my own body.

"Mara!"

From somewhere in the distance, she heard her name. Or did she?

"Mara! Stop. Get out of there!"

It sounded like Sage. Mara opened her eyes and saw the curtain drawn back. The blue column had turned a deep indigo and was huge between her legs, almost halfway in. She felt hands on her shoulders, being lifted from the chair. The indigo mass retreated to the mirror, shrunk, and vanished inside it. Mara felt Sage pull her from the necrotorium into the cellar.

"What happened?" Mara felt exhausted, weak, though she had been sitting the whole time. "What time is it?"

Sage was holding her tight against her. She felt the softness of her breasts and belly and smelled cinnamon from her hair.

"Mara. I stopped by and your door was unlocked. I heard noises coming from the cellar and I knew you were in trouble. The growling and animal noises were so loud. It was what I thought. Come on. Let's get out of here."

Sage led Mara to the stairs, then up. She sat Mara down in her kitchen and turned the stove on under the teapot.

"You'll be okay, now."

"What just happened? I was trying to get more information from Dr. Fisher, and something happened. It felt like I was being crowded out, pushed out of my own body. Sage, what happened?"

"I should have known. I should have picked up on the timeline. It's all coming together now.

"Samhain." Sage pronounced it *Sow-an*. "It's the end of October. Samhain is today. From sunset on October 31 until sunset on November 1. The time when the veil is thinnest. When the dead can change places with the living more easily."

Mara's head was still coming up from the depths of the necrotorium. Bits and pieces of what Sage was saying were starting to register.

"Wait. This *sowan* you're talking about. October 31, that's Halloween, right?" And that's today, Mara remembered. I've been so busy, I hadn't even thought about the date.

"Halloween is a sanitized version of Samhain. The original holiday started God-knows-when. Some say in Ireland before it was Ireland. Some date it to pagan rituals. There are ancient structures, tombs considered passages to the Underworld—or Otherworld—that are aligned with the sunrise at Samhain. On a rise called Tara in Ireland there is such a tomb, ominously named The Mound of Hostages. Samhain predates writing, which obviously goes pretty far back. It comes from herders who brought their livestock in from the pastures before winter set in, chose those that were to be culled, and began the slaughter."

"So it's just a calendar event, a demarcation between fall and winter?"

"Much more than that. The veil between this world and the next is the thinnest at that date. The boundary between the two worlds could be crossed with ease by spirit energies and the gods, good and evil.

"Oh, come on now Sage. That's all just a silly superstition."

Sage continued, not even acknowledging Mara's comment.

"Souls, remnants of the deceased, were believed to come home and the living felt compelled to feed the hungry ghosts. If they were not appeased, they would steal the living and take them back with them to the realm of the dead. That's where disguising one's self comes from, so the dead relatives cannot recognize you and take you with them. It wasn't until the 800s that Christianity hijacked the date from the pagans and sanitized it into 'All Saints'

Day.' Believe me, its roots are far more sinister than a children's playtime. It was—is—a festival for the dead."

The tea was steeping in front of Mara. She watched the steam rise and inhaled the smell of chamomile. Sage continued.

"Tales tell of the undead, horse-mounted messengers from the god of the dead. Archaeologists have found mummified humans in Ireland that appear to be royalty sacrificed as a ritual and tossed to sink into the bogs. There's a myth that challenges anyone courageous enough to tie a ribbon around the ankle of a man freshly executed by hanging. Demons are involved as protectors of the dead man who somehow comes back to life.

"Sex is also involved."

Mara suddenly perked up.

"A phantom warrior queen named Morrigu, who is associated with one's fate in battle, has sex with the Druid chieftain Dagda, who allegedly ruled over a supernatural race. Morrigu apparently required him to have sex with her before she would give him a victorious battle plan for defeating his mortal enemies. The sex was consummated on Samhain."

A few sips of tea and Mara's head had started to clear. Her writer's skepticism kicked in. "Sage, are you trying to tell me that there is a specific *time* during the year that is more dangerous than any other and that I should be careful because the dead can come and get me?"

"I'm just giving you the history of the date. As far as the reality of it is concerned, I think there is something to a passage between dimensions; your friend Dr. Landry said as much. The ancients felt there were natural portals that occur in the earth. You can still find them at sacred places around the planet. There's the Cave of the Cats in Ireland where supernatural beings emerge from the earth during Samhain. There's a known portal in Pennsylvania. That's why I'm concerned about this house. Before this was a battlefield, what else could it have been? In fact, what if it had been fated all along to be a battlefield? That all these men had been drawn here to this specific place just to meet their deaths?"

Sage's back was turned, pouring another cup of tea for herself. She swung back to face Mara.

"Mara, we're talking about midnight, tonight. Just a few hours from now. This is a ticking time bomb for spirit invasion. The worst part is I'm seeing them in masses of spirits, in legions.

"And what if the portal in your house is in the process of opening up? Can you think of a scientific reason for a portal between dimensions right here?"

Mara flashed back to what had opened up when she saw into the hospital scene from the elevator. She suddenly remembered her discussion with Katherine and Torres. Two thoughts entered her mind, one more frightening than the other.

Was Ricard Fisher attempting to tell her exactly how *she* could pass between dimensions?

Was there someone else—something else—that had also found the portal to her?

CHAPTER 77

Sage had left and Mara had just begun typing when Oscar's smiling face flashed in her head and another serious crying jag had her reaching for the entire box of tissues. As the tears rolled, she heard herself talking out loud. "What kind of a screwed-up place is this life, anyway? We work, we sleep, we love, only to end up with nothing. No future, no memories, no past, nothing left to show for it." She almost wished Sage's image of a dwelling-place for the dead was true.

Her mind went out to the fields of slaughter surrounding the house, and she saw it from kind of a drone's eye view: floating across the lush verdant valleys once corrupted by the foul slain, banking along the hillsides used by fate as anvils, hammering men's lives into tiny fragments, souls sparking off into the black abyss, then descending into the very cellar below her, not long ago the crude sarcophagus of young men plunged into extinction, decomposing in those hideous holes, lives cut short by other young men who are now moldering in graves themselves.

She thought about the site nearby where men fought in trenches through the pouring rain, trampling the wounded and the dead together underfoot and how the corpses became mere clotted gore, lumps of meat you'd see at a butcher. The dead struck by bullets time and time again, over and over, and eventually chopped into hash, no longer appearing anything like human but more like gobs of bloody jelly. "What did it get them? Where are they now? Nowhere. Nothing." *Nada. Nada.*

Blotting her lashes and tossing the tissue at the trash can, she thought: I've got to get this bio done. *For Oscar.* For all the help he gave me on it. For his friendship over the years. For understanding. For not being a Rex. Or a Brad.

Her phone rang. She picked it up and looked at the number. It was Brad. She threw it back down on the kitchen table.

No. Wait. I've had enough. I've been through enough. I'll talk to him.

"Yeah."

"Mara? Finally! I thought you had lost your phone or something. I've been trying to reach you for a couple of days now."

"Yeah." Silence.

"Sounds like you're still in the middle of that chapter you said you were working on."

"No. I've got time to talk. Especially about the other night."

She swore she could hear him talking through a smile.

"Yeah. That was fun, wasn't it?"

Again, silence. Mara seethed.

"Mara?"

"You call raping me fun? You call bruising me, biting me, hurting me fun? You son-of-a-bit...."

"Mara. What are you talking about? If you're mad because I left, I got a call and I didn't want to wake you."

"No. It was when you came back. You're just like the others. Suddenly you think you can...."

"Mara. What *are* you talking about? I never came back. My brother called. He said he'd gotten a call about a fire at his shop and wanted me to come over. It was a false alarm, and I went home after. I didn't want to disturb you."

Mara's thoughts flew through her head like leaves in a fall storm. Is he lying? It would be easy enough to check the fire log in the paper. But if he didn't come back, what about the bruises and bite marks? Where did those come from?

"You didn't come back and try to have sex with me?"

"No. I wouldn't do that. I think there's been a misunderstanding. Oh, damn. Hang on. I'm getting a text from Jerry."

If Brad didn't come back, what the hell happened?

"Hey, babe. I gotta go. We can talk about this later. You okay?"

"Yeah. Yeah, Brad. I'll be okay."

But until she found out what had happened to her the other night, she knew she wouldn't be.

CHAPTER 78

Reynolds was chomping away noisily at his dinner as Mara sat at her computer with her sixth—or was it her seventh—cup of coffee for the day. *It's okay,* she thought. *I've got to get this done even if I'm up all night. I'm so close to finishing....*

But after fifteen minutes of writing and backspacing over what she just wrote, she put her head in her hands and rubbed her eyes. She looked at the pile of folders on the table before her and thought: *Maybe a bit of cleaning up will help.*

As she stacked Ricard Fisher's folders and picked them up from the table, she was startled by a clatter on the floor. It was a flashdrive, apparently fallen out of one of the folders. *I don't remember seeing that in any of the folders the first time I went through them.*

A thought passed through her mind that, like the newspaper and voices on her recorder and dream visitations, Ricard had dropped this drive into her world from another dimension. *Don't be an idiot. He's dead. He can't do any of that stuff.*

Mara picked the drive up, turned it over in her hand. "What the hell," she said to Reynolds, and sat back down at her computer. Plugging the drive in, she waited for it to register and clicked the icon. Only one file was on it. A video, so she clicked it.

In a moment there was Ricard and Eleanor sitting in his apartment. She turned the volume up and began to listen to their discussion.

"Are you willing to be my sounding board?"

"Eleanor. You know I am. Since we were children, when no one else understood you, who had been your closest confidant?"

Obviously, this video was made sometime in the recent past, while Ricard was still alive and before Eleanor was plunged into mourning. Mara saw Eleanor smile warmly at her famous brother.

The lights on his sculpture garden were dimmed. It was as if they had an inanimate audience for their meeting.

"I just want to see if this makes as much sense to you as it does to me."

She blew on the surface of the tea he'd just handed her, took a sip and began to talk. Mara felt a little like an eavesdropper.

"The energy that still exists even at absolute zero, as you know, is the Zero-Point Field. I postulate that all electromagnetic waves are propagated through it."

From her talks with Mitch, Sage, Katherine and Dr. Torres, Mara knew that was the "ZPF" in much of Ricard's work, plastered all over his files.

"Eleanor. Are you suggesting something akin to the ancient concept of the 'aether'? You know that the Michelson-Morley Experiment supposedly debunked the theory of an omniscient, invisible substance through which all waves propagate."

"And you know, my dear brother, that their experiment measured the so-called 'ether' as if it were a liquid or a gas and *not* electromagnetically-based. It was flawed."

Ricard Fisher smiled a cocked grin. Eleanor continued.

"And I feel that through the ZPF, because of the vast variations of frequencies and the potentials for resonance, certain types of energy may be transmigrating to other dimensions."

"Are you talking about a wormhole into another dimension?"

"Yes. Exactly."

"Well." Mara watched Ricard begin shaking his head. "It is my understanding that wormholes are for outer space and that creating one requires more energy than is currently available on earth. That, my dear sister, is a tall order."

Eleanor stood and walked to one of the several white-boards on easels facing the camera and drew a series of wave-peaks and valleys and horizontal lines indicating—Mara wasn't sure what. She could practically smell the sweet odor of the marker-pen ink from her undergrad days as Eleanor sketched and talked.

"We may not be talking about the same type of wormhole. If the Zero-Point Field is the medium that propagates wave energy, couldn't the same forces occurring in a liquid medium potentially occur in an ethereal, electromagnetic medium? Whirlpools, vortexes, and waves. Is it possible that some of these could combine to create enough energy to develop passages through which certain unique energies—if tuned to the right harmonic frequencies—can move to leave as well as enter this plane we're on? Like a whirlpool can take us to the depths of the ocean."

Ricard scrunched up his face at her proposal. "I rather doubt it. But please continue your analogy. Could this be taking us where I think it is?"

With her back to Ricard, Eleanor scrawled some calculations on the board with powers to huge numbers. Mara heard the staccato tapping of the marker pen on the board as she spoke.

"As you know, Ricard, the Zero-Point Field occupies the space between everything: between the particles in atoms and between the cosmos. Quite literally an infinite amount of space in which energy may reside—small amounts, granted, but quadrillions of times over.

"That the Zero-Point Field is electromagnetically-based we know. As well, we know that animal physical and mental activity is electrically-based, thereby gives off electromagnetic waves. In the proper environment, perhaps during meditation, as when yogis claim to travel out of their bodies, or during extreme stress, one creates one's own miniature whirlpool, or vortex, or super-wave in the Zero-Point Field using harmonic frequencies of electromagnetism.

"And death is just such a unique experience, a one-of-a-kind moment. I believe bodily energy frequencies have been biologically selected to align themselves at death with universal frequencies to allow human remnant-energy to seamlessly pass into another dimension."

"'Biologically selected'? As in Darwin? Over millennia?" Ricard gave her his best skeptical look. Clearly, Mara thought, he wasn't buying her theory.

"This, I believe, is how human residual energies are continually being removed from earth to another dimension, a 'spirit plane,' if you will, in strict obedience to the laws of thermodynamics—that energy can never be lost or destroyed but remains a constant in the universe."

Mara saw Ricard stand and begin pacing, apparently to facilitate his thought processes. He stopped next to a marble statue of a nude woman.

"It sort of smacks of Eastern religions," he said. *"Religion,"* he re-emphasized.

"Yes. As a matter of fact, of thousands of years of Eastern religious beliefs. As I mentioned, yogis have meditated themselves into death-like trances and claim to have traveled inter-dimensionally. For now, return to my liquid analogy with me and let us reverse the process. Have you ever heard of 'super-waves'?"

"Of course. Tsunamis."

"Not exactly. A tsunami is the tidal wave generated by an undersea earthquake or volcano. A super-wave happens when, just by chance, in the infinite randomness of waves rising and falling, perhaps with the pull of un-anticipated celestial forces, suddenly their frequencies harmonize and produce one huge wave replete with massive amounts of energy."

Again she drew more waves on the board, some intersecting with others and amplifying their magnitude. Mara heard more tapping, an occasional squeak from the pen.

"If that sort of thing happens fairly often in the ocean, I propose the same could happen in the ethereal ocean, the Zero-Point Field. When the conditions are just right, it could be a huge event that opens the portal in reverse and lets energy pass between dimensions.

Her brother just sat and looked at her, running his finger around the rim of his teacup.

"Am I boring you, Ricci?"

"No, dear sister. Just wondering: is there a purpose for this?"

Mara thought: *Just what I was about to ask.*

"The greatest question—fear—of mankind is what happens after death. I think using the energy I spoke of before—to be proven by further calculations—it would be possible for a human being to die, continue to do research and send that research back to living humans so they may gain the greatest knowledge of all. I propose that the human crossing over into this dimension be called a 'necronaut,' or 'death traveler.' I believe also, as I'm certain my calculations will soon prove, that this necronaut, if the energy is created and all alignments are calculated, may return from death through that wormhole unscathed."

Ricard Fisher sat staring at his sister. Mara could not tell whether the look on his face indicated complete rejection of this radical proposal or admiration. Then he broke into derisive laughter. "Necronaut? What a silly title. Especially for what you are proposing. Do you know what you're saying? Do you know what you are asking this so-called 'necronaut' to do?"

Mara saw Eleanor physically recoil from Ricard's rebuff. "I'm not asking just *anyone* to become the world's first necronaut. I wouldn't ask someone to do anything I wouldn't do."

Mara heard herself say out loud—"Well?"—during the extra-long pause before Ricard asked, "You're *not* going to publish this anytime soon are you? I'm sure the world is not quite ready for it."

"No, it's too soon. I have more calculations and experimentation to finish. But *this* may be the final connection, science to spirit, that this weary world needs."

Ricard shook his head again. "I am skeptical, to say the least."

"More thought experiments?"

"More than just thought experiments, I'm afraid."

"Yes. And some real laboratory experiments. Would you care to help?"

"No, Eleanor. I'm afraid your little theory is going to need much more proof to get me involved. Are you going to continue work on it? Finding and training your so-called necronaut?"

To Mara, Eleanor seemed resolved. "Certainly, Ricard. Just let me get through this little surgery I have coming up and I'll be anxious to get to work."

"More tea, dear sister?"

"Only if you wish me to float away."

Mara watched as Eleanor and Ricard stood and walked out of camera-range. She could not hear what they were saying, but heard the heavy door to Fisher's apartment close. He walked back into the camera frame, up to the camera.

As he fumbled around trying to find the record button to turn it off Mara began to realize he had been recording their conversation without Eleanor's knowledge.

Mara heard him say, under his breath, "Necronauts. Oh my brilliant, naïve sister. Thanks for providing me with my next ground-breaking theory which should bring me…."

The scene went to black.

So that, at least, gave Mara a time line as to when their meeting took place—sometime just before Eleanor had her surgery.

It also made her realize where some of Ricard Fisher's genius came from.

But more frightening was the scientific link to the conversation she'd had with Sage not too long ago, about the ancient acknowledgment of Samhain and the thinning of the veil between the living and the dead. What did Sage say? The legions of dead.

And how easy it would be for them to cross it.

CHAPTER 79

Mara was finally getting around to washing the mugs she and Sage had used for tea when her phone rang. By the time she dried her hands and reached the phone Lillian had left a message. Mara put the phone on speaker and played it back.

"Okay, kiddo. This is it. You're not going to believe this, but Sonye Productions called. Yeah. The movie studio. They've heard about your book and they want to option it. Something in the low six figures. But they'll only deal if…I got another call coming in. You know what to do."

Mara shook her head. One thought flashed:

Dr. Faustus calling.

CHAPTER 80

At a dead end.
That's exactly where I am.
I've been sitting here for two and a half hours staring at my screen, typing and wearing out my backspace button. This is worse than writer's block. I can't create, I can't even think.
Some writer you are. You get a serious deadline, with some serious money on the line and you can't compose one decent sentence. Mara, what the hell is wrong with you?

She stood up and looked at the coffee maker. The taste of too many cups was already wicked in her mouth. She kicked an empty box across the kitchen. All that did was scare Reynolds who sulked into the living room.

Goddamn! What is it? Why can't I write? It's the big paycheck I've been waiting for.
Why do I feel so crappy about it? And why can't I write?
I know. Because it's a deal with the devil. Faustian. The last thing I thought about after I heard Lillian's message. I can't write a half-assed book. But I need the money. What do I do?

She leaned her head against the doorframe.
What do I do, Pop-pop?

Her eye found the small digital recorder lying partially covered by a file folder. She reached down and picked it up. *I know. I'll ask Pop-pop. Here's his chance to help me.*

She clicked the record button.

"Pop-pop. It's me, Mara. If you're really still around—your spirit, I mean—please say something into this recorder. Please let me know you're here."

She stared at the small, red LED light, hoping to see it blinking, indicating it was recording something she couldn't hear.

It glowed steadily.

"Please, Pop-pop. Let me know you're here. Talk into this recorder. Help me to know, to believe there's something to this book I'm writing. Say anything. Please."

Still, the light burned. No recording. *Damn. This worked with Ricard Fisher not too long ago. At least I thought it did.*

"Oscar. How about you? Come on, O. You can talk to me. Please?"

She stood for a full minute, waiting for something to be recorded, before she hit "stop," then "play."

The only recording was of her own voice, one question after another with no space—and certainly no EVP—in between.

She tossed the recorder down, on top of the files, sat down and put her head in her hands.

You idiot. They're gone, all of them, into oblivion. There's nothing after this. Nothing.

It was as close to a channeling trance as she'd ever been while writing. She had no idea where the words and thoughts came from. She was writing from somewhere out of her mind, from a consciousness pool that seemed to seep into her brain and trickle out through her fingertips. It seemed like someone else was typing. She thought about something a fellow writer had once said about the creative act: *God does the writing; I just pick up the royalty checks.*

That's how the last few minutes felt.

She stopped, scrolled back up to the top of the screen, and began to read.

> *...but even after all the research, all the scientists and physicists and neuro-biologists and psychologists and spiritualists and realists I've talked to, it's still not enough, still not explained, still remains supernatural, mystical, magical, miraculous. It still boils down to simple, pure, childlike faith, and I still don't know for sure: With death as the inevitable, inexorable end, why are we here? Why do we humans even exist? For what purpose other than to give birth to another lineage just to feed the grave themselves. Never mind that we all die. If there is nothing that comes after death, why are we even born?*

CHAPTER 81

Once again deep into the reverie known only to writers, artists, sculptors and saints, Mara was startled when her phone rang. She looked at the clock. She had missed dinner.

"Hello?"

"Ms. McKay?"

"Yes?"

"It is Eleanor Fisher, Ricard's sister."

Mara was stunned.

"I think I'd like to talk to you again." Then, a long pause while Mara shook off the shock.

"Why now?" Mara said it and immediately regretted it thinking Eleanor might take it the wrong way. "I mean, what changed your mind?"

"I've been reviewing some information…Ricard began to video his notes and thoughts on experiments before performing them…this is hard to explain. I was going through his things and found the last notes he videoed. I think it may shed some light on Ricard's final actions. Would you be interested in seeing it?"

"Yes. Absolutely. Just name the time and the place."

"The university library. Is eight o'clock all right?"

Mara looked at her watch. Twenty minutes. Just enough time to get there, if she hurries. "Yes. I'll be there."

Eleanor hung up. Mara stared at her cell phone. Odd as she was, Eleanor was perhaps now willing to share just the information Mara needed to fill in Ricard Fisher's personality for her book.

Her book.

She patted Reynolds on the head, tossed her notebooks and recorder into her pack, and grabbed the three hundred and twenty-seven page manuscript she had printed out from the kitchen table.

The heavy door to the old house slammed behind her. Outside the door, she lifted the lid to the garbage can and recoiled at the potpourri of smells, of rotten vegetables turned into dark sour-smelling soup and fish into putrid gag-inducing gas.

Into the can she chucked the manuscript.

CHAPTER 82

Driving to the library, passing groups of miniature trick-or-treaters haunting the sidewalks, Mara recalled Sage's explanation of Samhain. Our innocent child's holiday of Halloween had sinister beginnings. Like all folklore, it had to have its roots in real events.

What Katherine, Dr. Torres, Mitch, Sage and—in essence—Ricard Fisher had shown her gave a scientific basis for travel into another dimension. She was struck by one life-shaking thought: Is that what happens when we die? Is that other dimension what we call Heaven?

Or Hell?

She found a parking space near the library. Her phone rang.

"Hey, good looking."

She looked down at herself. "Hi, Brad." I sure don't feel good looking right now, she thought.

"You'll never guess where I am."

"I give up."

"I'm in your favorite elevator, in the library."

"What?"

"I decided to investigate on my own. And...you're not going to believe this."

"Brad, what are you doing?"

"The doors just opened." His voice suddenly became serious. "I can't believe what I'm seeing. It's unreal."

"Brad! Don't...not tonight!"

"Mara, it's the operating room. From a hundred and fifty years ago. The blood. The smell is awful...."

"Brad, stay out of there. Do not...."

Mara's phone began to crackle and hiss.

"Brad!"

"I've got...see...there's...oh, God...."

"Brad! No!"
The connection went dead.

CHAPTER 83

Mara's backpack hooked on the door into the library ripping it off her shoulder and dumping it on the floor. "Shit," she said. It echoed through the quiet library. "Not now. Not now," she mumbled. *I've got to get to that elevator.*

She squat-shuffled across the floor, gathering bits and pieces of her life she just couldn't bring herself to discard: scraps of paper with notes on them, a half-dozen different colored sticky note pads, some thumb-drives holding God-knows-what. Her phone rang.

"Yeah?"

"Mara. It's Mitch. Hey, I was wondering if you'd like to get together for...."

"Mitch! Man, wrong time to call. Totally wrong time. I'm late for an appointment, just dropped my backpack. I can't even talk right now."

"Uh, okay. I'll give you a call...."

"Yeah. Bye."

One of Fisher's notes had glided across the polished marble floor. Mara looked at it as she started to cram it back in her pack. It was one of the last entries in his paranormal journal, dated a few days before he died. Folded over, only a couple of words were visible to Mara.

It's...reenactment...teach...load and fire...musket....

Mara started to unfold the paper with one hand as she juggled her pack into place over her shoulder and started walking.

It's a good thing E and I went to the Civil War reenactment demonstrations. Nice of them to teach her how to load and fire the musket. It gives us an idea of how.... The note ended.

Mara looked up. There was E—Eleanor—standing in front of the information desk, looking prim in her dress and short jacket.

"Eleanor. I'm glad you decided to meet with me here. I just found out I needed to come to the library anyway."

To Mara, Eleanor seemed as aloof and emotionally elusive as ever. But tonight her eyes seemed especially deep, bottomless. Mara started moving toward the elevator. Eleanor followed.

"Miss McKay. Perhaps we can find a spot upstairs somewhere in the stacks where we can talk."

They got in the elevator and Mara reached for the button, but Eleanor beat her to it and pushed the button for the third floor where there was a lounge area. *Shit,* Mara thought.

The doors opened to a lounge area with a table and four chairs. Eleanor pulled one of the chairs out for Mara and sat in the other next to her. She pulled a laptop from her bag.

"It's one of Ricci's note videos. He began doing that a lot. Sadly, it turned into his epitaph, so to speak."

"Eleanor, I hate to sound rude, but there's something I have to do. Will this take long?"

"No. It's only a few minutes."

CHAPTER 84

Mara squirmed in the hard-bottomed, slat-backed wooden library chair next to Eleanor. On the large table before them Eleanor placed her laptop.

"Ricci began to video his notes to review and refine them," she said. "This is apparently the last one he made. I found it earlier today. I knew you would be interested."

As Eleanor's computer warmed up, Mara called Brad. It rang until his voicemail came on. Frustrated, she ended the call.

The video came up on the screen showing Fisher with his head down, adjusting something under the desk. He cleared his throat and lifted his head. Mara thought: There's the face that, for lack of a better term, has been haunting me since I moved here. Fisher began to speak.

"For the last twenty months I have been working on the most controversial aspect of physics I have known: the concept of the survival of some part of the human being after the cessation of biological life. This quest has forced me to explore the paranormal and spiritual realms and subject them to the rigors of science and experimentation. It has led me to some remarkable conclusions."

Oh, Ricci. Sublime Ricci. Dearest brother Ricci. With your magnificent mind, you explored the great, unanswered question of mankind since the beginning of time: What lies beyond death?

Mara watched Eleanor move closer to the screen, as if trying to overcome the great, impenetrable wall death had placed between her and her brother. Her emotional investment was obvious.

"Human spirit energy exists. It was my study of our Civil War that convinced me there is more to this life than matter. The energy of the human spirit can be measured and recorded. I and others have documented sounds, visual apparitions, and have recorded electromagnetic surges in particular places associated with violence and trauma."

Leaving me behind, you now have proven to the world your pinnacle intellectual achievement, one to light the way for all who follow. Where Einstein left off, where all the others were thwarted, you succeeded in formulating and proving the unification of matter and energy.

Again, thought Mara, the faraway look I saw during our interview, the mourning that still goes on and will go on until she dies. Eleanor's mood is catching. Talk about depressed. What the hell did I just do, tossing the manuscript? What the hell has happened to me since I got to this damned town? And now what's happened to Brad?

"Travel between dimensions occurs. Eastern yogis proved that, through meditation, inter-dimensional travel is possible. Near death experiences have proven travel to another dimension—and retuning to this one—are both possible. Humans have believed in it for eons, the crossing over of spirit from the earthly plane to whatever comes after. It's just recently, though, that we have been able to measure and record cross-dimensional transference of energy, sounds, apparitions and even the passing of information. The next step should be obvious."

Yes, Ricci. We knew each other's thoughts so closely. How I practically created your concepts on immortality, on inter-dimensional passage, how I understood so well what you had to do, and how I knew what you needed that night.

"And in fact, I was preparing to use myself as the first necronaut—death journeyer—to confirm that my calculations and theories were correct, that information can be sent from another dimension to the one in which we presently exist, and a necronaut can return safely from that other dimension."

I saw you tie together dimensions, mathematize death, take faith out of religious mythology and replace it with pure scientific reason. I saw you aspire to the knowledge and power of the gods and grasp it. Though most of the praise should have been mine, and you ridiculed me for my work, still I helped.

It's painful, thought Mara, watching her watch this video. I can see anger on her face—anger at losing her brother. But, it's more than that. I see anger because of something else that I just can't place.

Mara hit the redial button on her phone. Eleanor was too absorbed to notice. Come on, Brad, answer. Her call went to voicemail again.

"Inter-dimensional travel takes more than just an application of energy. It takes a super-wave of energy and the rare frequency resonance that seems to be present at the moment of death. In particular, a violent, sudden, unexpected death."

You have sacrificed yourself for the sin of ignorance. You have given life to increase knowledge in the world. You took science to an art form and you died for your art. You, Ricci. You, my dearest, dearest brother.

"But after all, my calculations seem to be wrong. I checked and re-checked. There is something more that is needed, something more than mere mathematics, matter and tangibles. Some things of this world, but not in it. So, I must call off my experiment for now. The play Eleanor and I were to enact later, to bring my fear and denial to an emotional pique must be postponed until I can learn more, calculate more from this side. I've realized that we—ISAP—will need at least another year to perfect the trans-dimensional communication we will need."

No, Ricci. My calculations were correct. You took— stole—my concept, yet didn't trust my calculations. You should have....

Mara felt more depressed than ever. The work that Ricard was to do was supposed to prove, without a doubt, that there was life after death, and perhaps help perfect communications between the dimensions. Now he's dead before he could work it all out, the energy, the frequencies, the...whatever. So, even the greatest mind of our generation couldn't crack the code.

Mara's phone rang. It was Brad. She answered and heard the crackle of a bad connection again.

Ricard Fisher paused in recording his notes to take a quick drink of water.

Mara stood and called Brad's number back. It rolled to voicemail.

"Eleanor," Mara said to the side of Eleanor's head. So engrossed was she with the video that she didn't even turn.

"Eleanor, how much longer? I've got to...."

"Just another few seconds."

And dear Ricci, for you I helped move others out of the way. The pesky policeman who had to come to the apartment and threatened to expose your grand experiment and my role in it. He had to go. I helped with that, too.

"It is unfortunate. Eleanor and I had it all planned, how she was to help me pass through to the next dimension, to travel suddenly, violently, so that the energies were as high as they could get."

Mara perked up at the statement. Eleanor was to help? What does that mean? Help him pass to the next dimension? Does that mean what I think it does? She hit redial again. Still no answer. Brad, I really need you.

"I hear Eleanor entering the front door from here in the back room. I'll have to suspend my recording for now. I need to tell her we must postpone our experiment, my journey, until I have completed the research."

Eleanor was there. At his murder.

The video ended. I need to get back to the elevator, Mara thought. I need Brad.

Oh, Ricci. No. We had planned it out so that your death would come suddenly, unexpectedly, quickly, like some soldier on the battlefield. My calculations were correct, weren't they? Weren't they?

"Fascinating, Eleanor," Mara prodded. Will she say something incriminating? "Although from that first viewing, I'm not sure I can determine exactly why he committed suicide."

Ricard Fisher's sister stood, calmly closed the laptop, turned and started toward the elevator. "I shall send you a copy."

And we, Lassie, will make sure she never sees it again.

CHAPTER 85

Even her voice, thought Mara, seems to have changed. *Faster, Eleanor. I've got to get to the cellar.*

They entered the elevator and Mara reached for the button, but Eleanor beat her to it and pushed the button for the basement instead of the first floor. A fortunate mistake, Mara thought. The doors closed and she felt the sudden weightlessness as the elevator began to descend.

And now I must remove the shallow, pathetic writer. She who wants to write only the first layer of your—our— work, dear Ricci, who has no reason to show, to utilize the deeper, other-dimensional layer you—we—worked so hard to prove. She wants to ignore the real you and the accolades that you deserve. She wants to ignore me as well. She, too, must go.

What's that? Is that my voice I'm hearing?

"And now, Lassie, I will help."

Then came the smell, an otherworldly fetidness, flooding Mara's nose with odors of rancid flesh and moldering marrow. "Oh, my God," she gasped. "Where did that come from?" She gagged, turned to Eleanor and saw the source.

Before her was not the prissy college intellectual she had set out to meet. Something was wrong. Eleanor was physically morphing before her eyes.

Her face was taking on rough, lined, masculine features. The brow thickened, her skin darkened, her eyes slitted. Coarse hairs sprouted from her swarthy chin.

Mara backed to the wall. "Oh, God. Eleanor?"

A calloused, dirty hand seized Mara by the throat and slammed her against the side of the elevator. Struggling to breathe, she ripped at the hand. It smelled of rancid pork and old urine. Mara tried to scream but she couldn't get enough air into her lungs. She tore at the hand with her fingernails, but Eleanor's grip tightened. She leaned closer to Mara's face.

Through hazy, narrowing sight, Mara saw Eleanor's face continued to contort, her chin lengthening to a point, her eyes moving closer together, her hair becoming a hoary, gray, clotted mass whipping around her face.

Mara felt a woolen-clad knee jam between her thighs and heard the zipper tear as the other rough hand ripped her jeans open from waist to crotch. The hand was now against her, the fingers like sandpaper scraping inside.

No. No! I don't want to die! I can't die. It's too soon. Too quick.

Mara smelled the sour breath as Eleanor's face pressed against hers. Eleanor's expression darkened, demon-like.

Another malevolent figure was joining Eleanor. The two figures morph into unspeakable, unrecognizable, indefinable creatures. Mara heard a rasp in a ragged hoarseness, *"I...will...be...you."*

The words were familiar. They were on her recorder. But now the fear of the moment for Mara was subsiding, fading to helpful unconsciousness. From somewhere in her being she felt that it would be so easy just to sleep now. Just to sleep.

To sleep.

CHAPTER 86

I float across the ceiling of the elevator, seeing Eleanor and my body below. Eleanor is unrecognizable. She looks like a man with dark, grizzled, hairy cheeks and large humped shoulders. She reaches down, tries to drag me out of the elevator. Suddenly she stops and grabs me roughly and tries to pull me out of my jeans.

I glance outside the elevator and it's the scene from my first night here: the gory, blood-spattered hospital. Squirming, writhing men in contorted postures, and three or four in crimson-stained, dirty aprons walk around. There, in the back, I recognize Ricard Fisher in his lab coat. And, nearer the elevator, beautiful, handsome Brad.

What's that at the top of the elevator? Brightness comes from above.

A large hole in the ceiling radiates light. I want to go there. I have to go there. I hear a humming, a buzzing, like high-tension wires. Low vibrations turn into tinkling bells and music, and change into a soft, melodic chant.

I move upward through the hole in the ceiling into a beautiful, luminous tunnel.

I recognize hazy places, things, softly focused faces—people, I think. Forms. Individuals coming out of the walls of the tunnel. And an animal.

Rocky, my Labrador Retriever. He died when I was fifteen. He's leaping and playing and trotting to me. I feel tears well up. And behind him, Aunt Bella, smiling her beautiful smile. And Bobby. Bobby, my love from high school, killed in Afghanistan three years ago. They said they couldn't open the coffin because there wasn't enough left of his face to reconstruct, but there he is, fine, healthy, whole, as handsome as I remember. I start to say something to him, but there is another being coming. I know who it is. My grandmother. She died when I was two years old. I'd never known her, but I know it is she, not from her face, but from her spirit, her essence, her energy.

There are layers I see, feel I have to pass through. And other beings made of bright energy who somehow I just know. They are old friends and soul mates, guides to show me where to go.

I'm approached by an energy, a being made entirely of...light. It's loving and warm. I can feel it, and for some reason I think it is male. He says nothing. I can't hear but *feel* questions about my life.

I'm analyzing what I've done, what I've accomplished. I can see all of it, a vast panorama of my life from the earliest moments, like a replay, making me evaluate in a flash what transpired, how I've handled it, how I've treated other souls with whom I've interacted. Is it good, how I've lived?

Then, I recognize another being of light.

I can finally speak.

"Pop-pop. I've missed you so much."

"Yes, baby," I can't really hear but rather feel it coming from him. "I missed you too, honey-child."

I want more than anything I've ever wanted to rush to him and the others, through this beautiful gateway of light, but I am stopped. I look down and see a strange silver cord trailing from me down to my body, still being toiled over by Eleanor. I want to cut it, to tear it away, but I can't. I try to touch it but my hand goes right through it.

I feel a tug, then harder, a pulling energy. There's another place I'm forced toward, darker, sinister, evil. I can barely see into it, but what I see horrifies me. There are shadows moving along the tunnel, from the light into that darkness. I instinctively know they are the walking shadows of displaced souls. In the muddy darkness where they are headed I see some things scattered about. They are tiny shriveled souls, curled up around themselves, like desiccated worms.

It enters your body, replaces your soul and takes you over. It lives as you, deceiving until it can do harm....

It's Sage's voice. I'm hearing what she said.

I look down and see my body. I see the blackness I'm being forced toward.

"But I don't want to go to that. Pop-pop, help me."

I cannot see his face, but I feel the oppressive sadness emanating from him. I try to reach out. He fades. "Pop-pop," I cry.

I look down and see the silver cord turn dark, brown, black. Part of me, my energy, is fading, getting hazy as I move toward the murky cavern where I see the dead curled souls. My energy…abandoning me now.

Again, Sage, like a distant echo: *It kills your soul so it can never ever move to the other plane. Your soul is removed and replaced....*

Forever.

I see my body crumpled on the elevator floor, halfway out. The one who took over Eleanor spreads my legs. The other tries to slither between them. I see him begin to enter me, displace my life energy, my soul, and take over. I remember the benign name for this horror: *A walk-in. And it's happening to me....*

I see the black cord grow thinner, into a thread.

I'm moving nearer the curled up, worm-like, abandoned souls.

I look down and see colored, misty wisps, leave my body.

I see a round white orb begin to leave my mouth.

"I got you, Mac."

I recognize the voice right away.

Oscar.

I look down and see the two dark forms explode. The burst is not of light like on earth, but of darkness, blackness, hammering them. Roiling clouds cover my body and the slithering mass that is trying to get in me, possess me, is tossed, thrown out of the muddy cloud and fractures into several pieces, flattened as if stomped, pitched from the elevator into the darkest, bloodiest corner of the cellar. I see Eleanor's body go limp in the distance, tangled in the welter of blood, bones and flesh. I feel a hard tug on the silver cord. I look down, time flashes, things go black.

CHAPTER 87

She was slowly rising to the surface from the bottom of a pool of thick, dark liquid. She could breathe just fine, but her eyes wouldn't open.

"Mara."

What was that? A voice? I'm starting to rise. The liquid is getting easier to move through. It's getting lighter.

"Mara."

Yes. Keep calling my name so I know where to go. I'm rising, rising and it's getting lighter. My eyes aren't as heavy. I want to open them, but I just can't.

"Mara."

Her eyelids began to flutter. She could open her eyes, but everything was hazy, indistinct.

"Mara."

There was the voice again. Over there. She turned her head and got a jolt of pain across the back of her skull. It actually helped her focus on the figure before her. Who is it? *Please let it be somebody I know.*

"Mara."

It was Mitch. She groaned, opened her eyes, and focused.

"Hey, Beautiful."

"Aw. Mitch. You're here." Mara looked around and saw she was in a hospital room. "What the hell?"

Mara tried to lift her head. Again the pain, reminding her she was alive and present in this world. She looked at Mitch.

"Reynolds?"

"I've got him. He's at my house."

She started to get up and Mitch reached over to help her.

"You think you should be getting up?"

"Yeah. Help me get up. I've gotta pee."

She turned to get out of the bed and her eyes unfocused again. She had to grab Mitch's arm. She went to put her arm on the meal tray, but something got in the way. "What's this?"

"I saw your manuscript in the trash. It's a new notebook and pen. I thought you might like to start writing again as soon as you can. I mean, I know how much writing means to you, and...."

She looked up at Mitch and the tears came. "Thanks. You're really sweet. I still gotta pee."

"Here." He helped lift her out of the bed. With him alongside, she walked to the bathroom. She glanced at the mirror as she passed and gasped. Her left eye was blackened and swollen and she had a blue lump on the left side of her forehead. A large cut on her cheek was held together by three butterfly bandages. Her chin looked fine as did her lips. The hospital gown had shifted and she saw a huge bruise on one shoulder and raw welts on her neck. There was a distinct burning on her thighs and between her legs.

"Still think there's no such thing as 'haints?'" she asked, moving her body parts to detect any other injuries.

"Re-thinking."

Looking in the mirror at her purple eye and lumpy head, Mara remembered the first thing Mitch had said when she woke.

"Beautiful, huh?" she turned to Mitch who was smiling. "C'mere."

She pulled his face close to hers and gave him a long, passionate kiss, until it started to hurt her head. "Mitchell Landry. If you still think I'm beautiful looking like this, you're something special. Now get outta here. I *really* gotta pee."

CHAPTER 88

I've been here before. The sludge, the brown muddy air, the wet heat, the screams, pikes with heads and sloughing flesh for faces, bodies in cages, boiling liquid poured down their throats, birdlike creatures pecking out their eyes, eating their guts in strings and defecating it all back upon them.

Fires, and the smell of bloody iron and shit and body parts strewn hither and yon, but still pulsing, moving, below me. Devils whipping naked people, raping helpless women, pressing red hot swords to their naked bodies. Coming for me.

Booming sounds, and blasting like cannon so close the concussion hits hard. And I start to feel the heat.

Like steam from a boiler, scalding against my face, stabbing needles in my eyes and pinpricks where my balls once were. I've got to get out.

There's only one who can help me.

"Malachai! Malachai! Help me!"

"Where are you?

"Malachai. Help! It's Will. Help me!"

Silence.

CHAPTER 89

She finished moving the plush, beige chair against the wall, stood back and looked at it. Then she walked over and cornered it. "Ah," to herself. "Much better."

She had had the metal desk replaced with a mahogany one and the wooden stick-style chairs with three comfortable office chairs that would look just as appropriate in a living room. An antique oak file cabinet stood to the right of the door. A vase with flowers sat atop it.

The once bare walls were now adorned with several colorful prints. Manet and Jean Leon Gerome.

She sat at the desk. The full, brown leather chair faced the door. The desk was free of any paperwork. Just a framed photo of her brother rested on one corner.

There was a knock at the door.

"Come in."

Katherine Bircham's face peeked around the door. "Hello," she said cheerfully, then walked into the office. "I just wanted to officially welcome you to the staff."

"Thank you. I appreciate the visit, Katherine."

Katherine looked around and shook her head. "Wow. What a change. Wood and fabric. And flowers." She moved to the prints. "And artwork. What an interesting choice. Manet's 'Olympia' and 'Execution.'"

"And some Gerome."

"I see. 'Pygmalion and Galatea,' 'Bathers,' and…."

"'The Execution of Marshall Ney.'"

"Do I see a theme here? Female nudes and military executions?"

"It's all I had to spare from home. At least it's better than bare walls."

"So true. Well, I'd better go. I have to be in the lab in ten minutes. Just wanted to wish you good luck. Ricard will be missed. You've got some mighty big shoes to fill, Eleanor." Katherine closed the door behind her.

"I'll do my best," Eleanor said to the closed door.

And, Lassie, I will help.

CHAPTER 90

Another damned funeral.

Mara took Mitch's advice and let him push her in the hospital wheelchair to Oscar's service.

The church was packed with civilians and cops. A small unit of Civil War reenactors dressed in blue uniforms stood guard at the head and foot of the casket. Mara noticed they were all African-American and were listed in the program as "USCT." United States Colored Troops, which Mara knew from her discussions with Oscar about his family.

She could barely see into the flower-draped casket from the wheelchair, only Oscar's handsome profile, so she made Mitch stop and she stood. To Mara, he looked like he had a smile on his face.

The service was almost regal, with grand music echoing through the church, and hymns sung by the mourners. There were some old spirituals, too. The only time Mara began to crack was when Oscar's fifteen-year-old niece, with a voice pure and high, stood and sang "Going Home."

The department chaplain gave an eloquent memorial to "another public servant who gave his last full measure to protect and serve the people he loved."

"So today," he said, and waited for the echo of his voice to fade, "we say our final good bye to Detective Oscar Fosster. No more will we see his like ever again."

As tears streamed down her face, they touched a knowing, joyful smile: Mara was certain he was wrong.

CHAPTER 91

Mara had packed just about everything she'd brought to Virginia. Mitch was kind enough to stop by and help. She noticed he moved slowly, almost reluctantly. *He really doesn't want to see me leave. I'm not so sure I want to, either.* Just one more box. She looked at the trunk and back seat and sighed. Sad, she thought. Everything I need to work, play—live—I can fit in my car. A couple dozen boxes and just enough room for the dog, and I'm good to go.

She looked around the kitchen one last time. At the kitchen table. That's where I was supposed to begin the next phase of my dream. "Ain't this a crazy life?" she asked Reynolds who was already dancing to go out the door.

Mitch came from the living room with a box. "Just this, and that's it."

Mara picked up her phone from the table and realized that someone had called while she had been out packing her car. It was her publisher.

"Hi, Mara. My name is Julia. Lillian's gone to another publisher. I'm your new editor. Call when you can."

"What does that mean?" Mitch asked.

"I guess I'll have to call her." Mara opened the door for him to take the last box out to the car. She realized she had another message. She didn't recognize the area code so she punched the message button.

"Hey, Babe. It's me."

Shit!

"Yeah. I got traded again. You let in four measly goals your first game and suddenly you're not good enough for San Diego. So, I'm back with Cleveland. And Ramona and I are over. Just wanted you to know. You've got my number."

Mara opened the door and walked to her car. Mitch had just put the last box in the trunk and closed it.

"Well. There you go," he said, looking at the packed car. "Quick question."

"Yeah?"

"While you were in the hospital bed, your gown got a little…uh, twisted. And I noticed that cute tattoo you got on your…."

"Yeah," she interrupted. "Um. Can we change the subject?"

"Sure. One other thing. I was hoping…. I mean. I sort of wish…."

"Yeah?"

"You know. Back in the hospital. Maybe that was the drugs they had you on, but…I thought we might…."

The wind blew a couple of bronze strands of hair across Mara's lips. She tucked the hair back behind her ear.

"Mitch. Would you do me a favor?"

"Sure, Mara."

"Grab a couple of those boxes and help me move back in. I'm not so sure I want to leave just yet."

Mara watched as a smile began to spread across Mitch's face.

"I've got a better idea. A beach house I own about a half-hour from here. I go on weekends. It would be a great place to write. And it's not haunted."

"Mitch, you *are* a special friend. I'll take you up on that. But only as long as you charge me rent."

"You got it, Mac."

"Oh, and that tattoo?"

"Yeah?"

"I'm getting it removed tomorrow."

CHAPTER 92

Mara had to blink a couple of times as the sun reflected off the windshield of Mitch's boat tied to the dock below. *What a pleasant, relaxing place to write,* she thought as she looked out the large picture window and her computer flickered to life.

She picked up her digital recorder to finish dictating some mental notes about the paranormal aspects of her subject, Dr. Ricard Fisher, and the supernatural experiences she had been through the last three weeks. This version of the biography would be different than the last version. It would include Fisher's breakthroughs in the field of paranormal studies and her personal experiences.

Amazing what a new editor could do to a writer's confidence.

She got to the part where she had met Brad and paused, recorder still running.

"Brad...Brad...what do I write about you? How do I sum up what could have been? How do I explain what happened to you?"

As she sat partially mesmerized by the diamond glints off the water, she looked at the digital device in her hand and realized it was still recording. She hit stop and replayed what she had just recorded.

Her voice came through loud and clear. Then there was another voice, raspy, in the crackling background.

"No," she said out loud. Reynolds stood and walked into the next room. "Please, no."

Hesitatingly, she replayed it. She could tell the voice was definitely male.

One more play and she counted the syllables. Three.

The words became clear, and the voice.

"I...told...you."

The voice was Brad's.

One word flashed through Mara's mind.

She said it out loud:
"Necronaut."

ABOUT THE AUTHOR

I started my career in Gettysburg as a National Park Service Ranger/Historian back in the 1970s. I knew that I wanted to be a writer, so after five years with the NPS, I got the crazy idea that I should start my own research and writing company. I became fascinated by, and started collecting, the ghost stories of the Gettysburg area. My first *Ghosts of Gettysburg* book came out in 1991. Since then, I have written over twenty books covering topics of historical interest, as well as the paranormal. My stories have been seen on *The History Channel, A&E, The Discovery Channel, The Travel Channel, Unsolved Mysteries, The Biography Channel*, and numerous regional television shows and heard on *Coast to Coast AM*, and regional radio.

In 1994, I started the commercially successful *Ghosts of Gettysburg Candlelight Walking Tours*.

Other books in print and/or ebooks by Mark Nesbitt:
Ghosts of Gettysburg
Ghosts of Gettysburg II
Ghosts of Gettysburg III
Ghosts of Gettysburg IV
Ghosts of Gettysburg V
Ghosts of Gettysburg VI
Ghosts of Gettysburg VII
Ghosts of Gettysburg VIII

Civil War Ghost Trails
A Ghost Hunters Field Guide: Gettysburg & Beyond
Fredericksburg & Chancellorsville: A Ghost Hunters Field Guide

Haunted Pennsylvania
The Big Book of Pennsylvania Ghost Stories

Cursed in Pennsylvania
Cursed in Virginia

Blood & Ghosts: Haunted Crime Scene Investigations
Haunted Crime Scenes

If The South Won Gettysburg
35 Days to Gettysburg: The Campaign Diaries of Two American Enemies (Reprinted as The Gettysburg Diaries: War Journals of Two American Adversaries)
Rebel Rivers: A Guide to Civil War Sites on the Potomac, Rappahannock, York, and James
Saber and Scapegoat: J.E.B. Stuart and the Gettysburg Controversy
Through Blood and Fire: The Selected Civil War Papers of Major General Joshua Chamberlain

Connect with **Mark Nesbitt** on Social Media:
facebook.com/mark.v.nesbitt
twitter.com/hauntgburg
markvnesbitt.wordpress.com
instagram.com/hauntgburg
linkedin.com/in/scpublications
goodreads.com/author/show/19835.Mark_Nesbitt

Made in the USA
Middletown, DE
10 June 2020